Earth Under Siege

"…Everything I've come to expect from this author. It's packed full of action, drama, surprise and suspense at every turn."
~*Silvia at Goodreads*

"Highly Recommended. Five Mysterious Stars."
~*RBS Productions*

"*Collision* is a top ten book!"
~ *Step into Fiction*

"Wow, just wow."
~ *The Jeep Diva*

The Fringe Series

"Best science fiction I have read in a long while."
~Michael D. Griffiths, *SF Reader*

"*Fringe Runner* is epic fun with great characters, action, and suspense. Rachel Aukes is the next big name in the Space Opera genre!"
~ Nicholas Sansbury Smith, best-selling author of the *Extinction Cycle* series

"A perfect read for fans of the fantasy and sci-fi genres."
~ Ethan Gregory, *One Guy's Guide to Good Reads*

"I would recommend this novel to anyone who likes action-filled space operas and stories about fighting against the ruling government."
~ *Audiobook Reviewer*

Included on Suspense Magazine's "Best of 2013" list

Listed by the Huffington Post as one of the Best Zombie Books

"100 Days in Deadland is a stunning exploration of the human spirit: survival and greed, good and evil...a microcosm of today's society wrapped up in a dystopian novel. Rachel Aukes has written a modern take on a classic. I for one, cannot wait for her next book."
   ~ *Suspense Magazine*

"Another great zombie survival book made its way to our hungry brains! The book never slows down, the events are unpredictable and the characters are well built.... So go get the book, you'll love this one!"
   ~ *Zombie-Guide Magazine*

"This book is 5 stars all the way. It is unlike any zombie or apocalyptic story I have ever read... *100 Days in Deadland* doesn't just tell a story about zombies, it tells a story about a person's struggle to survival in a world that has fallen apart and how that person grows and changes through it all."
   ~ *Horror Web*

"A great read about survival in an undead world."
   ~ *Buy Zombie*

Earth Under Siege

Series by Rachel Aukes

Flight of the Javelin Series

Fringe Series

Bounty Hunter Series

The Deadland Saga

Guardians of the Seven Seals

The Tidy Guides Series (Nonfiction)

EARTH UNDER SIEGE

The Colliding Worlds Chronicles

RACHEL AUKES

WAYPOINT BOOKS

COLLIDING WORLDS

Copyright 2018 Rachel Aukes

All rights reserved.

Published by Waypoint Books LLC

Cover Art (C) Vivid Covers

Edited by Kriegler Editing Services and Terri King Editing Service

ISBN-13: 978-0-9899018-5-7

ISBN-10: 0-9899018-5-8

Contents

PART ONE:
COLLISION

Chapter 1

It wasn't the first time a good idea had come back to bite Sienna Wolfe in the ass, but it could be the last.

She checked her phone again. *No signal.* She shoved the phone back into her pocket. Sucking in a breath of autumn air laced with the stench of burning wires, she took one more look at the crashed aircraft. Then she clicked on her flashlight and stepped inside.

The light sliced through the smoke and fell upon the pilot slumped over the instrument panel. A flight suit and helmet covered him from head to toe, making it impossible to tell if he was still alive or not. Trembling, she stepped closer and checked his pulse.

Alive.

A persistent beep echoed through the cylindrical ship, which she tried to ignore. Even though she had a pilot's license, she'd never been around a plane crash. When she'd heard something smashing through trees in the woods, she hadn't known what to expect, but she certainly hadn't expected to find what she had: an aircraft *without* wings.

It had to be military—top-secret at that—given how unusual it was. The ship didn't even have an N-number. Rescue helicopters hadn't shown up, leaving her as the sole first responder.

She blew out a breath and rubbed her hands together.

While checking the pilot for injuries before attempting to move him, a small sound under the louder beeping distracted her. Shining the beam toward the rhythmic *plip-plop*, the light fell on rivulets flowing down the wall toward a crumpled mass of sparking instrument panel. Bending down on one knee, she dipped a finger in the liquid and smelled the clear, almost gel-like substance. It was foreign, like an exotic nighttime plant, but the underlying hint of kerosene was unmistakable; it had to be some sort of jet fuel.

It was then that the sound caught her. The beeps were speeding up; what used to be a second pause between each was now half that. Earlier, she'd assumed the beeps were a proximity alarm.

Her lips parted. "Oh, shit."

It made perfect sense that a classified aircraft would have an auto-destruct to keep it from falling into the wrong hands. In a rush, she fidgeted with a seatbelt that had no visible latches. Her fingers brushed over a switch, and in a blur, the belts retracted into the floor.

At the risk of injuring him further, she dragged him toward the door. His boots dragged across the floor, the friction pushing the limits of her strength. Her hands slipped, and she nearly dropped him. She took another step but stopped cold when movement caught her eye. The trail of fuel had now become a river and was running down toward a section of smoking wires. Her eyes widened. Interlacing her fingers around the man's chest in a Heimlich-maneuver style hold, she put everything she had into hefting him through the doorway and outside the ship.

Not knowing how far away she needed to be, she kept dragging him. Her legs shook and her arms shook. Her back felt like it could give out at any moment.

"What are you doing?"

Sienna snapped around to find another man nearly hidden by the trees. Relief flooded her. "Oh, thank God. Help me, please. He's hurt bad."

He made no move.

She'd heard about that type of response; how onlookers froze at the sight of an accident. She snapped her fingers. "Hey! I need your help over here."

He stepped forward then. Tall as a basketball player, he wore an odd soldier's outfit—maybe like that of a Scotsman? His silver hair glistened in the moonlight. But what most drew her attention were the flesh-like, tattoo-covered wings that spanned behind him. Strange, since it was nowhere close to Halloween and costume parties weren't common in the area.

She shook it off. Didn't matter. "Do you have a car nearby? Otherwise, we can get him onto my ATV—Hey!"

He grabbed her wrist and yanked her to him. Pinning her arms against her, he patted her pockets down with his free hand.

Fear brought forth a surge of adrenaline. She bucked and kicked at him. "What are you doing? Let go!"

He pulled out her phone and then sent her tumbling to the ground. He dropped the phone, pulled out a gun, and fired. The blast, strangely quiet, obliterated her phone with the same results as a large caliber.

Sienna froze.

He holstered his weapon. "You've seen things you should not have seen. You need to come with me."

She clawed against his iron grip, but he continued to pull her in the direction opposite from her cabin.

"No!" she yelled and grabbed a tree not much larger than a sapling. The small branches sliced her palm as she was pulled away. A blast of heat shot past her, and the grip on her wrist loosened. She rolled onto her knees and looked up to see her assailant lying on the ground, smoke rising from a gaping chest wound.

Shock numbed her as she looked over her shoulder to find the pilot, now conscious, leaning against a tree a few feet away, and shakily aiming a gun in her direction.

She held up both hands. "Please, don't shoot."

She couldn't see his expression, what with his face still covered, but he lowered the gun, and she let out a sigh of relief. Keeping an eye on the pilot, she gingerly leaned over the newcomer to check for a pulse. Not that she needed to; a hole had burned straight through his chest. Her finger brushed against a wing as she leaned back, and she jerked away from the unexpected warmth emanating from the flesh-like prop.

Coming numbly to her feet, she focused on her breathing, and turned to face the pilot.

The face mask, as before, blocked any expression.

She kept her hands where he could see them. "Your ship has a fuel leak. I'm scared it's going to blow."

"Are you aligned with the Draeken?" he asked.

Draeken. An odd word. It was for that reason she recognized it, from something her mother had said a couple of months back. "I don't know what you mean."

He lifted the gun again, directly at her heart. This time, his aim didn't waiver.

Sienna didn't think, or realize what she was doing, as she swung her leg out and kicked the pilot in the head. The weapon flew from his hand. She dove, fumbling through the leaves to grab the gun. Standing above the pilot, she gripped the weapon with both hands and aimed it at his chest. Waited a moment. Nudged him with her toe. Waited another moment. Nudged him again.

Leave him.

That was the smart thing to do. The pilot had just killed a man and had been going to shoot her. In the distance, she could still hear the beeps, only now they were even closer together. She cursed at what she was about to do.

After tucking the weapon into the waistband of her cargos, she hoisted the pilot onto the back of the ATV. His legs dangled over the sides of the rack. She then climbed onto the seat in front of him and sped away. The engine roared, tires kicking up dirt and pine needles.

A massive boom rocked the ground and a shockwave nearly sent her tumbling from her vehicle. Heat then sucked everything back toward the explosion. There was no air to breathe, let alone scream. She hunkered down over the handlebars and pushed the throttle in all the way. The ATV chewed its way forward through the ravenous suction.

Then, as suddenly as it came, the wind vanished and the woods hushed, like someone had hit the mute button. Slowing the ATV, she looked over her shoulder and then slammed the brakes. She hopped off and stood, staring blankly at the crash site.

Confusion settled over her. There was no fire. No debris. No sign of wreckage. It was as though nothing had been there, like the ship and the shredded trees around it had imploded into nothingness.

Aside from the eerie absence of nighttime forest noises, everything appeared normal. Nothing to even hint that a ship had crashed there less than an hour earlier.

"Impossible," she whispered.

Sienna didn't know how long she stood there. Regular glances back at her still-present passenger proved that everything had been real and not some hallucination. Her heart felt like it was pumping lead, making it difficult to catch her breath. If she left the injured man, he'd likely die. He'd been about to kill her, but she told herself that he'd been unconscious a few seconds before that and could've been confused. She needed to get back to her place and contact the authorities. They'd figure out everything.

The quarter-mile drive through the winding pine woods felt interminable. She clutched the handlebars in a vice-grip as she tore around trees, ignoring small branches whipping at her face.

She slowed only to glance back every once in a while at her unconscious passenger.

When she finally pulled up to the front steps of her stone cabin, adrenaline still surged through her veins. She'd never, ever looked down the barrel of a gun before. It was a feeling she hoped to never experience again.

She dragged the pilot off the ATV and up the stone steps, the smooth material of his flight suit making her job all the harder to maintain her grip. Seconds felt like minutes as she hauled the dead weight into her home and dropped him on her couch. Her muscles shook with fatigue. Sweat ran down her temple and tickled her cheek.

She pulled out the gun with one hand as she swept back hair that had become plastered to her face. She stared blankly at the black weapon for only a second before she rushed into her bedroom, removed the Glock she stored in her nightstand, and checked to make sure it was still loaded and had a round already in the chamber. Its heft and familiarity comforted her, helping her to calm down. She then hid the pilot's weapon deep in her closet.

Eying her clothes, she yanked out a couple of flannel shirts, gave the fabric a quick tug, and hurried back to living room. There, she tied his wrists together with one shirt then used the second shirt to bind his wrists over his head and to the floor lamp. She knew it wouldn't hold him for more than a few seconds if he tried to attack, but seconds could make the difference between Sienna becoming a victim or firing her gun.

Finished, her stomach churned as she leveled her handgun on him. When he didn't move, she pulled out the chair at the computer desk across the room from the couch. She didn't have a landline phone, but she did have internet. After a quick search, she pulled up the Hot Springs emergency services website. She opened a chat window and entered details about the crash, the pilot, and her address.

She looked back at the pilot. She hoped someone would be

monitoring the messages, or else she'd be forced into driving the man to the hospital, which was nearly an hour away.

Sienna wished she'd listened to her mother more closely when she was rambling about militia-style factions currently operating in the country. Maybe then, Sienna would understand what was happening now. She leaned back in the chair and kept the gun level on her 'guest' as she waited for a response. Seconds passed like hours, and she found herself tapping her feet as she waited.

Still no response from either the emergency services or from the pilot.

After waiting a full minute without him showing any sign of consciousness, she headed to the bathroom and grabbed anything that could be used as a medical supply. She knew he could die without medical attention. Her legs didn't want to move, but she willed them forward, edging closer and closer until she reached him and dropped the supplies into a pile on the floor.

She was no medic, but she knew the first rule in any accident was to stabilize the patient. His breathing was steady, although not strong by any means. He likely had internal injuries. She felt around his neck for the edge of his mask. The mask was odd, mostly fabric but with padding and goggles. Locating the edge, ever so carefully she pulled it off.

And gasped.

His skin looked like he'd taken a shower in liquid gold. Dark tribal-style tattoos swirled over his skin, but there didn't seem to be a specific design to the way they curved around his neck and onto his face—a face with a nasty bruise forming around an even nastier swollen eye that was no doubt caused by her boot. She winced at the harm she'd caused, but then reminded herself that he'd been the aggressor, not her.

She leaned back.

Holy. Shit. First, the guy with wings; now this.

Tattoos were one thing, but this was something else. Even if they were some kind of military thing, there seemed no logical reason for the anti-stealth glimmer that covered his skin.

No way was this guy real. Despite a successful career in selling the possibility of it, she'd never really believed in it. There was no such thing as an… she could barely even think the word.

Alien.

Chapter 2

Sienna half-expected to see a cameraman pop out and yell "Surprise!", but no one did, which meant she was alone with someone who was like no one she'd seen before. She had assumed the pilot was military, maybe some kind of rich militia, but it was far more likely that both men were members of some rival cultish city gangs.

She was in way over her head—and she'd seen plenty of crazy in her life. For her first eighteen years, she'd followed her parents across the globe with their humanitarian efforts. After a relatively normal college career, she spent the next fifteen years consulting on missionary work.

She thought she'd seen it all...

A shiver ran across her skin as fear seeped into her. She stood over the man for another long moment. Convinced he wasn't playing possum, she set her gun down and checked for injuries. She was more careful and slow this time as she ran her hands over his arms, feeling for broken bones. She then moved to his chest and down his abdomen, stopping when she discovered a spot where the material was saturated.

She tried to cut down the front of the flight suit, but the thin fabric was stronger than she would have guessed. Even with both hands clasping the shears, cutting through the fabric was a painfully slow process. When the final bit of fabric covering his torso was cut away, she found the source of the wetness about an inch below his rib cage. Blood seeped from a deep gouge, but it was unlike any blood she'd ever seen before. It was thick and dark and definitely not crimson.

In a shocked daze, Sienna closed her mouth and watched his chest, covered in tattoos and small X-shaped scars, rise and fall and rise again, the wound continuing to ooze the strange fluid. This was something her unerring sense of logic couldn't defend. Here she was, watching dark liquid gold bleed from a wound.

Humans didn't bleed gold.

Maybe it was shock, but she found herself continuing, almost robotically. She leaned in to get a better look at the gouge. Grabbing a bottle of antiseptic and some cotton swabs, she dabbed the liquid across his skin. New "blood" rose with every gentle touch she made. The cut was too deep for a bandage. He needed a surgeon, not a Band-Aid.

She glanced back at her computer; still no response to her chat message.

Grimacing, she threaded a needle and placed her palm on his chest near the wound. The instant before she pierced the skin, heat bloomed under her hand. She jolted back and dropped the needle.

She looked at her hand, but it looked normal. She looked at his wound. Where her hand had been, his skin shimmered more brightly. Fresh, scarred skin now covered the edges of the wound. Her jaw slackened.

Maybe it was shock, maybe it was the after-effect of adrenaline wearing off, but she made only a half-hearted attempt to reason with herself before gingerly placing her palm against his skin again.

After a moment, heat hit her hand. She sat on the edge of the coffee table, feeling slightly woozy, but didn't remove her hand as she watched fresh scar tissue form over the bloody cut. It was like she was in a movie, watching herself. All the while, heat tickled her palm as though her hand rested on an anthill. When a fresh scar filled in where the bloody gouge had been, the tickling disappeared, and she pulled her hand away.

Lightheaded from the surreal experience, she leaned back, stared at her patient, and found eyes darker than midnight, without any surrounding white, watching her, squinting in the light.

In a flash she was off the table and standing several feet away, Glock leveled at him. "Don't move. I'll shoot you."

"Turn down the light. It hurts my eyes," he said. He tugged at his restraints while he muttered strange, almost-lyrical words that, judging by the look on his face, were more likely a string of cuss words.

"No," she answered. "Who are you?"

He stilled. "I am Legian. I mean no harm to you."

"Then why did you try to shoot me?"

"I thought you were aligned with the other one."

"Who was he?"

"A murderer. You can lower your weapon. I will not harm you."

She knew better than to believe him.

"Please, the light." He continued to squint.

She didn't lower her gun, but she did walk over and dim the lights.

"Why am I here?" he asked.

She swallowed. "I brought you here. You were hurt, and I couldn't leave you at your ship. It blew up."

After a moment, the pilot began tugging at his restraints again, showing no surprise at the fact that his ship had been destroyed.

She narrowed her eyes at the pilot. "Why are you here?"

"Release me," was all he said.

A soft snort escaped her. "Like hell. You were going to shoot me."

He yanked against his restraints and grunted before surrendering to the couch with a wince. It was then she saw a pool of blood she'd completely missed before.

"You're still bleeding."

"Release me."

"No way." She took tentative steps closer, all the while keeping the gun securely aimed at him. She shot a hard gaze at him. "I can try to help, but I *will* shoot you if you try anything."

He watched her with a clenched jaw for a moment before giving a tight nod.

With his wrists tied, she couldn't roll him all the way onto his stomach. Unable to see and stuck using only one hand, she had to work with touch alone, feeling for the wound. She moved her fingers over his skin until he sucked in a breath. Thick, warm moisture enveloped her fingers near his spine.

"Ow!" Sienna snapped back her finger to find a bead of crimson blood forming on the tip.

If he'd been a *normal* person, she'd leave the shrapnel in there until it could be removed by a professional, but this man was anything but normal. She softened her gaze. "There's something still in there. My guess is that you can't do your mojo thing with it in there. I'll pull it out on the count of three."

"Three what?"

"Never mind." She gripped the metal, and it came out with a quick tug. He grunted but didn't yank away. She pulled back and tossed the shard onto the coffee table. It made a metallic ping when it bounced off the hard oak.

Fresh blood began spilling out. Watching him watching her, she flattened her hand on his back. Just like the first time, heat surged. A familiar blanket of dizziness fell over her, and she fought to keep the gun steady. After several more seconds, the bleeding slowed, and then stopped altogether.

Exhausted, she shakily held the gun trained on him as she took a seat on the table, using her knee to steady her aim.

His brows furrowed. "You helped me. Why did you not break contact?"

She shrugged. "You needed help." She paused. "How do you do that?"

"My people can use energy to heal." He examined Sienna from his prone position. "Release me. Please." He gritted out the words through clenched teeth, making them sound more like an ultimatum than a request.

She shook her head. "Not until help gets here."

Suddenly, he lunged forward. His hands pulled free from the restraints faster than she'd thought possible.

He knocked her to the floor, and her head banged back against the hardwood. Her vision tunneled, and the gun was yanked from her hand. Still, she managed to kick and punch him. Not that it did any good, so she hit him with the only thing she could still move—her forehead. Stars danced across her vision, and shards of pain ran through her brain. He grimaced, but never even flinched. Still pinned as tightly as ever, all she could do now was glare. "Let me go."

He frowned. "Why did you help me?" he asked, deflecting her command.

In response, she struggled harder, and his grip tightened. It felt like her bones were about to shatter. She cried out in pain. He loosened his grip just enough.

"Why did you help me?" he repeated.

Sienna laid her head back on the floor. He had her, and he knew it. "I wouldn't leave someone to die." She glared. "No matter how much of an asshole they are."

He watched her for a moment then the weight lifted from her, and he released her wrists. She sat up and pulled her wrists to her chest, rubbing circulation back into them. Movement in the doorway made her jump, and fear stabbed her when she saw a second man, dressed head to toe in the same type of suit the pilot was dressed in, standing next to Legian. The newcomer was holding the same kind of gun Legian had carried, and it was pointed directly at her.

The two men began speaking in their strange melodic language, seemingly ignoring Sienna, yet the gun never wavered in the newcomer's grip. She thought about making a move for her gun, which was now sitting on the side table, but thought better of the plan since Legian stood a mere foot away from it. As the men conversed, the only word she could make out was *Draeken*, though she suspected much of the conversation revolved around her—or more aptly, what to do with her.

Her breathing was hard and tight until the newcomer holstered his gun, and she felt some relief.

After a length, the room went quiet, and both men watched her. Dread seeped like icy water through every molecule. Then, Legian stepped forward and held out a hand to help her stand. She slapped it away.

"This is Bente," Legian said. "He will bring us back to our base."

She pushed herself shakily to her feet.

She gulped. "Us?"

"You must come with us. We cannot risk our presence to be known. Surely, you must understand," Legian replied.

She held up her hands as she backed against the wall. "Listen, I won't say anything. You have my word. I swear," she said, her voice pleading.

"We can't take any risks," Bente replied. "You either come with us or we kill you."

Legian scowled. "Bente."

Fear built within her like a mouse stepping into a trap. She looked at the doorway then to the window, wondering if she could escape in time.

"You cannot stay here. It isn't safe," Legian continued. "I give you my word, you will not be harmed. You saved my life, and I will protect yours."

She wasn't an idiot. She didn't believe him for a second. The newcomer had already made it quite clear what would happen to her if she tried to run… it was the same thought she'd had going through her mind from the moment the pilot—Legian—had gained the upper hand. Feeling like a helpless, five-year-old girl, she nearly whimpered before looking up into dark eyes that contained no white. She forced herself to lift her chin, to fake strength. "Let's go."

Chapter 3

Legian didn't bother blindfolding Sienna, not that she could've have seen much, anyway; the inside of the windowless ship was as dark as the nighttime forest outside. Legian had buckled her into a seat behind the cockpit and now sat across from her. She could just make out his shape and had no doubt he watched her the entire trip to their base.

The ship flew differently than the small planes she'd piloted. Airplanes needed runways and momentum to build lift, while this ship rose from the ground like a Harrier but was far quieter and smoother. The curiosity within her wanted to check out the cockpit, to see if the controls and instruments would be familiar. After all, the laws of gravity and aerodynamics were universal.

The ship landed no more than ten minutes after takeoff. The short flight surprised her, and she wondered if their base was close to her cabin, or if the ship just flew incredibly fast. Probably a bit of both.

Bente opened the door and stepped out into the dim light filtering in through the space. He removed his mask, revealing the same golden skin and dark eyes as Legian.

"It will be a moment," Legian said as he unbuckled the straps on her seat. "Bente needs to update our *tahcaya*."

She pushed to her feet and took a step to the door.

"Trust me. You have my word that you will be safe," he said.

She chortled and broke eye contact, and listened to the sound of voices trickling into the ship. She tried to make out the words, but it seemed to be all in the same language she'd heard the pair speaking back at her cabin.

After what seemed like minutes, the one named Bente popped his head back into the ship and looked at Sienna. "Come."

With Bente in front of her and Legian behind, they escorted their prisoner even though she wore no restraints. As she stepped out of the ship, she found herself in a large enclosed hangar. The lights were dim there as well, and she'd wished they were a bit brighter so that she could make out more details.

Bente stopped and stepped to her side while Legian stepped to her other side. They were at the edge of the hangar. Dozens of ships like the one they'd arrived in were parked around the walls, draped in shadows, while several larger ships occupied the center.

Before her stood a male in a plain black uniform with no insignia, even though he bore the air of a leader. He was tall like Legian and Bente, but his hair was longer, and tattoos covered much of his visible skin; one in particular vined around his eye and gave him the look of a pirate. Several more aliens—some male, some female—stood behind him. All had golden skin and pure black eyes and wore the simple black uniform.

Legian spoke in the alien language, and this time she clearly heard her name among the words. When Legian finished, he turned to her. "Sienna, this is Apolo, our *tahcaya*—our leader."

The man stepped closer, and she girded herself to not take a step back.

"Hello, Sienna. You may call me Apolo." His English was near-perfect. "I lead the Sephian forces on this small planet. And, as you have helped one of my own, you have the privilege of being the first of your race to meet with me. However, your appearance has raised a complication that I'd hoped not to deal with so soon. As such, now I must decide what to do with you."

You mean you have to decide whether to kill me or let me live, she thought to herself, but said nothing.

Apolo gestured to the people behind him. "You must understand, there are lives on this base dependent on secrecy."

"Apolo," Legian said. "Sienna saved my life, and I have pledged her safety here. She accompanied us without coercion. I believe she means us no harm."

Sienna practically guffawed. 'Without coercion' was a stretch.

Apolo gave Legian a surprised look and turned to Bente. "Is this true? He has already made a pledge?"

Bente nodded. "Yeah. Trust me, I thought the same thing when I heard it."

Apolo thought for a moment. "Well, then, it is settled. Legian, Sienna is your responsibility. Do you understand?"

"Yes," Legian said without hesitation.

"So, it is done," Apolo said, and turned to Sienna. "You will remain here as our guest. You will not be harmed unless you intend harm to any of my people. In return, I request that you meet with me to help me learn more about your people and culture. Can you meet these expectations?"

As he spoke the words, she knew that what she was hearing was an ultimatum. Her second one tonight. Frustration and exhaustion roiled through her at the unfairness of the situation. She hadn't asked for any of this. She looked at Apolo, tamping down any emotion that may show in her features, and said simply, "I accept your conditions."

His gaze narrowed as though he could see through her façade. Then he smiled. "Excellent. We will speak in an hour. Bente will gather some of your belongings when he ensures your home is cleansed of our presence."

He turned and left with his entourage, while Bente and two others headed back to the ship.

Chills raced over her skin at the thought of strangers rifling through her things. She spun around to see Bente disappear onboard, and she fought the urge to follow him, even though she knew she could never go home.

"Come," Legian said. "I will show you to your room."

She stood a little taller as she turned toward Legian then fell in alongside him as they walked through the hangar and down several hallways. With the lights down so low, it felt like she was walking through a large building with only nightlights on. Every door they passed was closed, giving her no inkling as to a possible exit. Each door had a small touchpad set in the wall next to it which she suspected needed a badge of some kind to open them. Her hopes fell more and more as she realized this place was the perfect prison.

Legian turned, and she stumbled into him. She grunted. "Sorry. It's hard to see in here."

"My apologies," he said. "I hadn't thought of that. On my world, my people are accustomed to moving about in the dark. Our days and nights are opposite to humans' cycles. We sleep during the light hours. I will get you glasses to help you see."

He stopped at a door and tapped on the pad, as though playing the beat of some tune she didn't recognize. The door opened, and he gestured inside. "This is your room."

The lights came on at the same dim level as the hallways. Legian spoke. "Lights, increase twenty percent." The room lit up enough for Sienna to see, but caused Legian to squint.

She stepped over the threshold. The room was sparsely furnished with a bed, couch, what looked like a bar, and a door to what she hoped was a human-like bathroom. As she looked over the weapons hung on the wall, the unmade bed, and the drinks at the bar, she froze. It took a deep breath before she could swallow her fear enough to speak. "Someone lives here already."

"It is my room," he said. "You stay with me now."

Her jaw slackened. She spun to face him. "What?"

"I am sorry. We have no free residences, and even if we did, you are my responsibility."

"No. It's because I'm your prisoner."

"If you were a prisoner, you'd be in a holding cell."

"I'd rather be in a holding cell than sharing a room with you!"

He took a step back and held his hands out as though surrendering. "I am sorry for the situation you've found yourself in. I have given you my word. I will not harm you, and I mean that in all ways, but this room is the only option for you at this time. I claimed you as my responsibility, which means I am responsible for your life, wellbeing, and behavior at all times. Perhaps, once Apolo allows it, we can make new arrangements. Until then, you will remain with me. You may sleep on the bed. I will sleep on the sofa."

She stared at him for a lengthy moment. She had no control, and she wanted to scream at losing every semblance of her life and her freedom in under an hour. She should've left him to die with his ship. "Fine," she gritted out. "Where do I get cleaned up?"

He led her to a bathroom. "Bente will return shortly with clean clothes from your home. Until then, you can wear your current clothes, or I can find you something else here."

"I'll wear my clothes," she said quickly.

After he showed her how to use the shower, he left her alone, though she wondered if she was being watched even then. She constantly scanned the ceiling and every corner for cameras. She showered, changed, and left the bathroom to find Legian gone as well as the weapons on the wall. She laughed drily to herself. Can't have the "guest" within arm's reach of a weapon. She spent the next several minutes pacing the room, handling every item she found to see if anything could be used as a weapon or aid in her escape.

By the time Legian returned with a snack that tasted much like an expired protein bar, she'd scoured the small room, finding nothing that could be used. He then delivered her to Apolo.

Apolo's questioning wasn't nearly as painful as Sienna had expected. The medical examination, on the other hand, was far worse. She'd nearly cried when she'd first seen the table full of probe-like instruments laid out when she entered, making it look like a scene from a B-grade sci-fi movie.

Lucky for her, those instruments were just parts for a faulty wall panel being repaired. Unlucky for her, the scanner the doctor used wasn't calibrated for human physiology, and she ended up with second-degree burns over much of her back. The base's primary doctor, Fayel, whom she decided to call Doc, had the disposition of most doctors she'd met in her life. Apologetic for the harm he'd caused, he'd used salves to ease her burns, and she found it easy to not fear him as much as she feared the others.

She'd been given the day to recuperate, but that was simply because that was when the Sephians slept. Exhausted, she fell asleep. It helped that Legian didn't snore to remind her that she wasn't alone in the room. Even so, she shot awake often as new memories mixed with unfamiliar surroundings to create new and horrible dreams. She had lain awake in bed for a couple of hours before Legian woke and got ready for the night. Before he left, a Sephian female arrived.

"Hello, Sienna. I'm Nalea. I'm here to give you a tour of the base," she'd said. She could have been a double for a young Sigourney Weaver; almost a double, but not quite. Nalea sported glittery skin, pure ebony eyes, and long pitch-black hair.

They stepped into the dim hallway, and Nalea handed her a pair of sunglasses. "Here, these Draeken *tensatlen* will help you see."

Sienna slid them on. Immediately, the hallway lightened to where she could see all the details. She did a three-sixty, taking in everything. She lowered the glasses for a moment before pushing them back up her nose. They weren't night-vision goggles because they didn't distort any colors. "Wow. Sunglasses that *brighten* everything."

Sienna walked alongside Nalea through the long hallway, noticing screens on the walls and touchpads at every door. "This base isn't really a base," she said. "It's simply our ship. That's why the doors and walls may seem overbuilt."

"It's huge," Sienna said.

Nalea shrugged. "It's the largest Sephian ship, but it's tiny compared to a Draeken core ship."

As they continued their tour, Sienna noticed Nalea watching her. "What?" Sienna asked.

"Have you figured out any escape routes yet?"

Sienna became rigid. "What are you talking about?"

"Oh, please. I'd be doing the same if I was in your shoes. I saw you checking out every nick and cranny."

"Nook and cranny," Sienna said without thinking.

"What?"

"You said it wrong. It's 'nook and cranny'. Nick is a man's name."

"Oh," Nalea frowned. "I don't blame you for looking for ways out. But even though you can't leave, you aren't a prisoner."

Sienna's brows rose. "Being held against my will is the exact definition of 'prisoner'."

"Or 'slave'," Nalea said. "You know, that's why we came to your planet, to chase down the Draeken who'd enslaved our world, to keep them from doing the same to yours."

"You were slaves?"

Nalea nodded. "The Draeken arrived on Sephia many, many years ago, because their world, Draeka, was about to be destroyed by a supernova. Rather than coming in peace, they conquered us—their technology was far superior to our—and my people became their slaves. It took hundreds of years, but my people finally defeated them, and we drove the Draeken from our world. What we didn't plan was for the Draeken to have come here, to Earth.

When we learned Earth was already inhabited by an advanced race, we knew we needed to stop the Draeken before they did to you what they did to us. And that's why we're here: to protect the Earth and annihilate the Draeken threat once and for all."

She motioned to a large circular room lined with tables. "This is the Commons. It's the only room, other than the hangar, large enough to hold everyone at once. We eat here and have ship-wide meetings here. It's the heart of the vessel. As you can see, all hallways merge here." She motioned to the hub-and-spoke architecture before turning back to Sienna. "You must be hungry. Let me show you how to get food and drink."

Nalea led Sienna through the food line, which was incredibly similar to how a school cafeteria would work, except the food here was made to order. The cook spoke English, but Sienna recognized none of the dishes—everything looked like brown mush. Nalea ordered for Sienna. "*Mulhean* is our most popular dish. I think you'll like it."

Sienna and Nalea sat at a table near one of the hallway entrances. Sienna's stomach growled. With the exception of a couple of protein-like bars Legian had given her in the morning, it'd been a full day since she'd eaten.

Nalea dug in. Sienna took a big bite of the paste. It had a mashed consistency with crunchy, crystalline *something* to add texture. The only flavor she could glean was akin to Lima beans. She slowed her chewing.

"Do you like it?" Nalea asked.

Sienna forced herself to swallow. "It's… interesting. A bit bland. Do you have any salt?"

Nalea shook her head and frowned. "No. This is our most flavorful dish. Want me to get you something else?"

Sienna shook her head. "No. This is fine." She forced down the rest of the meal and drank a full glass of water. At least the water tasted normal.

As Nalea talked, Sienna found herself entranced by the

woman's tattoos, which were lighter than those she'd seen on Legian, Bente, and Apolo. Nalea glanced at her hands and back up at Sienna. "Ah, my *soullare* intrigues you."

"*Soullare*? Is that what you call your tattoos?" Sienna asked.

Nalea smiled. "*Soullare* is not a tattoo. We are born with it. They say it was our ancestors' form of camouflage, but all Sephians still have it, and it's darker on men. Our *soullare* is unique to each of us and is a source of pride."

Sienna found herself almost feeling as if she were talking to just another person, and she began to wonder if the Sephians weren't so different from humans... or if she was developing Stockholm Syndrome. She suspected it was the latter.

As the days passed, Sienna looked for exits less and, instead, sought opportunities to learn more about the Sephians and the Draeken menace. She realized that focusing on herself did no one any good when a genocidal threat was stalking the shadows. While she didn't know what she could do to help humanity, she found herself trying, nonetheless. By the third week, her body had adjusted to Sephian food, and she finally felt at full strength in the opposite circadian schedule.

She had also picked up on the now-familiar scent every Sephian naturally carried. It had taken a week before she noticed the base smelled like a faint, soft rain. Now she couldn't imagine how she hadn't noticed it right away.

She no longer feared Legian, although she still didn't know what to make of him. He had an aggressive personality and often bossed her around, telling her what to do and where to go, but as soon as she snapped back, he'd back down. She hadn't seen him do that around others and wondered if he feared her because she was the alien to him.

Then, one evening, she walked into the bathroom, not realizing he was in there. She plowed right into his bare chest as he stepped out of the shower.

"Sorr—" she began, but the word melted away as she took in his nakedness.

He stood there. "When you look at me like that, I want to— you shouldn't look at me like that."

She looked up to find him watching her intently. In a rush, she spun around, closed the door, grabbed a drink, and sat on the edge of the bed, looking away from the bathroom. Hyped-up new feelings made her feel like a traitor to herself and to her kind. It had been over three years since her husband, Bobby, was killed by a driver too busy texting her BFF. Three years since she left the city life behind and moved away from humanity, away from senselessness. And three long years since she thought about touching a man. She missed the touch.

Then she reminded herself that Legian wasn't really a man. He was an alien.

After the shower incident, conversations were awkward, and it seemed that Legian and Sienna often only saw each other during the days. But every time he looked at her, he had the same look that he'd had in the shower. She found it frightening… and exhilarating.

Over the next month, she'd come back to their room and sometimes find a surprise he'd left for her. One time it was the Xbox and games from her cabin. Another time it was a painting of a forest to remind her of what was beyond the walls of the windowless base. She needed those moments since she was still the outcast; many Sephians eyed her like she was the alien.

It was near the end of her second month at the base when she made up her mind. She had to do something or else she'd go insane. She stripped out of her clothes and waited on the bed. When he opened the door, he stood and stared.

"Close the door," Sienna ordered, "You sleep in bed today."

His look of shock morphed into one of pure interest, and he then spent the day proving to Sienna that some pleasures were universal.

Legian never slept on the sofa again.

———

"You've been here for nearly a year already," Sienna said. "The Draeken have been here even longer, and who knows what they have planned. Time is running out to get my people on your side. It won't matter that you followed the Draeken here to stop them."

"It is still too early," Apolo said.

"If I was a Sephian—"

"But you are *not* a Sephian," he corrected.

Her lips thinned. "You're right; I'm not. I'm a human, and I know I'd want to meet aliens face-to-face rather than find out they've been skulking around in my country for over a year."

"We'll talk more tomorrow," Apolo said and turned from her.

She glared, stood, and left his room. Legian followed her to their room. Once inside, she plopped onto the sofa. "I'm tired of no one listening to me because I'm human. They should give me a chance *because* I'm human."

"I agree with you," Legian said softly as he sat down next to her.

"That's great," she said dryly. "Now all we have to do is get Apolo to agree, and that's not going to happen."

"I've been thinking about that." He paused for a deep breath. "I know of a way."

She spun to face him. "What is it?"

He reached out and clasped her hand in his. "If you were to accept to be my *tahren*, you would be recognized as a Sephian and become a member of the Sephian community."

She frowned. "*Tahren?* Wait, like, soul mate? I thought that was a biological thing. I thought you can't choose your *tahren*. I thought the whole Sephian energy force thing chooses your *tahren* for you. You can't just pick someone to be yours."

He gave a small smile. "And you are correct."

"Legian, thank you for offering, but you can't do that for me. What if you find your *tahren?* No. I'll find another way."

He chuckled. "Sienna, I wish you could feel energy like I do I knew you were my *tahren* the moment you touched me. I first thought it was impossible for a Sephian and a human to become *tahren*, but I know now that it's very much possible, and opens up new prospects for both our peoples. I know not what lies ahead, but I do know that I'm not willing to sacrifice an opportunity given to me—to us—by the gods. You *are* my *tahren*. There is no mistaking that. I've only been holding off on informing Apolo until you had a chance to understand my people better."

She sat there and said nothing as she considered his words. In his mind, clearly, his proposal included no subterfuge. She had feelings for him, but she wasn't sure if it was love or simply a blend of passion, friendship, and proximity. Her brows knit together. Maybe there wasn't much of a difference in that comparison after all. After losing Bobby, she'd never wanted to care for someone enough to go through that kind of pain again. The problem was, she already did care for Legian too much.

She reached out and grabbed his hand. "Okay, you're my *tahren*. What do we do now?"

Chapter 4

Sienna walked into the country bar and scanned past the dancers for the man she'd come to see, nearly missing him for the cowboy hat he wore. He had bellied up to the bar, drinking a frosty draught.

Tonight was her first mission. Unfortunately, as humans went, she brought few connections, leaving her best option with Bobby's military unit. Taking a deep breath, Sienna gave her late husband's friend a quick smile. Before walking over to him, she scanned the bar for anyone else from Jax's platoon. In her email, she'd pleaded for Jax to come alone, but he was a soldier first, which meant he wouldn't be alone.

Her gaze stopped on a man sitting in the booth at the other end of the bar. Sporting a buzz cut and sitting too uptight for a night out, the fifty-something man didn't fit. She had no doubt more of the 51st Division, a joint Army-Air Force operations task force focused on space warfare, was here.

Straightening her posture, she considered walking right back out the way she came in. But Apolo was counting on her. Last week, a Draeken scout ship had been spotted flying over the base.

If the Sephian base hadn't been discovered yet, it would be soon. It was just a matter of time.

Unfortunately, the U.S. military didn't have the benefit of the *tahren* bond to start a relationship. It didn't matter if the Sephians said they'd followed the Draeken—a far more violent race—to Earth. Having not one but two alien races on American soil would be the last straw. There'd be violence, hate, murder, and suicide, and that would be day one alone.

Straightening her posture, Sienna spun on her heel to walk right back out the way she came in before this turned back to Jax and found his chair empty. Frowning, she spun around, only to come to a hard stop against a cowboy who filled out all ten gallons of that hat of his. A large hand latched onto her bicep, and she looked up into Jax's eyes. His hand lowered to her wrist. Their feet crunched on broken peanut shells littered across the hardwood floors as he led her through the bar and toward Buzzcut. Inside, fear prickled her.

"I told you to come alone," she ground out.

"Couldn't. This is bigger than both of us."

"I'm trying to keep things from escalating too fast."

"I think it's too late for that," Jax said.

Buzzcut looked up from a barely touched beer when they stopped at his booth. The older man pivoted on his red bench seat, hopped to his feet, gave an overly generous smile, and held out a hand. "You must be Sienna Wolfe."

She inhaled before accepting the offered hand. "You must lead Jax's company."

"Among other companies. Major Sommers; at your service." He motioned to the booth, and she slid in as he sat back down. Jax slid in next to her, effectively locking her in the booth.

Sommers put both elbows on the table and leaned forward over his beer. "Jax mentioned that you might like some assistance with some *illegal aliens.*"

"I like to think of them as friends in from out of town," she said. While anyone overhearing the conversation would assume they were talking about workers coming over from Mexico, they both understood the true meaning of his words. She glanced at Jax before turning back to Sommers. "How much do you know?"

He shrugged. "I know our *friends* have been here for some time, long before the night they took you."

She'd kept warning Apolo that the U.S. military wasn't half as dumb as he thought, but the Sephians had one major flaw: they thought they were smarter than everyone else. Not exactly an ego boost for a lone human in a bunker of five hundred-plus aliens. Then again, they'd won their freedom against near-impossible odds through blood, tears, and death. They earned a little self-righteousness, no matter how frustrating that could be at times.

"Why don't you fill me in on what you know?" Sommers asked.

Clasping her fingers, she leaned forward. She spoke as if her insides weren't tied in knots. "I was asked by Apolo—he's the Sephian leader here on Earth—to reach out to someone I knew and trusted in the military."

Sommers nodded. "And you chose Lieutenant Jerrick because you knew him through your late husband."

She gave a quick glance to Jax. "Yes. Bobby trusted him, so I trust him."

"Your late husband was an NCO in the 51st. He had an excellent service record. I wish I'd had the chance to meet him," Sommers said before continuing. "Why don't you tell me more about this Apolo and why he asked you to contact Jax."

There was so much to say, she struggled with where to begin. "Apolo wants to make contact."

Sommers raised his brows. "Then why hasn't he contacted us?"

"It's not that easy. The Sephians don't exactly blend in. Apolo knows that once they're out of the so-called closet, there's no going back. He wanted to take things slow and play their cards right."

"Invading our country is an act of war. I would hardly call that playing their cards right," Sommers cautioned.

Her jaw tightened. "They're not invading. They didn't even want to come here."

"They why are they here?" Sommers asked.

"They followed the Draeken here to prevent them from doing to us what they did to Sephia."

"And what did these Draeken do to Sephia?" Sommers asked.

"They enslaved the Sephians," she replied. "From what I've learned, the Draeken arrived on Sephia and conquered it during what they call the Great War. This war was worse than all of ours thrown together, condensed into one massive attack. Anyway, the Draeken had advanced technology. They slashed the Sephian population in half within a couple of weeks. For a couple of centuries, the Draeken ruled over Sephia, the Sephians as their slaves. Then, about twenty years ago, the Sephians rebelled in a drawn-out guerilla war that decimated both races. It was called the Noble War, and that was when they finally drove the Draeken from their world."

During all this Sommers listened but said nothing, so she continued.

"The Sephians won their planet back. It was bad news for us, because the next habitable planet along the space highway is Earth. Fortunately, the Sephians found out the Draeken had come here, so Apolo led a group of five hundred or so Sephians to a world they'd never heard of, a world they had no reason to care about, because they didn't want to see another world enslaved. And that pretty much sums up why the Sephians are here."

There was a long drawn out silence as Sommers seemed to ponder her words. "How many Draeken are here?"

"I don't know. Apolo seemed to think they escaped with only

one ship and that it wasn't full. But it could still mean a few thousand of them."

He frowned. "If the Draeken came here to take over the world, then why haven't they tried to do so already?"

She shrugged. "Apolo thinks they're lying low to build infrastructure to implement their plans. He's been searching for their earthside base but hasn't found it yet."

"Hm." Sommers watched Sienna for some time. "You were held by the Sephians for a long time. How can you be sure you weren't fed a line of bullshit or that you weren't brainwashed? What if the Sephians are the ones after our world?"

"No." She shook her head. "They may have forced me to come to their base to keep their secret, but they've never harmed me, and everything I've seen fits with their story. I don't agree with Apolo's decision to wait, but I understand why he did. Earth has no recorded visits from other worlds. Apolo was afraid we wouldn't be able to handle that knowledge. He's trying to do the right thing. When you meet with him, you can see the truth for yourself. He's ready to meet whenever you are."

Sommers leaned back. "I'm ready. Take me to his base tonight."

She stammered. "I can't."

"You can't or won't?" Sommers countered.

She swallowed. "Apolo does want to meet, but not at the base. He has concerns that the military would attack the base, and there are families—children—there. He can't share the location of the base yet, but he'll meet at a neutral location."

Sommers cocked his head. "This fellow wants to meet, but only on his own terms. That's awfully convenient for him."

"Listen, I'm doing what I can. Give me your card, next steps, whatever you want, and I'll relay it to Apolo."

"That's not good enough. I've got brass on my ass to get this situation under control. I need an assurance that Apolo will contact me *tonight*, and that his kind will show no hostilities."

"I'll stress the importance to him," she said, "but I'm just the messenger. Believe me, if I could get you in front of Apolo this very moment, I would."

Sommers eyed her for a moment before giving a tight nod.

She let out a sigh of relief. "Thank you."

Jax stood, allowing her to slide out and stand. As she turned to walk away, she noticed Sommers had said something as he lifted his beer. It wouldn't have been odd, except Jax was standing next to her, leaving no one near the major. *Earpiece.* How many had just listened in on their conversation?

Jax followed her to the door. "I'll get you out of there, Sienna. I promised Bobby I'd look out for you, and I will."

She forced a small smile and placed her hand on his bicep. "I'm where I need to be, Jax. The Sephians need me. I can save lives."

"Always the humanitarian," he said.

She gave a small smile, turned, opened the door, and stepped into the cool night air. Grabbing the helmet off the seat, she hopped onto her Can-Am Spyder and peeled away from the curb, not quite confident whether she had just helped the Sephians or opened their back door to the proverbial wolf.

As she sped under flashes of streetlamps, it hit her that Jax and Sommers were the first humans she had spoken to in many long months. It seemed like forever ago since she hadn't been the one the Sephians looked at like she was the alien. The normalcy of something as simple as a bar reminded her of the quiet, easy life she used to have.

She sped to burn out the tension in her body. There was no going back, and she didn't want to. She didn't regret her choice to join the Sephians, not that she'd really had one to begin with. But fate had brought her to Legian for a reason. She was good at helping out those in need, and she knew that she could make a difference—no matter how small—in both human and Sephian lives.

A bike identical to hers pulled up alongside. Legian's all-black garb and body shape was one she knew all too well. They drove side by side down the highway then down a winding country road, making turns every couple of miles until they reached a dead-end —their rendezvous point.

She climbed off her bike, pulled off her helmet, and scowled at Legian. "You were supposed to stay off the highway. What if someone saw you?"

He'd removed his helmet and rubbed his head, the moonlight glistening off his skin. He motioned to his full suit. "And they would've assumed I was just another biker."

She shook her head. "You're lucky we weren't followed."

He reached into a chest pocket and pulled a small black device with two buttons, one blue and one red. He clicked the blue button. It lit up immediately.

Her jaw slackened. "Jax. I can't believe he bugged me."

"Your race is better trained than I anticipated," he said as he ran his hands over her.

"I guess the major was serious about wanting to know the location of the base," she said, holding out her arms. "Damn it, I should've expected that."

Legian stepped away and held up a tiny device. Legian dropped the tracker and shot it, sending dirt and leaves scattering. He watched the charred device smoke for a couple of seconds before he holstered his blaster and clicked the red button. "This should block the signal from any other bugs."

She frowned. "You should've turned it on the moment I left the bar."

"I have no idea if it blocks human tech."

"Do you think they'll know we destroyed the tracker?"

"Yes." He turned to look down the dark road. "They're coming."

"I don't hear anything." She looked down the road, but couldn't see anything beyond the first curve. With the bike headlights off, the country night was black under a thick cloud cover. Exactly how Sephians liked it best.

"Three vehicles. About a mile off. Closing in fast."

"Call the base for an earlier pickup?" she asked.

"No time."

Chapter 5

"Into the woods," Legian said and took lead.

There was no mistaking the engine noise now. They were coming up fast and hard. Multiple big vehicles. Sienna followed Legian in the blackness, putting all her faith in his ability to find them a way out of this mess.

Legian helped her weave around trees. The engine noises cut, so he picked up the pace, and branches whipped at her from all directions. She could hear voices then the rustling of leaves as their pursuers began closing the distance between them. Adrenaline gave her added acuity, but she was still no match for the speed of the military unit on their tails.

"Stay safe."

"What?"

Without any additional warning, Legian shoved her, and she was sliding down a sharp decline. She landed hard and rolled back onto her feet. Legian had pushed her into a gully of some kind. She cautiously cocked her head from side to side. No whiplash. No broken bones. Still, her body was going to remind her of the fall in the morning. Legian tended to forget that she lacked the Sephian ability to heal.

"Legian?" she whispered.

No answer.

With the moon hidden behind clouds, she couldn't make out much in the darkness. She held out her arms and began to walk forward as fast as a nearly blind woman could in a forest at night. She heard someone breathing fast above her and froze. When the sound disappeared, she hurried forward, only to tumble over something and onto the ground.

Grabbing her now-throbbing shin, she leaned back against the fallen tree she'd catapulted over. To make matters worse, she found a soldier standing over her. His eyes were covered with night vision goggles, meaning he could see fine in the dark. He held a GPS-style device in one hand with a flashing bleep right in the center. The red light glinting off the nine-millimeter gun he held in the other. Damn. She had a second bug on her.

"Halo Two reporting. Target One attained. At least one unaccounted for. No tracking," the soldier spoke into the night air. It was Jax's voice. "Halo One. Come in." He paused for a moment and looked around, his gun still trained on her. He tried to reach his unit several more times, and by the number of F-bombs he dropped, he wasn't getting the response he was looking for. "Are you okay?"

Sienna realized he was now talking to her. "Yeah, I think so."

"Good. Where's the one that was with you?"

"I'm alone."

"Then how'd you get two bikes out here?"

"He ditched me."

Jax continued to try to reach his unit.

She pulled herself up onto the log, yelped, and grabbed her leg. She winced and looked up at him. "I think my leg's broken."

Jax watched her for a moment then abruptly slid the gun into his holster and reached down to her.

As he went to examine her leg, she whipped out the Taser from the waistband of her jeans, shoved him off her, and zapped him.

Electrical buzz filled the air as the two wires sent a violent charge into his chest. The shot lasted five seconds, but she imagined it felt like an eternity for Jax. When the burst stopped, he fell to the ground. She almost felt bad for him… almost.

Sienna pulled out a small cylinder that looked like a mini lipstick tube. Colorless, odorless, and potent. She bent over Jax and shook her head while he convulsed on the ground. "Sorry, but that's what you get for bugging me." She took off the cap and ran it across his neck the moment his hand grabbed her calf. Instantly, his grip relaxed, and his eyes fell shut. Jax would be out for hours.

Her leg throbbed. She may have exaggerated that her leg was broken, but it was close. She pulled the wires from his chest, retracted them into the Taser, and slid the weapon back into her waistband. She then felt around his neck for a transmitter and realized it was an all-in-one earpiece. She tossed it into the darkness.

"Hey." A voice startled her from behind. She swung out, and he ducked. "Good form." Legian sounded more pleased than pissed that she'd tried to punch him.

She pulled out her black bandana and wiped the sweat from her face, and then she looked up at Legian. "Where'd you go?"

"Leading the rest off-trail. I blocked their transmissions. Should buy us a minute or two before they regroup."

"So that's why Jax couldn't get a hold of them."

"This is Jax?"

She nodded. "But the blocker didn't work. He must've got a second bug on me because he used a GPS to find me."

She didn't want to ask, but she had to. "What do we do with Jax?"

"Leave him. We don't have time. I have a new rendezvous point."

"We can't leave him here. What if they don't find him? What if he gets bit by a rattlesnake or eaten by a bear?"

"The bears in this area are small. They could only gnaw on him."

An idea struck her. "We'll take him to the base. Introduce him to Apolo."

"We could use a hostage."

"As a guest," she corrected. "Sommers didn't believe me that the Sephians are allies. Maybe he'll believe one of his guys more."

After a brief moment of thinking through her words, Legian responded with his unique cross between a grumble and a sigh.

With a grunt, more for effect than strain, Legian lifted the unconscious soldier onto his shoulders, and they made their winding escape through the woods. The sounds of breaking twigs and crunching leaves were not far behind them.

Legian, carrying two hundred extra pounds, moved at a pace Sienna could keep up with. He remained in lead, using his natural night vision to guide them around trees and gullies. Sienna's leg throbbed with every step, but after several minutes, the pain lessened to a dull ache.

As they jogged, Legian called the base for an immediate pickup. She knew the soldiers would catch up them—they were trained for this sort of thing, and so it became a race to put enough distance between them to allow for a pickup.

Both Legian and Sienna panted as they continued through the woods.

Legian stopped and looked behind them. "They must be tracking us," he said in between breaths. "They're getting closer."

"It's me," Sienna said. "We should split up. I'm not a risk, but if they caught you..." Her words died in her mouth as she considered what the military could do to the first alien in their custody.

"Never," Legian said.

With perfect timing, a pale glow flashed three times just above them.

Sienna grinned. "They're here."

The silent shuttle touched down in a wider spot on a dry creek bed several dozen feet from them. The sound of slate cracking under its weight was welcoming. The door opened, and Legian and Sienna sprinted toward the ship. Legian, carrying Jax, entered first.

Shots rang out in the night, and Sienna ducked as she jumped on board. The door closed behind her, cutting off the sound of gunfire. She nearly collapsed with the feeling of safety in the dark ship.

"Made some friends tonight?" Nalea asked from the pilot's seat as she handed Sienna a pair of what she nicknamed *drades*, the goggles that allowed night vision.

Sienna sighed as she slid on the glasses and the ship's interior came into full view. "I'll tell you about it later."

"I'm counting on it." Nalea lifted the ship from the ground.

Through the pilot's screen, Sienna could see at least a dozen troops entering the clearing, shooting at the bulletproof hull as they did so.

Nalea pointed to the screen. "Look, they keep shooting at us like they can damage something."

"I need a second pair of *drades* for Jax," Sienna said.

"He doesn't need them," Legian grumbled from the back.

"He's a *guest*," Sienna reminded him.

"Hold your hollies." Nalea rustled through a compartment. "I know I have an extra pair up here."

"It's horses," Sienna replied with a smirk to her friend. Nalea spoke excellent English, but for some unknown reason, clichés and jargon threw her off every time.

Nalea rubbed her head. "Horses? Son of a bitch. I always mess that one up. Hold your damn horses, Sienna."

Sienna grinned and shook her head.

After a minute or so of opening and closing compartments, Nalea held out a second pair of glasses. "Strap in," Nalea said. "We'll be at the base in no time."

"Divert," Legian said from the back where he was disarming and securing Jax. "Sienna has a tracer somewhere on her."

"Sounds like you *really* made some friends," Nalea said. "Okay, I'm diverting now."

The ship twisted onto a new flight path, and Sienna held on to keep from falling.

Nalea pointed to a compartment near the ceiling. "There should be a scanner in there."

Sienna fumbled with the latch. Once open, she rummaged through the devices and pulled out one.

"No," Nalea said. "It's the black one."

"They're all black," Sienna said.

"No, most of them are gray. How have your people managed to survive for so long?" Nalea countered.

Sienna held up another one.

"No."

A third one.

"Yes," Nalea said.

Sienna clicked the only button on the device and scanned her clothes. It flashed near her hip. She examined her waistband and found it on her belt.

She handed the tracker to Legian who dropped it into a trash compactor. Meanwhile, she scanned herself one more time to make sure Jax hadn't planted a *third* bug.

She went to put away the scanner, but Legian stopped her. He motioned to the unconscious soldier. "Scan him."

She stepped over to Jax and ran the scanner over him. The scanner vibrated over his forearm. She pulled up his shirtsleeve and ran it over him again. Dammit, he was microchipped. "Uh, guys?"

"Use a blocker," Nalea said as she flew the ship.

"Blockers don't work," Sienna said.

"Use your knife," Legian said.

Her eyes widened. "You serious?"

"I'll do it," Legian said.

"No, I'll do it," Sienna said quickly. She didn't trust Legian to be gentle. She set down the scanner, pulled out her Swiss Army knife, and gulped. She ran her fingers across his skin several times. Only once she was sure she found the rice-sized microchip did she make a small slice and push it out. Immediately, she took her bandana and tied it over the bleeding wound.

Legian disposed of the microchip.

"All bugs are taken care of," Sienna called out.

"Returning to base flight path," Nalea said.

Sienna looked at Jax to see his eyes were now open. He was looking around, but she knew he couldn't see anything without night vision. "You're awake."

"You trying to slit my wrists?" Jax asked.

"You planted bugs on me. Call us even," she snapped back.

"You tased me. You know how much that hurts?" he asked. "We're nowhere close to being even."

She slid the glasses onto his face for him since his hands were bound. Jax took in the high-tech cabin. Everything was so different from human planes. There were no keyboards of any kind. Every unused space was covered by smooth panels of dim screens. Sienna wouldn't have known they were computer screens as opposed to just wall panels, let alone been able to read them, without the glasses. The ship was controlled by mental commands made through a band worn around the pilot's neck. Legian swore the technology was simple, but when he tried to explain it to her, it sounded anything but.

"Where am I?" Jax asked after a length.

"You're on a Sephian ship," Sienna answered. "You get to meet Apolo."

He didn't answer, and he certainly didn't look pleased. If anything, he looked like the grim reaper had come for him.

Chapter 6

"You're not a prisoner," Sienna said.

"Then untie me," Jax said.

"No," Legian said.

Sienna moved to remove his restraints.

"Sienna, leave them," Legian said.

She looked up to see Legian, sitting directly across from Jax and pointing his blaster at him. She glared, knowing he would never shoot inside a ship. "Apolo wanted me to contact Jax. He's a guest, not a prisoner." She removed the rubber-like bindings, and Legian, surprisingly, didn't stop her.

She took a seat and watched Jax rub his wrists. She knew he must have had the same thoughts going through his mind that she'd had three months earlier when she stood outside a Sephian ship. Make a run for it or play along… for now.

He continued to look around the ship, clearly trying to ignore the blaster aimed at him.

Sienna broke the silence. "Impressive, isn't it? The first time I was in one of these, I didn't have those night vision glasses so I was blind."

He pulled down the glasses then slid them back on.

"Draeken night shades," she said. "I call them *drades* for short."

"That's the worst slang word I've ever heard," Nalea said from the cockpit.

Sienna shrugged. "You're just jealous you didn't think of it."

"The Draeken came from a planet with a sun like ours, so they had to wear *drades* all the time on Sephia, where everyone lived on the dark side of the world. The Sephians are the opposite. They can see at night, but light burns their eyes."

"Sienna, that's enough for now," Legian cautioned.

"We're arriving at the base," Nalea said.

A minute later, the ship landed softly and silently on the base's hangar deck.

Sienna unbuckled her belts and helped Jax with his. When she headed to the door, Legian blocked her way. "Let me speak with Apolo first."

She frowned. "Okay."

He and Nalea stepped out to greet Apolo, while Sienna stayed back with Jax.

"What are the odds I get out of this alive?" Jax said softly near her ear.

"Good," she said quickly.

"You don't sound confident."

Problem was, she was feeling a bit doubtful herself. She knew now that Legian had saved her life when he brought her to the base, by taking her as his responsibility. He hadn't done the same for Jax, and she was suddenly worried that she'd doomed Jax.

Chapter 7

Sienna and Jax waited inside the ship as Apolo conversed with Legian and Nalea, two members of his trinity. His third member, Bente, stood to his right. Every Sephian leader had a trinity—a trio of their closest advisors. As usual, the Sephian leader wore the plain black Sephian uniform. No logos, decals, or emblems of any kind; there were no differences between uniforms. After being slaves for so long, it seemed as though the Sephians wanted little to do with hierarchy, though they did have a few ranks.

Apolo was the highest ranking Sephian male on both Earth and Sephia; his mate, the Sephian leader, was back on their home world. No doubt the distance from his *tahren* accounted some for Apolo's dour mood. Tonight his dark hair, a touch longer than Legian's, was mussed, likely from running his hands through it. He oozed raw sex appeal. No wonder he had been snagged by the most powerful woman of the Sephian race.

After several minutes, Apolo placed a hand on Legian's shoulder as he passed him and walked toward the ship, stopping a few feet from its steps. Apolo motioned Sienna and Jax to come forward, and Sienna stepped through the doorway first, putting herself between Apolo and Jax.

Apolo tilted his head in her direction. "Thank you for taking such great risk for the Sephian people tonight. I'm glad to see you are unharmed, and I look forward to hearing what you've learned."

He then looked around Sienna to Jax and brought a hand to his heart. "Welcome to our base, Lieutenant." His words were, as usual, spoken in near-perfect English, with only the slightest Sephian lilt. "I apologize in the manner that you were brought here. It is my hope that we become trusted allies. You may call me Apolo. I know your people have two names. My people do not as we refuse to wear the slave names given to our ancestors by the Draeken. I am the *tahcaya* of the Sephian people. In your language, my position is somewhat comparable to a general."

Apolo then gestured to the large hangar. "As you can see, this base is our ship, which we've buried under the landscape for anonymity."

Jax remained silent. Sienna suspected the soldier still considered himself a prisoner of war rather than a visitor, much like how she'd felt when she first arrived.

Apolo continued, unfazed. "Despite the circumstances of your journey, I am pleased you are here. We have much to learn from one another. Rather than bombard you with questions, I believe you may be most comfortable first becoming acclimated to this environment. As your people say, make yourself at home. I will see to it that you have access to anything you need." He motioned to the third member of his trinity, who stepped forward. "Bente here will be your guide during your stay with us. First, he will see to it that you can communicate with your commander so that he is aware of the circumstances."

"What if I want to return to my unit?" Jax asked.

"I'll see that arrangements are made, should you wish to

return. However, I hope you will stay for at least a few hours so that we can discuss how best for me to meet your commander."

Jax's eyes narrowed. "Whatever my commander says. No longer."

Apolo gave a small nod. His wrist-comm chimed, and he frowned. "I need to see to something. We will talk after you check in with your commander." Without waiting for a response from Jax, the Sephian leader turned and walked away.

"I'll show you where you can make a call," Bente said. He sounded polite enough, except Sienna knew Bente was anything but a nice guy. If Sienna were a gambler, she'd lay her money on the two being at each other's throats in five minutes flat.

"I'll go with you," she offered.

"Sure," Bente replied, and then motioned Jax down a hallway. "Pick up your feet, soldier. Try to keep up."

Where Nalea struggled with American vernacular, Bente had picked it up with ease. Sienna could almost see Jax's curious glare burning into the Sephian's back as he turned on his heel and followed his Sephian guide.

<hr>

3 minutes later.

Bente shoved Jax against the wall. Jax twisted and slammed Bente against the wall.

Bente chuckled dryly. "You must have one hell of a death wish, human. You think you could take me on? Even if you got past me," he said with no sound of humor in his threat, "there's a base full of Sephians here who'd skin you alive. You think you can take us all on?"

Jax wasn't backing down. Not one inch. "Try to knock me around again, and I guarantee you're going to be hurting."

Bente shoved him away. "If you put my people at risk, I don't give a flying fuck how you fight. I will put you down."

Sienna rolled her eyes. "Enough already." When neither moved, she glared at Bente. "Great job at making friends with humans, Bente. Way to go. Apolo would be impressed"

Bente narrowed his eyes before backing up a step. "Truce. For now." He held out his hand.

Jax looked at it for a very long moment then shook it. Bente patted Jax's shoulder, and it was like some pressure valve had been released. A bit, at least.

Bente started walking down the hall, and Sienna walked alongside Jax behind the Sephian. "I feel a man crush coming on. You two need some time alone?"

Bente belted out a laugh and then muttered a curse in English.

"Geez, Ben. I know I didn't teach you that one. You've been watching too much TV," she said.

He shrugged. "Not much else to do around here."

"Does everyone here speak English?" Jax asked.

"And Spanish," Sienna answered. "Many can speak six or seven other languages already."

Jax frowned. "How long have they been here?"

"We studied your primary languages on our journey here. We also have weekly required language and humanities lessons," Bente replied, not answering Jax's question.

"The Sephian language is so complicated, picking up new languages is a piece of cake for them. Hell, I've been trying to learn Sephian for three months and only have the basics. And I've got two degrees and three languages under my belt."

"Or, maybe it's because we're smarter," Bente said before stopping at a closed door. He swiped his hand over a touchpad on the wall, and the door opened with a whoosh. Inside, a young comm-tech sitting before several screens looked over his shoulder.

"Tanel," Bente began. "This is Jax. He needs to make a phone call."

"Oh. Okay," the comm-tech replied and motioned for Jax to

come in. "I can place a call through the Internet using voice over IP. I just need a phone number."

Jax turned to Bente. "Or, you could just give me back my phone, and I could use that."

"You get your gear back when Apolo says and not before," Bente said. "So, do you want to make a call or not?"

Jax's eye ticked. "Yeah, I'll make the call." He headed into the room. When Bente followed, Jax added. "A little privacy?"

Bente smirked and stepped back out. "I can always listen to the call later."

"Bente," Sienna scolded. "You are not recording his call. How's that going to inspire trust?"

"Don't bother, Sienna," Jax said. "I wouldn't have believed him if he said otherwise." He turned back to the comm-tech and made his call.

Bente and Sienna stood in the hallway. She could overhear the call, but Jax spoke in code—numbers and random words—indecipherable to her, but she imagined the comm-tech would spend the next few hours translating it. During the last bit of the call, Jax switched to normal dialogue. "They're treating me fine, and I'm going to talk with their leader, Apolo, soon. I'll call you again as soon as I can."

Sienna gave Jax a thoughtful look when he stepped into the hallway. "How's Major Sommers handling you being here?"

"I think he was surprised I'm still alive."

"Probably because if positions were reversed, ours would be dead already," Bente said.

"Nah," Jax said. "We'd run all kinds of tests first, then kill you."

"We'd better get going. Apolo's room is on the other side of the base." Sienna rushed the words out before Bente could snap back a retort.

Bente motioned to Sienna. "After you."

She led them down the hallway. "This base is just the ship they came here in, so once you look at it like it's a spaceship, every-thing makes more sense. You can use the screens on the walls to pull up maps, find out where someone is, or call someone."

"But you don't have access," Bente added to Jax.

"*Yet.* You don't have access yet," Sienna clarified.

Jax's eyes narrowed. "You can see where anyone is at any time?"

Sienna nodded. "Yes. There are cameras everywhere except inside quarters, and the computers log every time you enter a room." She pointed to a touchpad. "See? Every room has one."

Jax looked at a touchpad on the wall like he was trying to process all the details of the place. "Everyone here military, or are there civilians based here as well?"

Bente answered. "All Sephians, regardless of age, are consid-ered warriors. We do not have a formalized military division like you have."

"I noticed."

Sienna cocked her head. "What do you mean?"

He paused before answering. "Well, I haven't seen many guards. Most of the folks seem pretty casual. Very few are carrying weapons, not concealed, that is. This place doesn't look like a very secure base, especially if it's an HQ."

Bente shrugged. "We're shorthanded. The Draeken controlled our world longer than our historical records date. All Sephians who have reached adulthood were born into slavery, so, for many of us, our military training was surviving the Noble War. We learn as we go." Bente pointed at Jax. "But make no mistake. Our lack of training is not a sign of weakness. Everyone around you is a survivor and will do anything it takes to stay that way."

Jax ignored the veiled threat. "The Noble War. That where you fought the Draeken?"

"Yes, and we beat them. Our race was nearly destroyed, but the Draeken fared even worse. We estimate the few thousand who survived the Noble War jumped off-world in a mass exodus executed in a single night. We destroyed every short-range vessel that attempted to escape, but one of their core ships got away. We tracked it to Earth, which is how we ended up here to save you pale-skins."

Jax raised a brow. "We pale-skins have done a pretty good job at taking care of ourselves before you came along, Goldilocks."

"You haven't met the Draeken yet," Bente said.

Sienna walked faster to move them along. Jax slowed as they passed a closed door that beautifully strange a cappella music emanated from.

Bente pointed at the door. "That room's off limits."

"It's where Sephians worship their gods. They are very protective of their beliefs," Sienna said. "The gardens are the next level down. They're gorgeous. Most of the Sephian food is grown down there. Hopefully, you stay long enough to see it."

"He isn't staying," Bente said.

She let out a breath. A little help from Bente would've been nice at improving race relations. Instead, he posed in his classic I-don't-give-a-shit stance. She ignored him and took the next right, which opened up into a massive space. She walked through the middle, ignoring the tables of Sephians watching them. "Here's the Commons, where everyone eats. Pretty much just like any other cafeteria you've seen. Sephians are vegans, not that there's anything wrong with that, but they could learn a thing or two about spices. At least they have beer."

She opened the cooler and grabbed three beers, handing one to Jax and one to Bente. "Thought we could use some refreshments along the way."

Jax opened his can and took a single drink. She suspected he'd drink little more.

Paying no attention to Jax or Sienna, Bente drank his beer as he watched a table of Sephian females who looked up from their chatter every now and then to flash him flirty smiles.

"Good to see your fan club made it, Ben," Sienna said.

He tossed the empty can into a receptacle. "Let's get you to Apolo's." He took lead through the Commons and the hallways beyond.

As they continued their walk, Jax looked around, taking in everything. Sienna wondered what his trained eyes noticed that she never had.

"This is a massive ship," Jax said.

"I still get lost." She motioned around them. "The rest of the base is mostly living quarters or storage rooms.

"Do you have a brig here?" Jax asked.

Sienna thought for a moment then shrugged. "I don't think so. I've never seen any cells."

"We have a brig," Bente said.

"Do you have any Draeken in the brig?" Jax asked.

"Nope," Bente replied. "The only good Draeken is a dead Draeken."

Jax's gaze flashed to Bente before turning away. "Not much use for a brig then, unless it's to keep your own people in line."

"Or it's to keep annoying hu—"

"I've only seen one Draeken," Sienna interrupted. "They'd have a harder time blending in than Sephians because of their wings."

"It's true," Bente said. "The Draeken have sickly pale skin, much like humans, but they tend to be taller. And, yes, they have wings."

"Wings would make any attempt to secretly infiltrate our world much more difficult," Jax said. There was a lot of thinking going on in Jax's head by the look on his face. After taking another drink, he looked directly at Bente. "Can the wings be amputated?"

Bente nodded. "They can, and we've seen it done. But it's rare. Generally only half-breeds have it done. More out of shame than anything. It's rare a pure-blood would ever do it. Their wings are a source of pride, and proof of lineage is displayed across the skin. With how low their numbers now are, they would have to be desperate to go to such measures. Also, the wings are fully functional. To remove them is akin to removing a major organ, like their legs. Their ability to take flight has given them a significant advantage in many battles."

"What are their key weaknesses? How did you defeat them?" Jax asked

"We beat them with just enough luck and far too much sacrifice," a voice said from a doorway.

All heads jerked around to see Apolo step out into the hall. "Lieutenant, it's my hope that you can help bridge our worlds so that your people do not have to fight the same fight."

Jax gave a small nod. "Let's hear what you have to say."

Apolo gestured to his room. "I said we would talk; however, I gained some valuable information not long after you landed that we must address first. I welcome you to join me on this mission so you can see first-hand what we're up against." He looked across the three faces. "I have just learned the location of a Draeken camp."

Chapter 8

Sephians. Draeken. Aliens. In no way could either pass as human, yet both were now inexplicably connected to Sienna's people. And here she sat, left behind in a makeshift underground base, as the two fought over her kind. One for domination, the other for freedom.

She felt so useless.

Sienna, as a noncombatant, was staying behind. Finding herself fidgeting, she headed over to the training room to burn off some energy.

As she hefted the blaster in her hand, she couldn't help but appreciate Sephian technology. She could shoot the hell out of a target without ever having to reload. And that was exactly what she did. She didn't know how long she fired, all she knew was that by the time she released pressure on the trigger, the target was nothing but smoking black ash. A burnt-metal scent and haze filled the room, but her patience hadn't improved.

At least she could hit the target. Shooting laser guns was completely different from shooting regular guns. Give her a twenty-two pistol and she could hit a beer bottle at twenty yards. Laser guns, on the other hand, were much more sensitive and precise, even without the kick, making it nearly impossible to hit a target more than several feet away without concentration. Good for a sniper, bad for Sienna "Shotgun" Wolfe.

Even practicing for a full hour every day, she still didn't have as good an aim with a blaster as she had with her Glock.

"Nice shooting."

She snapped around and grabbed at her heart with one hand. "Jesus, Lea. I could have shot you."

Nalea pursed her lips. "That would have been a mean thing to do. I don't think I would be your friend anymore if you did that."

"Yeah. Because you'd be dead."

"Your aim's not that good yet," she retorted.

"It's better than your clichés." She sighed and looked down at her watch. The ships should be arriving at the base any minute now. She walked over and set the blaster in its charger on the weapons wall. "I hope everything goes well."

"It will," Nalea said. "We hit the jackpop this time. Apolo's informant provided us the location of their primary camp, and he's never fed us bad information before."

"First, it's jack*pot*, which further proves my point that my aim is far better than your clichés. Second, that's great news. If we could take a camp that big, we could handicap them in one blow."

"That's the plan."

Sienna thought for a second. "We could shoot some more while we wait, or... I have an unopened bottle of wine in my room."

Nalea smiled. "Wine, definitely."

"We'll grab it and head down to the gardens," Sienna said.

"That's the best idea I've heard all day."

They headed down the dim hallways toward her room. About halfway there, alarms screeched and lights blinked in muted neon colors down the hallway.

"What's going on?" Sienna asked, glancing around.

The intercom answered her first. The wards have been

breached was repeated over and over. Lucky for her, the Sephians had switched everything to English in a step toward integration.

Nalea and Sienna shot each other a quick look before the pair raced toward the tech-hub, and were the first to join the comm-tech on duty.

"Status," Nalea commanded.

The comm-tech started speaking in Sephian until he saw Sienna and switched to heavily accented English. "Security has been disconnected at checkpoints Ohni, Ufen, and Teni. No reports from any checkpoints yet. Com-screens are also down everywhere. The entire base is off-grid."

"System failure?" Nalea asked.

"No. We verified. All systems are online," the comm-tech replied, stress crackling his voice.

"How could security just disappear in so many places at once?" Sienna asked.

"Invasion?" The words were no more than a whisper as they passed from Nalea's lips.

Sienna froze. Most of their troops were on the mission. The base was protected by nothing more than a skeleton force right now. They didn't stand a chance against any kind of large attack. "Have you notified Apolo?" she asked.

He gave her a blank stare. Sienna put her hand on the comm-tech's shoulders. "Tanel? That's your name, right?"

He nodded.

She looked him straight in the eye. "Tanel, have you contacted Apolo?"

Tanel wiped his brow with his forearm. "I tried, but all communications are blocked. I don't know what else to do."

"Keep trying. Let Lea or me know as soon as you get stats on what we're up against." She turned to Nalea. "We got to find out if it's Draeken or my people. Or Sephian. And how many."

Nalea nodded. "We need weapons."

"What is the protocol for emergencies?" Sienna asked Tanel.

"Um… Um…" Tanel stammered several times before reciting the emergency management plan. "All non-troops should lock themselves in their rooms—they should know that already. Then… Gods, I don't know. Apolo always handles everything."

The comm-tech looked like he was going to freak out. She grabbed his shoulders and looked him in the eye. "Okay, Tanel. It's going to be all right. Check the protocols. Use the base-wide communications to remind everyone of protocol. Lea and I will cover things until you can reach Apolo. Do you have some kind of portable unit that can't be cut?"

Tanel scrambled through a drawer and grabbed a couple of small devices. "These coms are used for system tests, so they're kept decoupled from the network. They're voice-equipped, so you can used them for communications."

"Good. If you need to reach us, use these." Sienna and Nalea helped each other fasten the devices to their clothing.

"Lock the door," Sienna commanded. "Let no one in except us. Got it?"

He nodded.

"You'll be safe here," Sienna called over her shoulder before stepping into the hall. The nervous Tanel was out of his chair and at the lock pad before Nalea was through the door.

Nalea pointed to a map on the wall. "The armory is near checkpoint Ufen."

They jogged down the empty hallway. They had yet to see another soldier. Shit had seriously hit the fan.

"Ufen, Ufen. That's D. Can't risk it; that one's off the grid." Sienna spoke her thoughts aloud. She came to a screeching halt and grabbed Nalea's arm, stopping her instantly. "The training room. It has plenty of weapons, and it's closer."

Nalea nodded. "Good idea."

And with that, they cut down the hallway to their left and were in the training room seconds later. They cautiously stepped into the large room and spread out. The facility was empty, and they ran to the weapons cabinet. Fortunately, all the lock pads still worked, and she followed Nalea's lead in grabbing weapons and gearing up even though Sienna hadn't trained with many of the weapons yet.

At that moment, Tanel's shaky voice came over the intercom, telling everyone to lock themselves in their rooms.

"Ready?" Nalea asked.

Sienna shoved a handful of hand restraints into the one cargo pocket that wasn't chock full of weapons. She did one final check before looking up. "Ready."

Nalea poked her head into the hallway. "Clear."

Sienna stepped forward, and her back pocket zapped her with a tiny electrical bolt. She fumbled for the comm that could double as a portable bug killer. Nalea had hers out and to her ear already.

"Go," Sienna commanded into the flimsy bookmark-shaped device.

"It's the Draeken," the comm-tech said in a rush. "They're everywhere. It's impossible. How'd they—?"

"Calm down, Tanel," Sienna spoke into her com. "How many are there?"

"Don't know. Dozens. More."

Not good. "Where are they now?"

"Looks like they are all moving toward the Commons from the three checkpoints."

Nalea frowned. "But there's nothing at the Commons. Why are they moving away from the armory?"

"They have to go through there to get to the tech-hub and the officer quarters. Or, ah, shit. Of course."

"What?" Nalea asked.

"They plan to set up shop in the Commons to divide and conquer the base." With the exception of a few smaller hallways that connected the larger hallways like strands of a spider's web, the ship was set up according to a hub-and-spoke pattern, with everything coming together at the Commons. The Draeken would effectively cut off all areas of the base from each other then sit and wait for Apolo to return. They could decimate the Sephian force in one blow with minimal casualties on their side.

"Good work, Tanel. Keep us posted." Sienna slid the comm back into her pocket.

"We can't let them take the Commons. If Tanel can't get a hold of Apolo to warn him…" Nalea didn't finish. Sienna couldn't blame her; they both knew the outcome already, and it didn't need to be put into words.

The lights all brightened. Nalea winced, and Sienna pocketed her *drades*. "They've accessed the light systems," Nalea said, shielding her eyes with one hand.

With the Sephians blinded, the Draeken could practically waltz in and take the base with no casualties on their end. For this situation to happen when half the Sephians were off base, there was no way it was coincidental. Decision time. She grabbed Nalea's arm. "Okay. You find some sunglasses and head to the checkpoints that didn't show breaches to pull together what's left of our forces into something that can take on the Draeken. Since I can see, I'll try to beat the Draeken to the Commons and block them."

"You can't possibly think to hold off the Draeken on your own."

"Maybe, maybe not; but I can at least buy you time to bring in the cavalry."

Nalea watched her for a moment then nodded. "Kill on sight."

"Damn straight." As they split to go down separate hallways, Sienna paused and turned to face her friend. "Hey, Lea?"

"Yeah?"

"You better not drink that wine without me."

"Wouldn't dream of it." She gave Sienna a smile that was all too quickly erased by battle-hardened features before disappearing around the bend of the hall.

Sienna was alone; completely, utterly alone against an alien force she didn't stand a chance against. She'd only seen one

Draeken before—the scout Legian had killed who, without Legian's action, would've killed Sienna. She reached for the com. "Update," she commanded.

"Looks like each group is a full squad. Twelve in each. There are at least four groups, maybe more. The Ohni group will be there soon, within a few minutes at most. Some med-techs blocked the hallway. It slowed them down a bit. The other two groups are farther back. Looks like some of our folks are fighting back."

Without another word, Sienna sprinted toward the Commons. There was no sound as she approached the large, open area, not even the usual noise of pots and pans clanging in the kitchen.

Looking around the room filled with enough tables and chairs to seat half the base, she turned back to the kitchen. It was the only place where she wouldn't be a sitting duck. With a hop, Sienna hoisted herself over the waist-high counter and gauged her surroundings. The ceiling was ten feet high. It would limit the intruders' ability to fly, and she could use all the help she could get.

She set two blasters on the counter in front of her. One human against thirty or more winged aliens—she'd have better odds of winning the lottery. She shook her head. All she needed to do was delay the Draeken until Nalea brought in the reinforcements.

A noise came from hallway Ufen. The temperature in the Commons seemed to skyrocket, though she knew it was from her adrenaline. More sounds followed: boots thudding, weapons clanging, clothes rustling. It grated against her nerves. *Show time.*

She wiped sweaty hands on her pants before reaching into a pocket and pulling out a small disc. A Draeken chaos-charge. She examined it with irony. A taste of their own medicine would serve the bastards right.

When the first Draeken came into sight, she nearly dropped the charge. Sienna had forgotten how intimidating they were. Taller than even the Sephians, with silver hair, gray eyes, and skin covered by complicated weaves of colored designs; not to mention those wings. There was nothing else like it. The wings were huge, taller than each soldier. Even tucked in, they were the same width as each Draeken. It was terrifying and beautiful in a fallen angel kind of way.

As they started to spread out, she swiped her finger down the ignition pad and threw the disc into the center of the squad. The charge was designed for use against Sephians, but she was counting on the fact that the thing wouldn't be pleasant for its creators, too. The moment the charge hit the ground, she crouched behind the counter, closed her eyes, and held her hands to her ears. Even so, the sound was deafening when the charge exploded in an eruption of light brighter than the sun and a sound like a harpy's screech.

When she could bear it, she pulled her hands from her ears and picked up the blasters. She jumped up and began shooting like she'd gone insane. The Draeken, with blood oozing from their ears, staggered from the blast, knocking down tables and crawling behind them. Two Draeken went down beneath her first spray of shots. The remaining Draeken fired back, and she ducked behind the counter. Their shots cut through the wall like fire through papier-mâché. Her heart lurched in her chest. What the hell kind of technology did these guys have?

Scrambling to the next counter, Sienna pulled out a second charge. Only this one wasn't a Draeken charge. This one had been created by the Sephians, and she hated it; it reminded her of the dark ages, when lives had mattered so very little.

Voices, sounding muffled, were approaching.

Don't hesitate. She raised herself enough to send another barrage of shots across the open area. At least one shot made it home, because she heard a grunt followed by yelling. She shimmied across the floor back to the original counter. Can't let them get a bead on me.

Sienna simultaneously pushed two buttons on the blood-charge before throwing it over the counter. Like the chaos-charge, accuracy didn't matter on this one. She curled into a fetal position. Shouts and sounds of scrambling Draeken filled the air. Clenching her fists, she prayed she was safe behind the counter.

There was no sound when the blood-charge exploded. The screams were the only way she knew it had gone off. And there were plenty of those. She waited for several seconds after everything became deathly silent before she warily pulled herself to her knees and peered over the counter. The entire squad had been killed. Hundreds of tiny x-shaped spurs stuck out of their bodies and wings.

The marks left on their skin were identical to the scars Legian had gained during the war. His squad had been discovered while sabotaging a Draeken base. The only two survivors, Bente had dragged Legian into the woods, where they had played hide-and-seek with the Draeken for days until they were rescued. Legian had been lucky. If it hadn't been for Bente to pull energy from, he never would have lived.

A couple of the Draeken still moaned. She pitied them. The spurs were coated with a deadly cocktail of anticoagulant and poison designed specifically for Draeken physiology. They were already dead; their bodies just didn't know it yet.

Her pity didn't last long. A shot whizzed by her ear, signaling a second squad already spreading out into the room.

Dammit. Where's Nalea?

She felt in her pockets for another charge. No more.

"Nuleet," a Draeken called out. He said something else, but she couldn't make out the strange curt words that reminded her of the German language. Everything fell silent.

Building courage, she peeked around the corner of the counter, and found herself looking right into the eyes of a large Draeken with long, mussed silver hair.

He arched his brow. "Human?" He spoke in clear, nearly perfect English, with barely a hint of that German-like accent. The

Draeken sounded genuinely surprised at seeing her. "Surrender. You are sorely outnumbered."

"Don't be so sure. That last squad didn't last long," Sienna called out from behind the counter.

"There's no honor in using a blood-charge. Only Sephian scum would resort to that." The Draeken had the nerve to sound pissed off.

"Then how about you surrender?" she replied.

The Draeken guffawed. "To whom? I don't see Apolo here."

She gritted her teeth.

"If you surrender now, we will not hurt you. We have no intentions of harming humans. We came to this planet in peace."

"Yeah, sure you did," Sienna replied dryly, but her insides were twisted like a wet towel wrung too tight. She wasn't going to delude herself; she knew there was no getting out of the mess she was in.

His wings ruffled in obvious irritation. "Have it your way then."

He made a motion with his hands, and his squad spread out. At that moment, the third squad appeared, looking a little worse for wear. One against twenty-four. Even after obliterating the entire first squad, her odds hadn't improved much.

A hurricane of shots flew through the kitchen, and she scurried to hide between the ovens and refrigerators. Before she reached a safe place, heat blasted her, and a sharp pain cut through her left thigh. She cried out and dropped to the ground. Blood poured from the wound, even though the blast had cauterized the skin around it. So much blood. *No!* Don't let it be an artery.

She had to stop the bleeding fast. She pulled out a hand restraint and tightened it around her thigh. The makeshift tourniquet would buy her a few extra minutes at most before she passed out from blood loss.

Her attackers must have heard her scream because the

shooting stopped. She clenched a gun in her hand. The silence scared her more than the gunfire.

"Keep moving," Sienna repeated like a mantra. With a heave, she dragged herself back to the front. Out of nowhere, a boot came down on her injured leg, and she screamed in blinding agony.

When her vision cleared, she found herself lying on her back, the Draeken who had spoken before now towering over her. He got down on one knee, watching her with silver eyes, then grabbed her gun and yanked her to him.

"So, have the humans allied with the Sephians?"

Her strength siphoning from her body, she didn't respond. He continued to watch her. A laser cut through a wing and he swung back against the sink, the plastic shattering.

"Sienna!"

She pulled herself up to see Nalea running toward her. Sienna had never seen a more beautiful sight in her life. The sounds of battle echoed from the cafeteria.

"It's about time." She reached out for the gun the Draeken had taken from her, which he'd dropped when Nalea shot him.

Nalea gave her a full smile before giving the fallen Draeken a solid kick to the gut. He let out a grunt. She grabbed a fist of his hair and yanked. "Roden." She spat the name with vile surprise.

Even though his brow was furrowed in pain, he smiled. "I see my reputation precedes me."

"You'll pay for what you've done to my people." She pulled out her gun and aimed. His leg kicked out, knocking her down.

"Lea!" Sienna's scream came out more like a whisper. Somehow, she pulled herself up on an elbow to helplessly watch as the two clashed, too weak to help. They were too close for her to shoot. All she could do was wait for a clear shot as her friend fought an opponent who clearly outmatched her in both size and skill.

Time seemed to slow as the two fought. Roden knocked Nalea

to the ground, his wings blocking Sienna's view. They paused for a lengthy second as though frozen then Nalea twisted and came up with a blade, slicing across his shirt. His punch connected, and Nalea fell back.

With the last of her strength, Sienna fired a shot above his head, and pieces of ceiling rained down onto his wings, hitting his wound. He hissed and strode toward her.

"No." Sienna fired again. Missed. He kicked the gun out of her hand, and his boot shoved her hard. She felt herself hit the wall, and her breath burst from her lungs.

As she lost sensation in her limbs, Nalea filled her vision.

"Glad you could make it," Sienna whispered hoarsely, no longer having enough strength to talk.

"Stay with me, Sienna. Stay with me."

"We make a good team, don't we?"

"Yeah, Sienna. We do."

Those were the last words she heard before the world closed in on her.

———————————————

Chapter 9

———————————————

ell. I'm in hell.

That was Sienna's first thought when she regained consciousness. Her head throbbed. Her mouth tasted like cotton. Every muscle in her body ached. She opened her dry eyes, but the room was dark.

When she moved to pull her body upright, hot pain shot through her leg.

"Ow," she muttered hoarsely.

"Careful, *tahren*." Legian's arms enveloped her and pulled her gently into a seating position. "Here." She felt Legian wrap her hand around a glass. He coaxed it to her lips, and she nearly coughed when the cool liquid splashed her throat.

"That's enough for now." He pulled the glass away too soon and wiped water from her chin with his finger.

Sienna lay her head back against the pillow.

She was alive, which meant that, by no small miracle, they'd held back the Draeken. And Legian was here. He'd survived. She reached out, and he grabbed her hand.

"It's too dark," she said.

She heard a click, and suddenly she could see him in the light from a small beaded lamp at her side. He squinted in the light but continued to look at her.

He was frowning. "I wish you had the Sephian ability to pull energy from others to heal yourself."

"I wish so, too." She instinctively looked around for a window, even though she knew there were none. Where everything else on the base was shades of gray and black, in the medical ward, silky fabric draped the walls and all the furniture was soft. Even the plush mattress she lay on was nothing like a hospital bed. Everything was more like a surreal lounge instead of the chemical-laden cleanliness of hospitals she'd known.

Jax yawned in the corner and came to his feet. "You're awake."

Sienna turned, but her neck muscles were too stiff, and she closed her eyes. "How long have I been out?"

"You've been in the med-hub for four days," Jax said.

Four days?

Legian spoke. "The first two days were hard. Fayel didn't think you would pull through. But I told him you would. You don't know how to give up."

"I told him the same thing," Jax said.

She gave a weak smile. "I'm glad you stuck around, Jax, instead of heading back to your unit."

He shrugged. "Sommers wants to keep a unit on the ground here. My team was reassigned to advise Apolo."

More likely, he was reassigned to keep tabs on Apolo, Sienna thought to herself. "So, what did I miss? Did everyone make it?"

"Nalea brought you here after the attack," Legian said. "She saved your life. We suffered minimal casualties on the base; all thanks to you, from what I've heard. But gods, Sienna. When I learned you faced the Draeken... on your own, no less..."

As his words trailed off, Sienna closed her eyes when she remembered. "All I did was cause a distraction until Nalea could get there with reinforcements."

"Distraction?" Jax guffawed. "You took out an entire Draeken squad on your own."

Legian smiled. "It seems that my tahren is the now the most beloved human on this planet."

"Hi, Jax," a woman said sweetly.

Jax gave her a friendly wave. "Hey."

Sienna looked up to see a petite, Sephian female enter the room. Like all med-techs, she wore colorful clothes. On Sephia, everything was tied to energy. Med-techs were more about donating energy to those who needed it than actual patch-ups. It was a glossy example of how, in some ways, Sephians and humans really were from two different worlds.

"Don't mind me," she said when she approached the foot of Sienna's bed. "I'm Risa. I'm just here to check your bandage."

"Do you mind, Legian?" Risa asked, shielding her eyes from her lamp.

Legian clicked off the lamp.

Now enveloped in darkness like that of a night with a full moon, Sienna felt the med-tech fidget with the bandage that covered most of her left thigh. Her teeth clenched, and she sucked in a breath.

"You're lucky to still have your leg, let alone your life," Risa said. "If Jax hadn't been here to transfuse blood, you might not be here. We were very lucky his blood worked. It's too bad you don't have our ability to heal. It would save you a lot of time and pain."

"So I've heard," Sienna gritted out, and threw out, "Thanks, Jax. Now, we're even."

"Not even close," he said.

Risa continued. "You're human. Do what humans do. Embrace the pain. It means you're on the road to recovery. Though, you'll be lucky to walk again."

Sienna frowned. "I don't believe you."

"Who's wearing the medical uniform?" she replied curtly.

Sienna swallowed. "Doc thinks I will be able to walk again, right?"

"You'll walk again," Jax said with confidence.

Legian spoke. "Sienna, there was considerable muscle damage. Fayel believes that, with physical therapy, you may be able to walk again with the help of a leg brace."

"I'll walk again," she said to reassure herself before changing the subject. "How'd the mission go?" When no one responded, she asked, "What happened?"

"Your leg is looking better. I'll be back to check on you a little later." Risa grabbed her gear and left the room in a rush.

Sienna turned back to Legian. It was then that Sienna recalled Roden saying there was no camp. She'd prayed their mission was a dull hop around the patch. Her gut told her that her prayers hadn't been answered. "Legian, turn on the light so I can see you."

The lamp clicked on, but he had his face turned away from her.

Jax watched Legian with a hooded gaze, clearly waiting for the other man to speak.

She turned to Legian. "Tell me what happened."

When she thought he wasn't going to answer her, Legian finally spoke. "It was a trap, and like blind children, we walked right into it. The intel showed the Draeken camp to be in a deep valley. We thought it was perfect for an attack. We didn't realize until it was too late that there was only one way in and out of the valley. It was a bottleneck. Perfect for an ambush, not an attack. They came at us from above and below. We didn't stand a chance. Over half of our ships were destroyed in the first minutes. Only four ships escaped safely."

Four? There had been five times that many. "Oh, Legian, I'm so sorry," she whispered. She wanted to hold him, but he had distanced himself.

He continued. "We lost nearly two hundred troops and any military advantage we may have had. Jax and I escaped only because we were with Apolo. Another ship allowed themselves to be slaughtered so we could escape. Fifty Sephians sacrificed their lives to save ours." His hands covered his face. "We ran, while our people were slaughtered."

"Don't," she whispered, frowning. "Don't tarnish their sacrifice. It was their choice. They gave you a chance to survive to defeat the Draeken next time."

He paused at her words then continued. "In one brilliant strike, the Draeken crippled us. We were overconfident after pushing them off Sephia. We don't stand a chance against them now." He stopped, turned to her, and then turned the other way. Like he was trying to escape the demons in his mind.

"It will be okay," she said, not knowing what else to say. Without Apolo, the Sephians would be lost, but she knew that as long as Apolo lived, the Sephians wouldn't break apart.

He swung back to her. "No, Sienna. Don't you understand? We have failed. I have failed you, your world, and your people. I should have seen the trap. Instead, I let myself become proud. Too proud to think the Draeken may be one step ahead. Too proud to consider we might not stop them. We've never been able to stop them, only run them off... and now it's too late for your world."

"You're wrong; you haven't failed. We'll stop them. My people outnumber them by billions. Our military is strong—"

"Do you really think your people stand a chance against the Draeken if they want this world?"

"Yes, I do," she said with conviction.

"I do, too," Jax echoed. "We're stronger than the Sephians give us credit for."

Legian shook his head. "You don't know the Draeken. Not like I do. They're not like any opponent your world has ever faced. Their technology is too advanced. Everything we have, we've taken from them." He paused. "I had a sister. Did I ever tell you that?"

Sienna blinked. "No, you didn't. What's her name?"

"Her name was Cepa. She was beautiful. Some even compared

her to Krysea. Cepa was five years younger than me and had more spirit than a pack of wild *fregee*. Ah, the messes she got us in." He chuckled, shaking his head, and then sobered. "A Draeken wanted her for himself. It was the master's son. It didn't matter that she'd already found her tahren."

Sienna sucked in a breath. In the corner, Jax's features were tight as he listened.

Legian continued, as if he were talking to himself. "When the master's son came to take her, Cepa's tahren managed to kill him. But he was killed as well. Cepa was devastated. She tried to end her life, but the master claimed her for himself as punishment and proclaimed that she was not to be allowed to die. During the final battle, when I found her, what I found was a shell that looked like my sister. Cepa's spirit had fled with her tahren's. I did the only thing left a brother could do. I helped her body join her spirit."

"Oh, Legian. I'm so sorry," Sienna said.

His head lifted as though it weighed a hundred pounds. "That's what the Draeken do. They claim everything, and they won't grant you peace of death until they've taken everything worth taking. How can you beat that?" Legian looked pointedly at Sienna and Jax in turn.

Sienna swallowed. "Your people beat them once. Now it's my people's turn. We'll succeed. With Sephian knowledge and guidance, we can beat them. Together, we will beat them."

He crossed his arms over his chest as though to challenge her. "And you believe that?"

She nodded. "Absolutely."

Chapter 10

Two weeks later.

Sienna leaned on her cane for support. She was at Legian's side, finding it impossible to stand still. Her adrenaline was too amped up. She'd never been to any event as important as this one.

Getting to stand at Apolo's side, she was being afforded an incredible honor, even though she knew it was only for show. Similarly, Jax stood at Apolo's other side. She glanced over at Apolo and Jax. Straight as soldiers, neither looked the least bit stressed.

They reminded her so much of Bobby right then. He'd been a gunnery sergeant under Jax. Bobby and she hadn't been married long enough for her to get to know many in his unit. She'd been ready to follow Bobby wherever he was stationed, but a teenager who was driving while texting had changed everything in an instant.

The doctors had said Bobby never felt a thing. One second he was walking across a crosswalk, the next, he was taken from her forever. Just an ordinary accident. Sienna had quit her job the following week; two months later she sold their loft, and began construction on her cabin. She'd had enough of a world that no longer made sense. She wanted to be alone. Alone was safe. Alone didn't break her heart.

Then something happened that went against all the plans she'd made and all the promises she'd pledged to herself. Just when she thought she had reclaimed control, Legian had literally crashed into her life and thrown all those plans to hell. She knew now though that helping the Sephians gave her renewed purpose. She was exactly where she needed to be.

The huge hangar doors began to open, jarring her from her reflections. The loud whoomp-whoomp of a large helicopter reverberated around the space. She watched in awe as the Chinook settled through the doors and onto the open ramp below. It dwarfed the Sephian ships, and she wondered if Apolo was ready for the change touching down on the landing pad.

It seemed to take forever for the huge blades to stop moving. Sienna's heart thumped in her chest as she willed herself to calm down. She'd told Apolo so many times that he could trust humans. Apolo was stuck behind the proverbial eight ball; his troops had been decimated, he'd lost touch with his spy, and they didn't stand a chance against the Draeken alone. Now, humanity's future teetered on humans accepting the Sephians. Jax had updated his CO every day, and several more soldiers had been sent to join him, but still, today would be a moment of reckoning.

At least two dozen troops, all dressed in black fatigues with matching emblems on their shoulders, poured out of the helicopter. The lieutenant-colonel had come prepared. Even though the Sephians still outnumbered them twenty to one, Sienna had no doubt the officer had more than enough reinforcements waiting an arm's reach away to take the base if necessary. She prayed it wouldn't become necessary.

One of the last of the group to emerge, the lieutenant-colonel stepped out of the helicopter, safely encircled by his soldiers. It was easy to recognize him; even in basic black, there was a presence about him, that indefinable air of confidence that surrounded all strong leaders.

Sienna immediately recognized Major Sommers behind the officer, and realized this was Jax's platoon, plus more.

The pair walked toward Apolo's group, a wall of men flanking them on both sides. The lieutenant-colonel stepped with intent as though he was attending a ribbon cutting ceremony rather than stepping on alien territory for the first time.

Jax stepped forward, meeting them halfway, and saluted. "Welcome to the Sephian base, Lieutenant-Colonel Jerrick, sir."

Jerrick? She furrowed her brow while she examined the officer. Gray buzz cut where Jax's was brown. Both had the same deep-brown eyes. Same nose, same chin. The older man even had the same saunter. That was why he had seemed so familiar. He had twenty plus years on his son, but the resemblance was uncanny.

The lieutenant-colonel was speaking. "Good to see you, Lieutenant. How have they been treating you and your squad?"

"We have been treated fairly and with respect, sir."

The officer watched him for a moment, as if he were gauging the sincerity of Jax's words. Then he nodded. "Good to hear. Now, let's get this show started." He turned his attention on Apolo and approached the Sephian leader.

Jax motioned to Apolo. "Lieutenant-Colonel Jerrick, this is Apolo, leader of the Sephian force here on Earth." Jax said the last word with a slight hesitation, like he'd never used it in an introduction before, which he probably hadn't. "Apolo, this is Lieutenant-Colonel Jeremiah Jerrick, commanding officer of the 51st Joint Special Operations Task Force, a battalion operating within the U.S. Space and Strategic Defense Command."

Apolo held an open hand out to the officer. "It is a pleasure to meet you, Lieutenant-Colonel. Having your son as our guest these past two weeks has been a tremendous opportunity for us to learn from one another."

The officer returned a hearty handshake. "I look forward to our conversations. And I'll warn you—I won't beat around the bush. That's not my style. I have plenty of questions. And I'm expecting straight answers."

Apolo nodded. "I would expect as much. I have placed the safety of this base and its three hundred souls in your trust."

"A gesture well received," the officer replied.

"Now, if you'd like to come with me, I have a room for us to talk candidly. We have much to discuss." Apolo gestured down a hallway.

The officer nodded. Bente and one of the officer's men stepped in front, and the two leaders walked away side by side, with their officers falling in behind and the remaining soldiers forming up around them.

A dark-skinned soldier sidled up next to Jax. He gave Jax a salute then a smile that was quickly returned.

"Staff Sergeant, it's good to see you," Jax said.

"Lieutenant," he replied.

The pair stepped in line behind the officer and Apolo, and Legian and Sienna followed after.

Sienna was far enough behind the leaders that she couldn't make out their words. Not that she tried. She assumed it was casual chit-chat, as they would wait to reach Apolo's secure quarters to get into negotiations. She hobbled with her cane to keep up with the group.

"*Yltar!*" a young Sephian yelled as he jumped out into the hallway. Everyone froze. Standing before Apolo and the officer was a young Sephian man holding a blood-charge. Bente and a soldier stood on either side of the man, both poised to attack. The sounds of bootsteps and movement erupted around Sienna.

"Giphers. Give me the charge," Apolo commanded as he stepped between the officer and the newcomer.

The Sephian shook his head, and he started to cry. "I'm sorry. I have no choice. They've got her. They've got Giras."

"Who has your sister, Giphers?" Apolo asked gently, yet his voice clearly demanding an answer.

"They'll kill her if I fail. My life for hers, they said." Tears streamed down his face, and he scowled. "We shouldn't have come here. They need us on Sephia. Let the humans deal with the Draeken. We don't owe them anything." And with that, Giphers moved his fingers, and the blood-charge lit up. He tossed the device in the air. He lowered his head to his hands and wept.

Legian threw Sienna to the ground. He landed on her leg, and sharp pain tore through it. She gasped as she tried frantically to move.

Everything seemed to move in slow motion as the charge armed over a two-second timer. Apolo dove for the hovering charge while Jax and the staff sergeant tackled the officer. Apolo grabbed the charge and threw it away down the hall as Bente covered him. It exploded in mid-flight, exactly as it was designed to do.

Sienna had never seen a blood-charge go off before. Not even when the Draeken had attacked the base. It was bizarre seeing an explosion without any sound. At first, it looked like dust filled the air. But she knew that small x-shaped barbs were in that poisoned dust, and they flew everywhere.

Giphers collapsed. Apolo and Bente hit the floor hard. Several others still on their feet fell to the ground, grasping at wounds she could not yet see.

Then the world returned to normal. Blood splattered the walls. Men yelled and moaned.

"Sienna? Sienna, are you hurt?"

She looked up into Legian's concerned eyes at the same time she felt his hand against her cheek. "I'm fine." Her dazed words came out like a shout. "You okay?"

His look of relief was instant and brief. The next instant, his frown returned, and he jumped up and ran toward Apolo.

Sienna saw Sommers on the floor, and she scrambled to him.

He held a bloody hand to his shoulder. She reached out to him. "Are you okay, Major?"

He winced. "Been through worse. What the hell was that?"

Rather than answer, she yanked off the bandana tied around her wrist and pressed it against his shoulder. "We need to get you to the med-hub."

"Don't move!" The muzzle of a gun pressed into her temple.

Sienna froze.

"I'd advise all of you to not move," the major said. He placed his hand over hers and pulled away with a wince, keeping pressure on his wound while removing her hand from under his. Her bloodied hand fell to her pants, and the cold metal barrel nudged harder against her temple.

She looked out of the corner of her eye since she couldn't turn her head. Golden and crimson blood splattered the walls, mixing together to form bizarre abstract art. Men lay on the floor and leaned against walls, gritting their teeth against the pain of their injuries. Sephians aimed blasters at the soldiers, who in turn aimed guns at the Sephians. The whole situation had become a face-off.

Sienna spotted Legian out of the corner of her eye, and he looked furious while he knelt by a wobbly Apolo and pressed his hand over his leader's arm. Blood continued to ooze out, which meant it had been a very serious injury. Bente was down, and at least a dozen rifles were pointing at them.

With Legian's help, Apolo pulled himself to his feet. She was impressed that the man was even conscious after losing so much blood. He seemed unfazed by the guns pointing at him. He turned to face the lieutenant-colonel, who fortunately looked like he had pulled through the incident unscathed though it was difficult to tell.

With the worst timing, the entire staff of med-techs came racing around the corner. Many weapons swung in their direction, but through either a miracle or training, no shots were fired. The med-techs stumbled to a stop, dropping supplies and nearly tripping over each other. They stared wide-eyed, looking from Apolo to the fiasco and back again. Risa was near the back of the group, flat against the wall.

Apolo held his uninjured arm toward the med-techs. "Allow my people to help your injured men. Their blood will not clot without the antitoxin. Anyone injured will die without assistance."

The lieutenant-colonel looked over his bloodied men then nodded tightly.

Apolo motioned to the dozen or so med-techs. "It was a blood-charge. Help the humans first. And get Bente to the med-hub fast." Two raced toward Bente, who lay unconscious on the ground, blood pouring from his back. They had him on a stretcher before the others gingerly stepped forward and spread out among the injured.

A young med-tech rushed to Apolo and swabbed him—the Sephian version of injections—with the antitoxin. Apolo stopped her when she rolled up her sleeve. "Help the humans first. Put the call out for more donors to heal the wounded Sephians."

"But... you're hurt," the med-tech stammered. "You are our highest priority."

Apolo glared at her. She paled, turned, and hustled to a fallen American soldier. Legian grabbed a cloth binding out of her bag and wrapped it around Apolo's arm to staunch the blood. Then, without a pause, he bared his chest to the Sephian leader.

Apolo shook his head. "No, friend. I need you at full strength. I will take no more of your energy today. My wound is minor. I'll wait for a donor once I know the more seriously injured are secure."

In response, Legian gave him a hard look. He slowly fastened his shirt and stood at Apolo's side. The lieutenant-colonel stood firm a few feet away.

As the leaders watched over them, Sienna turned her attention to watching the hallway turn into a makeshift hospital. Med-techs swabbed every injured soldier with the antitoxin before bandaging their wounds. Astonishingly, only Giphers had been killed, although several looked seriously injured. This wasn't over yet. Not by a long shot.

Sienna no longer felt pressure against her temple, and she looked up to see Jax watching her, his hand on the staff sergeant's gun, still inches from her head. After a tight nod from the major, the NCO backed off, slid the gun back into its holster, and helped Sommers to his feet.

A hand appeared in front of her and she grabbed it. Jax pulled her to her feet, saving her a lot of work, since her leg brace had been royally screwed up when she'd been knocked to the ground.

Jax motioned to the staff sergeant. "Ace, this is Gunny's widow. Don't point a gun at her again."

"Apologies, ma'am," Ace said. "Gunny was a good man."

"He was," she agreed as she leaned against the wall.

Without another word, the men moved. The major walked toward the leaders with Jax and Ace on either side. He paused to give her the bloodied bandana.

Apolo eyed the lieutenant-colonel, the *soullare* that vined around his eye making his gaze all the more intense. "I give you my word that I will get to the bottom of this outrage, and I promise you, justice will be both swift and merciless."

The officer, however, appeared less than swayed. "I have no doubt, but how can you represent Sephians if you can't even control your own people?"

"If I may speak, sir?" Jax asked.

The officer nodded.

Jax spoke. "I have seen the enemy, sir. The Draeken are like nothing we've ever faced. I saw them kill over two hundred Sephians in under eight minutes. What I saw will destroy us all if we don't stand together."

The lieutenant-colonel cocked his head. "If they are as vile as you say, why haven't they attacked us? Why have they only attacked Sephians?"

"Why haven't they attacked us until today, you mean? Look around you, sir. The Draeken have just declared war on your people."

The officer glanced over the hallway and waved a hand in the air. "I saw no Draeken today. We have no proof. It could've been a mutiny by Apolo's own people."

"My people are loyal." Apolo stepped forward out of Legian's supporting arms. "I will get to the bottom of today's attack. Let's continue our discussion in my room."

Lieutenant-Colonel Jerrick shook his head. "I think we've talked enough for one day."

Apolo's lips thinned. "It is my greatest hope that we can form an alliance… for the safety of your world."

The lieutenant-colonel watched Apolo for another second then nodded to Sommers, who in turn organized the soldiers. He then took a deep breath and looked around, his gaze settling on Jax. "Lieutenant, you remain here with your full platoon until further instructed. Report in to both Captain Fisher and Major Sommers at least three times per day."

"Yes, sir." Jax saluted and called out to his team.

"Apolo," Jerrick said. "I'm continuing to leave my men with you as an act of good faith. I expect you to ensure they are treated with the utmost respect, and receive open access to your base, people, information, and materials."

Apolo nodded. "You have my word. They will be given the same level of authority as my trinity." He paused and motioned to a Sephian couple, who stepped forward as though expecting to be called. "I would like to send two of my people with you for your questions, and I'm sure your doctors would like to better understand Sephian physiology. Sirlyn and Tejan are *tahren*—a bonded couple. As such, they are best equipped for you to learn about the key differences between Sephians and humans. And, I expect them to be treated as you expect your people to be treated here."

"Of course," the lieutenant-colonel replied.

Apolo continued. "In another act of good faith, I will not consider moving my base. You have our location. What you do with it will become a critical turning point in your world's history."

The lieutenant-colonel narrowed his eyes ever so slightly before giving a tight nod. "Until we talk again." Jerrick turned from Apolo and walked away surrounded by his soldiers, minus Jax's team of eight.

When Sienna felt the soldiers were a comfortable distance away, she rolled up her sleeves as she hobbled toward Apolo, who was now wavering on his feet. "Let's get you to the med-hub. And I hope you'll accept some of our energy on the way." She leaned into him, trying to hold him up as Legian came to support both of them.

"That could've gone better," the Sephian leader muttered, his voice sounding weak.

Sienna blinked as Apolo drained her energy. "It will next time." And she hoped her words held true.

So many thoughts swirled through Sienna's head as she sat in Apolo's room alongside Legian, Jax, and Nalea.

The door opened, and Sienna looked up to see a haggard Apolo enter the room. He now sported a fresh six-inch scar on his bicep, and a jagged line where a spur from the blood-charge must have slid across his arm rather than going straight in. Sienna had noticed the Sephians scarred more easily than their human counterparts and wondered if it had something to do with their accelerated healing abilities. Regardless of how fast a body healed, it still retained reminders. Instead of arthritis, the Sephians got scars.

Legian leaned forward, putting his elbows on the table. "Do you have an update on Bente?"

Some of Apolo's stress looked like it washed away with the question. "They got to him before he lost too much blood. When I checked in on him, he'd gone through three donors already and was onto a fourth. If his body accepts the new blood, he'll recover."

Nalea leaned back in her chair and looked up to the ceiling. "Praise the gods."

Legian nodded toward Apolo. "It looks like you could use another donor as well."

"We have more important business to discuss," Apolo replied with a sharp tone.

Legian gave his leader a disapproving look but, wisely, said nothing.

Apolo's fist knuckled the table. "After today's unfortunate incident, I believe it is safe to say that we remain on our own in our fight against the Draeken." He turned to Jax. "It isn't a lost cause; not yet. You and I will discuss how best to proceed tonight."

Jax nodded tightly.

"However, the alliance is not our immediate concern," Apolo continued. After a moment, he lowered his head and ran a hand through his long hair. "The Draeken influence is a festering wound in this base. Despite our best attempts, our comm-techs have found nothing. We are no closer today than we were before the ambush. We can no longer afford to wait for the traitor—or traitors—to make a mistake."

"You don't think Giphers was it," Legian said it in a way that sounded like he already knew the answer.

"That kid didn't have enough brains or balls for it," Nalea added.

"Any news from your spy?" Sienna asked.

Apolo frowned. "I lost contact with him immediately following the first base attack. Since the information he provided on the Draeken camp was faulty, I think it is safe to assume he has been compromised. We no longer have a viable source of information on the Draeken."

"*Suvaste*," Legian muttered.

Apolo nodded. "All the more reason to act now. Today's events made it clear. I believe the time has come to entice the *fregee* out of hiding." He rubbed his nearly healed arm and sat down. "Before he was compromised, my informant believed Hillas died en route to Earth from injuries he sustained before he left Sephia."

Nalea leaned forward. "If Hillas is dead, Roden is in charge of all Draeken."

Legian scowled. "Unfortunately, we can't know that for sure. We don't know when your informant was compromised. They could have been feeding him misinformation longer than we realized."

Apolo shook his head. "Possibly, although I doubt it. He's too smart for that. The last communication I received from him was distorted and audio only, which I should have seen as a red flag. All we know for now is that we can no longer make assumptions about their military strategy."

From what Sienna had heard, Hillas, the all-powerful Draeken despot, was an in-your-face brutalist. The Draeken leader was a brilliant planner, but he had no respect for life. He'd charge right into battle with no thought as to casualties on either side.

Roden, on the other hand, was a wild card, thought to be insane. No one could figure out how he operated. He often avoided full frontal assaults, yet was known to be fond of sending soldiers on suicide missions. He served as one of Hillas's generals and was believed to be the only remaining high-ranking Draeken from the Noble War. Oh, and torture was his hobby.

Her leg throbbed at the thought of him.

"With Hillas, we knew what to expect. He's always operated with some sense of moral code. We cannot make such theories if Roden is now in command. Going forward, we will operate under the assumption that they may employ any strategy necessary," Apolo added. "Although we did gain one valuable piece of information today."

Sienna's eyes widened. "What's that?"

"The traitorous dog leaving its stench around this base is on a Draeken leash. I am convinced the humans had no hand in either the ambush or the incident today. It narrows our scope considerably. The traitor is a Sephian with ties to the Draeken. Ties that have remained hidden to us. We will entice the traitor come to us."

Sienna winced. He'd thought the traitor could have been a human?

"To draw out the *fregee*, we need to offer something it cannot resist," Legian said.

Sienna tapped a finger to her lips as she thought. "How about letting it leak that the lieutenant-colonel shared the location of the Draeken core ship? That kind of intel should be irresistible to someone sympathetic to the Draeken."

Apolo tapped a forefinger to his lip. "We have kindling. Now we need a spark."

"Perhaps you conveniently keep the location and attack plans in your room," Legian added.

Apolo considered for a moment. "Yes. That should do it. We'll need to be careful about how we share this information. We don't want the traitor to become suspicious."

"My team can help with that," Jax said.

After another hour of planning, the group stepped out into the hall. The trap was ready to be set, and each person had a role to play. The traitor would be stopped tonight, no matter what.

Chapter 13

It was a dull, recurring dance. Sit, stand, pace, sit again. Boredom threatened to overtake the group holed up in the tech-hub.

Bente was furious at Apolo for making him stay in the med-hub. His temper played into the plan perfectly, although Sienna felt sorry for the med-techs on duty. He'd proven to be the worst patient she'd ever seen. She'd picked up some new Sephian cuss words when they had restrained him, which must have been pretty colorful, since even Nalea refused to translate them for her.

The restraints wouldn't have held Bente if he'd really wanted out, so it was a good thing he'd obeyed his leader and remained there to play his part. Apolo had apprised Bente of the plan, which had only fueled Bente's anger at being bedridden during an important night.

On the downside, not having Bente in the room threw off the group's cadence. Even with the constant white noise of audio filtering in over the monitors across the base, the tech-hub was quieter without his quips, making the minutes drag. Her eyes glazed over while she stared at the dozen monitors on the wall, each of them showing different angles Apolo's rooms and the hallways outside it.

If the information they had leaked made it to the right ears, Bente was miserably stuck in the med-hub—fact—while Apolo, Legian, and Nalea were to be off base tonight negotiating a new source for supplies—fiction.

The plan was beautiful in its simplicity. First, Legian and Nalea had grabbed a bite to eat at the Commons and told a few key people—the gossips—they were heading out tonight with Apolo. That kind of thing happened often, so the news was sure not to raise any red flags. Part one accomplished.

Two was where Jax's team came into play. Jax and his men had hit the training room during its busiest time to make sure they had plenty of company. After a half-hearted attempt at a work-out, they'd chatted about how Jax had got the okay to move into the officers' hall, converting the storage room next to Bente's into living space. They went into how it was great to hear some of the scoop firsthand, such as the news of a bona fide Draeken base being found, and how Apolo was sitting on the news to play it safe.

To add a cherry on top, they had spilled that they were heading into town after Jax had moved his gear to his new room. It wouldn't take a scientist to figure out the officers' hall would be left empty, leaving only the tech-hub staffed. And the comm-techs were notorious for staying holed up in the room until their shifts were up.

The Sephians already had a disdainful view of human intelligence, so for Jax and his team to leak important information fit right into their preconceived stereotypes. With three hundred Sephians cooped up in an underground bunker, the news had likely zigzagged the entire base before they'd even left the training room. Aside from the continuously staffed tech-hub, this left the small officers' hallway vacant and ripe for the disreputable to pluck.

The plan had gone into effect three hours ago, when all the participants faked their departures then retreated to the tech-hub. Now it was a waiting game. What was going to happen, Sienna wasn't sure, but something *had* to happen. They'd been on the losing team too long. They needed this win.

With her feet propped up on the table, Sienna rocked her chair on two legs. It had never occurred to her before how boring security guards' jobs could be. Waiting, watching monitors, and waiting some more. No one spoke, except for Jax who checked in with his team every few minutes.

"How's the leg?" Nalea asked her.

"Well, it's still attached. But I've discovered I could make a second career doing weather. My leg throbs every time it's going to rain." Sienna shrugged. "Then again, it throbs every day."

"We have computers that track and forecast the weather for us," Tanel said. "They are one hundred percent accurate. I believe your leg cannot be as accurate."

"You'd be surprised," she muttered.

With no warning, the lights flickered on several screens, and then went out. Sienna hastily wiped her fingers across her jeans and glanced over at the wall of monitors. She frowned. Lights were still on across the base except in the vacant officers' hallway. Being underground as the base was, the hallway had no windows, leaving the screens pitch black. Even the nocturnal Sephians couldn't see in that kind of dark without some kind of help.

"We're blind," she spoke aloud. When she didn't get a response, she looked up at Apolo, who didn't look the least bit surprised. "You were expecting this?"

He nodded. "I suspected our prey may try this, and I had a taciturn system installed today in this hallway."

Seconds felt like minutes. Legian, Nalea and Jax scanned the monitors, and Sienna followed their lead. Tanel's fingers danced energetically across the digital keyboard. Then, a neon-outlined shape emerged on the screen. She had no idea what a taciturn system was, but it wasn't infrared. Whatever it was showed a lot more features and colors than any infrared image she'd seen before. She could see a man's shape, the outline detailed enough to show he was wearing some kind of goggles.

"And there is our prey," Apolo said to no one in particular.

Jax apprised his men through his earpiece. "Bravo Team, Tango has entered the box."

Everyone in the tech-hub watched in silence as the shape jogged down the hallway and stopped right outside Apolo's door. Sure enough, a moment later, after looking from side to side, the shape punched in a code and entered.

"Pull the bios on the intruder. When we get to my room, reset the power," Apolo commanded the comm-tech before turning to the two members of his trinity. "Let's go."

Apolo, Legian, and Nalea took the lead. Jax handed Sienna a flashlight, and Sienna grabbed her cane. She and Jax stepped in behind the trio, but Legian held out an arm, blocking them both.

"This is a Sephian matter. We need to resolve this."

Jax gave a nod and took a step back. "I'll have my team in the hallway on standby."

After the door closed, Sienna stepped up behind Tanel. His fingers ran across the flat keyboard, and the humanoid shape on the monitor to his left flashed as a string of symbols measured its shape and size and compared it against the stats of all the Sephians on the base. Names and pictures scrolled down the screen faster than she could follow.

She took off her glasses and cleaned the lenses with the edge of her shirt. Sliding them back on, she turned her attention to the larger monitor in front and watched as three neon shapes moved down the hallway. She blew out a long breath. "They move like vampires."

"They have a history together. It shows," Jax answered.

"The bio information on the intruder is coming up now," Tanel announced into the hand-held mic as he continued to type on the console in front of him. "His name is Pilin. He's an op-tec, a level four operations engineer."

"A handyman. And not a very good one if he's only a level four," Sienna said, speaking out loud as much for her benefit as for Jax's.

Jax leaned closer to the screens. "It would take some skill to cut the power in just the officer's hall."

"And even more skill to cut the power and get to Apolo's room in under a minute."

"He's got a partner," they said in stereo.

Sienna thought for only a second. "Tanel, can you pull up the video feed near the power boxes just before the power went out?'

"It will take a couple of minutes," Tanel replied.

Jax used his earpiece. "Bravo Team, possible second Tango in quadrant *tini*. Search for anyone who tickles your nose hairs."

Jax turned to Sienna and nodded. As they waited, Apolo's team reached the door to Apolo's rooms. He swiped his hand over the wall, and the door opened.

Apolo spoke some words in Sephian through the hand-held com. Tanel tapped several places on the keyboard at the same time, and the lights in the hallway came back on. Sienna and Jax watched as Legian and Nalea moved to stand alongside Apolo. The Sephian male was staring at the three like a deer caught in headlights now that the power was back on.

He tried to bolt, but Legian tackled him before he could take more than two steps toward the door. Apolo pulled the traitor to his feet and punched him. Even on the small screen, Sienna could see blood fly from the force of Apolo's hit. It was the angriest she'd ever seen him.

"I'm pulling up the video feed on monitor four now," Tanel said.

Sienna and Jax watched the video of an empty hallway. Several seconds into the feed, the screen became a blur.

Tanel pounded the screen. "*Suvaste*. They used a dampener."

"Can you clean up the image?" Jax asked.

The comm-tech shook his head. "No. I won't be able to identify anyone off this. Sorry."

The trio continued to watch the screen. The traitor was on his knees, whimpering as blood poured from his broken nose. His hands were banded behind his back. Nalea held a blaster to his head while she kept her other hand on his clothed shoulder. Sienna realized she was being careful to not come into direct contact, thus preventing Pilin from healing himself.

Legian stood back several feet and also had a blaster leveled on Pilin. Apolo was pacing back and forth in front of the prisoner, pausing long enough to glare at him midway through each lap. After a few more laps, he stopped before the kneeling Sephian and gave him a hard look. "How could you betray your own people?"

"Wha—what? I don't know what you're talking about."

The words were spoken in Sephian, and Sienna struggled to translate. "Tanel, turn on the translator."

Tanel tapped a couple of commands. "There. I have the English translator on."

"Thanks," Sienna said as she watched the screen. On it, Apolo stared down at Pilin then kicked him in the gut. She cringed as the prisoner cried out then lost his lunch.

Oblivious to the mess, Apolo scowled and grabbed the man's collar. "How could you betray your own people?"

The prisoner coughed, fighting for breath. "I didn't. I swear it."

"You are a liar and a traitor. Your name will forever be a scar upon our people."

Tears ran down Pilin's face. He tried to get up, but Nalea knocked him back down.

"I remember you, Pilin. You have been in the detention block before. It was theft, if I recall. Oh, yes; you had stolen alcohol from the Commons. Is that how they got to you? Through your addiction?"

"I don't know what you're talking about. I am faithful to our people. I swear it."

"And, I suppose now you're telling me that breaking into my room is a simple misunderstanding?"

"Yes!"

Apolo didn't appear to like that answer, because he back-handed the Sephian across the face.

The prisoner cried out, "Please, please."

"You beg for mercy now? From the same people you sought to betray? Why would you betray your people, Pilin?"

He shook his head violently. "I would never betray our people."

Apolo slapped him. "I don't believe you. Every time I think you're lying, I will mark you. Do you understand?"

The man whimpered. Apolo nodded to Nalea, who bent Pilin's arms back in what had to be an unnatural position. The Sephian screamed in pain.

"Do you understand?"

"Yes!"

"Good. That's a start."

"Who do you work for, Pilin?"

"No one," he cried.

Apolo raised his hand and Pilin winced. The sound of the slap made Sienna wince in sympathy pain. *Tell the truth, man.*

"I'm going to ask you one more time. Who do you work for?"

Pilin's shoulders shook from his uncontrollable sobs. "I swear, Apolo. I came here for a bottle of whiskey. I heard you kept the good stuff here. That's all. I swear it."

Apolo lifted his hand, and Pilin let out a yelp. But Apolo didn't slap him this time; instead, he bent down to come eye to eye with the prisoner. "Who told you that, son?"

He shook his head with his sobs. "It was a rumor I heard at the Commons."

"And who cut the power?"

"I—I don't know. The engineering log showed a power test was scheduled to be conducted in the officers' hall at ten o'clock. That's what it said. Precisely ten o'clock. I grabbed night gear just in case. I thought it was a lucky break. That's all."

Apolo grabbed Pilin's chin who yelped. "You know the punishment for treason, Pilin?"

The poor man looked up with a look of shock. "Tr—treason?"

"Yes, treason. What you did tonight, regardless of intentions, was treason. Tell me. Who sent you here?"

He sobbed. "No one. I swear it," he stammered before breaking down into an uncontrollable crying fit.

Apolo came to his feet. "Sephian law states the punishment for treason is immediate death, Pilin. I will make yours swift out of pity because you were played the fool."

In a blur of movement, Apolo grabbed and twisted the man's head. A loud crack broke the silence. Sienna inhaled sharply, covering her mouth with the back of her hand. She'd never seen an execution before.

At that moment, she was glad she was leaning against the comm-tech's desk. Otherwise, she was sure her knees would have given out. She couldn't take her eyes off the man now lying on the floor, his neck bent at an unnatural angle. She didn't even hear Jax move until a hand touched her shoulder.

She jumped.

He brushed a hand down her cheek. "You okay?"

The question sounded more like a command, and she nodded with as much confidence as she could muster. "I'm fine."

He stayed at her side while she continued to watch. No one in the room seemed fazed by what Apolo had done. They all watched Apolo, unmoving, as he stared at the wall, his mind obviously somewhere else.

"How will we know who gave him the information?" Legian asked.

Apolo answered instead. "That was the one thing he could

never tell us. He didn't know. He was simply a pawn. There was nothing else we could have learned from him." The look on Apolo's pained face betrayed his strong voice. "The traitor knows that we tried to trap him."

"How so?" Nalea asked.

"Pilin came here looking for whiskey, not for information," Apolo said.

Legian frowned. "Pilin was set up to fail. But why?"

Apolo answered. "Pilin must have known who the traitor is, even if he wasn't aware that he knew. He'd likely been used by the traitor before without knowing."

Apolo paused to speak to Tanel. "Pull everything you have on Pilin in the week before and after the base attack, as well as today's attack. Search everything. Make a list of every single Sephian he came into contact with and every single activity he did —no matter how small. If he defecated, I want to know. Do you understand?"

Tanel spoke so fast in Sephian that Sienna couldn't make out the words.

Apolo turned back to look down at the dead man. "Sending the drunk here would be an easy way to clean up loose ends. The traitor would know there is no leeway in dealing with treason. We're too low in numbers. The disappearance of any Sephian would be noticed quickly."

Nalea spoke. "If the traitor is cleaning house, it could mean he thinks he has something all ready to go."

Apolo nodded tightly. "Or, he's found a new pawn to use. I believe it's time for us to make the next move."

Chapter 14

"Do you yield?" Legian boomed.

"Never," Sienna shoved out through clenched teeth while she knelt on her hands and knees, panting. The pain in her leg was agonizing. She'd always had some cellulite, but now she felt like a jellyfish. This session felt worse than her first one. She was weak and hurting. And the worst part? Legian knew it.

Her sparring partner held out a hand, his face tight. "Yield, Sienna. Please."

She slapped his hand away.

She pulled herself up, trying not to favor her bad leg. It burned like acid with each movement. She grunted through the pain and somehow managed to get to her feet. Legian gave her space while she came to her full height across from him on the training mats.

She knew what she looked like. She'd been getting her ass handed to her all morning. She looked around the massive training room as she took the time to catch her breath. Padded sparring rings covered the floor, each a different color. Weapons of various shapes and sizes filled racks lined against the dark walls. A muted sound from the filtration system filled the air, like white noise, only less obtrusive. More like a gentle sigh.

Today, they used no weapons, instead working on fundamentals. Her leg couldn't support her own weight, let alone any sharp moves. She wore a stiff brace, and even with it she could barely stand. Without it, she was crippled.

But she would do this. She had to do this. She motioned to Legian. "Again."

He raised an eyebrow and stared at her. When he realized she was serious, he gave a proud smile… then he attacked. His arm shot out, and she dodged to the left. He kicked out a leg, and she jumped. She landed with a wince, but that wasn't what pissed her off.

"You're holding back," she snarled when a blow rolled off her shoulder.

"You're injured," he said, matter-of-factly.

"Doesn't matter. I could be injured during a battle and would still need to fight."

He stepped back. "You sure about this?"

"Sure as your skin sparkles, Tinkerbell."

He narrowed his eyes while he examined her for a moment before he shrugged and attacked. This time for real; she was flat on her back in under a second.

Sienna embraced the pain. Turning it into a war-scream, she twisted and grabbed Legian's legs in a double-takedown maneuver. Except he didn't go down. Just as she'd planned. She switched her pressure, pulling back rather than pushing. It knocked him off balance, and he fell toward her.

She twisted on the ground in time to keep him from toppling onto her, but he ducked his chin and rolled head-first to the side. He was on his feet and attacking before she was standing. Diving to the left, she narrowly missed his swing. He snapped around. She held her breath and leapt at him. He moved to the right like she expected, and she spun her good leg out the moment she hit the ground. She knocked him off balance and fell on him.

With a full-out smile, she looked down to a surprised Legian.

"Do you yield?" Sienna asked in her best smart-ass tone as she straddled him.

He looked up with a wide grin, and her smile dropped.

Suddenly, she was the one with her back to the mat, staring up at the lights. "Damn it. Not again."

"I was having too much fun seeing the look of success in your eyes. You actually thought you had me," he replied, standing victor over her.

"How's training going?"

She looked up to see Apolo saunter into the training room.

Legian turned to face Apolo. "Sienna's doing good for a human."

Apolo walked around Legian and bent down, leaning his forearm on one knee no more than a foot or so from her. She pulled herself to one elbow and looked him in the eye. She refused to cower under intimidation, and she wanted to make sure he knew it. "But the real question is, will your leg be a weakness we can afford out there?"

"I won't be weak," Sienna said.

He backed away. "Show me that your leg won't be a detriment."

Legian stepped forward. "She's not ready."

"She's a human as well as the *tahren* of one of my trinity. As such, she will be at the forefront of sensitive negotiations. We don't have the luxury of waiting for her to be ready," the Sephian leader said.

Legian lowered his head and stepped off the mat. Sienna eyed him, and he looked at her, tense, unmoving.

Apolo motioned her to him. "Any time you're ready, human." He didn't even widen his stance. He assumed she was harmless.

She turned her pain into rage and launched at him. He didn't bother to move out of the way. Instead, he held his arms out and embraced her as she rammed into him. She dropped and swept out his legs. Apolo fell to the floor with a look of surprise, as if he hadn't expected her to take him down. She took advantage of his hesitation and clapped her hands on his sensitive ears.

That pissed him off. In the next second, she found herself slammed against the mat so hard she could have sworn a tooth got knocked loose, a knee against her throat. She clawed at his leg. He watched her gasp for air, smiled, and the weight was gone. She grabbed the hand in front of her, and Apolo pulled her to her feet. The brace clanked as her leg straightened, pulling her healing muscles too tight. She bit her lips to keep from flinching.

Apolo showed her no mercy because she was female. He held true to the Sephian belief that females were as capable as their male counterparts. A belief Sienna firmly supported, although right now she was feeling markedly less than anyone's equal.

She turned to face him, taking in shallow breaths while he scrutinized her. After a moment, he gave her a slight tilt of his head, like he approved. Of what, she had no idea.

Apolo nodded at Legian. "Continue with training," he said and walked out.

The moment he left, she collapsed back to the floor and inhaled sharply. Her eyes burned from sweat. She yanked off her bandana, wiped off her face, and tied it back around her wrist. With a quick tug, she tightened her ponytail then fell to her back. Legian sat down next to her as she stared at the ceiling.

"Apolo is our greatest warrior," Legian said. "There's no shame in losing to him."

She grunted. "Why did he lead the Sephian force here? There has to be so much that he could do back on Sephia."

"Krysea asked him to lead us here. I would follow him to my death, as would any other Sephian. Other than Krysea, there are no other Sephian who command such respect."

She shook her head. "I get why she asked him, but, I mean, why did he accept?"

"He would never turn down an assignment Krysea gave him. Our leader has always done what's best for our people. He knows that and accepts it."

"Yeah, but what about what's best for her? For Apolo?"

Legian brought himself up on an elbow and ran a hand over her skin. "That's not her way. Or his, for that matter."

She bent her leg slowly until the muscles released.

"Your leg needs rest. Why don't we stop for today?"

Her lips thinned. "And if my leg never heals?"

"Human healing takes time."

"But what if?"

Legian frowned like he didn't understand.

"What if I never heal? Apolo's right. He can't afford any sign of weakness."

"Sienna, I would love it if you never stepped foot in combat. I raced to find you when I heard the base was attacked. You are many things, but you have never been weak."

She took hold of each of his hands and he helped her to her feet. She gave him a soft kiss. He went to embrace her, but she turned away. She hobbled over to the weapons rack and grabbed a long wooden stick and twirled it in her hand.

"Again."

Chapter 15

Nalea motioned Legian and Sienna into the room. Bente, Jax, and Apclo were already there, sitting around the black table and looking down at a screen that covered nearly the entire flat surface. Standing behind Jax were three of his team, who Sienna knew only by their last names: Hurt, Quincy, and White.

She pushed the glasses up her nose before she hobbled into the room, using her cane for support. Legian closed and locked the door behind them. No one else looked up when they entered. They were too absorbed with whatever was on the screen, mumbling as they hunched over the table.

Legian pulled a chair out for Sienna and she sat down, hanging the cane by its handle on the back of the chair. He took the seat next to her. Her eyes were drawn to the image on the screen. It was a detailed 3-D floor plan of what looked to be a large office building or warehouse. It was colored differently than any floor plan she'd seen, but the outline was the same. Sections were filled in with bright colors. Chartreuse for hallways, fuchsia for the open area. It was like seeing a rainbow for the first time. Beautiful, yet every color had its place.

The image looked so real, she fought back the urge to reach out and touch it. Sephians had the coolest technology. Actually, it was Draeken technology, since the Sephians had been nothing more than their worker bees for a couple of centuries. Designed by Draeken, built by Sephians. It made for a nice sense of irony that the slaves had used their masters' technology to gain their freedom.

And use it the Sephians did. The base was filled with technology adapted to their needs. They were experts at survival, and adjusting to other cultures seemed a tool of the trade. Since she had come on the base, she'd begun to see familiar objects pop up everywhere, from video games to guns, and laptops to magazines. The Sephians were starved for anything they could get their hands on. She figured it had something to do with growing up in slavery. There wasn't a Sephian on this base who had owned much of anything before they broke free from Draeken control. Some, like Legian, maintained a minimalist attitude, while many others turned into pack rats.

Sienna wanted to spend more time pondering what made the Sephians tick, but there were more important things at hand. She leaned back in her seat and made eye contact with Apolo. "What am I looking at here?"

Apolo shot her a quick look before his eyes dropped to his wrist computer, which reminded her of a wide smart watch with metallic straps. He hit a series of buttons, and a strange silver glow with a muted vibration fell over the room. It seemed to come from nowhere and everywhere at the same time.

"Dampener device," Apolo said in Jax's direction. "It prevents any type of audio from being tapped from this room."

Squinting, Sienna examined the walls and ceilings for some small contraption, but she couldn't find the source.

Apolo gestured over the image. "What you see before you is the last piece of viable intel I received from my Draeken informant before he went silent."

Sienna narrowed her eyes, waiting for Apolo to continue. He didn't, so she spoke up. "How do we know we can trust that what your inside guy gave us was any good? They could have gotten to him long before the base attack."

Apolo's attention snapped to her. "This intel came in two weeks before the ambush, and came through with visual and audio unlike the faulty intel we received later." Suddenly, he hit the table with his fist, causing the image to shiver. Everyone froze in their chairs while he clenched his fists. Apolo's moods were worsening, and rumors were spreading that he may eventually lose his mind after being separated from his *tahren* for so long. The odds weren't in his favor.

The plastic-like material ended up with a perfect knuckle-sized indentation before slowly regaining its original smoothness. When Apolo finally continued, he didn't look up. "I should have known better than to trust that intel. Instead, I grabbed onto an opportunity that seemed too good to pass up. The chance to stop the Draeken in one fell swoop. Someone played me for a fool." He clenched and unclenched his fists as he spoke. "The intel that led us into the attack on the base was the last communication I received from him. Before that, he reported in multiple times a month."

He paused and glanced at each face around the table. "This data, although incomplete, is good; I'm sure of it. I have been holding on to it until my informant could send more information. At this point, we know he's gone silent or has been compromised, and so I must assume we will be unable to collect more data."

"If they got to your informant, it makes sense that's how they found the location of our base," Bente added, softening his usual brusque tone.

Apolo shook his head. "Impossible. My man does not know the location of this base. He is nearly unbreakable—"

Bente raised a finger.

Apolo replied to Bente's unvoiced interruption by patting

down the air with his hands. "Yes, I know everyone can be broken. That was why I ensured my informant knew nothing of our base location. It's safe to assume we have our traitor to thank for leaking the location of the base to the Draeken. If only my informant wasn't so protective of his own people and had shared the location of the Draeken camp before…"

Apolo came to his feet, clasped his hands behind his back, and walked around the table. Everyone sat in silence and watched the leader pace. He was seemingly oblivious to anyone else in the room. On his third time around the table, he paused and pointed at the image. "We need to focus on what we can control. So far, we have nothing more besides this floor plan and a partial address."

His fingers brushed over the image, and the screen zoomed in on a section of rooms. "Bente, you've spent more time in Draeken facilities than any of us. Look closely at this block of rooms. My informant believed this to be the location of something along the lines of a Draeken-human interaction center.

"After looking at the floor plan, we believe it may be a medical center. A human breeding facility, to be exact."

Sienna shoved her chair back from the table in a rush. "Human breeding? You can't mean…" Her voice trailed off.

Apolo nodded tightly. "Yes. I do. We know the Draeken female population was decimated in the Noble War. Their numbers are desperately low. It makes sense that they are pursuing the survival of their race through cross-breeding. In fact, we believe this may be the primary reason they chose this planet. As we've discovered ourselves recently,"—Apolo waved a hand in Legian's and her general direction—"humans are genetically compatible with our race. There's no reason not to believe it is also the case for the Draeken."

"It's like a bad sci-fi movie," Quincy said from behind Jax.

"Yeah," Smith added. "Not only do they want our world, but they want our women? No effing way."

"That's assuming they're willing to stoop that low and taint their Draeken bloodlines," Bente added from the side.

"If their numbers are low enough, they can't afford pride," Jax retorted.

Bente scowled. "You sure this is a medical facility? It's not laid out like one." He went back to looking at the screen. His eyes narrowed, and then he pointed at a long hallway with a series of rooms on the screen. "This area looks suspicious."

"My informant couldn't confirm its use," Apolo said, "but he was confident it was neither a military installation nor a place that brought harm to humans. He advised me of the location with the intention that I avoid it rather than go after it."

"We're going in, aren't we?"

"Yes," Apolo said.

Nalea pointed to the same area of the floor plan that Bente had noted. "This area should be our primary target. Outside of the larger area, all the smaller rooms attach to this hallway. It's the hub. Most of their medical equipment and prisoners are likely to be contained here."

"Is there any way we can verify what your informant said is true?" Sienna asked.

Bente leaned forward stiffly and examined the image. "Recon."

"Do we know if they're drawing the human women to this location, or are they capturing them then bringing them there?" Legian asked.

"We believe they are being drawn there. Tanel researched the location and said that this large room is used as an entertainment venue." Apolo's fingers brushed over the display he wore on his forearm. He paused to read it. "It's called Mayhem. Tanel says it's called a gothic dance club. He's researching it further now."

"It's 'goth,' not 'gothic.' That means it's a night club where folks in dark clothes get together to hang out, dance, drink, and what not," Sienna explained.

Jax nodded. "It would be easy to drug women's drinks in a dimly lit bar."

She jerked at the truth in his words. The idea of drugging someone pissed her off. It was one thing to fight someone face to face, but taking advantage of someone like that was dishonorable. "You're right. They probably use something like roofies. From there, they could restrain the poor girls throughout the pregnancy." She fidgeted with the bandana on her wrist as she spoke.

"But the simplest plan would be to let the girls go," White continued. "They wouldn't even need to keep their victims more than a couple of hours. Just long enough to tag 'em and bag 'em. The girls would never know what hit them. Basically, it would be a breed-and-release program. If they picked carefully, the girls would think they got knocked up during a one-night stand. The Draeken could sit back and wait until their nine months were up then go in and take the infants."

Sienna leaned back and shook her head. "That's wrong in so many ways."

"I think the victims would catch on when ultrasounds showed extra appendages," Jax added on.

Legian wrapped an arm around Sienna. He did that whenever he was stressed. And with a clenched jaw, he was definitely looking stressed. "Hybrids likely wouldn't develop wings, but we can't know for sure. They likely restrain the victims."

"We can get intel from a distance to see the amount of traffic the place gets, but we'd need to get up close and personal to know for sure," Nalea said.

Sienna glanced up at her friend. She hadn't noticed how Nalea had nearly lost her Sephian accent. Before long, she'd be like any other American. Well, except the golden skin and black eyes. That would still be a bit of a problem. Contacts would hide the eyes, but there was no realistic makeup to do the trick to their skin.

Apolo nodded. "We need to get an inside look." He looked from Jax to Sienna. Legian's grip tightened on her shoulder. "Jax's team and Sienna will be our scouts. Jax and Sienna will enter the club as a couple, with Bravo Team armed and ready outside. We need to verify the Draeken have set up a facility."

Jax used his fingers to move through the floor plan. Even with this being his first time using the technology, he operated it like a pro. "We need to know what we're looking for, as well as their usual security measures."

Nalea rubbed her neck. "Trust me. You'll know. While Draeken technology is far more advanced than human technology, it is also noticeable. I can show you common equipment to look for. As for security, assume the worst."

Bente looked Sienna up and down, and she frowned at him. He frowned back. "If it is a Draeken facility, they will have surveillance throughout and around the building. It will be critical to blend in. You do not look like the usual clientele."

"And Roden's seen her before. If they have any kind of professional op going on, we'll be busted before we walk through the door. Besides, it's too dangerous for her," Jax chimed in. "Sienna should stay behind. My team can handle this."

Sienna held up a finger. "First, with some hair color and makeup, my own mother wouldn't recognize me." She held up a second finger. "And nine tough guys walking into a Goth club will look a hell of a lot more suspicious than a couple."

"But with a shit leg, you still put the mission at risk."

She narrowed her eyes at Bente, aka Mr. Pessimist. "Doc has been working up a new brace for my leg. He thought he could have it ready by tomorrow. I'll be able to go without a cane. He says I might not even have a limp when I wear it. Besides, I'll have Jax with me. He's trained for this sort of thing. He's a commando."

"Special Operations," Jax corrected.

"Sienna's going in," Apolo said. "If this is a breeding facility, a human woman will help Jax gain access to the club. A single man, let alone multiple single men, may not be able to enter the club without drawing notice." Whatever he typed next caused the screen to go blank. "We'll have analysis back from the comm-tech by tomorrow. We'll reconvene after second meal to finalize preparations. In the meantime, get some rest. You'll need it."

Then he tapped out a few more keystrokes. The lights switched back to normal and the mild vibration disappeared. Apolo exited through the door to his bedroom without another word. Everyone stood—Bente taking as long as Sienna to get to his feet—then left, Legian and Sienna silently following the others out of the room.

Going deep into Draeken territory terrified her, but she wasn't going to complain. Hell, she was finally getting a chance to make a difference.

There was no way she'd let her new people down.

Chapter 16

Jax pulled the car to a stop, and then looked over at her. "I'm impressed, Sienna. You'll fit in perfect."

"You clean up pretty decent yourself." In fact, Sienna was surprised at how well Jax gothed up. They had used matching deep red and black hair color, and he'd even let her use kohl eyeliner on him. He wore black leather pants, motorcycle boots, and a tight black tee.

She, on the other hand, was dressed all in black, from the leather strapless corset over a black satin shirt to the full-length skirt hiding her new leg brace.

A hodgepodge of black plastic-like straps, the brace looked more like some kind of bondage toy than a medical device—oddly appropriate. The kinetic bands harvested energy from her body, which was then converted into power for the brace. She didn't even limp, let alone feel much pain, with the brace; it was an extension of her body.

The cane was now unnecessary, but she'd kept it anyway, hanging it on her wall to remind her of the risks she'd faced.

A valet opened the car door, held out his gloved hand, and

helped her out of the car. Her steel-toed black leather boots made a solid thump on the sidewalk. She then waited at the curb.

Jax walked around the car and held out an arm, which she looped her hand through. His nose ring caught the light as he watched her, like he was measuring how badly she was going to screw up. "Ready to do this?"

"I have a knife in each boot, a gun tucked into my garter, a tracker in my corset, and I'm wearing an earpiece. I think I'm ready."

Sienna could barely hear Legian's warning to be careful in her ear over the bass radiating from the club. She stayed on Jax's arm as they approached the front door. Jax handed the doorman a couple of large bills. The man unhooked a red rope and they stepped under the neon *Mayhem* sign written in dripping blood-red letters. They strolled past two more large doormen then down a long, dark hallway that opened up onto a huge ballroom. Everything was exactly as the floor plan had shown.

So far, so good.

It was Sienna's first time in a Goth club, and she took in the decadent scenery. Tall crimson velvet curtains were draped down the twenty-foot black walls. Deep red couches and dark cherry tables were scattered across a floor packed wall-to-wall with dark-haired, dark-dressed people.

Some people lounged on the couches, drinking, talking, making out, and all combinations of those things. Many more were on the dance floor, gyrating to rave music with a bold, dark beat. Looking down from the top of the stairs, the dance floor reminded her of a subdued mosh pit. She felt herself swaying to the haunting, almost drug-like beat that vibrated through her body.

Jax nuzzled her ear with his nose. "Don't stare. This is our kind of place, remember?"

She closed her eyes and inhaled the cool air, which contained a hint of incense. "Just getting the vibe of the place." She put a painted fingernail to her lips. "I wonder if the guards at the door are to keep folks out or to keep folks in."

Jax's lips tightened, and he didn't look like he was entirely sure himself.

"C'mon," she said, leading him toward the stairs. "Let's get a drink."

With a nod, he took the lead, sweeping her down the wide stairs and straight to the bar. The bartender gave Sienna a full-body once-over look. Whatever he saw must have satisfied him because he leaned closer with a flirty grin. "What will you have, sweets?"

"I'll have a tawny port. Aged twenty-years, preferably," she said, licking her lips under a flirty gaze.

He winked at her, and then turned a cool appraisal onto Jax.

"Templeton Rye on the rocks."

The bartender nodded and went about getting their drinks while Sienna swayed in time to music that would leave her ears ringing for days.

A glint of metal caught her eye. She glanced over at a girl with a dozen piercings. Dressed in a micro-mini leather skirt and strapless corset covered in a skull print, she fit right in with the crowd. What kept Sienna's attention, however, was the tattoo that spanned the girl's shoulder. It was of an angel in flight. Only this angel's wings didn't have feathers. Instead, its dragon-like wings were covered in tattoos.

Sienna eyed Jax, and he gave a glance that told her he was thinking the same thing. She nudged the petite girl. "Wicked ink."

The girl grinned and glanced over her shoulder as though she could see the tattoo. "Thanks. Got it done last week."

"Haven't seen a demon done like that before. With all the marks and stuff."

"I know. Isn't he sexy? His name is Laze. He takes the best care of me. And he is incredible." She said the last word with an over-exaggerated bend of her knees.

Sienna batted playfully at her. "No way. You met a real demon? Get outta here."

She rolled her eyes. "You're new here, aren't you?"

"New in town."

The girl nodded. "Hang out here long enough, maybe you'll see for yourself."

Sienna must have looked doubtful because the girl grabbed Sienna by her arms and looked her in the eye. "At first, they come to you when the fog machines smoke up the place. It's so surreal, it could be a dream. Only it's not a dream. And the things they do to you…" She shivered before playfully running a finger down Sienna's neck, sending sensual goosebumps across her skin. The girl smiled. "You're a bit old, but you're hot. Maybe you'll find out for yourself. After all, they need us," she whispered with a brush of her lips against Sienna's ear.

Sienna cocked her head. "Need us?"

Tat-girl gave her a knowing smile. "You'll find out if you're chosen. Trust me, you would never have to worry about money or anything ever again. That's how good they take care of us."

The girl was probably already pregnant by her demon lover and didn't even know it yet. Sienna made a mental note of the name Laze.

When Sienna opened her mouth to speak, Jax handed her the sipper of wine, and then wrapped an arm around her waist. Jax gave the other girl a flirty half-smile. "If you don't mind, I need this woman to myself."

With that, he tugged Sienna forward.

Jax put a hand on her hip and Sienna led the way to an open sofa near the wall. Old-fashioned drop-lights hung from the ceiling, shedding just enough yellowish light that she didn't trip over anyone. She'd become decent over the past few months at not crashing into things in the dark. Moving around this club was a piece of cake compared to getting around the base without her *drades*.

The leather corset creaked against the leather sofa as she sat down and propped her boots up on the coffee table, crossing her ankles. Jax sat next to her, wrapping an arm around her. To anyone else, they looked like any other hot-and-heavy couple watching the scene.

"Why the rush?" Sienna asked. "I was getting good intel at the bar."

"The bartender was beginning to eye you like you were a news reporter," Jax replied before narrowing his eyes in concentration.

"Oh."

Static sounded through her earpiece, but she couldn't make out any words. Taking the smallest sip of wine, she did her best to fit in while listening for more to come out through her earpiece.

"Repeat last." Jax spoke to her, although she knew he wasn't talking to her.

Again, a garbled response came through her earpiece.

"No joy," Jax replied with a frown and eyed Sienna. "Looks like we're on our own in here."

"At least the cavalry is just outside."

"A lot can happen in a couple hundred feet." He leaned back, resting an arm over the back of the couch. He watched the crowd for several moments before speaking again. "Things are a mess right now."

"Not everything," Sienna said. "From what I hear, you and Risa are hitting it off."

He thought for a moment. "I don't know what the fuck I'm doing."

"I know that feeling," she said.

"At least Doc's no longer an issue."

Sienna frowned, then her eyes widened. "Oh, I thought Doc just liked to flirt with her."

Jax shook his head. "There was more than flirting going on. And I got tired of that shit fast."

"How long did you know?"

He turned back to her and raised an eyebrow.

"Yeah. I guess you probably knew from the get-go. The base is small. And you are a super commando type." She put a hand on his knee. "Well, I'm glad she got her act together. You could use some fun in your life."

Jax replied by taking a drink of his whiskey.

Sienna looked back toward the bar. "This club is a perfect setting for the Draeken to meet women. I don't think it's a breeding facility in the way it sounded. It sounds more like a way for the Draeken to introduce themselves to humans who'd be accepting of them in the right atmosphere. Pretty brilliant plan if you ask me. That girl sounded like a pretty satisfied customer."

"Could be, but if they're worried about extinction, I wouldn't be surprised if they don't have more going on." Jax nodded and stared off into the crowd, running a hand up and down Sienna's arm while he scanned the club. He had one leg crossed over the other. Even though she knew he felt otherwise, he looked right at home. He handled himself so well she couldn't help but relax against him.

She had become entranced by an androgynous couple on the dance floor when a waitress with way too much eyeliner stepped into her line of sight.

"Can I get you two anything?"

"We're good." Jax brushed her off, and the waitress moved on to the next table without so much as a smile.

Sienna rested her head on his shoulder and glanced across the dance floor. "I don't see any doors, so I'm thinking they must be hidden behind these curtains."

"That's my thought, too."

She closed her eyes and rubbed her temple as she struggled to recall the exact floor plan. This was one of those times when a photographic memory would come in handy. To their left was the hallway to the restrooms. From there, the entrance above. She looked to the right. Directly behind the dance floor. There. It had to be there.

"The door is behind the second curtain on that wall."

"Playing The Price is Right?" Jax asked with a raised eyebrow.

She gave him a look of frustration. "See how the light is burned out above that one. It's the only light not working in this whole place. I bet it's intentional. It's so dark, it would be impossible to see someone coming and going."

He casually scanned the club before standing and holding out a hand. "Let's dance."

After a quick perusal of the crowded floor, she placed her hand in his. They weaved through the tables between them and the dance floor. When they reached the crowded dance floor, Jax pulled her hand above her head and gave her a twirl.

"Déjà vu," she said. "Minus the cowboy hat. What did you ever do with that? I liked it."

He smiled and gave her another twirl. "No one said we can't have a little fun while working."

Sienna laughed. It felt good. She couldn't remember the last time she had a full, real laugh. Lately, there hadn't been a lot to laugh at.

The song switched over, and the crowd migrated to the dance floor.

"I can't believe I know this song!" she yelled into his ear over the noise.

"I'm going to dance you toward the wall."

Jax steered them charmingly through the sea of slowly gyrating bodies and toward the edge of the dance floor. The room was beginning to swim when Jax stopped abruptly. Her head hit his chest.

"I'll cover you while you check the curtain."

He gave Sienna the lightest push, but her left leg missed a step and she torpedoed toward the wall. She stopped herself from meeting the wall face first and turned around. Jax was nowhere to be found. Tightening her lips, she dove behind the curtain, and, sure enough, there was a large steel door with no handle, only a flat electronic screen on the wall.

She backed up to tell Jax, but a large body blocked her.

"Ah!"

Jax held her steady. "Shh."

She poked him in the chest, accentuating each word. "Don't scare me like that. What are you trying to do? Give a girl a heart attack?"

He ignored her, and instead leaned her against the wall and stepped up to the screen.

"Apolo gave us a direct order to not do anything to raise suspicion," she said when she saw him pull out a small pen-like device.

"We can't get intel unless we take some risk," he replied, and raised the device to the screen.

She crossed her fingers. The comm-tech had sworn the thing would work and was one-of-a-kind. He'd also went on and on about it being worth more than Jax and her combined, but she liked to think Tanel was being a touch overprotective of his gadgets. Then again, knowing the Sephian's complete lack of any sense of humor, maybe not.

A light flashed on the screen, and the door opened with a whoosh.

"You good?" he asked.

She hiked up her skirt and pulled out her gun. "Let's do this."

From the other side of the doorway, Jax held up three fingers, then two, then one.

Show time.

They stepped through the door and into a brightly lit room. She swung her gun around, her back to Jax, as they scanned the empty room. After a full three-sixty, she lowered her gun. A row of kegs lined one wall, while the others were lined with boxes of liquor.

She didn't know what she'd expected, but this wasn't it. "Do you think they got to Apolo's spy earlier than Apolo thought?"

"Maybe. Maybe the intel was bad. From the looks of things, they could've closed down months ago—if they were even here."

Sienna shook her head. "No way. That girl's ink was brand new. Something's off." She did another full turn to take in the room. "Wait a sec. In the floor plan, this room was longer than this."

Jax scanned the walls then walked to the far end of the room and began pulling boxes out. She followed suit. After moving a couple of dozen cases, she froze. "I found something."

At that moment, something metallic clinked between them. She glanced down at the object. "Chaos-charge! Cover your—"

Too late. The thing must have been on a short timer; the room erupted in light and screaming. She fell like a leaf in a tornado of bright light and noise.

"Legian!" she screamed, even though she knew he probably couldn't hear her. She could faintly hear Jax's yell for backup.

She rolled over and was trying to figure out which way was up when something grabbed her hand. Or, more precisely, something grabbed the gun from her hand while a tremendous pressure held her down. She tried to slap away her assailant, but with the vertigo, her hands wouldn't listen to her brain and she pretty much lay there, useless, as she was disarmed. She listened to the clinks of knives and charges being dropped onto the floor. Her weapons.

"Bastard," Sienna muttered, and a deep chuckle broke the now painful ringing silence in her ears. She wouldn't be surprised if both eardrums had burst, given the way they throbbed and the ringing that had set up in her ears. She looked around, taking several moments for the room to quit spinning. After what seemed like forever, her eyes slowly focused on the shape of a seven-foot Draeken standing over her. Her head jerked around as she searched for Jax, and she found him prone on the floor alongside her.

She jerked up, only to have a large hand shove her back onto the floor. She hadn't seen the other Draeken that knelt by her. She struggled against him, but he held her down with one hand, seemingly without effort.

She recalled the tattoo she'd seen earlier and recognized the wings. "You must be Laze."

He raised an eyebrow. "Come here to find me, did you?"

The Draeken next to him chuckled. "Your reputation precedes you. Perhaps she wants to experience a real man."

Sienna renewed her struggles. "I'd rather eat a forty-five than touch you."

"Spunk. I like that. But you're not my type. You smell of slaves." Laze's eyes narrowed. "How did you find us?"

"The Yellow Pages."

Laze grabbed her jaw and she winced. "I don't like to repeat myself. How did you find us?"

"She doesn't know anything. She came with me," Jax called out from several feet away.

She heard the sound of a punch, followed by a grunt. She couldn't turn her head toward the sound. She could only look up or close her eyes. And there was no way in hell she was going to let the Draeken think she was scared of him. She watched him turn toward Jax and grin. "Relax, human. We'll get to you soon enough." The devious smile was turned back onto her. "You will both tell me what you know. That, I promise."

She struggled harder, and he laughed. Then a loud sound cut the air, and warm liquid splattered her face. The Draeken fell like a heavy wall on her, and she fought to get out from under him, unable to breathe.

As quickly as it happened, the weight was gone, and she gulped fresh air. Legian fell to his knees and pulled her from the Draeken.

"Glad you could make it," she said, with as much humor as she could muster.

Legian bent down and kissed her then pulled away. "Let's get you out of here."

"Sounds good to me. After we finish checking this place out.'

He helped her to her feet, only to throw her toward the wall again. A laser shot whizzed by her head. Coming to her hands and knees, she turned to see Legian reach for his gun. "Get out of here. *Run.*"

Chapter 17

ike hell I'm leaving you.

That was Sienna's first thought when shots fired from the now-open door that'd been hidden behind crates in the far wall. Both Legian and Nalea—who'd come in with Legian, Jax's team, and a couple of other Sephians—were directly in the line of fire.

He fired a couple of shots at the doorway. "Go outside! There's a dampener in this building. Our coms don't work. Call Apolo for backup."

He turned his attention back to the battle. She ran a few steps and crashed into the fallen Draeken—Laze—who moaned. She turned to see Legian pop off more shots, but then he shot a look right back to her. "Get Apolo."

Sienna nodded and scrambled toward the door. She hated to leave, but she knew that they needed backup or none of them may get out of there alive. She was the least-experienced fighter there, so it made sense she should be the gopher. Something grabbed her leg. She snapped her head around to see Laze, though groggy, with a firm grip on her.

"No, you don't," he muttered, spitting out blood.

She swung out with her free leg, and the heel of her boot connected squarely with his jaw. His head snapped back, but he didn't let go. She kicked again and knocked him loose. Jumping to her feet, she dove toward the entrance, only to be tackled into the wall by Laze. Her head crashed into the brick wall and white spears shot through her vision. Momentarily dazed, she swung out an instant too late. Laze swiped his hand over the screen on the wall near the steel door, and her escape route slammed shut.

She elbowed him where his shirt was soaked with blood, and he was on his back a second later. He tried to get up but was knocked back when Nalea stepped on a wing. He cried out and slapped at Nalea's leg, but a second Sephian grabbed the downed Draeken's hands, banded them, and then did the same to his ankles. He gasped for air when she removed her boot from his wing.

It was then that Sienna remembered her training. Draeken wings were the most sensitive part on their bodies. She mentally kicked herself for fighting him like he was a human, and for not focusing on his weakness.

A hand grabbed her neck, and she fell back against Legian.

"Stay down," Legian growled.

She looked into feral eyes and knew there was no reasoning with him. "I need a gun."

He reached inside his coat and pulled out a small blaster. It was Legian's least favorite of all the Sephian weapons, which mean he'd carried it for her. With a smile, she grabbed it, checked it, and slid it in the waistband of her skirt then turned and shoved over a stack of boxes. They didn't offer any shielding, but at least they wouldn't be sitting ducks.

"I don't suppose you brought any charges with you?" she asked above the sounds of battle.

Legian shook his head. "Blood-charges, but they won't do us any good in these close quarters."

She pulled the gun out of her belt and fired random shots

through the door in the wall. She could see no Draeken, but she had no problem seeing their weapons when they stuck them around the doorway to fire. They had to be out of chaos-charges or else she would have been drowning in light and noise.

There was no way to tell if they outnumbered the Draeken or not. They were stuck in a Catch-22. They were pinned down, but at least the Draeken were faring no better. It was obvious Apolo's intel had been good.

Sienna looked around them. Definitely time for Plan B... if only she had a Plan B.

No sooner had she thought it than an earthquake shook the floor. Pieces of concrete and plaster rained down on her, even as she covered Legian with her body. Wiping dust from her eyes, she peered over the box of broken liquor bottles and saw a gaping hole where the steel door had been.

Soldiers—far more than just Bravo Team—poured into the room, hitting the deck when the Draeken started firing in their direction. "Yes!" Sienna shouted as they spanned out, many behind boxes, others running under cover fire toward the wall with the secret door.

The sound of gunfire amped up by the power of ten when machine guns went off around her. Bullets hit the brick wall outside the door, but no shots were very close. It was like the Americans were trying to miss. Her brow furrowed. Why wouldn't they want to take out the Draeken shooters?

Her eye caught an object flying through the air and through the door. Smoke hissed out through the small doorway, and the Americans stopped firing. She followed suit and watched the doorway. There were fewer shots coming through the door than before. A wing brushed through the gray haze, and she saw a Draeken turn and run, his buddy providing cover fire.

"They're getting away!"

The soldiers were moving toward the door in a synchronized manner, but they were still too far away. Sienna was closest. She jumped over the boxes. When she landed, she hit a wet patch of spilled liquor and fell. The momentum of her jump propelled her right through the door. Her foot hit the Draeken in the shin, and he went down.

No longer under fire, everyone else sprinted forward, and Legian was on the fallen Draeken at the same time a blade went for her throat. She clutched the Draeken's hand with both hers. When he was yanked back, she was able to pry the blade from his grip.

Legian yanked her to her feet. "When we get out of this—"

"I know. You'll show me how much you love me," she winked then winced, reaching for her leg. She slowly bent her knee, only to find a loose binding. With a grimace, she shoved the broken strap into the rest of the brace, checked her weapon, and motioned down the hallway, which was becoming visible through the dissipating smoke.

"I saw more Draeken head this way," she called out to the approaching soldiers.

"How many?" one of them asked.

Sienna held up two fingers. "At least two. Maybe three."

He nodded and yelled a command to those behind him. Then several troops stepped past them and followed him.

The group disappeared around a corner. When shots sounded, she moved forward, only to be held back by Legian.

"They've got it covered."

Sienna swallowed, trying to tamp down her adrenaline rush. She turned her attention back to the Draeken she'd drop-kicked, who was being shackled and injected with something courtesy of the Americans. It took a second before his struggles ceased and he was out cold.

The two soldiers at the downed Draeken made way for Major Sommers. He knelt by the Draeken.

Tucking the gun back into her skirt, Sienna brushed hair from her plaster dust-coated face and looked around. The place looked like Armageddon and stank like the devil had drunk himself into a stupor. "One hell of a happy hour at this place," she said to no one in particular.

She turned to Legian. "We better clear out this place before the cops show. It'll be hard to explain all this."

"There won't be any police," Major Sommers replied. "I've got that covered; it'll be harder to reign in the press. And by now, they will have received some tips. We don't need pictures of aliens circulating the papers."

Sienna shrugged. "Aliens are a daily occurrence in the tabloids."

"Yeah, but real pictures would be harder to explain," Jax cut in.

"Bag 'em," the major called out, causing Sienna to jerk around in time to see Nalea walking toward them, the men behind her dragging three more Draeken behind them.

"No blood?" she asked.

"Tranq guns," Jax replied. "Cleaner and safer."

"And smarter; now you have prisoners," she chimed in.

Sommers gave her a half-grin that disappeared as quickly as it had appeared. "Let's get out of here. Cleanup crew is on the way." He turned and strode away.

Sienna fell in behind him as he stepped over broken bottles and pieces of wall. Her jaw dropped as she looked around. Only one Sephian had been shot, and he was being bandaged by a curious human medic. With all that shooting, she'd expected to see a whole lot more blood. Not a single casualty. It was like an old A-Team episode. A thousand shots fired without any blood.

She limped behind Jax as he and the major stepped through the giant hole in the wall where the door had been minutes earlier. Steel shards jabbed out, snagging her skirt. Without pausing his stride, Legian bent down, tore the skirt, and helped her through the wall.

She looked around the vacant club. "Wow. I can't believe it's empty."

"Called in a tip of a drug bust. Cleared out the place in minutes."

She admired his ingenuity.

Sommers continued walking through the bar, and she hobbled faster to keep up. "Major?"

He slowed and glanced her way.

"Back there, the Sephians and our people worked well together, didn't they?"

"Not bad." Sommers looked from Legian to Jax and back to her. He narrowed his eyes briefly before giving a small smile. "It's a start."

Chapter 18

Sienna stopped outside the door and leaned on the wall to steady herself. The new brace worked wonders, but her leg would never return to normal. Even after Doc refitted the brace after Club Mayhem—talk about a name that was so apropos —her best speed was no better than a half fast jog.

"Are you well?"

She stepped back so she could face Legian. "I'm fine." Turning around before he could reply, she punched in the code to open the door. She pushed the *drades* up her nose, and they stepped inside to the darkened room beyond.

They were early for the trinity meeting so as to give Apolo a full debrief on what had gone down with the major. She entered the lounge with Legian at her back.

Apolo stood alone, leaning with his hands on the table. He was talking to a beautiful Sephian woman on the screen. Upon Sienna and Legian's entry, he jerked around. The emotion in his eyes nearly knocked her back.

"Sorry for the disruption. We'll wait outside." She snapped around to walk away, rubbing her palms together even though the temperature in the room was almost balmy.

"Bah. Come in." He waved them in and returned his attention to the screen.

Even Legian looked timid as he stepped gingerly into the room. Sienna could make out little of the conversation, and she could tell Legian was trying to not listen while he casually inspected everything in the room except the screen. Whatever they were discussing was obviously private, and she sensed a deep longing in the words.

Krysea.

Apolo's *tahren*. The bond between the two was obvious. Every day must be torture for them. Whenever she was apart from Legian for more than a few hours, she began to notice the loss in connection. She couldn't imagine being separated from her *tahren* for months, let alone potentially years. That kind of dedication to their people went far beyond anything she could imagine. Could she give up Legian to save the human race? Honestly? She really didn't know.

Sienna couldn't help but stare at the screen. Krysea was gorgeous. She'd expected a battle-worn, scarred woman. The Sephian leader surely couldn't be this beautiful.

Legian bumped her, nearly knocking her glasses off. She scowled at him and his eyes looked forward. She followed his eyes and found Apolo watching her.

"Krysea wishes to speak to you." Apolo spoke with no hint of emotion.

Sienna gulped as she and Legian stepped closer to the screen and faced the leader of the Sephian people. Legian spoke first, bowing his head and greeting the leader in Sephian. Sienna followed suit. Since her Sephian sucked, she then remained silent.

"I have begun to learn your language but have much to learn. My *tahren* will translate," Krysea said in drawn out, stilted English. Then she continued in flowing, beautiful Sephian.

Apolo translated. "Krysea blesses your bond and prays for a blissful future."

"Thank you," Sienna said. Legian echoed her.

Krysea nodded with a warm smile before continuing.

"She has been apprised of your actions and approves my choice," Apolo added, his voice and manner all-business.

Sienna glanced over at him. "Choice?"

Apolo narrowed his eyes onto her. "Regarding you."

He said something else, but she missed it, and jerked her attention back to the screen. Krysea was still speaking. The leader smiled, and the screen when black.

Apolo stared at the blank screen. The tightness in his body betrayed his emotionless face.

"How do you do it? Stay apart from Krysea, I mean," Sienna asked softly in his direction.

He jerked out of his trance and looked up to face her. "I do it because I must."

Apolo let out a deep breath. To her, it sounded like hopelessness. He looked up, and she could have sworn his eyes were damp.

"It took us several months at full power to fly here; we nearly used up our long-range power cells. That was intentional. The cells are rechargeable, and initial planetary analysis showed that your star generated energy similar to ours, which can recharge our power cells. Unfortunately, when we arrived, we learned that was not the case. Your sun does not generate compatible energy. Even if we tried to return on our lowest power settings, we'd never make it. We are running our base off our short-range power cells now, but they won't last a year. At that point we will be fully dependent on this planet's resources."

Sienna brought a hand over her mouth. "You're stranded here?"

Apolo shook his head. "We are looking for other options, but haven't found anything viable. The only good news is that the Draeken run off the same energy source and likely discovered the same problem when they arrived here."

"Earth is our home now." Legian spoke quietly, his voice barely a whisper.

"Can't Krysea send more ships with large power cells?"

Legian shook his head. "The cells are too large to transport. They can't send enough to bring us all back, and any ship sent here would be stranded as well."

"I'm so sorry." Sienna's voice cracked as her heart broke. She and Apolo may not see eye to eye all the time, but no *tahren* should be separated. To be separated like that was an unending torture. A death sentence.

Apolo cracked his neck and walked around the table. "Take a seat until the rest of the trinity and Jax arrive."

She glanced up at Legian, who nodded to her. "Apolo, we would like to debrief you about what happened at Mayhem."

Apolo waved her off. "Excellent progress with the humans; the debrief can wait until after the meeting." He started to pace.

Frowning, Sienna sat in the nearest chair. Legian sat down next to her, and together they endured the ominous silence. It took five interminable minutes before the others arrived, and during that time she watched a frazzled Apolo transition back into the stoic leader she'd come to respect.

First to the room were Bente and Jax, who'd become friends over past few weeks. Nalea finally arrived, a few minutes late. Ever since the base attack, she seemed distracted, unfocused. Something was up, but her friend's style was to keep things bottled up, festering, until they exploded like a Molotov cocktail. Sienna made a mental note to schedule some time with her. Legian had told her once about the last time Nalea had lost it. It wasn't pretty. Evidently, people died when Nalea blew.

Sienna didn't know exactly what had happened the previous time; Legian said it had had something to do with Nalea's family. Nalea never spoke of her family. In fact, no one knew anything about her childhood. That was, until a guy showed up who swore he'd worked under the same Draeken house as Nalea, and that he knew her secret. No one had thought anything of it until the next day when Nalea and the guy went missing, along with a ship. She'd shown back up a week later. Alone, nearly starved, and without a ship. She had claimed they'd gone on a recon flight and were shot down, but no one knew the truth, other than the fact that no recon flight had been scheduled. Legian suspected it was intentional that she came back alone, but he'd never dared confront her on it.

Nalea nodded to Sienna on her way around the table to her chair.

Apolo started before everyone sat down. "The Mayhem mission dealt a small blow to the Draeken. From what I've heard, we can thank Jax for the human assistance at the club. Without them, we very likely would have suffered losses. As it stands, we were very fortunate to incur no casualties, with only one of us acquiring minor wounds."

Applause lightened the atmosphere.

Apolo continued. "The mission reopened the door for discussions. I have spoken with Lieutenant-Colonel Jerrick and have arranged for an official alliance meeting that will include him as well as a political leader. The meeting should be at a location that has connections to both our people. Therefore, I have requested Sienna's cabin."

Sienna jerked upright. "My cabin? Are you sure?"

Apolo smiled. He had *that* look again. The one he always had before he dropped a bomb.

"What?" she asked, the word barely a whisper.

"Since you became Legian's *tahren*, you have been thrown through a quantum hole. Most would have broken. Many would not have survived. Yet, your prowess at both defending the base during the attack and on the Mayhem mission has earned the respect of the Sephians based here on this planet, of me, and most importantly, of our *tahcayaren*, Krysea. You and I often have different views, and it is those differences that I have come to value the most. Earth is our new home. It is time we acclimate to our new world and, hopefully, new people."

Apolo looked at each member of his trinity in turn. "I will always do what is best for my people. And, it is in their best interest that I made my decision. From this point forward, Sienna shall become the human face for the Sephians on Earth."

Sienna frowned. "I don't understand."

"Sephians are a matriarchal society. It is time to bring a human female to the helm of this base. It brings strength to our troops. While Jax advises me from a military perspective, I will look to you, Sienna, to advise me on how best to integrate our peoples."

"I don't know what to say." And she didn't. Of all the words out of Apolo's mouth, what she'd just heard was far from what she'd expected. While her logical mind knew it was purely a political ploy to set the stage for human-Sephian relations, her emotional heart remained in shock.

"Do you accept this responsibility?" Apolo asked.

She looked around the room. Every eye was on her. She had always been a loner. An introvert. This kind of responsibility should belong to someone who was bred for it, not some country girl who played Xbox. But she also didn't believe in coincidences; Legian crashing in her backyard had been the first step, leading to where she now stood.

She squeezed Legian's hand before looking back to Apolo. "I graciously accept this honor."

Apolo walked over and held out his arm, and they sealed the pact Sephian-style—by clasping each other's forearms.

"According to Sephian tradition, I have a trinity, a body of three minds to guide me and with whom I can discuss all topics of importance." Apolo turned to Legian, Bente, and Nalea before turning back to Sienna. "While you can consult with me any time, I hope you will also look to my trinity to guide you."

Sienna made eye contact with each of the trinity members. "Of course. I look forward to your guidance, friendship, and honest thoughts." She turned to Jax. "I'll look to Jax as well." She smiled. "You haven't let me down yet."

Apolo nodded. "I believe their counsel will guide you well." His voice held a hint of respect. "Now, let's make the announcement and break out the drinks."

She strode over to Legian and he embraced her. Even if it was purely for show, one thing was for sure: she wouldn't let them down. She'd make a good poster child for relations. She would see it through to the end. No matter what.

Chapter 19

Sienna had never been more stressed in her life. More than when she discovered aliens weren't some made-up sci-fi creatures from Mars. More than when she left the only life she knew behind and went traipsing off into the unknown with one of those aliens. More than when the base was attacked and she'd nearly been killed. More than any of that.

She now knew what Atlas must have felt like to bear the weight of the world on his shoulders. Of course, her responsibility didn't come near that. She was a figurehead rather than an actual decision-maker. Still, she was the walking commercial for integrating Sephians into the world. After all, she was the first human to have a *tahren*.

She wished she could fade into the SUV's black leather so she wouldn't have to go back to her cabin. They were already driving down familiar rough side roads. It wouldn't be much longer now.

The truth was she'd never had to be responsible for anyone else but herself before. Even with Bobby. He had been away on duty too often and at home too little. It had left her to remain carefree and—she hated to admit it—selfish. But suddenly, for the first time in her life, how she acted could impact others' lives.

Her greatest fear wasn't looking bad in front of others; that she could live with. Her greatest fear also wasn't Apolo realizing he had made a mistake. Or of those closest to her seeing that she couldn't hack it. Or even those who had seen and done shit she'd only imagined who would see through her in a heartbeat if she faltered and would know that she had been faking it all along, that she didn't have the guts to make the tough calls.

No, her greatest fear was that her actions could lead to death. That was something she wasn't sure she could handle.

Legian squeezed her hand. "Is everything okay?"

She put on a fake smile. "First day on the job jitters, that's all."

He kissed the top of her head. "You'll do fine. Apolo will be there. You won't be alone. You will never be alone."

"Yeah." Sienna grinned, and then stared out the window at the passing trees. It was true. She knew she wasn't alone. With them, she would never feel alone.

Sienna leaned forward and squeezed Jax's shoulder. "Thanks for driving."

"No problem. I'm a piss-poor backseat driver. I'll take driving any day over being a passenger."

"What do we need to do before your father arrives?" Risa asked Jax from beside him in the front seat.

"We'll need to set up a perimeter in case the news leaked to the Draeken," Legian answered.

Jax answered. "Ace checked out the place a couple of days ago, so we should be all set. The cabin and surrounding woods will be secure."

"He's your army buddy, right?" Risa asked.

Jax nodded.

"So, Lea," Sienna said. "If I remember right, we're due for a girls' night involving some wine you've been hiding in your room."

Nalea smiled in response, snapping her attention back inside the vehicle. "The wine's still there, safe and sound."

"Then it's a date."

"Are there pillow fights involved in this girls' night?" Jax asked with a shit-ass grin.

Risa halfheartedly pushed against him. "Men. Doesn't matter what world you're from. You're all the same."

"We're here," Jax called out from the front, his voice turning soldier-serious in a split second.

Conversation over, she looked out the window. Her heart gave a little jump. Home. Only it wasn't home. Not anymore. Sienna had never thought she'd see the cabin again. It looked exactly as she'd left it. The small stone cabin stood in a scant clearing within dense pine woods. She'd built it for the privacy and had always found solace there, surrounded by sounds of bird songs and pine needles rustling in the breeze.

She couldn't even begin to fathom how homesick the Sephians must be, knowing they never would see their home again. She stepped out of the SUV and inhaled the forest air. It was cool and laden with the woodsy scent of evergreen. Spring was beginning to show its blooms, though winter was still hanging on for all it was worth. She walked around the matching SUVs already parked nearby and took in the building before her.

Home.

The lieutenant-colonel and others weren't scheduled to arrive until twilight when the Sephians could cope without dark glasses. She'd wanted to come early to have some time at her cabin. But as she stepped through the door, a bustle of activity filled the small space. Her home had become claustrophobic, and she bit back the tension. There hadn't been this many people here even when the construction crew had built the place.

With her mother off touring the world, she'd never found the time to see the house her daughter built. Not that Sienna hadn't expected that. Kat had always made it clear that work was more important. Sienna loved her mother—that was never in question —but her mother wasn't the warm and fuzzy type. She believed good parenting involved exposing children to the ugliness in the world by the time they could walk.

Once Sienna hit eighteen, her parents had shipped her off to college. She'd wanted to stay with them and join their humanitarian crew, but they'd had different ideas. They seemed to think college was a necessity. Considering her an adult, they put Sienna on the first flight back to the States.

She may not have had a loving childhood, but for the first time in her life she was thankful for her parents. They had taught her life was tough. They had also fervently believed that there was life beyond the stars. What would have happened to Legian if he'd crashed in a skeptic's backyard? And she'd learned one critical thing while raising herself out of a suitcase: no matter what happened, she could deal with it. It was a lesson she'd used over and over again with the Sephians.

She sensed Legian come up behind her before he touched her. "You are my rock," she murmured as he wrapped his arms around her.

"I don't understand the statement. I don't consider myself like a stone, although parts of me become hard as one."

She twirled in his arms to find a grin on his face.

"Let's go for a walk." He gruffly took her hand and led her outdoors.

Nearly an hour later, they sauntered back into the cabin.

Nalea winked at her. "You still have a branch in your hair."

"Nice to see you two could make it," Jax said, walking from the kitchen eating a real, honest-to-goodness cheeseburger.

Her stomach growled, and she grabbed the half-eaten burger from his hand.

"I was eating that."

She took a big bite of the juicy burger. "Perks of being a model citizen," she said with a very full mouth.

He shrugged, walked back into the kitchen and returned

seconds later with another one. "The security perimeter has been set up. We have full video. Had it three hours now."

She stopped chewing. "How far out does the perimeter go?"

He smirked. "Far enough to see which tree you carved your names into."

Another hour later—because Legian definitely did not behave in the shower—Sienna reached for the doorknob, poised for the meeting. She paused, turned, and looked around.

Nothing had changed. Everything looked exactly as she'd left it. Surprising, since Jax's team—and possibly the police—had rifled through every square inch of the cabin. Sienna moved to the dresser, opened the small wood box on the top of it, and pulled out the silver charm bracelet. A charm for every trip she and Bobby had taken, a charm for every special occasion. At least, that had been the plan. Only a couple of the links had charms. Their time had been cut far too short. When he died, she'd thought she had, too. Maybe that was the real reason why she'd built a cabin so far out in the woods. To avoid connecting with anyone else.

And then life went on. She'd found out she hadn't died with Bobby. Instead, she had plenty of life left. It had just been buried under grit and grime.

"Ready for this?" Legian asked as he came up behind her.

She placed the bracelet back in the box, closed it, and stepped toward the door. She smoothed her hands down her loose linen sweater and khaki cargos before reaching for the doorknob again. "I am ready." She took a deep breath, opened the door, and stepped into the hallway beyond.

A fire was lit in the living room, giving the area a comfortable, homey feel. Apolo had been right. Her home was a perfect location for this meeting. You couldn't get more human than a cabin.

"Hey, Sienna."

She turned to see Nalea standing nearby. "Sorry. I didn't see you."

"The humans will be here any minute, but there's still no sign of Apolo. Have you heard from him?"

Sienna grabbed her phone, even though Apolo had never called her on it before. No missed calls. "No one's heard from him?"

"I'm afraid not. He's usually early to all functions."

At that moment, Apolo's SUV pulled into the drive and Sienna rushed out to meet them.

The back door of the SUV swung open and she grabbed it. Apolo looked pissed off, but otherwise unharmed. "Where have you been?"

Apolo motioned toward the front of the vehicle. "Bente got us lost."

"Fucking address isn't on the nav system," Bente spewed out as he stalked past her.

She smiled and caught up with Bente. "You could fly light years through space and find a wee little planet in the middle of the universe, but you couldn't find a cabin in the woods less than fifty miles from the base?"

"Piss off," was the Sephian's reply, and he opened the screen door, letting it snap back shut in front of her. Bente wasn't exactly a gentleman. He could make bad guys in the movies look warm and cuddly. Then again, she guessed warm and cuddly would've been pretty useless during a war. No wonder he was so popular with Sephian women. If he wasn't there to kill you, a girl could feel pretty safe with him around.

She caught the door into the cabin before it smacked her in the face.

"What the hell kind of food is this?" Bente grumbled from the kitchen, and she walked toward his voice.

He was holding a cheeseburger in one hand, examining it like it had wiggled.

"It's called food. And trust me, our guests are going to like these a whole lot better than the crap you like so much," she said with a visible shudder.

Nalea looked up from her chair by the window and came to her feet. "You made it."

Apolo grimaced. "Yes, just some minor delays. Any word from our guests?"

"Ace says they're less than a mile out," Jax replied. Jax lifted his hand. "Wait. No. They're driving in now." He stepped outside without another word.

"Game on." She stood and followed Apolo outside.

Several black Humvees pulled up in a semi-circle around the front of the cabin and soldiers poured out. She recognized Lieutenant-Colonel Jerrick and Major Sommers right away. A couple of suits walked with them, each protected on all sides by soldiers in two different types of uniforms. American and British.

Jax stepped up first and saluted his father. The older Jerrick returned it with a haphazard salute before continuing toward the house. He stopped a few feet away.

Sienna nodded to each in turn. "Good to see you again, Lieutenant-Colonel. Major. Welcome to my home."

The lieutenant-colonel held out his hand, which she accepted. "Thank you for hosting us, Ms. Wolfe." He turned to Apolo. "Apolo. I can only hope that tonight's meeting is less exciting and far more productive."

"As do I, Lieutenant-Colonel. The perimeter has been secured by both your and my people. I believe you will find security up to your standards."

The officer nodded then motioned to the men standing at his side. "I'd like to introduce Senator Dane Sokolos of the U.S. Senate and Lieutenant-Colonel Geoffrey Bryant of the British Army."

After a flurry of introductions, Sienna opened the door. "Shall we go inside where it is more comfortable, gentlemen?"

The group filled the living room. Apolo stood to her left with

Jax and Bente on his other side. Legian and Nalea stepped in on her right.

"The Draeken showed first aggression at the club," the lieutenant-colonel said as he sat down on the sofa. Evidently not one to mince words, he got right down to business. "As such, we believe is it in the best interest of our countries to treat the Draeken as a likely threat. We also believe that an arrangement would be beneficial between our people and yours."

Apolo smiled with a slight nod. "That is what we desire. By combining forces, we can eradicate the Draeken threat."

Jerrick lifted a finger. "Our stance is not to eradicate an entire race. Rather, we want to gather more information and perhaps engage the Draeken, while insulating our people against harm."

"Ideally," Lieutenant-Colonel Bryant interjected in a smooth British accent. "While the United Kingdom has no desire in becoming embroiled in a costly war, we will not stand idly by if the Draeken attack our allies and attempt to build an empire across the ocean."

Apolo spoke slowly and warmly. "Then our goals are common. I believe a partnership can be devised to secure our common interests."

Jerrick leaned forward. "And I'm most curious about what some of those interests may be, Apolo."

Apolo gave a slight tilt of his head. "I see you appreciate candor, Lieutenant-Colonel, so I'll lay it out. We exhausted our power supplies when we followed the Draeken to your world. We cannot return to Sephia. We offer our knowledge and technology in return for amnesty and full citizenship."

Jerrick rubbed his chin while the room sat in silence, considering Apolo's words. The senator, who Sienna recognized as being from Arkansas, spoke first. "An agreement like that would need to be formalized first by the American President, and then the United Nations Security Council would need to accept it. Following that, it must be communicated to the public in the right way and at the right time. It won't be easy introducing your people to the general population. We can expect riots, both from the human rights and the religious fronts, as well as the racists. And that's just for starters."

Sienna swallowed before speaking. "It will change the way we've always looked at ourselves. We're no longer alone in the universe, and we have to learn to accept that there are other races as intelligent as us. It wasn't easy for me, and I imagine it was no easier for you. It will be the biggest change ever to be announced to the world. However, as leaders, you have the power to embrace the opportunity and announce us to the world in your own way and at a time of your choosing, or else have the Draeken do it for you. You can usher in a new age for humanity."

"Sienna speaks the truth," Apolo added. "We are not forcing your decision. The decision is yours. We will maintain a covert base as long as the Draeken threat permits, knowing we remain under your goodwill. However, the Draeken have made no such promises. And from what we saw at the club, the Draeken will quickly become much more than urban legends. What have you learned from the Draeken prisoners you attained at the club?"

"Unfortunately, very little," Sommers replied. "We had no proof of their existence until last week. We have begun to study the Draeken we captured. They haven't spoken yet, but biologically speaking, they have been a goldmine of information so far."

Sienna cringed inwardly at the implication of his words. Visions of mice in cages surrounded by white lab coats came to mind. No one, not even the Draeken, deserved to be lab experiments.

She picked up a small briefcase. "Within weeks of landing on our world, Sephian computer systems designed a vaccine for the common cold. Sephian knowledge and technology are generations ahead of ours, and they are willing to share all that in exchange for an alliance. This case contains several vials of the vaccine, and memory sticks with the formula and all the medical data you need to prove that it works with no negative side effects. I have taken it and suffered no ill effect. Consider this token as a gift to show the depth of Sephian intent and goodwill." She opened the case and walked around to show it to the men in the room.

Jerrick accepted the case, snapped it shut, and handed it to the soldier at his right. "I believe our intentions are aligned. I have the authority to formalize a temporary arrangement with the Sephians from a military perspective. We will work together to mitigate the Draeken threat, under certain conditions, of course."

"Of course," Apolo said and shook the lieutenant-colonel's hand.

It was the senator's turn next. "While we cannot commit to a formal agreement today, I give you my word that the proposal will be brought to the President. Your act of good faith will go far in earning our trust. I'll be in touch to discuss an arrangement in more detail."

Senator Sokolos held out his hand, and again Apolo accepted.

"Lieutenant-Colonel Bryant," Apolo spoke, and the British officer turned his attention to the Sephian leader. "I have a proposal for you."

"Go ahead," Bryant replied.

"Having the entire Sephian force in one location is a risk that has plagued me since we came to your world. A risk that became a reality when the Draeken attacked our base. I propose we will split the Sephian force, with half staying in North America, and half relocating to the UK. You would select the location, of course. You may also station key personnel at the location to learn from us. It would provide an opportunity for us to work alongside one another while better protecting the Sephian people and our knowledge of the Draeken. What say you to this?"

Bryant sat quiet for a moment, and then came to his feet abruptly. "Since there's plenty of hand shaking going on today, why not some more." He smiled. "I came here to propose the same. In fact, I already have a location being prepared. As such, I accept your proposal, and I believe we will learn much from one another."

The two men shook hands.

One of the soldiers stepped forward holding something in his hand. Sienna jumped at the movement.

The senator gestured to the soldier. "We'd like some photographs of this momentous occasion. This meeting will be considered First Contact in the history books."

"Of course," Apolo said.

The men came to stand near Apolo. The trinity, Jax, and Sienna stood behind Apolo. Sienna stood with a practiced smile, oblivious to the flashes of the camera. She had bigger things on her mind. Alliances were being formed, but what if they failed?

Chapter 20

Sienna's day began with an envelope. A small, discreet manila envelope slid under her bedroom door.

She lifted Legian's arm and slid out from under him and climbed out of bed, the old wrought iron bed creaking as she did so. A large hand reached out and wrapped around her waist, pulling her back toward him.

"Come back to bed," he mumbled dreamily.

She twirled out of his arm and he grumbled. Ignoring him, she pulled on the old terry cloth robe she'd had for twenty years. It had been hanging on the hook by the bed, exactly where she'd left it on the night she joined the Sephians.

Not ready to spend ten minutes putting her brace on, she reached for the walking stick that was propped in the corner. Using it for support, she limped over to the door and picked up the envelope and turned it over. It was sealed shut. An intricate design decorated the front. No writing.

Legian pulled himself up to an elbow. "What is it?"

"Don't know. The envelope only has a symbol on it. Do you recognize it?" She held it up, and his face visibly paled.

In a burst, he jumped out of bed, grabbed her wrist, and pulled the envelope from her hand. He became hard as a statue.

"I take it you recognize the symbol?"

Legian grimaced. She could feel his fear down to her toes.

She pulled back and looked into his eyes. "What is it?"

"It's the imperial symbol of the Draeken."

She suddenly had a hard time swallowing. "How'd it get here? We have twenty-four-hour security and surveillance on the cabin. There's no way in hell a Draeken got in here."

"Nevertheless, you are holding a letter with the Draeken imperial symbol on it." He rushed to put on his clothes. "I will go over the video from the past several hours. If we have a traitor here, I will find him."

She nodded mutely before looking from the envelope to him and back again. "We've got to open it."

Legian nodded tightly.

She gently tugged the envelope from his grip then tore off the end and held the open end down. A small piece of paper slid out onto her palm.

"What's it say?" he asked while she examined both sides of the paper.

"It says *Cave. Noon. Today.*"

Legian frowned. "Do you have any idea where this cave is?"

She stared out the window. "Yes. There's only one around here. It's spooky, so I hung a God's eye at the entrance. It's not far from where your ship crashed. That's the only cave it could be."

He gave her a look like she was a barbarian. "You hung the eyes of some creature at a cave?"

"What? Oh, wait. It's not what you think. I can't believe you think... anyway, a God's eye is made out of yarn and sticks. It's a Native American thing. You make them to scare off bad spirits. Believe me, that cave needed it. It's always given me the creeps."

Neither spoke for what seemed like eternity. Finally, she broke the silence. "I'm thinking we should go to see what's up."

"It's a trap."

"If they wanted to ambush us, why not do it at the cabin while we slept? If they could slide an envelope under my door without being noticed, they could just as easily assassinate us in our sleep. Besides, if it were a trap, why would they be so obvious about it? Invite us to a trap? That's so cliché."

Legian started to pace. Like Apolo, he did that whenever he thought. She swore he'd worn a path into the floor in their room back at the base. He stopped before she expected him to. "We'll set troops up around the area. I'll go in at noon to draw them out."

She put her hands on her hips and glared. "No. This letter has to be meant for both of us. You recognized the Draeken seal, and I'm the only one who'd know about the cave."

"We can't risk it."

She drew in a deep breath and let it out slowly. She didn't want to do it, but she had to. "Would you say the same to anyone else?"

His lack of response was answer enough.

"Fine," she continued. "You're my tahren. I want and respect your advice. But it's my life and my decision. The letter is meant for us. I'm going."

"That is not practical," Legian gritted out through clenched teeth.

"It's safe to say they know about last night's meeting if they know we're here. What if they're ready to surrender or make some kind of peace offering?"

"You don't know the Draeken like I do."

"I know. That's why I trust your guidance. But you're not being objective. You want me to stay back for my protection, not for the good of our people."

"That's not true."

"It's true," she snapped. "If this is something that can shorten this war, I want to be there. End of discussion. The video should show us who delivered it. We can ask more questions then. In the meantime, I trust you and Jax to make sure the perimeter is safe so we're not walking into a trap."

He glared at her for a moment. "As you wish," he muttered before handing the note back to her and stomping off to the bathroom.

She stared at the closed bathroom door for a moment. She knew Legian only had her safety in mind, but she couldn't be respected if she let him coddle her.

She didn't bother with getting dressed. She stepped out into the hall and hobbled through to the living room. Jax and Risa were already sitting on the couch, eating egg sandwiches. Nalea sat across from them, eying their food with suspicion.

Risa took a bite out of her sandwich.

Nalea cringed. "How can you eat the egg of an animal? That is so wrong."

"Easy," Risa replied. "Like this." And at that moment, both she and Jax took oversized bites out of their sandwiches.

Now Nalea shuddered. "This planet has barbaric practices."

"Barbaric, but tasty," Sienna replied.

"Let me make you one." Risa jumped up, licking butter from her fingers. "I'm really getting into this cooking thing."

"And she's pretty good at it," Jax added, leaning back contentedly on the couch.

"Yeah, I'll take one. Thanks." Sienna collapsed into a seat. "Hey, have either of you seen anything odd around here this morning?"

"No, why?" Nalea asked.

Sienna handed over the letter and envelope to Nalea.

Her face paled, as Legian's had done minutes earlier. "Where did you get this?"

"Someone slid it under my bedroom door. Legian is going to check out the videos."

Jax popped to his feet, walked over, and grabbed the letter.

"It's from the Draeken."

He frowned and grabbed his radio. "Ace, check in."

"Ace, here."

"Alert the teams. I need a full perimeter check. We have a breach. Possible Draeken," Jax said into the radio.

"Copy that," Ace replied.

Jax turned back to face Sienna. "Are you going?"

She nodded. "Can you and Legian to make sure we're ready for whatever they try?"

"Of course," Jax replied. "I need you to show me the area on a map. I'll have the area secure within the hour. We'll have eyes on the ground. And, I'll be with you at the meeting."

"I'm coming, too," Nalea replied, matter-of-factly.

Sienna smiled. "Thank you. I can't ask any of you to come. Like Legian said, it could be a trap, but—"

"We stand together," Legian interrupted as he approached.

Relief washed over Sienna when Nalea and Jax nodded their agreement, and she returned a smile. "Thanks, guys."

"What'd I miss?"

Sienna glanced up to see Risa walking into the room, carrying a plate with a steaming egg sandwich on it. The med-tech gasped and dropped the plate. Glass shattered across the stone floor. She pointed to the envelope as she knelt and began to pick up the glass shards. "What's that?"

"It seems Sienna has received an invitation to a party," Nalea replied.

Jax knelt and helped Risa collect pieces on the floor.

Nalea ran a hand through her hair. "But it doesn't make sense. How did the letter get into this cabin in the first place? We have a full perimeter line set up."

"My guess?" Sienna replied. "It came from the inside."

"You mean the traitor's here? With us? I thought we were safe." Risa started to shake. Jax rubbed her back while whispering soothing words in her ear.

Sienna paid no attention to Risa, and instead focused on

calming her own nerves. The one thing she didn't need today was more stress. Jax could deal with his woman. "It's a half-hour ride out to the cave on ATVs. We have a lot to do and only five hours to do it in. Let's get busy." She turned around and headed down the hall. She had plenty to do, starting with a long, hot shower to get some thinking done.

Sienna strapped on a helmet and climbed onto her ATV. Legian climbed on behind her while Nalea rode with Jax on one of the new ATVs they'd brought when setting up security around the cabin. Even though it was a cloudy day, both Sephians wore dark sunglasses to protect their eyes.

Nalea and Jax both wore earpieces and spoke with the Sephians and soldiers posted around the perimeter. The entire makeshift base was on full alert, and guards were positioned throughout the woods around the cave. The air buzzed with energy. Unfortunately, they were going in none the wiser than when she'd found the letter in the morning. The cameras had conspicuously cut out for an entire hour before sunrise, leaving them with a big fat zilch for leads. They weren't even one step closer to knowing who—or what—had delivered that letter.

With a swift movement of her foot, the ATV jumped into gear, and they began the ride deeper into the woods.

They all wore black Sephian uniforms. Not for a fashion statement, but because they were durable and did a great job of keeping off sharp tree branches and tiny critters, both of which infested these woods. The thin fabric also worked better than anything with her leg brace. Any of her other pants jammed up in the bands.

The weather was perfect, and it took under twenty minutes to get to the cave. Still concealed by brush, they had to get within ten feet of the entrance to see it. Legian jumped off the quad before she stopped, and began looking for signs of others in the area. Jax and Nalea were right behind him. Sienna moved more gingerly, taking in anything that may have changed since the last time she was here. She glanced toward the cave. The large blue and red God's eye still hung from the tree branch that had grown across the top of the cave entrance, as if it were holding the darkness within.

She didn't have to wait long. The God's eye moved when the bony tip of a dragon-like wing bumped it. Tattooed wings spread out as a Draeken she recognized stepped into view. She stood firm. Her friends swiftly came to her, setting up a living, breathing wall of protection.

"Hello, Roden." Sienna was as polite as possible, while a phantom pain in her leg was busy reminding her of why she disliked that particular Draeken so much.

"Sienna Wolfe." He continued walking toward her, a Draeken woman and a Draeken man flanking his sides. He hadn't changed a bit. His silver hair was still long, and he looked like he could knock out Wolverine in a single punch. His wing even looked like it had healed completely. Not even the tattoos were marred. She wished she'd been so lucky. He wore a dark kilt, boots, and a tight shirt—all with pockets and weapons strapped to them.

Sienna scanned his bodyguards. Both were dressed similarly to Roden. Easily six feet tall, the woman reminded her of a Valkyrie with her long silver hair—the wings suiting her perfectly. The man on Roden's other side looked feral, his cold eyes vacant of all emotion, of all humanity. He's already dead. Except his body's still going.

Roden glanced over everyone with Sienna until his eyes stopped on the woman standing to her left. "Ah. Nalea. I was hoping you'd make an appearance. Did you come here to continue what we started?" He drawled out her name with sugary seduction. It gave Sienna a sick feeling. The bastard knew exactly how to push buttons. He was dangerous.

Nalea's nostrils flared, and she pulled out a blaster.

Sienna placed her hand on her friend's forearm, and Nalea slowly lowered her blaster a couple of inches. "Ignore him," Sienna muttered under her breath.

"Easier said than done," the Draeken crooned in a deep, masculine voice.

She pointed a finger at Roden. "You. Behave. Or I'll let her shoot you. Now, are you going to tell us why we're here, or did you schedule this little meeting simply to make jabs?"

A corner of his mouth curled upward. "No wonder you aligned with the Sephians. You have the same violent streak. Have you noticed? You'll never see Draeken drawing first blood in any conflict. Regardless of the inherent violence in you and your chosen race, I have a proposition for you, dear Sienna."

Legian sidestepped and became a wall in front of her. He spoke with his fists clenched. "That is my tahren you speak to, Draeken. Take care with your words."

Roden snarled back. "Your tahren is the reason I'm here, Sephian scum."

She put a hand on Legian's shoulder and stepped forward. "You have quite the way with folks, Roden."

He took a casual step closer to her, as if she didn't have three armed bodyguards at her side. "It's simple. Death starts wars. Life ends wars. I have a proposal to end the genocide of my people."

She raised an eyebrow.

"Surely your *tahren* told you how my people have been driven to near extinction? Those few of us who remain survived only by fleeing our home."

Nalea nearly spat the words. "Sephia was never your home."

"I disagree, woman."

"The name's Nalea," Sienna said. "And you digress."

"No, Sienna. It's important that you understand our history if we are to attain peace," he replied. The woman next to him lifted her chin slightly, never once taking her eyes off Sienna.

Jax and Legian remained alongside her, but she suspected Legian was doing the best he could to not rip the heads off the Draeken right then and there. She considered letting him do it. Maybe it would end the war. Then again, it could cause an all-out war on Earth.

"I'm sure you have heard of the Great Rebellion—what the Sephians call the Noble War?" Roden asked.

"I have. It was where the Sephians reclaimed their world from their enslavers."

He narrowed his eyes slightly. "Hmm. But have you been told of how we came to Sephia in the first place?"

"No one knows the truth, Draeken," Legian spat out through clenched teeth.

Roden scowled. "No one knows, because the Sephians destroyed the records shortly after the Great War. But answer this, Sephian. Why would they destroy their own historical records unless those files showed something they didn't want their successors to remember?"

The Draeken then turned from Legian to Sienna. "You see, the star that illuminated our home world had grown old. Our people were given a choice. Flee our dying planet and possibly die in the frozen expansion of space, or stay and die at home in a guaranteed fiery death. Millions fled in large ships. Some went off on their own, but most ships stayed together and traveled through the light years."

"Get on with it. I grow tired of your stories," Legian muttered.

"I would if I didn't keep getting interrupted," the Draeken replied dryly. "Now, where was I? Oh, yes. Eventually, our ships ran low on provisions. After all, they were massively over capacity and couldn't support the numbers on them long-term. Fortunately, our systems showed our people to a planet with no suns. It was a bleak world, far different from our bright, warm world, but it sustained life. That was what mattered. The Draeken leaders offered alms in the form of technology and knowledge to the Sephians in return for approval to form a settlement on-world. The Sephians callously rejected our offer. Then our people begged. Again, they were rejected. My people were running out of food and had months to live. Again, they were forced to make a hard choice. They chose to fight for survival."

Nalea moved but didn't leave Sienna's side. "That is just a legend. We have our own, and it doesn't paint the Draeken nearly as pretty."

He shrugged. "So you say. But what matters is that we won the Great War, and therefore won the right to live on Sephia."

"And we won the Noble War," Legian replied, "and reclaimed our home. And we vowed you would never turn another people into your slaves again."

Roden shrugged. "Your world had slavery before we ever got there. We just continued that Sephian tradition. And who says that's what we're doing on this world?" he snapped.

"You're Draeken. That's what you do." Nalea's words sizzled with scorn. The tension was so palpable, Sienna felt herself breathing more rapidly.

"We're Draeken. We survive. *That* is what we do, Nalea." He murmured her name softly, and Sienna watched her friend prickle in response.

"Thanks for the history lesson, Roden," Sienna said. "So, why did you really come here today?"

Roden cracked his knuckles, and she noticed Jax put his hand on his holster at the movement. The Draeken noticed it, too, because the woman next to Roden matched Jax's stance.

"I offer a quid pro quo, Sienna. You know the position I carry, and the power I wield. With a snap of my fingers, I could have you killed. Or, I could use that power to end the war."

"Likewise," Sienna snarled.

"The war is over," Legian said. "You lost. Now we're just doing cleanup."

Roden glared at Legian. "The war will never be over. Not until the two races align."

"And how do you plan to accomplish that?" Sienna asked.

"As I declared before, life ends wars."

Sienna's eyebrows lifted. "You're going to have to elaborate. Spell it out for me."

"Simple. We unite the people by uniting the leaders. You will become my mate—"

Sienna couldn't hear anything else because Legian lurched forward and grabbed Roden by the neck. Roden punched him, knocking him back. The other two Draeken stepped forward, keeping their hands on their holsters. Jax jumped in and pulled Legian back.

Roden sported a bloody nose, and Legian looked like he was going to have a heck of a shiner.

Sienna scowled. "Are you two done? Now can we talk again?" She looked straight at Roden. "You were saying?"

He grinned, and then he frowned and spat blood. "I know you have a tahren. On this world, you could have chosen none higher in status. Except for Apolo that is, but he is already taken and Krysea's not here, so that no longer matters. By taking me as your consort, you—the human—unite both the Sephians and the Draeken while also bringing in the human element."

She squinted. "What part of tahren don't you understand?"

"I take it your tahren failed to mention that, in both our races, women in authority can have more than one cohort. It has been done in the past to unite people. I have no doubt it would work here."

Sienna's knees grew wobbly, though she remained standing. Out of everything she had prepared for today, a marriage proposal wasn't one of them. Especially from a being who had tried to kill her.

Roden's gaze moved to Nalea. He looked up and down like he was undressing her. "However, one of Apolo's elite trinity would serve as a suitable second choice to unite our two races on this new world. The human element is merely a nice political statement."

Nalea snarled and Roden smiled. "I'm nobody's second choice," she gritted out before lunging at him.

Sienna saw a shimmer in the light and noticed the knife Nalea gripped. "Lea, no!"

The other two Draeken pulled out their blasters, and Legian and Jax did the same. Sienna expected to feel the pain of being shot. Instead, she was knocked to the ground. She looked up to see Legian roll off her and start firing at the Draeken. Shots were returned.

Dark gold liquid flowed from his shoulder. "Damn it, Legian. You got shot."

"Only a flesh wound," he muttered.

She pushed him behind the trunk of the tree. Sienna couldn't see anything. Legian blocked her view. "Stay here," she ordered, and then jumped behind the next tree. She looked around the large trunk and caught a glimpse of Jax firing his gun while running in a crouched position toward where the Draeken had been standing before she was knocked to the ground.

She fired several shots into the air in case the Sephians had lost contact with Nalea. Something caught her eye. She turned in time to be grabbed by the Draeken male.

He tackled her to the ground, and her bad leg twisted under his weight. Agony shot through her, but she pushed the pain back by biting her lip. Her attacker had been shot at least twice, but he moved like he was in no pain. He lifted a knife. She let out a war cry, jerked her gun to him, and squeezed the trigger point blank at his chest.

She couldn't say how many times she shot him. All she knew was that she held the trigger down until there was a hole where his chest had been. As his body fell, Legian caught it and threw it to the side. He then pulled her to her feet and looked her over for wounds. Only after he had convinced himself she was okay did he pull her to him.

Sienna clutched Legian's arms around her waist as she stared at the corpse. She'd never killed so close before. She thought she was going to be sick.

Voices jarred her from her thoughts. She turned to Legian. Her eyes widened when she remembered he was wounded and slapped her hand over his shoulder.

He winced and wrapped his hand around her wrist but didn't pull it away. "Save your strength," he murmured.

"Trust me. I've got enough energy for both of us," she replied and kept her hand in place, the warmth buzzing under her palm. With her adrenaline high, she felt like she could heal every wounded Sephian in a ten-mile radius. For seconds—or minutes— they watched each other, unafraid of each other's gaze.

Once the heat between Legian's shoulder and her hand returned to normal, she pulled away and put her hand in his. Together, they walked back toward the cave. Reinforcements had arrived and were scanning the area. Jax sported several cuts, but was now busy tying up the Draeken woman, while Nalea was nowhere to be seen.

"Where's Lea?" she asked to no one in particular.

"We haven't been able to find either her or Roden yet. We searched the area. It doesn't look like there were any other Draeken," one of the soldiers reported while he eyed her warily.

Her second greatest fear furrowed in her stomach. "Lea's gone." She grabbed Legian's hands. "We've got to get her back."

Numbly, Sienna looked once more at the Draeken she'd killed. She realized that killing was easy; it was the losing a bit of her soul that was the hard part.

Chapter 21

Sienna scolded herself every time she ended up in another training session with Legian. He looked like he was enjoying himself, as if these training sessions were his revenge for every time she pissed him off. *He's getting his vengeance all right,* she thought as she tied the bandana around her head to catch the sweat burning her eyes.

She couldn't see his eyes through the dark sunglasses he wore, which made it even harder to guess his moves. To make matters worse, her leg brace was still being recalibrated by Doc. And she didn't have her old brace at the cabin, leaving her to train by balancing on one leg. Serious handicap, but Legian seemed to think it was a good idea in case she was ever caught without a brace.

He lunged, and she dove to the side. He caught her ankle and she kicked back, hitting him square in the chest. He fell back, but was on his feet a split second later.

"That may work on me, but Draeken are stronger and faster. They age faster, but that does you no good in battle unless you plan to lecture them to death on English slang."

"Ha ha," she quipped.

"You can't beat them with a frontal attack. You aren't strong enough. You've got to go for their wings. They are extremely sensitive and the fastest way to take one down. You can take down a Draeken three times your size if you get hold of a wing."

"That's a bit tricky to practice, since you don't have wings," she snapped back.

He ignored her. "They protect their wings. Keep them close to their bodies. You have to find other ways to take them down, too."

"I can't do this." She let out an exasperated sigh, sat down on the floor and rubbed her bad leg.

"Yes, you can." Legian stepped closer and held out a hand.

Seizing the moment, Sienna grabbed his hand and yanked him forward as she reached for her cane. He fell, and she straddled him, pressing the cane against his neck. His eyes widened.

He smiled then he cussed. "You cheated."

"Yeah. So? I'm not the one lying on his back right now."

With a grunt in response, he brought a hand up and gingerly pushed the cane away. "I think we've had enough training for one day." He ignored her offered hand, instead pushing himself to his feet.

She smiled. "Sore loser."

"Don't think a Draeken will fall for that trick," he scolded.

"And don't think that's the only trick up my sleeve," she replied.

Inside, Jax and Ace were playing a game of gin rummy. Risa sat next to a scowling Jax. Ace was grinning.

"Let me guess. Ace is winning," Sienna said, stepping through the doorway.

"I think he's cheating," Jax said.

Ace snorted. "Poor man's down because I'm kicking his ass."

"What do you have there?" she asked, motioning to the cheese dip and nachos on the table next to Ace.

"My snack," the soldier replied without looking up. "Get your own."

She put her hands on her hips. "I don't know if you know this, but you're a guest at my home right now," she said to the man sitting on her couch.

"Doesn't mean you get my nachos."

"Fine. I'll remember that at Christmas time." She headed into the kitchen to make her own snack. She cubed the cheese and mixed in a can of diced tomatoes and peppers. As it bubbled in the microwave, she thought of Nalea. It had been three days. Apolo had been furious. He'd said that of all the trinity members, they couldn't lose Nalea to the Draeken—whatever that meant. He'd tried to check with his informant, but again received no response. It was a safe bet his cover had been blown and he was bear bait in Canada right about now. The Draeken prisoner in the basement had been even less help.

They'd sent out scouts, but they'd found nothing. It was difficult to follow a trail when there were no tracks. Everyone assumed Roden must have flown away, taking his Sephian prisoner with him and leaving them with very little to go on. Nalea's name had become taboo around the cabin. Her disappearance sat heavily, like a proverbial white elephant in the room. No one spoke of it, yet everyone was thinking about it.

Juggling her cheese and a bag of nachos in one hand and the cane in the other, Sienna hobbled back into the living room. She sat down next to Ace and crunched her chips extra loudly. When he looked at her, she smiled sweetly. "My snack. Back off."

Legian leaned forward and grabbed a couple of chips. He ate them plain. Sephian food was bland, and he hadn't grown accustomed to anything spicier than Doritos yet.

Jax threw his cards down and pushed back from the table. "This is bullshit. I swear you could play Russian roulette with a fully loaded revolver and win."

Ace shrugged and leaned back in his chair. "And you like the beatings. You're a regular sub. I know what you need."

"What's that?" Jax asked.

"You need a woman to pull out the whips and chains," he replied with a wicked-ass grin.

With that, Jax barked out a laugh. "Yeah, whatever man. I'm out of here. Time for a perimeter check."

"Sure. Take out your sexual frustrations on the poor guards," Ace said.

Jax flipped his friend the bird as he stood. Risa kissed Jax, and he headed out the door, letting the screen door slam shut behind him.

Sienna sat and smiled through their banter. She needed his humor and normalcy more than she liked to admit.

Risa stretched. "I could use a nap," she mumbled through a yawn, covering her mouth.

"See you later," Sienna called out after the med-tech as she headed down the hall.

"Hold up." Ace pulled himself to his feet, the grin dropping from his face. "We gotta talk."

Risa turned, eyed him warily, and then smiled warmly. "Of course."

Ace sauntered down the hall, and the two disappeared in the guest bedroom. Sienna had set it aside for Apolo, but he'd ended up staying at the base. Jax—and therefore Risa—had claimed the open room right away to keep a close eye on Sienna, leaving everyone else in temporary shelters erected around the cabin.

She looked at Legian. "Speaking of naps, I could use one, too."

"If by nap, you mean us naked and me inside you, I'll come with you."

"No. I was thinking of that full body massage you owe me."

A scream rang out from across the hall. Sienna surged up. Legian leapt toward the door. He turned the handle and turned back to her.

"Go!" She hopped behind him.

He tore the door open and had disappeared inside before Sienna made it three steps closer. Shuffling sounds and crying emanated from the room. She pulled open the drawer to her nightstand and cursed when she remembered she'd taken that gun to the base when she first left the cabin with Legian. Slamming it shut, she hurried as quickly as her lame leg allowed. Grabbing the doorway, she stumbled into the room and froze.

Legian had a choke-hold on Ace, who was holding his gun point blank at Risa's heart.

"Jesus Christ. What's going on here?" Sienna demanded.

"Oh, thank the gods." Risa ran toward Sienna and wrapped her arms around her.

"Get away from her, traitor," Ace belted out, and Legian tightened his grip, causing the man to cough.

Sienna faced the men, still holding Risa, who was trembling. "Legian, release him."

Legian backed off slowly and Ace jumped to one side. Risa looked at him and cowered into her. "Keep him away from me," she whimpered into her neck.

Sienna patted the med-tech on the back as she eyed Ace. "What the hell happened?"

Ace opened his mouth to speak, but Risa jumped in to speak first. "He tried to seduce me. When I rejected him, he tried to rape me."

"*Bullshit.*" Ace held a hand against his shoulder, a dark red stain outlining his hand. "She tried to kill me."

Risa trembled in her arms. "He's lying. I tried to protect myself. He's jealous of Jax. He said he was going to hurt me when I fought back. I swear it."

"If I wanted her dead, she'd be dead already," Ace gritted out through clenched teeth.

At that moment, Jax strolled into the room. He stopped, stared, and muttered, "What the hell's going on?"

"Jax! Gods, I'm so glad you're here." Risa ran to him and pointed at her lover's best friend. "That man tried to rape me!"

Jax looked in shock from Risa to Ace and back again. Ace said nothing, but his entire body tensed like a cable pulled too tight. Sienna prayed silently that he wouldn't snap. Then, ever so slowly, Jax's hands dropped from holding Risa. He backed away and raw anger poured over his face.

"Jax?" Risa pleaded in a whimper, reaching out to him.

"What did you do?" Jax ground out the words.

Risa's jaw dropped. "What do you mean?"

"What did she do?" he asked Ace, never taking his eyes off her.

"She tried to kill me," Ace replied. "I told her that I saw her around the video feeds the morning they went offline, and she freaked."

The video... "The letter." Sienna stared at Risa. Like a rain shower, the pieces fell into place.

"He's lying," Risa sobbed out as she backed away from Jax.

Jax scowled. "Ace never lies." He edged closer to her, his hand reaching behind his back. "And he would never, ever try to rape a woman. Anyone who knows him knows what happened to his sister." A hard look fell over him. He had made a decision. And from the way he looked at Risa, it didn't bode well for her.

In a rush, Risa charged Sienna. Sienna jumped back, stopping against the wall. Risa pulled out a blaster, and Sienna froze. There was no escape this time. Risa grabbed her arm and stepped behind her, using her as living body armor.

"Stop or else I'll kill her," Risa threatened, and the three men stopped in their tracks. "I'm sorry," she said to Jax.

"You're sorry?" Jax asked incredulously. He shook his head. "I was your perfect sap. I got you access to the officers' hall, Apolo's room.... Don't apologize for something you planned out detail by fucking detail. No. I give you kudos. You played me good. You're one hell of an actress."

Sienna could feel Risa trembling behind her. "It's not like that."

Jax glared. "Give the act up already."

"How could you, Risa? How could you betray your own people

like this?" Sienna asked, trying to distract the med-tech as she thought through ideas of how to get the blaster pointing at her head to be pointing at anything but her head or the men in the room.

Risa guffawed. "The Sephians aren't my people. They were never my people. The woman who gave birth to me left me to die in an alley, like I was nothing but garbage. It was a Draeken who saved me. They protected us from ourselves. And how did we show our appreciation? We stabbed them in the backs."

"You were their slaves," Sienna replied.

"No, not slaves. Not all of us. Hillas raised me as his own."

"Hillas." The single word fell from Legian's lips in no more than a whisper.

Risa turned Sienna to face Legian. "Yes, Hillas is my father. He may not be the one who impregnated my mother, but he treats me like his daughter. He is a far better father than any Sephian could be."

"He used you," Legian replied.

"No. Never."

Sienna felt the blaster nudge against her temple.

"He loves me. He didn't ask me to take this mission, but I volunteered. I did it. To protect him."

"But Hillas is dead," Sienna said.

"Hillas is not dead. But you will be."

Chapter 22

The blaster moved against Sienna's temple as Risa adjusted her grip. Sienna seized her chance. Throwing her head back, she connected with something that made a loud crunch.

"Uh!" Risa's grip loosened, and Sienna jerked away the instant the blaster went off. Heat blasted by her face, and the smell of burnt hair filled her nostrils. In slow motion, she watched Risa aim the blaster at Jax.

Jax dove for Risa.

Risa fired.

Jax didn't stop. He chopped the med-tech in the throat, knocking her to her knees. The blaster dropped to the carpeted floor with a thud. Risa's hands clawed at her throat as she struggled for air that wouldn't come. Jax had showed Sienna that move a week ago. It was sure death, he'd said. Her windpipe had been crushed. It was just a matter of time now.

Blood poured from Risa's broken nose. Jax just stood there and stared while Risa fought to breathe. As her eyes bulged, she reached out to Jax. He did nothing as she grabbed his pant legs before sliding down into a crumpled heap on the floor.

Silence fell over the room. No one moved for what seemed like an eternity in a black hole. Finally, Jax moved forward, only to stumble. Everyone lunged forward to grab him, but Ace got there first. Sliding an arm around Jax's back, Ace helped him to the bed before sitting down on the cedar chest.

Sienna glanced toward the hall. "I'll grab a first-aid kit."

She returned from the bathroom a seconds later with her cane in hand and an armful of supplies. Legian had torn away Jax's shirt to reveal a nasty burn on his hip.

Ace continued to hold a hand against his shoulder. "You're lucky she was a bad shot. It grazed you."

Jax remained silent while he stared out the window.

Dumping the supplies on the bed, Sienna grabbed some scissors and faced Ace. He lowered his hand and fresh blood seeped through his shirt.

"Knife wound," was all he said.

"I'll call Doc, but it could take him some time to get here. In the meantime, we need to staunch the bleeding." She cut off his shirt, and then dabbed at the wound.

"It's not too deep."

She pressed a cloth against the wound, and he grimaced. "You'll need stitches."

"Nothing new to me."

And that was something she had no doubt about after seeing Ace without a shirt. Scars of all shapes and sizes littered his skin, his latest addition not making the top three for worst scars on his torso.

She stood there for a minute, keeping pressure on the wound, as she watched Legian rub salve on Jax's burn. Every now and then Jax would wince, but otherwise showed no sign of emotion.

Suddenly Ace pushed her away. "For fuck's sake, give me a needle and thread already," he muttered.

"But Doc should do that," she replied.

"I got this." He gave her a half-smile before winking.

With a wary eye, Sienna backed off and sifted through the supplies for a small pre-sealed bag labeled *Suture Kit*. She tore it open and held it out for Ace. He grabbed the bag and threaded the needle like a pro. She stared while he played doctor on his own body. "Sure I can't help?"

"Nah," he replied. His hands were steady, although his voice was tight. Stitching his own wound had to hurt like hell.

Sienna heard the screen door open, and she stepped out into the hallway to see a Sephian soldier walking into the kitchen.

"Wait up, Sana," Sienna called out to the soldier.

The Sephian woman stopped, turned, and faced her. "What can I do for you, Sienna?"

"Get Apolo and Doc up here right away. Also, on your way out, send in two able -bodied Sephians."

Sana jumped into gear quickly and without question.

Sienna stepped into the kitchen and rummaged through the cabinets. She stopped when she found what she was looking for. An old bottle of whiskey she'd bought when she wanted to kill her pain, back when she had dumbly thought booze could drown the memories of Bobby. Instead, all the stuff had done was guarantee a lousy hangover.

She carried the Texas fifth into the bedroom. She could hear water running in the bathroom. Ace came out moments later, the blood washed from his hands. His eyes lit up. "That's my kind of medicine," he said as he reached out for the bottle.

Sienna handed him the bottle and bent down to examine his new stitches. "Impressive."

"They don't call me Ace for nothing," he replied, and took a long draw before handing the bottle back to her.

Sienna stepped over to the bed where Legian had also finished patching up Jax. She offered the bottle. Without looking at her, Jax swung his legs over the side of the bed. He grunted and held his side as he dragged himself to his feet then he grabbed the bottle and stumbled out the room without even looking her in the eye. She watched him leave, and Ace jogged to catch up. He looped Jax's arm over his shoulder, and the pair disappeared down the hallway.

Adrenaline making her hands shaky, Sienna pulled together the supplies and shoved them back into the plastic pouch. She noticed the blood on her hands. Strange that she hadn't even noticed it before. The sight of it didn't bother her any longer. And that scared her. She'd changed, but she wasn't sure it was for the better.

Two Sephians stepped into the bedroom and froze when they saw the body on the floor.

Sienna pointed to the body. "Get rid of that traitor."

There were some days she wished she could get a do-over. Today would have been one of those days. Whoever had said ignorance was bliss had really nailed it. Yesterday, Risa had been one of her friends. Today, Risa had tried to kill her.

Sienna had been through a lot in the past few months, but today was the first time she truly felt she'd lost her innocence. She would never again be the trusting Sienna she used to be. She was different, jaded.

She watched without emotion as one of the men grabbed Risa's body by the shoulders and the other by her feet. They carried her out of the cabin and out of her sight. She didn't know what they would do with the body. The truth was, she didn't care. Someone she'd considered a friend had caused the deaths of hundreds of Sephians. That was unforgiveable.

Sienna walked into the bathroom and scrubbed her hands. Even after she knew they were clean, she kept scrubbing, trying to wash away Risa's betrayal. The med-tech's actions made no sense to her. Her hand had led to the ambush, the base attack, and who knew what else. Hundreds of deaths would rest on her soul. What in the world could lead someone to do something so terrible?

Sienna didn't stop scrubbing until her hands had turned red. She turned off the water and grabbed a towel. She couldn't help feeling as though that death surrounded her, followed her. She hung the towel back on its hook and didn't realize Legian had come in until he wrapped his arms around her. She let herself relax into his embrace.

"You okay?" he asked.

"Seems like I need to redefine 'okay' every day."

He held her, saying nothing.

"I'm okay. You?" She turned around and wrapped her arms around his waist. She clung to him. With Legian, she felt safe. But safe didn't cut it. Not anymore. With a deep breath, she broke the connection. "I should check on Jax."

"Want me to come with you?"

She shook her head. "It may be better if just one of us go. How about you stay here and search through Risa's things. See if you can find out if she had anything else underway. Or, if we have any more traitors in our midst."

***

It took Sienna the better part of an hour to find Jax, passed out with the empty bottle of whiskey by his side. With a bit of help from a soldier on patrol, she was able to get Jax back into his bedroom, although she wasn't sure he'd appreciate the reminder once he awoke.

"Unexpected turn of events," Apolo said as she pulled a blanket up to cover Jax.

They made eye contact, and she stepped out the room, clicking the door shut behind her. Apolo followed her to the living room where Bente, Doc, and Legian waited.

"Doc, Jax has a laser burn on his hip, and Ace patched up a cut on his own shoulder. They both need to be checked," she said before she sat down next to Legian.

"As you know, I'm not skilled in human medicine, but I'll see what I can do. Where do I go?"

She nodded down the hallway, and he hustled off in that direction.

She sat there and scanned the faces in the room. Finally, she blurted out the words. "We found the traitor."

Apolo leaned forward, eyeing her with interest.

"It was Risa, the med-tech."

Murmurs filled the room.

She heard a gasp from the hallway. She looked to see Doc holding a hand to his mouth in shock. He clenched his fists, closed his eyes, and shook his head.

"Doc, Jax needs you now," Sienna called out.

The doctor jerked up. He nodded and muttered "Yes, yes," as he stumbled toward the guest room and disappeared. She had no doubt he'd blame himself—just like Jax—for not figuring Risa out earlier. She imagined there would be too much self-blame going around for a while. That's what happened when someone close betrayed you. Someone had to be blamed. And with Risa dead, people would blame themselves.

But not Sienna. She had enough stuff beating her up already. Guilt wasn't going to get added to that list. She turned back to the room and continued. "Unfortunately, we were forced to kill her before we could get much information from her. We still have no guarantees that she was operating on her own."

"What we did learn was disturbing, though," Legian added, and she turned to him. "Risa told us that Hillas lives."

The murmurs in the room turned into an uproar as the Sephians present cussed and questioned Legian.

Sienna patted the air down with her hands, trying to quiet the room. "She could have been lying, although she had no reason to lie at that point."

Apolo clenched his eyes closed for a moment before opening them. "This changes nothing. We have always suspected the

Draeken tyrant survived the war. This news substantiates that suspicion. But in the past, Hillas never allowed Roden the kind of authority he's shown lately. There is something afoot in the Draeken camp."

"We'll question the prisoner." At Sienna's words, the entire room turned to her.

Apolo began pacing the floor. "We'll question Talla, sure enough. But I know that one. She won't give us anything we need." He turned on his heel when he came to the window, stopped, and faced the room. "Without my informant, we are blind. We can only hope we repaid the favor in kind today."

"Still no news yet?" Sienna asked with an optimistic raise of her eyebrows.

He shook his head. "I have to assume he is no longer viable."

"Sorry to hear that." Her words were barely above a whisper. Even though Apolo remained stoic, the news—or lack thereof—from his informant had hit him hard. Legian had told her the pair had worked together for many years. Even though he was Draeken, he was one of Apolo's closest, most trusted friends. But, because he was Draeken, Apolo would never be able to admit that to anyone. It sucked, wasn't fair, and was too much like she'd seen happen time and again on her own planet. Instead of wings, it was religion or color or some other bullshit excuse.

She leaned back into the comfort of the couch while Apolo spoke about the new alliance. Both the Americans and the Brits were on board, but she didn't think for one instant that it would be easy. Nightmares of power struggles, red tape, and deception already lurked at the outskirts of her dreams.

The next morning, after spending the entire night talking about the Draeken threat, Apolo returned to the base. Sienna was exhausted but happy. A lot had been discussed and even more had been accomplished. It had been a good night.

Jax stumbled out of the bedroom. Legian and Sienna sat on the couch, watching him as they ate breakfast. He looked like hell had frozen over as he sifted through the cabinets. After going through several cabinets, he slammed one shut, grabbed at his side with a wince, and turned to glare at her.

"Don't you have anything to fucking drink in this place?"

She handed her plate to Legian and walked into the kitchen, using her cane for support. She opened the fridge, pulled out a soda, and tossed it to Jax.

Jax ignored the can as it flew past his shoulder. His bloodshot eyes fired daggers. "That's not what I meant."

"I know exactly what you meant, and that won't fly here," she replied. "Come with me."

At first, he looked like he wanted to shoot her, but then the soldier in him manned up and he followed her through the kitchen and down the stairs to the basement. The basement was small, used more as a wine cellar than anything. It had cost her a small fortune to build one in the rock-laden ground of Arkansas, and the construction company had balked at her request. But she had grown up in the Midwest and considered a basement a must-have anywhere with even a remote chance of a tornado. She'd never imagined it could double as a makeshift prison.

The Draeken prisoner sat on the floor with the black band-like material the Sephians used around her neck and wrists. The other end of the band was locked onto a steel I-beam. There was enough room in the cord for her to walk around without there being enough for her to attempt suicide. She could just reach the toilet. A basement bathroom was something Sienna had specifically requested from the construction company. And she felt completely redeemed seeing its value now, even though the guards had removed the door to keep the prisoner always in their view. The

Sephians had been going to give the prisoner a bucket, which went against Sienna's morals, let alone the Geneva Conventions.

The Draeken prisoner's name was the only information she'd shared willingly, and the only thing they'd already known. Talla Kohlm didn't even look up when Sienna reached the bottom of the stairs. The Sephian guarding her, on the other hand, came to attention immediately. Sana, the consummate soldier. Way too rigid, that one.

"We won't need any more guards down here right now." At the sound of her voice, everyone in the room looked at her, including the prisoner. Sienna turned to Jax. "The prisoner is Lieutenant Jerrick's responsibility now."

Jax frowned. "I don't think this is a good idea, Sienna," he gritted out.

She stood her ground, at full height. She could feel every eye in that underground room on her. "You were there for me, and I'm here for you now, even if it doesn't feel like it. I don't care how you do it, but this prisoner is now on your shoulders. Got it?"

His eyes narrowed at her, and they stayed in the standoff for what felt like minutes before he sneered. "Yes, ma'am."

"Sana will keep an eye on the prisoner until you clean up. Get some greasy food and caffeine in you."

It was his turn to stand his ground. "No. I'm good."

"Fine. You can grab something when you assign other guards."

Without a word, he walked over to Sana, who handed him a com. She headed upstairs with a look of relief. Jax fastened the device around his throat, grabbed a folding chair, and carried it over. He opened it and sat down, his forearms resting on the seat back, and faced Talla. She sat there, glaring first at Jax then at Sienna.

Sienna held out the soda she'd grabbed before coming down. "Got this covered, Jax?"

"Covered," he muttered from his chair and took the can from her hand.

She took one last look at Talla, who was now deep in a stare down with Jax. Her wings ruffled in agitation. Sienna turned to the stairs but paused before going up the first step. "Oh, and one more thing." She waited for Jax's eyes to meet hers. "Don't kill her... yet."

Chapter 23

Oddly, moving back to the Sephian base felt a bit like moving home. For the first time in Sienna's life, everything felt in balance. The base was now operating around the clock. Legian took over much of Apolo's role since Apolo was swamped with bureaucratic duties. After a week back on her original *human* sleep pattern, Sienna had been waking up more refreshed and energized. Several platoons, all under Major Sommers, had moved to the base, requiring many of the Sephians to bunk together to free up quarters for the soldiers. Too many changes, too many bodies in close quarters, and short tempers made most of Sienna's job schoolyard patrol.

Legian's arm lay loosely over her. She traced the mark that swirled around his forearm. "I wish we could stay like this forever."

"Someday."

Unfortunately, this wasn't *someday*. Nalea was still missing, and the shadow of the Draeken threat smothered her every thought.

Music blared from the nightstand. Startled, Sienna grabbed her new smartphone. "Sienna speaking."

"Sienna! So good to hear your voice."

Sienna pulled the phone away and stared at it a moment before bringing it back to her ear. It had been months since she'd heard that voice. "Kat?"

"Of course it's me, sweetie. I'm back in the States, and I look forward to catching up. We must talk, Sienna. We've so much to talk about."

"Things are a bit crazy right now, but—"

"No buts, dear. I'm already in Texarkana."

Sienna ran a hand through her hair. Her mother's timing seriously sucked, but Kat was still her mother, so Sienna would make things work. "Yeah, sure. I'll pick you up at Filly's at noon. Sound good?"

"Perfect. See you soon, sweetie. Love you."

"Love you too, Kat."

Sienna sat there for a moment before setting the phone down. She nudged Legian's arm. "Wake up, sleepyhead."

He mumbled some kind of response.

"You get to meet my mother today."

His eyes jerked open.

She laughed. "Don't worry. Kat's not *that* bad." She thought for a moment. "Well, yeah, she can be."

"I'll check with Sommers, and I'll have Kat brought in blindfolded, just like we do for press access," she said, changing the subject. Over the past week, Sienna had been working with Major Sommers to establish access badges for the visitors who were bound to start checking out Earth's latest additions. Inquisitive Kat would be a great way to test security.

Sienna turned, but Legian grabbed her wrist, pulling her down to him. "Until tonight then," he whispered, his breath soft against her neck. Then he kissed her long and soft on the lips before finally releasing her and rolling over, taking much of the blankets with him.

She smiled at the way he showed his love. Pausing, she brushed her thumb down his cheek. "Legian?"

"Hmm?"

"What are your thoughts on marriage?"

He rolled back over to face her, cocking his head while he watched her. "I don't understand. We are already married. The *tahren* bond proves it."

"The bond only proves that we're mated, not married."

He frowned. "I have read about the ritual and do not understand it. There's no soul bonding with it. It's just words and paper."

"It's more than words and paper. It has a magic to it, too." Where the *tahren* bond forced mates together, marriage was a voluntary decision. Its magic came with a mutual promise of lifelong commitment. She'd lost one husband, and she had sworn to herself that she would never love again. But that was her being afraid of her heart hurting so much again. Now she knew better. Everything she'd lived through was worth it. That was life.

"But we're already bonded in all ways that matter."

She stiffened, suddenly feeling a touch edgy. "I guess you're right," she said as she moved away and rummaged through her closet, randomly grabbing clothes. After throwing on a long-sleeved thermal, cargos, and hiking boots, Sienna grabbed her cane, left Legian, and hobbled straight to the Commons to grab breakfast. Fresh muffins sat cooling on the counter. She ate one as she watched the sunrise on one of the digital screens brought in for the humans' benefit. Warm blueberries burst like hot caviar bubbles in her mouth. After licking her fingers clean, she washed down the muffin with a glass of orange juice.

She then grabbed a couple of muffins and a carton of juice before looking at her cane. Setting it back down, she took a wicker basket full of fruit and dumped the contents. Adding back in a couple of bananas along with the muffins and orange juice, she walked clumsily down the hallway to the holding cells, carrying the basket in one hand while gripping her cane in the other.

When she reached the only inhabited cell, Talla looked at her.

Her wings, covered in the usual Draeken tattoos, hung loosely out from her sides. Her long, silver hair was fastened on top of her head. She looked exhausted, no doubt from the daily rounds of unending interrogation. A small part inside Sienna was glad to see that the prisoner had survived Jax's sour mood. Sienna hadn't been confident she would survive a night, let alone a month.

Even though Jax now had guards assigned to his prisoner, he still spent hours every day overseeing her "care".

"Here." She held out a muffin first to Jax and the other guard before offering one to Talla.

Jax didn't move an inch. "No thanks. Already ate." He sat with the folding chair turned around and leaned forward on the backrest, keeping his prisoner under close scrutiny.

Talla snatched the muffin from Sienna's hand and sat facing away from Jax to eat it. He watched the prisoner while she ate and ignored him.

Sienna almost grinned when Jax narrowed his eyes and gave her the classic Jax scowl. Yeah, Jax was back. "Can I get you anything else?" she asked, setting the basket on the floor next to his chair.

"Nah. We're good," Jax replied.

"You know, Talla, things would go easier if you were willing to meet us halfway," Sienna said.

The Draeken glared at Sienna before giving them her back once again.

"Have it your way, then. You and Jax have fun. Oh, and Talla…" Sienna waited for the Draeken to straighten. "You better rest up. You're scheduled for another round of interrogation today." With that, Sienna left the holding cells.

She was surprised to find Apolo waiting for her outside the door, peeling an orange. He held out an arm. Sienna took it, and he walked her into his old quarters, which had been converted into briefing rooms. She sat on the newly-added leather couch while he took an overstuffed chair across from her.

"I wanted to stop by before I leave for England tonight," he said before popping a slice of orange in his mouth.

Her brow furrowed. "You're leaving already? I thought it would take longer for them to prepare for your arrival."

"I did, too. Evidently the Brits are quite excited to get their hands on our technology."

Sienna nodded in silent agreement. *I bet they are.*

He smiled. "They are also quite accommodating. They've established an old wartime bunker for us. Sunlight-free."

"That's the British for you. I'm guessing you'll acquire an addiction to fine teas and crumpets in no time," Sienna said with a smile. "With my luck, the Americans will try to relocate our U. S. group to an army base where we can be monitored twenty-four/seven."

His lips thinned. "Make no mistake, we are already being monitored. Every second of every minute of every day." He glanced down the hallway. "Tell me, how does Jax fare?"

Sienna raised her eyebrows. "He's going to be fine. Doc says his burn is healing nicely."

"I'm not talking about his injury."

She leaned back into the couch. "Risa's betrayal knocked him down for a bit." *It knocked us all down.* "But he's getting right back on. I've assigned him to our Draeken prisoner to keep him busy. He's been quite diligent in his duties."

Apolo smiled. "It was wise to assign him to the prisoner. I think it was exactly what the soldier in him needed."

Sienna shrugged. "I figured only drunkenness or duty would work with him, and duty seemed like a healthier plan. Everything would be easier if only Nalea was back." Sienna winced, regretting saying those last words.

Apolo inhaled deeply. "Roden has her, and he's keeping her alive for a reason. There is hope. However, having a complete trinity is a critical strength of a leader. Being without one is a weakness in the eyes of the Sephians."

"But replacing Nalea would also be a sign of weakness," Sienna said. "It would show that you're giving up on her."

Apolo said, "And that, to me, that is unacceptable."

They sat in silence for several moments while Apolo finished the orange and Sienna stared at the wall.

"We will make it our priority to find Nalea, and I will work with the Brits on this as well. She is crucial."

"How so?"

He mused for a moment. "That is something she needs to tell you herself. What I know, I know in confidence. All I can say is, the longer the Draeken have her, the greater the risk."

Sienna eyed him strangely, but he said nothing more. "I wonder if Roden knows."

Apolo jerked. "Why do you think that?"

Sienna shrugged. "I don't know exactly. But there was something off about the meeting that day. It was almost as though Roden had planned all along to take Nalea. He seemed awfully focused on her."

"Perhaps Roden suspects something. All the more reason to search for her and stop Roden."

"Lieutenant-Colonel Jerrick has offered to help out with the search," Sienna said. "Let's hope he meant it."

"Time will tell. The Americans have shown strong initial support."

"By support, you mean the troops he's assigned to the base?" Sienna shook her head. "They're here to keep an eye on us, not to keep the Draeken out." She rested her head on the back of the couch as she stared up at the ceiling for a long moment before turning back to Apolo. "We have a long road ahead of us, don't we?"

Apolo smiled weakly. "While our alliance isn't yet written in stone, we're all on the same page when it comes to the Draeken. We'll have to build from that." He stood and looked around. "I'm short on time. I should be going. I'll give you my location and will set up communications once I'm settled in there. Even though our British hosts have offered a full telecommunications setup, I also desire something a little less *privy* to eager ears."

"Good luck. And, Apolo? Thank you. I treasure both your leadership and our friendship."

"As do I." With that, he gave her a formal Sephian handshake then turned and walked out the door without another word.

Sienna headed outside to wait for her mother's transport ship to land. Instead of standing idly around, she spent the time walking the perimeter, stopping at every checkpoint to chat with the Sephians, who looked to her in order to learn about humans.

As the ship touched down with her mother inside, Sienna leaned against the wall. At some point during the past several months, she realized that she considered the Sephians more her people than humans. The Sephians were her people, and she'd do anything for them. The idea didn't disturb her. Instead, it made her proud.

Chapter 24

"Are we good here?" Sienna asked.

"All scans came through clean. Your visitor is cleared for access," Quincy replied as he reached to remove her visitor's blindfold.

Her mother looked just like she had the day Sienna had seen her last, except her brown hair with striking waves of gray was shorter now. Kat had always been attractive, and age hadn't changed that one bit.

Kat rubbed her eyes, looked around, and then threw out her arms when she found her daughter. "Sienna!"

Sienna smiled, only to be pulled into a full hug. "Sorry about not being there to pick you up. I got a bit tied up here."

"It's okay. I've missed you so much, sweetie." Her mother pulled back to take in her surroundings. "This is unbelievable, Sienna," she said motioning around the hangar. "And you're in the middle of all this."

"C'mon." Sienna motioned to her mother. "I'll show you the gardens."

Kat frowned, bringing out the fine lines at her eyes. "Can I have a tour? I was hoping to see the rooms where all the technology is, like for communications."

"Only the gardens are approved for guests. I'll see if I can get you more clearance next time."

Kat smile flattened in disappointment. "All right then. To the gardens."

"They're really something. You'll see."

As they went down a level toward the gardens, they walked past several guards—both human and Sephian, though few of the interracial teams spoke to each other. The Sephians towered above the humans by several inches. Unlike humans, Sephian females stood as tall as their male counterparts. That genetic trait did nothing to help average-height Sienna earn respect. Her size and her inability to pull energy to heal only made the Sephians believe humans were all the more fragile, which meant she had to work twice as hard to get them to look up to her.

As the human face of the Sephian force, the soldiers came to her—or Jax—rather than going to any Sephian, and she doubted it had much to do with her authority. Racism was still running rampant across the base—on both sides—something she hoped would fade over time. At least they both saw the Draeken as a common threat.

"…I thought."

Sienna glanced over at Kat. "Sorry. What'd you say?"

"Still the daydreamer, I see." Kat smiled. "I was saying that this place is more normal than I'd expect. I don't know what I thought I'd see, but this,"—Kat motioned around her—"isn't much different than any military base."

Sienna shrugged. "Guess other than a few trillion or so miles separating our people, we're not that different from each other." Although there would always be some biological differences. They had brightened the lights when the troops came. Now the Sephians needed to wear sunglasses all the time, but it was a small price considering the alternative.

With a swoosh, the door to the gardens opened, and Kat sucked in a breath. "Oh my. Incredible."

"These gardens provide all the food for the Sephians on this base." While the gardens that spanned over an acre were an incredible sight, Sienna had been here long enough to notice that the plants were quickly growing more and more sparse. The knot in her stomach continued to grow.

The gardens weren't intended to provide sustenance while on-world. While the Sephians were slowly accustoming their biology to Earth foods, they would be hard-pressed to support themselves without the gardens—and the gardens couldn't last much longer. The Sephians needed to adapt fast, but having the proverbial Draeken wolf at the door didn't make things any easier.

They took a seat on a bench under a fruit tree. The air was heavier here. The Sephian home world's atmosphere had slightly higher concentrations of oxygen, and while the Sephians handled Earth's air just fine, their plants were more sensitive.

Kat sighed. "Oh, Sienna. I wish you weren't entangled in this mess."

Sienna frowned. "I thought coming face to face with life beyond Earth was your greatest dream."

"It was, but that was before you were pulled into this. But don't you worry, dear. I'm going to make everything better."

"What are you talking about?"

Her mother came to her feet and pulled something out of her purse.

"Kat?"

She made no response as she lay what looked like a piece of black plastic wrap over a control panel. Instantly it melted around the panel and started to grow.

Sienna's frozen as she stared at the growing black liquid.

Kat tugged Sienna's hand. "Come. It's finished. We must hurry."

Sienna yanked out of Kat's grip and stepped back. "What have you done?" She scrambled in her pocket, found the comm she always carried, and hit the panic button, which would now be sending a constant signal to both the tech-hub as well as Legian.

"I did what needed to be done, dear. The Sephians are here to commit genocide. Life beyond Earth is still my greatest dream. *All life.*" Kat unbuttoned her sleeve and pulled up her shirt, revealing a tattoo of the Draeken imperial family's symbol.

Sienna brought a hand up to cover her mouth. "Oh, Kat, you didn't."

Her mother smiled as she glanced down at the tattoo then her smile fell, and she snapped at her daughter. "We must hurry. We don't have long. We must get out of here before it's too late."

"Mom," Sienna snapped. "These are my people. I'm never leaving them."

Kat's lips thinned. "I'm sorry it has to be this way. But I won't sit by and watch the genocide of an entire race. Goodbye, Sienna." She turned to run, but Sienna tackled her.

"Sienna, no! You'll kill us both!" she cried out from under her daughter.

"Then deactivate that thing."

Kat looked confused. "I can't."

Footsteps pounded the floor, sending vibrations through her. She looked up to find the soldiers first on the scene.

She pointed to growing black liquid-like substance and yelled out, "She's attempting to sabotage the base!"

They looked at the substance and back to Sienna as if waiting for instruction. The door to her other side opened, and she watched Legian, shirtless and barefoot, lead in several Sephian troops. Oh, thank God.

Everything felt slow-motion as he took in Sienna, Kat, and then finally the black substance. The look on his face was pure dread.

Legian's eyebrows shot up as he faced Sienna. "Find cover! The bomb is small enough that we may be able to burn it in time." He visibly swallowed. "If it burns," he said quieter, clearly just to Sienna. "The blast will still be powerful enough to destroy this room."

And everyone in it. The terror emanating from every Sephian present was answer enough. As he lifted his gun, she wished she had her weapon, but protocol prevented her from carrying a weapon when with a visitor. "Get down!" she shouted to the human troops. But none listened. Instead, they pulled out their weapons as well, following suit with Legian.

She pushed her mother against the floor hard, and fortunately the woman didn't push back. Armageddon broke out when the Sephians opened blaster fire above Sienna.

The air grew hot as the weapons continued to fire for several long seconds. Sienna closed her eyes and pressed her head into her mother's back, who was shouting out accusations against the Sephians. She'd been too late. The bomb had grown too much—

The explosion sent Sienna flying off Kat and through the air. She crashed into a bench, knocking her breath from her lungs. Fire burned her skin, and she sucked in a breath.

Eyes, nose…

Throat…

No, her lungs were on fire.

She couldn't breathe.

Blackness.

Sienna came awake with a moan scratching her raw throat. Trying to open her burned eyes, tears began to pour against the cold air. All she saw was the large Sephian holding her, golden tears streaming down his darkened face.

She wanted to tell him how good it was to see him, how she knew he'd survive. But she settled for "Hey."

Much of her body hurt, like she'd been out in the sun all day and was now the center attraction in a dodgeball tournament. She frowned, or at least tried to. Strangely, some parts of her were completely numb. She glanced down at her blistered hands. They weren't numb, but her shoulder—and much of her face—felt weird. "Help me up."

"You're in shock. I need to get you to the med-hub." She hadn't heard that level of concern in Legian's voice since the base attack.

"I'll be okay," she replied, trying to pull herself up but finding no strength to do so.

Reluctantly, Legian pulled Sienna up, holding her carefully. She glanced around. Most of the human troops were spread across the floor, motionless, many clearly never getting up again. Several of the Sephians were down as well, but the med-techs were already helping them. From the look of Legian's skin, he'd gone through several donors while she was out. Then she spotted her mother sitting in the middle of the mess, her hair gone and blisters covering her face.

"You betrayed us, Kat."

Her mother made no response.

"You betrayed the Sephians, the United States, and your own daughter," she said, coughing between words.

"I told you, Sienna. I couldn't stand for genocide."

"It's not like that."

Kat looked up. "I love you, Sienna, but your friends have blinded you. I never wanted to hurt you."

"I know, Kat," she replied softly. She took in a breath, though it burned to do so. "Katherine Wolfe, you are a traitor. And by Sephian law, the penalty for treason is execution."

Sienna glanced up at Legian. His lips tightened. She nodded as much as her broken muscles would allow. With a grimace, he handed her his blaster.

Sienna lifted it, the weight causing it to wobble in her hand, but she was close enough that aim didn't matter.

A sad look of acceptance came over Kat's face. She held out her arms. "It's finished."

"No, Kat," Sienna replied. "It's just the beginning."

Then she squeezed the trigger.

Chapter 25

S ienna never cried.

She'd made sure Kat received a proper burial. Despite her last actions in life, her mother had helped out many people as a humanitarian. Kat had always been her mentor, teaching her the hard lessons of life. And it seemed she'd had one lesson left.

Being a leader means you have to make the hardest sacrifices.

She didn't hate her mother. She couldn't. With her hands braced on the sink, Sienna stared at her reflection in the mirror. The left side of her face was scabbed, with no hope of healing without massive scarring. She'd surprised everyone by not dying. With third degree burns over a third of her body, that she hadn't succumbed to infection was a miracle thanks to Sephian medicine.

Once she healed enough, she'd shave off what was left of her hair. In the meantime, she didn't care what she looked like. She had more important things to worry about.

Like ensuring the Sephians a safe future on Earth.

Pushing off from the sink, Sienna started her slow inspection of the base. She knew where to find Jax at least; at this same time every day, he'd be in the holding cell watching their Draeken prisoner.

Finally, long after sunset, she went back to her room and read for a while. She didn't know how long she stayed up, but she knew she'd been asleep for hours when Legian stepped into the room. She awoke at the sound of his footsteps. The book lay across her chest, still open to the page she last read. She set it on the nightstand and watched him walk over to the bed.

"You're home." She muffled a yawn and made room for him in the bed.

"Home," he murmured as he sat down on the mattress and gave her a soft kiss. "I like the sound of that."

It was then that he stood abruptly.

"Legian? What's wrong?"

He then went down on one knee before her. She reached out to him. "Are you okay?"

No answer. Instead, he reached into his pocket and pulled out something. He held out a piece of crumpled fabric before her.

She tentatively reached out and picked the fabric from his hand. She stared at the familiar black cotton with pink skulls. "You got me a new bandana? Just like my old one that I lost in the blast. Where'd you find it?"

He smiled at her questions, and she returned the smile and unraveled it. As it came undone, a small piece of metal fell out of it and into her lap.

She sat and stared at it in utter confusion.

He grabbed it and held it up before her. He grimaced slightly. "Ace told me this is how I do it. He even brought me to the store. I'm going kick his ass if he played me."

He continued to hold the ring before her and looked at her hand. "Which finger?"

She pointed to her ring finger. "This one." He slid it on, gently as to not abrade her healing skin. It fit perfectly. She wiggled her finger in the light and found symbols engraved across the silver band. Sephian symbols. She examined them more closely. She twisted the ring around her finger as she translated the four symbols. *Love. Tahren.* A word she couldn't make out. And, *Forever.* "What's this symbol mean?"

He bent down and looked it over. "*Caya.* It is the closest Sephian word to 'wife.'"

Holding her left hand in her right, she brought it to her heart. "Oh, Legian."

"Ace said this is where you accept or reject me."

"I accept. Of course I accept," she said in a rush and pulled him to her. He kissed her, and before she knew it, his clothes were on the floor and he was lying next to her.

"I love you, Sienna. You've saved my life. And I want you as both my *tahren* and my wife. I'd also like to take your last name."

She frowned. "But Sephians don't use last names."

"Humans do. And it would be an honor to carry my *tahren*'s name."

She cupped his cheek. "Of course. I love you, Legian. Always."

She leaned into him and drifted away, letting the Draeken threat wait until tomorrow.

END OF PART ONE

PART TWO:
IMPLOSION

Chapter 1

Draeken base in the northwest United States

N alea lay on her side, feigning sleep, as the guardsman walked past her cell, whistling an old tune that reminded her of Sephia. The tips of his leathery wings brushed the floor as though he was bored, which matched the slow, staccato rhythm of his steps echoing through the hall. His senses would be dulled from the monotony of his late-night shift; hers were primed.

She forced herself to breathe deep and steady as she waited until his footsteps faded into the silence. She'd had months to memorize the guardsmen's schedule. If the gods were on her side, the hallway would remain empty for at least another hour.

Now!

Tensing her body, she surged toward the barred door of her cell. Her muscles were alive and ready. Her hair was short, so it would stay out of her way. The lights were dimmed for the night, so they wouldn't blind her sensitive eyes—a good thing now that her dark glasses were destroyed. With one last silent prayer to the gods, she pressed against the bars that kept her imprisoned within her enemy's earthside stronghold.

The cold metal resisted movement. She pushed harder, and the barred door swung outward. Her escape mechanism fell to the floor with a *plink* and her breath hitched.

It had worked!

Hard to believe a little piece of plastic was all it took to bypass Draeken technology. Wync, the guardsman on the nightshift, had been so busy taunting her for being wingless as he escorted her back to her cell after interrogation that he'd failed to notice her sliding the lens from her dark glasses against the locking mechanism as he pulled her cell door closed.

An alarm should have sounded immediately. Fortunately, the Draeken were facing an energy shortage—just like the Sephians were—otherwise, the system would've alerted the guards if the bolt was blocked in any manner.

She smiled. She had no problem taking advantage of any chance for escape.

Nalea carefully pushed the door closed behind her to avoid raising suspicion. She didn't even glance back at the small cell she'd been forced to call home for nearly a year. After tonight, she'd never be on the other side of that door again.

Flattening herself against the wall, she peeked around the corner and down the hallway beyond, looking first left then right. To the left, she would find freedom and could be miles away before her captors noticed her absence. She turned right.

Some things were more important than freedom.

Her bare feet made no sound on the cold floor as she hurried down the hallway. Every step was deliberate and quick. She knew the way well: the empty cells, a locked supply room, even the guardsman station where Wync had undoubtedly stopped to catch a nap. Scowling, she wished she had more time to ensure the racist would breathe his last. *You'll get yours, Wync, someday.*

It wouldn't be much farther now. Long seconds passed before she reached the room she sought. She double-checked the sign to the right of the closed door. It read *Lord Commander Roden Zyll*.

Nalea clenched her fists, fighting to remain steady. Precious seconds bled out while she calmed her breathing. Her muscles burned with tension, as though they were warning her, *run!* The ends of her short hair clung to the edges of her sweaty cheeks.

Sephians normally wore their hair long, but Roden, thinking to punish her, had cut her hair short after she'd refused to allow him to brush its snarled length. Instead, she'd considered it a personal triumph. Every time she made her captor lose his temper was a step closer to finding his mortal weakness. She hadn't yet found that weakness, but she knew she was running out of time. *He's only a Draeken.*

Focusing on the touchpad, she inhaled deeply and closed her eyes, recalling the unique tone each button made as Roden entered them every time he brought her to 'dine' with him, which was his polite term for non-physical interrogation. He'd yet to raise a hand to her, instead preferring to mess with her mind, acting as her host rather than captor, all the while subtly plying for information she'd never surrender.

And so they'd been at a stalemate for nearly a year. Nalea refusing to betray her people, and Roden with something up his sleeve, for that could be the only reason he hadn't tortured or killed her yet. The only way to win this game was to make her move first.

Convinced of the passcode, which she'd played over and over in her mind a hundred times a day, she reopened her eyes and punched in the six digits her memory had shown her. The small light on the touchpad flashed blue before going dark. *Success!* The door opened with a nearly silent *whoosh* that translated into something more like a sonic boom to her ears. The air hardened in her lungs. Would Roden awaken at the sound? Worse, could he still be awake at this late hour?

Defeating the Draeken meant stopping Roden. Steeling her nerves, Nalea stepped inside just as the door closed behind her.

No one rushed her. No sound of movement. It was nearly pitch black in the room, thanks to clouds trying to smother the moonlight outside. As her vision easily adjusted to the soothing darkness, she scanned the room. Draeken, like humans, had to wear special glasses to see in the dark. Sephians, on the other hand, were nocturnal. They had evolved on a planet with three moons and weak sunlight. To put it mildly, Nalea had excellent night vision.

And, just as this planet's inhabitants absorbed the sun's rays through their pale Draeken-like skin, her people's golden skin was optimized to draw as much lunar energy as possible. The dark exhilarated her.

On her first day as a prisoner at this earthside base, Roden had surprised her by giving her a pair of dark glasses to ease her sensitivity to the light, almost certainly in an attempt to build false trust. Nalea had seen and heard plenty about Roden Zyll, a commander famous for his viciousness. Yet he was also an enigma. The only thing she knew was that he never did what anyone expected.

A Draeken lord, second only to Grand Lord Hillas Puftan, Roden's strategies were a dichotomy of ruthless assassinations, outright attacks, and—in her case—charming mindfucks. The moment he gave her the dark glasses, she *knew* he had something planned for her. And that thought had haunted her every waking moment since.

Without glasses for protection, Nalea needed to make her escape and find shelter before sunrise, where Earth's bright day star would blind her. Until dawn, in this room, she needed no glasses. The darkness felt natural, and it comforted her as her gaze fell upon the Draeken on the bed. With one arm resting over his head, his chest rose and fell slowly, his darkly colored tattooed wings spread out loosely beneath him.

Relief soothed Nalea's frayed nerves. Retribution was so very close now. She crept first to his desk, where his weapons were laid out symmetrically. Her hand skimmed over the blasters and glided across the knives, pausing at a long blade embellished with etchings. She hefted its weight in her hand. It would do.

Keeping her gaze fixed upon the sleeping Draeken, she closed in, step by slow step, holding the blade ready before her. The sliver of moonlight broke through the window and glinted off the knife's dark metal, producing shimmering lines across her golden skin. It would have been better if the clouds had completely blanketed the moon this night so Roden wouldn't be able to see her coming even if he wakened.

All it would take was one quick slice. One quick slice and Lord Commander Roden Zyll would no longer pose a risk to either the Sephians or to the inhabitants of this planet... or to her.

The light across her hand trembled, and she realized she was shaking. She gripped the blade with both hands to steady herself. She paused, inhaled, scolded herself for her weakness, and took another step. After all, it should be an easy thing to kill a godless Draeken. She'd killed dozens—hells, *hundreds*—of the bastards already. Why did this one have to be any different? She wanted to kill Roden. He'd been kind to her for too many months, and it messed with her mind. She *needed* to kill him more than any other Draeken she'd killed. Especially since this particular one happened to be her captor, and something far, far worse... her destined *tahren*. Her soulmate.

Of everyone in the universe for her dysfunctional soul to latch onto, why did it draw her to her most hated enemy? Since he was a Draeken, he would never be hindered by the *tahren* bond; he'd never feel her emotions like she could feel his, should she give in to the bond. If he discovered her secret, he'd have the cruelest form of torture available at his hands.

He was clever, and she needed to escape before he grew suspicious. He already questioned her with unending perseverance rather than turning her over to his underlings for more traditional torture methods. Had he thought to convert her to the Draeken side? Surely, he must know she'd die before betraying her people. More likely, he'd kept her alive to trade her for his officers the Sephians and humans captured last year.

No matter his intentions, only one option was acceptable.

Kill Roden Zyll.

Resolved, she lowered the blade toward his neck. Her body was fighting itself as the natural instinct to protect one's mate pushed against her resolve to kill with all its might.

The *tahren* bond, while slithering just below the surface, would not take hold unless she allowed it. Until Roden was dead, Nalea must be stronger than nature.

Suvaste, I control my own destiny!

Furious, she yanked her arms above her head and brought the knife down with the force of all her rage behind it. Just before the blade would have skewered his black heart, a vise gripped her wrist and twisted. Sharp pain shot up her arm and she grunted. She scrambled to get away but was yanked forward, spun, and shoved against the mattress. The air rushed out of her lungs.

Nalea fought against Roden, but he overpowered her and forced her arms above her head. Even though she was in her prime, he held her down as though she were just a little girl, both wrists bound all too easily in one of his larger hands. His body pressed hers against the bed, giving her no opportunity to move, let alone escape. He still had a hand free, which she suspected now held the deadly blade.

Her spirit crashed. *I've failed.*

"Lights," Roden ordered, and the room brightened in response.

Nalea clenched her eyes shut against the intensity. She'd failed her people, those of this world, and herself. She was lost.

"Look at me, Lea." He spoke gently, and she hated him all the more for it.

Her eyes snapped open to give him her harshest glare, except the brightness caused her to wince.

"Lights, dim."

The brightness no longer blinding, she glared while he frowned down at her. His wings, each tipped with a sharp bone spike, spread out behind him as though to shade her from the light. She'd often wondered how many opponents he'd slayed with those wing tips. She then wondered how many females had grabbed them during sex, and she chided herself for the thought.

His silver Draeken eyes scrutinized her in the now dimly lit room. "Ah, Lea, you vex me."

She wrenched her gaze away. "The name is Nalea, and I hope you rot in all twelve hells."

He gripped her jaw and made her look at him once again. Then he smiled, revealing a hint of white teeth. Simple biology made her wonder what those lips would feel like on her neck, wondered how those teeth would feel when they nipped at her skin. But, as it was Roden, he'd likely bite. And hurt. Reality was the best cure for her distracting thoughts.

"You know," he said, skimming a finger down her neck, "if you wanted to come to my bed, you had only to ask."

She tried to pull her wrists free to no avail. "The only thing I want is to see your blood flow through these halls like a river," she snarled.

"Such hostility," he murmured before leaning closer, his breath grazing her ear. "I'm sure you can think of something more interesting for your *tahren*."

Frozen, she gasped, slack jawed. She swallowed and focused on keeping the truth hidden from her features. "You're insane. Why would you think that?"

"I know a great many things," he whispered, as though reading her mind. "Remember the first time we met, when my people entered your earthside base?"

When she said nothing, he continued. "When we *tussled* and I disarmed you, it was at that moment, the moment when I touched you, and your beautiful onyx eyes widened. I knew then, in that instant, that something had shocked you to the very core. For a Sephian, what else could it be than you have found your destined mate?"

She remained a statue, keeping her lips pressed tightly closed.

He cocked his head slightly. "You didn't think I'd noticed? Tut, tut. I am not Lord Commander by not being perceptive. Why do you think I have personally led your interrogation all year?" His smile then grew intimate and his wings lowered slightly, as though to cocoon them. "Because, my dear, forcing you to be near your destined *tahren* day in and day out is the sweetest torture of all. Tell me, Lea, what does it feel like to yearn for your enemy's touch, to yearn for the touch of a Draeken?"

She snapped her teeth at him. "*Jihtee.*" *Fuck you.*

He pulled back, humor turning his lips upward as he shook his head slowly. "Fighting the bond is useless. You know you can't prevent it. It's only a matter of time. You are mine."

"I'll *never* be yours," she swore.

He smirked. "A challenge I accept." Then he leaned closer. "You will accept me, Lea. Willingly. Sublimely. Fervently." Each word was slow, whispered inches from her lips, and she trembled under the force of them. "That, I promise."

"*Never,*" she gritted out then sucked in a breath when she felt a sharp prick in her neck. Blackness swirled around her. As her world faded, her last recurring thought was that she should have killed Roden Zyll when she'd had the chance.

Chapter 2

Roden's lips curved upward as he strode back to his room after ensuring his prisoner could not escape again. He loved a good challenge, and Nalea brought the best kind. When he'd first realized he was her destined mate, the thought had appalled him. How could he, a great Draeken lord, be a common Sephian's *tahren*?

Though there was nothing common about Nalea. She was a member of Apolo's trinity, making her *almost* his equal by military standards. The more he'd considered the possibility, the more the idea had intrigued him. While there'd been Draeken-Sephian consorts over the years, the number was trivial when compared to the size of the two races. And, of that number, at least one mate was always of mixed Sephian-Draeken blood. Their DNA was similar enough for biological compatibility but simply too different for the Sephian *tahren* bond to recognize a Draeken.

Roden had confidence in his heritage; his bloodline was pure Draeken descent for as far back as records were kept. So then, the question begged: What was Nalea hiding? By all accounts she looked Sephian: golden skin, with the nearly transparent markings of the *soullare* branding her flesh, pure black eyes, black hair and, most importantly, no wings. She was tall for a Sephian, nearly six feet, but not tall enough to raise suspicion.

Still, he knew she was hiding something. And so he'd begun a search, a search more thorough than any he'd done before. The utter normalcy of the information he'd found on her was telling in itself. Nothing stood out about her life before the great slave rebellion—a clear sign that her profile had been tampered with.

With a few archival bypasses, Roden had retrieved the truth. His prisoner's darkest secret had taken root before she was born.

It was the same secret that made Nalea the key to his plans.

If Nalea had fled the base instead of coming to him, his plan would've been quashed. And he couldn't bear to consider the consequences of that. She had been beginning to stir when he laid her down on her cot and bolted her cell door; this time making sure the lock was secure. She wouldn't get out of her cell again—not without his permission.

A loud beep yanked Roden's attention to the wall comm. A light by the small rectangular screen in the wall flashed a prism of bright colors. Hitting the flashing button, he glared at the image of the guardsman standing in the hallway.

The guardsman on the screen flinched, his wings tucked closer to his body.

"You're early," Roden barked.

"Apologies, Commander." Wync stood stiffly at attention outside the door to Roden's quarters. "You asked to see me."

"And so I did." He sighed. He clicked off the screen before taking a seat behind his desk. He hit a switch on his desk and the door opened.

The guardsman stepped warily inside. "My lord?"

Roden crossed his arms in front of his chest and watched the nervous Wync, looking like he was about to wet himself, making it clear he knew why his commander wanted to see him. Wync was loyal and strong, but also young and stupid. Nalea never would've escaped her cell if Laze or Talla were here. But both had been taken by the Sephians and were likely dead already, and so he'd had to make do with what limited resources remained loyal to him.

There were too few Draeken left breathing after the Sephians began their crusade to obliterate his race. Earth was their last chance at survival. Roden couldn't afford mistakes that could cost more Draeken lives. Rubbing the back of his neck, he narrowed his eyes on the guardsman standing before his desk. "I'm disappointed in you, Wync."

The guardsman flinched before lifting his chin. "I followed all protocols with the slave, but—"

Roden tsked. "The Sephians are no longer slaves. If we don't adapt quickly, those *slaves* will end us. They've already aligned with this planet's inhabitants and are filling the humans' heads with lies as we speak. Do you understand how dire our situation is?"

Sweat had formed on the guardsman's forehead. He swallowed before giving a tight nod.

Roden leaned back in his chair and rubbed his temples. "We'll use up the last of our power cells on the earthside bases in only three cycles. The core ships can maintain life support and orbit, but little else. There are barely enough of us remaining to prevent extinction. Our race is dying, Wync. Without human mercy, we're doomed." He gave the young man a hard look. "Your ineptitude grinds on my nerves. As a guardsman, you must be perfect. No mistakes. Three lashes should provide a sufficient reminder on how to do your job."

Wync's mouth dropped open, but he—wisely—clamped it shut. Lashings were a brutal punishment to Draeken, with their sensitive wings, but allowing a prisoner to escape was often punishable by death. After a moment, Wync tilted his head and spoke. "As you command, my lord."

Roden glanced down at a random document on his desk. An inventory list. Every day the list grew shorter. His life had grown dull from never-ending hours of paperwork, babysitting, and politics. Would he ever get a good night's sleep again? Knowing Wync still stood at attention before him, he gave a distracted wave of his hand. "See Elng in the morning for your lashes. Now, go get some sleep."

Roden never looked up; he simply waited until the door opened then closed again. He punched the lock button. He desired no eavesdropping for his next meeting. The technology and security at this earthside base were mediocre at best.

When the tides turned against them in the Noble War, they'd been forced to flee Sephia with barely even the wings on their backs. It was a miracle they'd escaped with four of their largest core ships. If anything had gone wrong the night of their grand escape, the proud Draeken race—which only two decades ago had numbered in the millions—would have been wiped from the universe.

As it was, their race numbered in the mere thousands now. Not an optimistic sign, especially since the Sephians had followed them to this small planet with every intention of finishing the job they'd started over twenty years earlier.

And now he led one of two earthside bases, set up for his people to study the humans, and from which to engage at the right time. A time Roden thought had long since passed, but Grand Lord Hillas continued to delay.

Roden would much rather play with his feral prisoner than endure this current banal existence of running a base a hundredth the size of his last one on Sephia. Nalea had been beginning to stir when he laid her on her cot and bolted her cell door, this time making sure the lock was secure. Frowning, he punched in the code only one other Draeken knew, which established a secure link with the most restricted office of the other earthside camp, hidden deep in the Canadian wilderness. The link attempted to connect for twelve and a half tediously long minutes. He suspected the old fool made him wait intentionally as a way to show Roden who was the superior, uncaring that his Second had better things to do than sit on his ass listening to electronic noise.

Roden despised the games.

Just as he went to stand, a face appeared on the screen. Not a hair out of place, and impeccably dressed as ever. Their race might be dying, but Hillas Puftan always wore a good public face. Roden bit his tongue to keep from sneering at the Grand Lord's pride. "Your Highness," he said before Hillas could address him, finding some grain of pleasure in speaking first to a male too deeply ingrained with protocol and traditions.

Hillas pursed his lips as he looked Roden up and down with clear distaste. He held no love for Roden but desperately needed him, and they both knew it. Roden followed the Grand Lord's commands, more or less. Their stalemate worked. For now. A time would come when a precipice would be reached, and Roden suspected that time was drawing dangerously near.

Draeken numbers were far too few to take any unnecessary chances. If something *unfortunate* were to befall Hillas, suspicion would immediately fall on Roden as second in line to rule. The Draeken held strongly to tradition, and Hillas had been Grand Lord for decades, the Puftan family for centuries. Roden would have to be careful. But his plan was infallible; the number of days Hillas breathed grew short.

"The humans are behaving exactly as I predicted," Hillas said, his hands clasped before him. "Their so-called alliance with the Sephians has confined the gold-skins to human military bases. Their movements are already harshly restricted. Before long, the Sephians will be nothing more than test subjects in labs. When that time comes, there will no longer be any threat against us."

He speaks as though a race numbering in the billions is no threat. Roden leaned back a little more. "Consider this," he said carefully. "Every moment the Sephians are with the humans, they have an opportunity to fill their heads with lies about us. What's to keep the humans from coming after us like they did last summer? We lost several good Draeken and their human consorts, including children not yet born."

Hillas raised a hand. "Bah. A minor setback. We are still strong."

Roden raised a brow. He knew the name of every Draeken still breathing, and the loss of eight Draeken families was *minor*?

"Let the humans think what they want," Hillas continued. "Human technology is a thousand years behind ours. Even if the Sephians share the technology they stole from us, the humans could never replicate enough weapons for a mass assault before we crush them."

Roden's lips tightened. "They outnumber us millions to one. Their weapons may be archaic, but they're still weapons, and as brutal and deadly as any Sephian weapon. The sheer numbers alone could—"

"You're missing one critical point. Humans cannot work together. Throughout their history, there is not a single day recorded where their entire world was united. They *need* us to lead them. I'm not worried."

You should be. "They've never had a world-wide cause to unite against before," he said instead.

Hillas laughed. "Let them unite. We are in a different time now. We cannot afford the compassion our forefathers showed on Sephia. The time for mercy is over. If they do not wish us here, we could wipe humanity from this world with the firepower we have on just a single core ship. This world could become the new Draeka. We will rebuild and prosper."

"With only four core ships with drained power cells? None of them have power to support weapons usage."

Hillas gave a knowing smile.

"And you're forgetting one important thing," Roden said.

Hillas cocked his head then smiled. "Ah, yes, you believe that we are too few in number to rebuild our race without humans."

"And you don't?"

"I believe we take what we need," Hillas said, his tone matter-of-fact. "Human DNA, while close to ours, is inferior; they cannot take flight. We splice the genes of those with favorable characteristics, keep the rest for a controllable-sized serf pool, and rebuild the Draeken bloodlines."

Roden gritted his teeth. It was as he'd suspected: Hillas had no desire for peace. The Grand Lord had changed much over the years. Once, he'd been a leader of great vision. Now, if the Grand Lord had his way, it would be Sephia all over again: a new dynasty of chaos and oppression. Before the supernova, Draeka had been a place of peace and wisdom. He often wondered if Draeka's conscience had died along with that star.

When his people had gone to Sephia seeking a new home—millennia before Roden's time—they'd had the strength to win the war the Sephians had forced upon them. Now Hillas, for some reason, wanted to do the same on Earth. Except that now, that way of thinking wouldn't work. They couldn't afford a drawn-out war—or any war of any kind. Whatever was to be done had to be done with minimal casualties, or there'd be no Draeken remaining to continue their race.

The precipice was upon them. Roden watched Hillas closely. "Gene splicing has had mixed results. There's no guarantee it will be successful on a large scale."

"That was because we tried it with Sephian genes, but human DNA is a closer fit to ours. If it weren't for their lack of wings, they could be considered our brethren."

Roden fought to retain his calm. "Now is our chance to reclaim the glory of Draeka. War is not the answer. Slavery is a Sephian legacy; it was never ours. It's a nasty habit we picked up from the Sephians, and it's time we let it go."

Hillas' eyes narrowed. "If you were Grand Lord, the humans would breed Draeka right out of us. In mere generations, our people could lose their power to take flight."

"Or we could create a *new* race with the power to take flight."

"Bah." Hillas waved a hand. "You would surrender too much for our people's survival. And that's why you'll never lead them."

That hurts. But Hillas had a point for once. Roden was willing surrender much, including his own life—and most definitely the Grand Lord's life—for his people's survival. He sighed. "Regardless, there's nothing we can do without power cells. Our core ships are essentially disabled. They can't enter Earth's orbit without stealth control, let alone land. What would you have me do?"

"The time for action will come, Commander. Preparations are already underway."

"Preparations?" he asked, a feeling of dread weighing him down.

Hillas ran his fingers over his bejeweled hand. "Nothing that concerns you—not yet anyway; I will contact you when the time is ripe. In the meantime, continue to search for the spy in your camp."

Roden paused. Apprehension shot through him, and he forced a relaxed expression. "There have been no signs of espionage since the Club Mayhem incident. I believe the spy, whoever he was, was likely killed or taken at the club."

Hillas pounded a fist on the desk, and the image on the screen warbled. His face reddened, as though he were about to boil. "I don't care! Our people need to feel safe. That means I need a traitor found and soon. I want an execution that is very public and very painful. Consider finding the traitor your top priority."

So the Grand Lord didn't care *who* Roden brought to him, as long as it was someone to appease his sense of justice. Hillas had done that sort of thing before, but now Roden considered whether the activity was to give the Draeken a sense of comfort or to keep his Second busy.

Sleight of hand.

The thought prickled at Roden's nerves. Why was Hillas trying to distract the only lord with the power to usurp his plans with an impractical order? What was Hillas up to that didn't involve his Second? It was then Roden realized that the precipice he feared had been reached and passed. He could wait no longer. He gave a slight nod. "Your Highness. I will find your traitor. Will that be all?"

Hillas smiled, seemingly content with Roden's response. "One more thing," the old Draeken said. "Is it true you have a Sephian female currently in your cells?"

Roden inhaled deeply to maintain an aura of nonchalance. "There is a Sephian currently held on my base. I did not realize I needed to apprise you of every minute detail that takes place under my command."

"Nalea Homs is a member of Apolo's trinity, and therefore my business," Hillas said. "Bring her to me. No need for fanfare. You, alone, bring her directly to my earthside quarters. I expect to see you on the eve of two day's hence."

Roden forced a tight nod. "Of course, Your Highness."

"That will be all."

Roden punched the disconnect button and scowled. The Grand Lord had shown little interest in any prisoner before. Quite the opposite, in fact; the old male preferred the chase and bored quickly once his prey was conquered. Hillas clearly held suspicions regarding Nalea. But he didn't yet know the truth. If he had known, he would've sent an assassin to finish her long ago. Hillas simply could not have the risk she posed hanging over his head.

Roden had been biding his time with Nalea, counting on the fact that Hillas knew nothing when it came to this particular Sephian. Regardless, between Hillas' suspicions and his other preparations, Roden could wait no longer. Unfortunately, that meant he could no longer toy with his prisoner either.

As for Hillas' other order, Roden had no intent of hunting for a traitor. Oh, he knew the traitor still lived, but it wouldn't matter much longer. Everything was about to change. He'd go through the motions to keep Hillas off his back, at least long enough to keep the Grand Lord from discovering his plans.

Hmm. He rubbed his smooth chin. His original plan would have to be modified, as the timeline was now condensed. He'd need Nalea to make it work, and the risk was great to them both. He frowned, rubbing his neck as though to tamp out the uncomfortably strange emotion. The thought that she likely wouldn't be alive three days from now was... distasteful.

Pushing back from his desk, his wings quivered in anticipation as he pulled on his boots, stepped through the door, and headed toward a particular cell. He needed a break, and his stress eased with every step he took closer to *her*.

Roden would question Nalea one more time; even though he knew she'd never willingly confirm what he already knew. Perhaps then he could forget about the Grand Lord for a brief time. No matter how wearisome Hillas could be, he was still Grand Lord and revered by most Draeken. Hillas carried a strong presence and clung to old protocols. Few suspected what Roden already knew to be true.

The Draeken Grand Lord was going insane.

Chapter 3

"Why does the Grand Lord wish to see you?"

Roden's curt question did nothing to ease Nalea's pounding headache courtesy of the tranq shot he'd given her earlier. She pulled herself into a sitting position, rubbing her temples as she did so. At least he'd left the lights dimmed in her cell, especially since she suspected she wouldn't be getting another pair of dark glasses any time soon.

She glowered. "How would I know what goes on inside a Draeken's head? Do I look like a psycho to you?"

He smirked. "I think you meant 'psychic', and do you really want me to answer that?"

"Kiss my ass."

"Another time, perhaps."

She shook her head, instantly regretting the movement. "Is this your idea of torture? Talking your prisoners to death?"

He stepped closer, his lips curling into a sneer. "Ah, my dear, when I torture you, believe me, you'll know."

When, not if. Shivers flitted across her skin as she stared into those silver eyes, currently filled with taunting humor. Every living Sephian had heard stories of Roden's cruelty. Thousands had been killed in battles he'd orchestrated. How many Sephians had had their *soullare*—the brand that covered each Sephian body since birth—flayed from their bodies at his command? How many Sephians had been forced to watch their mates get slaughtered?

And perhaps the cruelest gesture of all was that this Draeken—universally hated by her kind—was destined to be her *tahren*. Either the gods had a perverted sense of humor or they knew her soul was irreparably stained and had chosen to punish her.

Frustrated, Nalea rubbed her eyes then glanced back up to find that intense gaze still scrutinizing her.

"Sugar helps with the after-effects," he said and threw her a red apple, which she let sail by her head as she watched him. The fruit bounced off the wall behind her and landed with a rolling thud.

"Why would you care?" she asked.

He watched her for a second then pulled out two more apples. He bit into one with a loud crunch. Her mouth watered in response.

He held out the other apple through the bars. She watched him for several seconds before coming to her feet. Still eying him warily, she took a step and snatched the fruit off the floor before retreating to the deeper safety of her cell.

They stood facing one another for a moment before he sat down with his usual nonchalance and took another bite out of his apple.

She chewed the fruit, mirroring his demeanor. *Two can play that game.* This continued until he threw the apple core into a waste receptacle in the wall.

After wiping his hands on his thighs, he leaned forward, eyed her for a moment, and then sighed. "What's the Grand Lord's interest in you?"

"My answer hasn't changed. I have no idea," she said, holding his gaze without blinking.

He cocked his head. "While I am a patient lord, our time is growing short."

Nalea's heart hammered in her chest. Roden could scar her body, destroy her mind, and crush her soul. He would never know why she hated Hillas more than any other Draeken; even more than the one standing before her. She shook her head. "Why don't you go ask him yourself?"

He said nothing, those silver eyes piercing her as though he could dig through her mind himself to find the answers he needed. Finally, he spoke. "I am going to miss our chats. I find them quite entertaining. But I warn you, Lea, I dislike secrets very much."

Her brows rose. "Isn't that the pot calling the pestle black?"

His lips curved upward. He opened his mouth then closed it, grinning as though he knew some inside joke. "I should say I dislike other people having secrets. I rather enjoy mine. And, believe me when I say this, I will find immense pleasure in plucking those secrets from you."

She held up her middle finger. "Fuck you."

"Tsk, tsk. You've picked up bad habits from the humans. And to think that we were getting along so well."

Her jaw clenched. "I've never even seen the Grand Lord in person, so how would I have any idea what he's thinking? Maybe he's run out of Sephians to maim… like you're any different. How many of my people have you beaten, cut, and murdered?"

Roden eyed her for a moment then turned away. As he stepped into the hallway, he glanced back. "Careful, Nalea, or I'll show you exactly what I am capable of."

Chapter 4

Apolo stared at the screen, jaw set hard, as Legian and Sienna Wolfe apprised him on the latest restrictions placed on Sephians at the American base. He and his troops in Britain weren't faring much better. None of them liked the current arrangement.

They'd shared their technology and knowledge. The humans had allowed them to remain on Earth—not that they could go anywhere else with drained power cells—but they were restricted to the two military bases. Fortunately, like the Sephians, Draeken power cells were built to recharge off indirect solar energy similar to that found near Sephia. They'd both assumed Earth's star bore the same energy signature, and they'd both miscalculated. Now they were stranded far from Sephia.

"Curfews have been expanded to twenty-four hours," Legian said.

Apolo scowled and nodded. "It is the same here." Only the Draeken were still moving freely about on the planet. Every day, new restrictions were placed on Apolo's people. First the curfews; now they couldn't even leave the bases due to the excuse that they may be seen by the local population.

Apolo didn't believe any of the rationale for an instant. The humans liked control, and they were getting trigger-happy at the thought that the Draeken were still out there somewhere, yet they were nowhere closer to finding either the locations of the Draeken's earthside bases or their powerful core ship.

"Any words of wisdom for your people here?" Sienna asked, looking as exhausted as he felt.

He sighed. "Hang in there."

She *harrumphed.* "Easier said than done. Talk to you tomorrow."

Legian nodded in farewell, and Apolo returned the gesture.

With that, the screen went blank. Apolo leaned back. At the rate things were going, the façade that his people held any rights would soon vanish and they'd become slaves to new masters. Right now, their future did not bode well. He rubbed his hands over his face in frustration.

He needed a miracle.

Chapter 5

The Draeken dimmed the lights, double-checked the locks, and ensured the electronic dampener was functioning at full power. Only when Kreed was confident prying ears couldn't break through the dampener did he dial the secure code. Privacy was critical for this meeting.

Though he was expecting it, his muscles still flinched when the golden visage appeared on the monitor. There was no way around it: meeting with the Sephian leader would be seen as a betrayal to his people. Doubt skimmed across his mind, hinting that taking such a risk was too dangerous and he should make the break sooner versus later. If his actions were discovered before the Grand Lord's death, then everything would be for naught. He'd be branded a traitor. But if he didn't do this, his people would never find peace. He was their best chance.

Kreed studied the image on the screen. Apolo's black *soullare* vined around one eye, giving the well-groomed male a dangerous demeanor. Even though Sephians lived decades longer than their Draeken brethren, Apolo looked worn out, as though the past two years had aged him three-fold. Being away from his *tahren* was taking its toll. Knowing he'd never see her again must make it a torture to wake every day.

Apolo's eyes widened and his jaw dropped before quickly closing. "It's good to see you, Kreed."

He nodded. "It's been too long, old friend."

Relief washed over the Sephian's features. "After you went silent, I feared you'd been compromised."

Kreed grimaced. "Close." *Too close.* "I needed to lay low for a while. When I found out I had been impersonated, I knew Hillas had learned of my existence." After a drawn-out sigh, he ran a hand through his hair. "Listen. About what happened—"

"The ambush wasn't your fault," Apolo interjected. "I know you never would've given me faulty information."

Guilt stabbed at Kreed. *If you only knew, old friend.*

"What's done is done," Apolo continued. "But I could use some good news here. Have you tracked down Nalea?"

Even as a child, his friend had always been impatient. A trait Apolo had never outgrown.

"Nalea was terminated not long after she was brought to the base," Kreed said quietly. Safer to say that than the truth. If Apolo knew of Roden's keen interest in her, he'd launch a rescue mission immediately, and Kreed couldn't allow that. That mission could destroy everything he'd worked for. His old friend didn't need the weight that came with that knowledge. In some cases, ignorance was a blessed balm.

Apolo closed his eyes. "*Suvaste.* She will be avenged. Roden Zyll will pay." After a moment, he sighed. "Do you have any other information that can help us?"

Kreed gave a tight nod and continued to share what little—but critical—intel he'd acquired. Information from Hillas had become increasingly sparse, especially anything pertaining to their defense against the Sephians. He knew the Grand Lord was planning something big, and that couldn't bode well for either the Sephians or his own people. He may have been born Draeken, but he knew that unless his people changed their ways—and quickly—they faced certain genocide.

The Sephians had formed an early alliance with the humans, so there was still hope for Kreed's people. After all, his people had brought no violence to their new world. If anything, the Sephians were the aggressors here; though he admitted they had just cause —slavery tended to cause unrest.

Unfortunately, the Sephians had been first to align with the humans, bending their unwitting hosts' ears with misperceptions; a costly mistake to the Draeken. For his people to be accepted on Earth, he needed Apolo to earn the support of the human military. Without full human buy-in, Kreed's people were as good as dead. He glanced at the clock. Frustration burrowed in his gut. Time was running short. One of the base auto-scans that ran every twelve minutes could catch his electronic dampener's signal any moment. "I'll check in again when I can."

"If it gets too dangerous, get out of there and call for a pickup. The humans can be challenging, but fair."

Kreed went to hit the button.

Apolo lifted his chin. "One more thing."

"Yes?"

"Watch your back."

"*Sheescaten, ta deiti,*" Kreed said. *Peace, my brother.*

Apolo dipped his head. "*Deiti.*"

The screen went blank. Kreed paused. If he made the smallest error, he was dead, which made it all the more important that he make no mistakes. He punched in several commands to remove the electronic distortions to his face. Apolo and Kreed hadn't been face to face since they were boys, so the Sephian would no longer recognize his childhood friend. Wearing an altered face on-screen protected them both, and Apolo knew it. As long as no one knew what Kreed looked like, no one could be tortured to surrender the identity he now wore. He would remain safe as long as he was careful.

On the downside, when it came to revealing himself, things would get tricky. Apolo couldn't confirm his identity, which made his other identity crucial. Not that the odds of survival were in his favor.

Once the comm's settings leveled off to normal, he leaned back in his chair and massaged his temples. It'd been a long day. The last two scheduled supply drops from Hillas' earthside base hadn't yet arrived, and he knew it was because the Grand Lord grew jealous of Roden's power and the loyalty of Roden's guardsmen.

Right now, Hillas was the only being who stood in the way of peace. If things went right, the Draeken could reach peace with the humans and Sephians by year-end and blend somewhat into human culture. His people would be safe.

Only one problem.

Kreed knew things never went right.

Nalea knew Roden was there even though he made no sound. Keeping her back to him, she continued to face the wall where she'd been imagining swimming in the Golran Sea. Whenever Lord Homs had granted her a break from her duties, she'd gone there. It was one of the few vacation places not frequented by Draeken, as wings made swimming difficult. Nalea, on the other hand, was an excellent swimmer. The water, fed by hot springs, caressed her skin.

She'd been fortunate. Most Sephians had never enjoyed vacations. Lord Homs had been a kind master, treating all fourteen of his slaves as though they were a part of his family. He had gone so far as to refer to them as his family unit. But, even as a young girl, Nalea had known they could never be a family. Not as long as those born with wings had power over those born without. A fact she proved the night she sliced her master's throat.

Blood Night.

It was the night that had changed everything. She'd still been a child then, having not yet reached the age of thirteen. War didn't care; it sucked all ages into its deadly maw. On that night, slaves across Sephia had revolted to take back their freedom. That night started the twenty-year Noble War. Her people far outnumbered the Draeken, which resulted in many more Sephians being slaughtered than Draeken. But enough had survived to drive the winged scourge from their planet for good.

They'd reclaimed Sephia, but the Noble War wasn't over. The few remaining Draeken had fled, and Nalea had been one of the first to volunteer to join a group of six hundred Sephian soldiers to pursue the scourge—to the ends of the universe, if necessary. The Sephians would never be truly free of their captors until the Draeken were extinct.

"What goes through that mind of yours?" Roden announced from behind her.

Tension climbed her spine. Her nerves were frayed from the endless battles with Roden. She'd broken free from her cell before; she'd do it again. She remained facing the wall. "Can't get enough of me, Roden?"

A soft chuckle. "I admit I find you… intriguing; however, I'm simply trying to be a good host. I wouldn't want my guest to grow disenchanted in my care."

Nalea sighed. If she asked him to leave her alone, he'd be there even more than he already was. At least he hadn't tortured her… yet; something that made her both relieved and suspicious at the same time. "What do you want, Roden?"

"Always to the point, Lea; I appreciate that. I have brought a proposal for you. How would you like to earn your freedom?"

She forced herself to not turn, to not display interest, to not respond. She shook her head. "If to earn my freedom, you mean for me to betray my people, you may as well kill me now."

"I would never kill my consort."

Nalea snorted and folded her arms over her chest. "I'm not your consort. Nor will I ever be."

"Hm. I disagree. Alas, but that's not why I'm here. Back to my proposal; I ask nothing from you that would pit you against your own people, I give you my word. In fact, I offer you an opportunity to become a legend in the Noble War."

The sound of metal on metal caused her to twist around. Roden was stepping into her cell, its door wide open. Even with his pale wings held tight behind him, his presence seemed to fill much of the small cell.

"I know better than to accept the word of a liar, Roden Zyll."

He shrugged. "I speak the truth now." He motioned to her. "Come to my room so we can discuss this further."

She raised her brows. "Never in all twelve hells will you get me to come willingly to your room."

He gave her a wicked grin. "You came on your own volition last night."

"To kill you."

"It doesn't have to be that way."

"As long as you live, it does."

His posture stiffened. His wore a loose shirt, black kilt, and boots. For a lord, he dressed plainly, but there was nothing common about his highborn charisma. Where many nobles flouted their station in order to gain respect, Roden needed no adornment. He was a natural leader, making one race follow him in droves and another race try relentlessly to kill him.

He tapped out a few commands on his wrist-comm and glanced up at the camera entrenched in the ceiling. Nalea followed his gaze to see the light on the camera flicker off. She tensed. What didn't he want his guardsmen to see? Clenching her jaw, she eyed Roden in a silent face-off. *He will never break me.*

He cocked his head. "I know why Hillas wants you."

Her heart felt as though her blood had become lead. Of all the things to say, she'd never expected *that*. "You're bluffing," she said, trying to sound haughty.

His eyes narrowed, the corners of his lips curved upward, and he took a step closer. She fought the urge to take a step back.

Another step closer. She lifted her chin in defiance, forcing herself to look up to maintain his gaze.

When he came closer still, she found herself backed against the wall. He leaned closer, his heat branding every cell. When he spoke, his words were a whisper, his breath tickling her ear.

"The Grand Lord wants you because you're his daughter."

The smallest gasp. Fear and revulsion locked her in place, while the words shook her to her soul. Scrambling, she jutted out her chin. "I'm Sephian, Roden. Try again."

Roden smiled. That casual, crooked half-smile spoke of a highly intelligent adversary. She hated that smile almost as much as she hated him.

"You're a good actress, Lea. Even I wouldn't have suspected if you hadn't betrayed your feelings when I battled you. You were fortunate to have inherited many of your mother's traits. But not all." Then his features turned hard, and he frowned. "I've seen the scars."

"I have no idea what you're talking about," she threw out, and couldn't help but notice that she didn't sound convincing, even to herself.

The next instant he forced her face against the wall, pinning her. His hand slid under her shirt. She struggled in earnest only to freeze the instant his fingers touched her back—the exact spots where phantom pains still haunted her, where fantasies of taking flight prickled at her dreams. The scars were so old that they were no more than two faint hairlines, but they stood as the sickening truth of her lifelong secret.

Roden ground out his next words. "Tell me. What kind of mother would carve the wings from her own babe's back?"

Nalea shoved away from him. He made no move as she put space between them.

"How dare you judge," she bit out. "My mother saved my life. Exactly what kind of life do you think a hybrid gets to have?"

His brows furrowed. "Hybrids were common on Sephia. There is no sin in that. All children were cherished."

"Hybrids were cherished by *Draeken*. To my people, hybrids are brutal reminders of rapists and of slaves with no rights," Nalea corrected.

Roden growled. "Yes, there are criminals in every race; criminals that deserve to be put down. But don't forget that I grew up on Sephia too, and I saw for my own eyes many love-matches between Draeken and Sephians—most without a *tahren* bond to nudge the Sephian partners along—that produced beautiful hybrids." He lifted a hand. "You cannot deny that Draeken treasure all life, regardless of their ability to take flight. Slavery was a Sephian tradition we continued after the war out of necessity." He held up a clenched fist. "But never have I seen rape condoned. Punishment has always been swift and harsh for heinous crimes, regardless of race."

She laughed but bit it back when she saw his glower. "Look me in the eye and tell me you believe that Hillas Puftan—the righteous Grand Lord who promoted life and love while he persisted with slavery—would treasure his own bastard offspring?"

Roden's lips thinned.

"Tell me this. How many children do you think Hillas fathered by raping Sephian slaves? And yet today the Grand Lord has no heir—legitimate or otherwise—to rule when he's gone. What do you think happened to his younger brother who disappeared not long before the Noble War? What do you think happened to him?" Years of hating Draeken bubbled up within her. All the years of worrying about the moment her lineage was discovered was too much. She threw out her next desperate words for spite. "You're Draeken. You only ever care about Draeken."

Roden's fists shook as he held himself in place, and she sensed the restraint it was taking him to keep from attacking her. Sudden trepidation built with her. She attempted to stare him down. He lunged forward, grabbing her by the throat, and slammed her back against the wall. She clawed at his forearm, struggling to breathe.

"Your past has poisoned your mind. Get this straight," he hissed out. "Yes, I'm Draeken. And don't think I wouldn't kill you myself if it would help save my people." His grip loosened slightly, but he still held her in place. "But you're also wrong. I'm different. You'll see. That you still live is proof enough."

"Why?" she asked honestly.

He pulled his face away from hers while still allowing her no movement. His anger had ebbed, but she could see it, simmering just below the surface. "Because I'm going to take you to Hillas."

She belted out a callous laugh. "If he knows the truth about me, he'll kill me the first chance he gets."

His lips twisted upward. "Not if we kill him first."

She jerked. "What kind of trick is this?"

"No trick."

She opened her mouth to refute him then shut it and watched him as she tried to fit the pieces together. A moment later, she calmed. "Ah, I see," she mocked. "You want me there when he dies. Because, if Hillas is killed by a Sephian, no one would suspect it was actually an assassination by one of his own. And, as the most powerful lord next in line for the throne, you'll graciously step in to lead your people."

He shrugged. "Naturally, they need a strong leader." Then he looked at her hard. "Don't tell me you haven't dreamed of killing Hillas."

"Every night," she muttered.

"Now's your chance."

She continued to watch him. Emotion swirled in those silver eyes, but she couldn't read him. Finally, as though tired of being near her, he turned away. His wings, covered with dark-colored tribal tattoos, showed her exactly how powerful his lineage was. Blue and green markings lined his wings, detailing his royal heritage. Bold symbols proclaimed the godless logic he followed.

Images of bloody battles spoke of victories he'd led. This feudal lord was no minor Draeken to be trifled with. He would be a strong leader, perhaps stronger than Hillas, and that could only make her people's pursuit of the Draeken all the harder.

Her next words were soft. "Even with your power, if your people suspect you were behind his death, you'll be executed."

"Leave that to me." He paused then turned back to her. "Do exactly as I command, and you will be set free. I give you my word."

Nalea stood there as his words sank in. If she could believe his word—and she couldn't—Roden was giving her a chance at taking down the one Draeken she hated even more than him. *Her father.*

With one kill, she could free herself of her secret and drive the Noble War to a critical turning point. Only two people knew the truth about Nalea's heritage. Apolo, she trusted; Roden, never. If she didn't want the secret to get out, Roden would have to die.

While she still couldn't determine when Roden spoke truth or lies, she knew he'd lied to her about one thing. If she survived, she was the only remaining legal heir to the Draeken throne. The Draeken, with their traditions, would accept a bastard, wingless child of the Puftan bloodline over a lord from a different bloodline. Roden could never claim the throne as long as she lived. Either way, she had a death sentence.

Her choice was simple. *Not help Roden, die now. Help Roden, kill Hillas, hopefully kill Roden, and then die.*

She held out a hand. "I accept."

He looked down at her hand and broke out into a wide grin. "I prefer to seal our agreement with something more à propos."

Before she could move, he roughly grabbed her shoulders, yanked her to him, and pressed his lips to hers. She responded by shoving at him, which sent her stumbling backward.

He stepped back, and she wiped her lips with the back of her hand. "I hate you."

"I know," he replied. "But it doesn't change the fact that you need me." He tapped his wrist-comm again, and she knew the camera lights would be blinking back on any moment. Roden was done with her for now.

"I own you, Nalea Zyll," he said in a low voice, his back to her.

She didn't miss the fact that he'd added his surname. An intentional slight, as her people refused to use last names. Only their masters had used such names.

He paused just before walking away. "Never forget that."

With his feet propped on the desk, Roden leaned back in his chair, his wings spread out behind him, draping across the floor. He rolled his neck, trying to ease the tension in his shoulders. Between planning a mutiny, leading the search for the Draeken traitor, and keeping his people safely hidden from the humans, there was little time left to sleep.

After rubbing his temples, he leaned forward and tapped out several commands on his desk, and the key to his plans filled the screen. The heir to the Draeken throne was still safely locked away in her cell; her heritage unknown to everyone. The tension in his body eased, and he smiled.

He'd always known his Sephian prisoner harbored secrets. After he first battled her and suspected that he was to be her *tahren*, he'd researched her to see how he could leverage her weakness in the war. He'd scoured her files, finding nothing. And so he'd dug deeper.

It hadn't taken long to uncover the forged birth records. The Nalea he knew bore no legal birth record. The one in her files belonged to a still-born Sephian baby with the same name. And, since no father was recorded, it became clear her mother had been hiding something.

Her mother, Nexa, had been a beautiful Sephian with strong yet feminine features. Nexa had belonged to the Homs house, a Draeken lord Roden had met once in his youth and knew to be a good lord, known for neither politics nor secrets. But a neighboring house had a far different reputation: the Puftan house, childhood home to none other than Hillas Puftan himself. Roden had heard rumors about the Grand Lord's… appetites, and Nexa fit his tastes perfectly. The poor woman had never stood a chance.

Once Roden rationalized the hard truth, he'd hated his leader all the more for it. The bastard deserved to die for his crimes. How fitting it was to have the result of one of his crimes be his undoing.

While Roden was confident of his theory, he needed proof. Capturing her at the false meeting with Sienna Wolfe presented him with the perfect opportunity to confirm his suspicions without her being the wiser. After tranquilizing her, he'd scanned her blood for signs of a Draeken heritage. From there, it hadn't taken long to find the hairline scars that betrayed her secrets. Not only was it proof positive, but her DNA matched the Puftan bloodline: Nalea's father was the most powerful Draeken.

Still, there was no way Nexa could've forged birth certificates without Draeken help. Homs had put his own life in danger by hiding Nalea. Roden wondered if Nalea knew that the Draeken she'd killed had risked so much to protect her.

Nalea had been right about one thing: if Hillas had known about her, she would've been killed at birth. Hillas was ruthless at protecting his position. Even now, the Grand Lord clearly suspected something when it came to Nalea. Roden gambled that it was the inordinate amount of time he'd spent with her that had garnered Hillas' attention. Fortunately, that too played into Roden's plans.

Allowing Nalea to kill the Grand Lord was the greatest gift he could give her so that she would be more apt to accept her role in his plans. Nalea was the key to his endgame, but he'd have to move quickly. Even though he'd deleted all Nalea's files—including those in the archives—he had no doubt Hillas was capable of his own deductive reasoning, especially since Nalea bore far too many of her mother's facial features.

Roden chuckled when his attention returned to the screen. With every sit-up, Nalea glowered at the camera. It brought comfort to him knowing that he threw her off as much as she did him. He reached for the bottle of spiced rum he'd procured from Club Mayhem before the humans shut it down. The flavor reminded him of *bolgk*, his favorite drink, bringing back memories of home. He unscrewed the cap, paused, and then frowned. He sniffed the liquid yet detected nothing but the sweet smell of sugar alcohol.

He watched the bottle for a moment then set it down on the desk and examined it. Dark glass with amber liquid; a pretty package all too easily tainted. "What are you hiding in there?" No matter how tired he was, he was careful in his routines, and leaving the cap only loosely tightened certainly wasn't one of them. His boots landed on the floor with a solid *thud* as he came to his feet. Grabbing the bottle, he punched the unlock code, stepped into the hallway, and waited for the door to close and lock before heading down the corridor.

It was late and the base was quiet. His people had quickly grown accustomed to Earth's orbital schedule, and most would be sleeping. He continued past Nalea's cell, and down corridors riddled with sharp turns until he reached a second set of cells on the other side of the base. These cells Nalea knew nothing about.

He came to the first cell. The human male inside was still awake, oblivious to Roden as he tapped on a keyboard. Every night he kept busy, typing out his memoirs on the tablet Roden had approved to keep the detainee content. Christopher Jones was a journalist who'd happened across the back rooms of Club Mayhem not long after it opened. While it wasn't the Draeken way to kill innocents, they also couldn't have their plans announced to their new world without being fully prepared.

The human had been here for over a year now while Roden waited for Hillas' approval to approach the humans with terms of peace. During the daytime, Christopher was allowed free run of the base—except for Roden's corridor, of course—but at night he was relegated to his cell due to fewer Draeken guardsmen being on duty during the sleeping hours. Roden had been careful. He would never be accused of being cruel to humans.

He wondered what Nalea would do if she knew of this cell block. Would she have freed these people rather than come to his room the night of her escape? If so, she may have been miles from the base by the time Roden discovered her empty cell.

He chuckled drily to himself. Of course, the woman he knew would have come to his room that night no matter what. Her hate for him was too great to be ignored.

He cleared his throat, and the human startled then smiled. "Oh, hello, Commander. What brings you by this late hour?"

"Out for a stroll, Christopher." He held up the bottle before punching in the code to unlock the cell door. "We came across several crates of this beverage. A few tried it and found it too sweet. You want it?"

The human looked pensive then inquisitive as he came to his feet and reached out for the bottle. A quick look at the label brought a smile. "It's been ages since I've had a good rum."

Roden smiled as the human took a long draw. He only just swallowed it before he stumbled backward. The bottle crashed to the floor, sending glass splinters everywhere. The man's eyes rolled upward, and he followed the bottle to the floor. His body convulsed as it succumbed to the incredibly swift poison.

"*Fyet*," Roden cursed before the human's body stilled. He grimaced. He hadn't wanted the human to die. He hadn't disliked Christopher. Rather, he'd found the man respectful and likely a good ally for when Hillas would finally condone their plan to reveal themselves and their intentions to humans. Having Christopher test the rum had been a purely logical choice. Compared to the limited number of Draeken remaining, humans were simply more expendable.

He turned to leave but paused to glance at the human's tablet computer. Whatever the man had written on the tablet, it no longer mattered. On a whim, he picked the computer up and left the cell to return to his room. His mood had soured. While he hadn't killed Christopher—the blame for that fell squarely on the assassin—he disliked the needless loss of life.

After changing his locks and adding an old-fashioned chain lock to his door, a dark laugh erupted from deep within Roden's chest. Someone had had the gall to try to kill him. Him! He looked forward to tracking down the traitor and brushing up on his interrogation skills. After all, this assassin was merely a tool for the real killer. Someone with enough clearance to have access to his lock codes... and there was only one Draeken with more clearance than Roden.

Chapter 8

"I have the coordinates for Hillas' earthside base," Apolo said, scrutinizing the figures on the other screen for their reactions. Several sat at a long table facing the monitor. Three human officers sat on one side, with the other side taken by Legian, Sienna, and Jax Jerrick, their military advisor. Apolo hadn't yet had the heart to tell Sienna and Legian that Nalea had died at the hands of Roden Zyll. It would only make their vicious vendetta against the Draeken worse.

In a similar formation, Apolo sat with Bente—the third member of his trinity—and the senior British officers he worked with daily. He'd filled them in only minutes before the scheduled forum. Relations were fragile enough without the British playing hero and going after Hillas on their own.

"I thought your spy was dead," Sienna said, suspicion dripping from her voice.

"I was wrong."

"But he was compromised," she said. "The ambush—"

"Was a devastating loss," he interjected. "But I trust him. And we need his intel."

"Where's the base?" Major Sommers from the American side asked.

"Canada," Apolo said.

Sommers scowled. "It'd be easier if it were on American soil."

"I understand." Apolo looked over all the attendees before continuing. "Lieutenant-Colonel Bryant and I believe that once we have the surrounding area secured, an open recon mission is the wisest course of action. Let them see us coming. That way, we can't be accused of being the aggressors. Leaving it up to Hillas to take the next step."

"Are there any humans in the vicinity?" Sommers asked.

"No," Apolo responded. "They are quite isolated."

"Then we should consider bombing the base," Sienna said. "Wipe out the lot of them in one fell swoop. They didn't come here for peace."

Apolo frowned. Sienna had hardened during the last year. Ever since she'd been forced to execute her mother a year ago, her views had morphed into merciless judgments. Her soul was now as scarred as her skin. While Bryant suggested she was suffering from a human condition called PTSD, if she continued in this way of thinking, he would be forced to remove her from his inner circle. He hoped to all twelve hells he wouldn't have to. She was a natural leader with a strong spirit. His people as well as her own respected her.

"We will not bomb Canadian soil," Colonel Jerrick said.

"Just as with every race, not all Draeken are evil, Sienna," Apolo said in a low voice. There was just enough in the way she blinked that he knew he'd struck a chord.

"I agree with Apolo," Jerrick added. "We do not have conclusive evidence that the Draeken have foul intentions. They have shown no more hostility than Apolo's people. We will not draw first blood."

"Wasn't Club Mayhem a clear enough sign?" Legian asked.

Jerrick turned to him. "We still cannot verify that the Draeken intended any harm. All the humans at the club were there by choice."

Apolo inhaled. "Let's focus on what can be done now. A Draeken risked his life to get this new information to us."

"Let's discuss options to recon the base," Colonel Jerrick said.

Lieutenant-Colonel Bryant proceeded to relate his plan. When he'd finished, Sephians and humans alike broke into discussion.

"They'll see us coming from miles away," Sienna shot out across the table.

"Hillas has an advanced detection system," Apolo said, nodding. "But if we go in at precisely sunset tomorrow night, we can pass through undetected. If all goes as planned, there will be no injuries and we'll know the layout of the base for a large-scale attack, if needed."

"It sounds like a setup," she snapped back. "Too much like the ambush."

"We've been dancing for too long. It's time to either take the Draeken to bed or dump them," Jerrick said. "I trust Bryant, and I support the plan."

Legian's fist pounded the table. "The risk to our people is too great."

Apolo narrowed his eyes. "And to ensure everything goes according to Lieutenant-Colonel Bryant's plan, I'm going in with the recon team." He turned his hard look onto Sienna and Legian. "We followed the Draeken here to ensure they did not enslave another world, not to wipe them out."

Sienna's lips tightened. "I'm closer to the base. It makes more sense to have Legian or Jax go in."

Apolo's face hardened. "I will be there in two hours."

Lieutenant-Colonel Bryant said, "You don't yet have approval—"

"I don't give a bloody damn. My people need me," Apolo

snapped back before standing and walking out of the room. *Suvaste.* These idiot humans, in their need for control, were going to end up with a war on their hands.

———————————————

Chapter 9

———————————————

"*It's time, Lea.*"

Nalea inhaled Roden's masculine scent as his rough palm caressed her cheek. "Mm."

A deep chuckle…

She stilled. Something wasn't right. Finally, she remembered why.

She *hated* Roden Zyll.

Suvaste!

Nalea jerked awake to find herself looking up into silver eyes. She stared, horrified. With a rush, she sprang to her feet.

"I was asleep," she snapped.

His lips turned into a playful smile, and his laugh drifted across the walls of her cell. "You dream of me."

She looked down, not wanting to make eye contact. "I may have been dreaming, but it most definitely was *not* about you."

Another chuckle. "Then who?"

"Why are you here?"

His smile faded. "Hillas has demanded that you and I come to him. I'm afraid it truly is time, my dear."

She swallowed before holding out her hands to be restrained. "I'm ready."

Roden chuckled, grabbed her wrists, and pulled her into his embrace. His soft words against her ear sending tingles across her skin. "Didn't I mention that I told Hillas you're not my prisoner?"

She scowled and tried to pull away. "Then what the *suvaste* am I?"

His lips curved into a wicked grin.

Her eyes widened before narrowing. She pushed at his chest. "What did you tell him?"

He released her. "The truth. That you're my consort, of course."

Her blood ran cold. "You didn't."

His features tightened. He turned and opened the cell door, standing to one side. "I did, and you'd better be damned convincing or we're both dead."

Chapter 10

For the second time in as many days, Nalea stepped out of her cell. As before, it was late and the hallway was empty, and she turned toward Roden's room. Only this time, he led the way. She numbly followed him through the hallways, and waited while he entered his unlock code, noticing that this time he made a point of *not* hiding the code he entered. And, he'd changed the code since she'd last been there.

After the door shut behind them and the silence of her new prison enveloped her, the numbness morphed into anger. She spun. "What the hell are you thinking? Who would ever believe Lord Commander Roden Zyll could stoop so low as to take on a Sephian as a consort?"

He raised a brow. "A Draeken-Sephian of the royal Puftan bloodline. My dear, I am certain they'll accept you as my consort. In fact, I suspect our people will find the union both practical and fortuitous. The continuation of the Puftan line will be a blessing to our people and a new hope to end the Sephian's relentless genocide." He continued on his way to his desk. She remained standing there as he tapped on his computer.

After a long silence, he spoke. "If you're brought to the Grand Lord as a prisoner—or even as a member of my base—he has the authority to take you from my command and have you killed without anyone the wiser. If you're brought to him as my consort though, even as your father, Hillas can't demand to see you alone, let alone transfer you to his control; not without breaking Draeken protocol. He can't kill you—his second-in-command's consort—without raising suspicion." He lifted his chin a touch higher. "Rather brilliant, if I do say so myself."

"Brilliant?" she countered. "More like suicidal. You must've suffered a major head injury if you think you can convince the Grand Lord—not to mention every other Draeken, that you'd let any woman into your heart... and a half-breed at that!"

Roden sprang to his feet, a stern expression on his face. Nalea fought to stand her ground as he strolled to her, lifted her chin, and placed a slow, tender kiss upon her lips. A kiss she refused to return.

Just as she felt her control slipping, he broke away and returned to his desk. "You see, my dear, I can be quite convincing."

Suvaste. She shook her head, forcing herself to remember that to Roden it was all for show.

"With you being of the Puftan bloodline, there's little convincing to be done on my end." He watched her. "Now, you, on the other hand, could work on your acting skills. If I may make a suggestion... accept the *tahren* bond. There would be much less need to act."

"Ha!" Nalea burst out. "You overestimate the bond. Even if I gave in to the bond, it does nothing to change my emotions. The bond may be biological, but it holds no sway over my mind and heart."

He shrugged. "You could try it and see."

Nalea took a step closer. "Anyone who knows me will never believe that I could feel anything for a Draeken."

Some kind of emotion flashed through his eyes but was gone all too quickly. His lips curved upward into a foreboding smile. "Haven't I mentioned that Nalea of Apolo's trinity died not long after her capture? Aside from the few guardsmen I've entrusted to watch you, the world believes you're already dead. To any other Draeken, you're a Sephian I captured for my own pleasure. Of course, all the truth will come out once we meet with Hillas and your safety is secured."

The room spun and Nalea barely reached the chair in time. She sank down, staring at the Draeken typing away on his computer. Everyone she loved thought she was dead.

No one would ever come for her.

A vision of a funeral service passed through her mind. Her closest friend, Sienna—driven by her human emotions—would have cried while giving a moving eulogy. Legian would be strong at her side. But Apolo, with his *tahren* still on Sephia, would suffer even more. He'd closed himself off to nearly everyone. It'd taken Nalea over a decade to discover the person beneath the leader façade.

It'd been bad enough for her to be in close proximity to Roden over the past months, but to know that her friends had suffered needlessly because of his cruel games... She turned a hard glare onto Roden. "You heartless, cruel *bastard*," she ground out, slamming a fist on his desk.

He glanced up, looking confused. "I couldn't have your friends plan any kind of rescue mission, now could I? Not when we're so close to bringing peace to both our races."

With a shriek, she lunged across the desk. Surprise flashed across his face the instant before she tackled him, sending them both tumbling to the floor. She twisted around to straddle him so that his wings were pinned behind his back. She could've killed him just then, but she'd be no closer to ending Hillas. Instead, she swung back and slapped him.

The sound echoed through the room. Her palm burned and

tingled from the force of her blow. "I hate you," she shouted, the words breaking as she fought back tears she refused to shed.

The slightest hint of emotion flashed across his face, erased before she could recognize it. "I know," he replied softly.

He didn't strike her back. He didn't push her off him. Hells, he just sat there as she glared down at him. Nalea watched him, narrowing her eyes. After a while, she shook her head. "Who are you really, Roden Zyll?"

"Are we done here?" he asked. He then he knocked her off him, picked up his chair, sat down, and went back to his computer.

She muttered every swear word she knew as she paced around the dark room. As a small consideration, Roden had dimmed the lights enough she could see without squinting. First thing she noticed was the lack of weapons. There was little décor; not even a nail in the wall that could even be used as a weapon.

Her gaze fell on the bed and froze. Women's clothing had been laid out across it. Not just any clothing, but *Draeken-style* clothing. Where Sephians wore unisex styles, Draeken males and females dressed differently: males wore kilts and boots, while females wore lissome dresses and delicate shoes. As Draeken often flew places, they didn't need practical shoes, and they preferred their garments to flit and flutter in the breeze. Both happened to be the exact opposite of Nalea's preferences.

She fisted a scrap of material and held it up. "What the *fyet* is this?"

"A gown. It was quite difficult to obtain, but it's rather lovely, wouldn't you agree?"

She dropped it back onto the bed as though it had bitten her. "A bit presumptuous, aren't you?"

"No. I'm a realist and a pragmatist."

She stared at the gown. "I'd rather go naked than wear this."

Roden smirked. "That's your choice, but that may prove distracting."

Nalea glared.

"We must be convincing. A Draeken consort would be expected to look the part."

Sephian females were adored for their strength. They had no need to wear the fragile, colorful pieces of fabric Draeken females flaunted to attract lovers. If she wore this gown, most of her *soullare* would be on display for all to see. "How am I to hide any weapons under this thing?" she asked, holding the flimsy material before her and seeing *too* much light through it.

Roden barked out a laugh. "And give you a chance to cut my throat like you did to old Lord Homs?" He shook his head. "I don't think so."

Her breath hardened in her chest. That had happened on Blood Night. As far as she knew, there'd been too much chaos for any records to be tracked that night. She'd never told anyone about that night. Not even Apolo.

Roden rubbed his temples. "Will you always doubt my resourcefulness?" He then gave her a hard look. "Homs was a good Draeken, you know. He didn't deserve that."

"It's not what you think."

"So you didn't slice Homs's throat while he slept peacefully in his bed?" He rubbed his neck. "Hmm, somehow I think you could do *exactly* that sort of thing to an unarmed Draeken."

"You're right. I killed him," she admitted quietly. "I went into his room, picked his sharpest dagger, and slit his throat while he slept. He died while still deep in his dreams." She stepped forward, placing her palms on his desk. "But did your source also tell you that a Sephian death force had broken through his gates and were about to execute him using blood whips, just as they'd done to the three other Lords in the area?"

Roden looked a touch surprised but said nothing.

She leaned forward. "Do you realize how much he would have suffered? Blood whips tipped with barbs coated with anti-coagulant and poison; he could've burned and bled for days, even at his age, before the poison would've reached his heart."

"I assure you, I am quite aware of the pain caused by blood whips... as well as other Sephian weapons," Roden coolly replied. "Your people have developed quite the harsh arsenal."

She leaned back and crossed her arms over her chest. "*My* people have done what they needed to survive, but that's beside the point. What I did for Homs was an act of mercy."

"Hmm." He returned to typing on that infuriating computer.

She slammed her fists down on his desk, forcing him to look up. "What's that supposed to mean?"

His eyes narrowed upon her. "I think you have a talent for survival and to hells with anyone who gets in your way—especially if that person happens to be a Draeken. You didn't come to this planet to save humans. You came here to kill Draeken simply because they were born with wings. You don't care if they've no blood on their hands. You hate that you're half Draeken, and you bundle up all that hate and shoot it at all of my people as punishment for Hillas' sins. Face it, my dear; you're a bigger hypocrite than I am."

Nalea snapped back. "Homs was the closest I ever had to a father. He treated me and my mother as though we were family. You can take your godsdamned righteousness and stuff it."

One side of his lips curled upward, but there was no hint of humor. "Ah, so cold Nalea can care for a Draeken. Good. You better remember that feeling if you want to convince Hillas."

"You're not Homs," she spat out.

"No. I wasn't incompetent enough to let you slice my throat."

Her jaw clenched as he stood and side-stepped around her.

"I was twelve."

Roden glanced back. "What?"

"I was twelve years old. I would've done things differently now, but at that time, I wasn't strong enough to stand up against the death force. I would've been whipped right alongside Homs if I'd stood up for him." She winced at the memory. *Such a straight cut, yet so much blood poured out. The blue sheets, the dark crimson...* She lifted her chin. "I did what I thought was best for Homs. I was trying to protect him."

"Remorse does nothing to untangle that knot in the heart though, does it?"

Nalea turned to face Roden. For the first time, she truly saw a softness to his features, his silver eyes tinted with compassion. She frowned. "No, it doesn't."

He stepped closer then. "We all have regrets. It's what we learn from them that maps our future." He grabbed a pillow and blanket and walked past her.

"What are you doing?" she asked. "I thought we had to go see Hillas."

"Not until sunset," he replied curtly. "It's late. I need rest. The bed is yours as long as you don't talk."

She stared at him as he sat down, kicked off his boots, fluffed the pillow and gave her his back. His wings formed a wall, making it quite clear the conversation was over. He pulled the blanket over him and glanced over his shoulder. "Oh, and other than the blades I have on me, the others are safely locked away. I'd advise you to not make an attempt to kill me in my sleep."

With that he rolled back over, and silence filled the room.

Nalea lay down on the bed and watched him for several moments. Deep breaths were his only response. She rolled onto her back. Every night since Blood Night, she'd thought of Homs and what she'd done to the only other person she'd loved as much as she'd loved her mother. But, for the first time since that night, she no longer felt absolutely, abysmally alone.

She closed her eyes and a tear slipped free. The truth sat like a stone in her stomach.

The Draeken who lay on the floor several feet away had done horrendous things.

So had she.

He would do anything to accomplish his goals.

So would she.

She could no longer deny why the *tahren* bond had sought Lord Roden Zyll as her soulmate. Everything she accused him of, she was also guilty of.

They were both monsters.

R oden didn't understand why Sephians chose to cover their bodies with drab clothing. Their golden skin, with hues of the *scullare*, was meant to be on display; in his opinion, at least. He glanced over at his passenger who continued to adjust the gown.

"Keep your eyes on the flight path. You're going to get us killed before Hillas gets his chance." Nalea pointed ahead. "Watch out!"

He turned back to piloting the ship, pulling up just in time to avoid an exceedingly tall tree. Roden had to fly the ship at full power, making the speed too fast for a human eye to make out enough detail to know that these ships weren't native to their planet. If he slowed down, humans would find it odd to see a ship with the smallest of wings.

The speed of their flight brought bullets to mind, the small piece of metal shot from human weapons. While bullets were far less effective than Draeken blasters, bullets did have their value. His ship, shaped like one and moving like one, could end up in the side of a mountain if he wasn't attentive.

Draeken ships flew much better in the higher altitudes where the oxygen levels were lower and fewer obstacles posed risk. Unfortunately, the humans had developed a rather robust radar system, and Roden was forced to fly too low for his preference to avoid detection. A lesser pilot would have crashed by now.

Flying fast and low required careful focus, a task made more difficult with Nalea's movements on the edge of his vision. He wasn't used to such pleasant distractions while flying. Just as he'd expected, the gown fit her beautifully. He'd chosen classic silver, a perfect contrast to her golden skin. Her gown matched the threads weaved through the fabric of his shirt and kilt, not to mention his eyes and hair.

His only concession was to ensure her shoes were somewhat practical. They were heels, not too high that she couldn't run if they met danger, and most definitely not high enough to use the heel as a deadly weapon. Her shoulders were only slightly obscured by a black silken scarf with his royal lineage emblazoned in silver. He wanted to make it quite clear that if anyone harmed Nalea, they would face Roden's wrath.

She spent the next several minutes of the flight fidgeting and tugging at her gown.

The seat back was narrow, designed as it was for Draeken anatomy, giving him plenty of room to flex his wings. He stretched his right just far enough to brush against Nalea's bare arm.

She scowled, pushing his wing away. "You really think this is funny, don't you? Could you have found a skimpier dress?"

"If you're wearing something that is clearly for fashion and cannot hide the smallest blade, then Hillas will have nothing to fear from you." He cast a sideways glance her way. "We'll be there soon. You ready to play your part?"

She rolled her eyes. "This isn't my first dog and peony show."

"It's *pony* show. You know, I find it ironic that Hillas also struggles with the English language."

"I am *nothing* like him."

"No, you're not. That's why I believe you will do the right thing."

She scowled. "I'm not doing this for you. I'm doing this because Hillas is an evil menace who needs to pay."

"And because you wish to be free," Roden added.

Nalea didn't respond.

Roden sighed. "I gave you my word you'd be free, didn't I?"

"Freedom doesn't mean much when someone's dead," she replied.

His lips thinned. "If you don't survive, that means this whole thing went to hells, and I won't be left breathing either. Personally, I'd like to stay alive for a few more years. The plan won't be successful unless we *both* live. If we can't count on each other, we're dead already. We have to trust each other if we're going to succeed."

She narrowed her gaze at him. "I'll trust you as much as you trust me; how about that?"

He grinned. "I accept." As long as she played along, it didn't matter what she believed. The endgame was all-important, though her commitment and trust would become crucial if they did somehow survive until the next day. Yet when he told her what the real endgame was, he suspected he'd receive neither her commitment nor her trust... especially when she learned that he had no intentions of granting her freedom.

They were farther north now, somewhere over Canada, with only a couple of hundred more miles of forest to cover before they reached Hillas' earthside base. A light bleeped on the panel. His fingers flew across the screen as he punched in the entry access codes. "We're here. Are you ready to do this, dear?"

She blew him a kiss, the action looking more hostile than friendly.

After they docked, he typed in a special code to secure and hold the ship on standby should they need to make a quick escape. He then typed in one more code; one no one knew. He'd made some special modifications to his ship. Even Hillas couldn't bypass this code without destroying the ship in the process.

Nalea stood and stepped toward the door. He held out a hand. "Shall we?"

Her glare would've shredded a lesser Draeken's confidence. Fortunately, Roden was no insignificant male. He held up a pair of silver-rimmed dark glasses and waited until she snatched them from his hand, slid them on, and then—finally—slipped her hand into his before he entered the code to open the door. Her grip was firm, as though she desired to break his fingers. He ran a thumb over her skin, and her lips formed a hard line.

The door slid open to reveal three of Hillas' guardsmen awaiting their arrival. For protocol, only one was sufficient to escort Roden to the Grand Lord. Sending more was a brazen display of power. Three guardsmen? An affront to his pride; it would take at least a half dozen to take down Roden. Hillas clearly underestimated his Second. And that would be his downfall.

Brushing against his wings, Nalea moved around Roden to step out of the ship first, with Roden right behind, still holding his hand. When he stood at her side, she looked up at him and gave him a warm smile.

Fyet, the woman could act.

Chapter 12

Nalea expected betrayal. Or she at least expected Roden to kick his plan into action the moment the guardsmen closed the door behind them. She hadn't expected the *waiting*.

It'd been over an hour since they'd been left alone in a small office, and still no sign of Hillas. Oh, she had no doubt the Grand Lord was watching them that very moment. She tried to play her part, a part made no easier by the chilly temperature. Roden had said the Draeken were facing the same power shortage her people were, and the cold supported his statement. The lights were dim enough that she could remove the dark glasses Roden had given her earlier, but she'd left them on so that Roden couldn't see her eyes.

Unlike Nalea, stuck in a scrap of clothing and acting as a well-behaved consort, Roden had it easy. He didn't have to act. He was being his usual arrogant self. He sat opposite her, watching her while leisurely propped up on an elbow.

In between idle chat with her 'consort', she tugged at the dress as she tried to find a more comfortable seating position. Her chair was like Roden's, a classic Draeken style made of ornate metals with a narrow curving back to accommodate wings; in other words, uncomfortable. She blew out a breath. "He knew you were coming, right?"

"Yes." Roden frowned. "He's not usually so late."

An alarm blared, the deep tones reverberating through the room.

Roden and Nalea jumped to their feet.

"They found the base," he said, as though speaking his thoughts aloud.

Did he sound pleased? Nalea sucked in a breath. "Who?"

"Sephians," he replied, and then added drily, "And their new friends, I suspect."

Had her people aligned with the humans? Sienna and Apolo had been planning another meeting with several indigenous leaders before she'd been taken, but that had been months ago. She could only hope they'd aligned and not become slaves to yet another race.

A cacophony of gunshots and blaster shots sounded outside the main door. Roden pulled out a blaster, turned, and headed toward the side door. "Sounds like they're in the landing bay. This room is close enough that if they're any good, they'll get here within minutes. I suggest we move to somewhere a bit more secure."

He opened the door. He never saw the chair coming crashing down on his head from behind. He crumpled, his head hitting the floor with a loud *crack*. He wasn't out cold but was definitely incapacitated as he sought to regain his bearings.

Nalea dropped the chair and tried to bite back the guilt roiling in her as she stepped on Roden's wrist, relieving him of his weapon as he groggily reached out for her, then stepped over him and bolted through the doorway. Once in the hallway, the need for freedom quickly overcame guilt.

Knowing Roden would be back on his feet within seconds and extremely pissed off, she weaved as quickly as she could through the winding hallways without risking a twisted ankle. Taking the route they'd been led, she ran directly toward the sound of gunfire.

As she slowed to turn a sharp corner, a hole appeared in the wall near Nalea's right shoulder. She stumbled to an abrupt stop.

"Don't move," a familiar masculine voice called out with the welcome lilt of a Sephian accent.

Nalea sucked in a breath when she linked the Sephian with the voice. "Apolo?"

"Nalea?" Apolo scowled, then his eyes widened. He held out his arms and she sprang into them. He embraced her hard, and she didn't let go.

"*Suvaste*, I thought you were dead. Praise the gods he was wrong."

"You don't know how good it is to see you," she said. "How in the hells did you find this place?"

"My spy sent a beacon; lit up this base on the grid like an erupting volcano."

"Kreed is alive?" Nalea asked. The last she'd heard, Apolo's spy had gone dark. Everyone had assumed he'd been compromised.

Apolo nodded, then took a step back and frowned. "What in the gods' names are you wearing?"

"Long story," she muttered. "We need to hurry. Roden is right behind me."

At the mention of the Draeken's name, Apolo raised his blaster toward the hallway. He grimaced. "Justice will have to wait. Right now, we need to get you out of here."

Exhilaration shot through her, only to be smothered by a sense of impending doom. When Apolo pulled her forward, she dug in her heels.

The sound of multiple pairs of pounding boots broke through the silence. Apolo glanced down the hallway, and then turned back to her, frowning. "We have to move fast. This is just the first assault on this base. We may have caught them off guard, but they'll regroup quickly. We need to be out of here by then."

Furious at herself, she slammed her palm against the wall. "I have to stay here."

"What are you talking about?" Apolo said, tightening his grip.

She pulled him into another embrace and kissed his cheek. "I have a shot at Hillas, and I've got to take it." She wanted to leave more than anything, but running was selfish, pure and simple. Despite not trusting Roden, he had given her a chance to eliminate the Grand Lord and end the devil's reign.

"We'll go after him together. It's too dangerous here."

"I can't," she said, standing taller.

After a second of watching her, Apolo shook his head and stepped back. "I understand why you need to do it. I'll try to get Kreed to you. If it's possible, he'll get you out of this mess." His words sounded tired and laden with remorse.

She nodded. "Thanks."

With that, Apolo broke away from her and turned back the way he'd come. He looked back. "And, Nalea?"

She raised her brows. "What?"

He gave her a warm smile. "We'll get you back." Her leader gave her one last look before turning back toward the approaching boots.

Her mind swirled and her heart ached as though she'd never see Apolo again, but regardless of her feelings, she was doing the right thing. Like it or not, she and a particular Draeken lord were the best chance Earth had against a despot.

A vise gripped her neck and wrenched her backward, throwing her against the wall hard enough that her vision went black. She kicked out, knocking her opponent away. She swung up the blaster, only to have the weapon snatched from her hand. Her vision returned, revealing a furious Roden.

He maintained an iron grip on her wrist. She let him yank her through the hallways and away from the sounds of gunfire.

Still coughing for air, she said, "I was... coming back... for you."

He stopped abruptly and she stumbled against his back. His wings flicked angrily in response. He turned to face her. Blood still flowed from his head, a sign that didn't bode well for either Roden's current temper or his retaliation later. His eyes were hard and cold. "Lies don't suit you."

His eyes shone bright with fury, and he yanked her forward again. The sound of gunfire was closing on them. Nalea picked up the pace, but still struggled to keep up with the taller Draeken.

Roden pulled her through winding, empty hallways, and she let him. When they met Draeken guardsmen, they paused only long enough for Roden to send them off with a curt command.

He kept a firm grip on her as he rushed down hallways until the sounds behind them tapered off. They continued on, every now and then stopping to find a locked door. He would curse and move on, clearly little more familiar with this particular base than Nalea herself was.

He turned them down a darker hallway than the one they'd been in before. No lights were installed there yet. He moved to the side. "*Fyet*. Can you find a door?"

Nalea pulled free from Roden and stepped in front. Her eyes adjusted to the dark and she walked forward, slowly at first, then jogging as she headed toward indentions in the walls. Doors... and not just any doors; these didn't even have security tags on them yet.

Nalea skimmed past the first and chose the second. The door opened easily, and she stepped into the small room. Sized for a typical sleeping room, it wasn't much larger than a closet, just enough room for a bed and trunk. Hillas was expanding this base, but where was he going to find more guardsmen? *Was there more than one core ship?*

Roden pressed the door closed and turned to face her, although in the darkness she doubted he could see anything. She watched the blaster he held at his side. It was then she realized that the entire time he'd pulled her through the hallways, and even now, he'd never once pointed the weapon at her.

She stepped closer, wrapping her hand around the wrist of the hand holding the weapon. "The game's changed, Roden," she whispered. "I'm here now because I *chose* to stay. I'm no longer your prisoner. I'm your godsdamned *tahren,* and I'll never be your possession."

The small room suddenly felt smaller. Instinctively, Nalea placed her hand on Roden's chest to hold him at bay. His heart beat strong and steady beneath her palm, while hers beat shallow and fast.

"*Tahren?* Does that mean you're going to accept the bond?" he asked.

She took a deep breath. "For now." But not for the reason he thought.

He nuzzled her ear, his breath sending a shiver through her. "You start this, there will be no stopping. You'll always be connected to me."

"I know." She'd deal with the repercussions later. And rather than fear or fury, she felt anticipation. She grabbed him behind the neck and pulled him down to her lips. In the dark, she felt her way around him, her fingers discovered skin battered by scars. Draeken, with their advanced technology, rarely scarred. Roden Zyll was a man who'd clearly seen battles much of his life.

As she embraced him, she reached deep into herself and let her energy flow upward and outward, similar to how she'd healed fellow Sephians before. She could feel warmth under her fingers and through her lips as her energy seeped outward, a little at first, then more. Roden, not being a Sephian, couldn't send out his energy, yet hers seemed to have no trouble reaching into him.

The room began to get hotter, and she realized that the source was her. His emotions snuck up on her. They slithered around her soul like small snakes, tickling it, and then they penetrated her all at once. She gasped.

Roden grabbed onto her, never letting go, as she acclimated herself to the bond. It felt as though she'd walked from the night into the blinding sun. Suddenly, she was no longer alone within her body. Jammed right alongside her thoughts and feelings, she could feel something *more*. Roden's emotions, glimpses of his intentions, his very essence had imprinted itself on her soul. Her heart pounded.

"Are you all right?"

Roden's words were soft and gentle. His breathing was tight, as though he was also undergoing a transformation.

"It's done," she whispered.

"Regrets?"

"No." Now Roden couldn't lie to her; she'd be able to see his intentions before he acted. They were finally on a level playing field.

"Good."

She sensed pleasure in his response. "I still hate you," she said.

He kissed her shoulder. "I know." Not even the slightest disagreement. A spark of hurt flashed within her, but it was smothered all too quickly. "Apolo and his team will be gone by now. The hallways should be safe."

He opened the door and stepped into the hallway. After a moment, he holstered his weapon.

She frowned as she joined him. "How'd you know Apolo was here?"

"No doubt their recon mission didn't go as planned," he continued, ignoring her question. "Now that Hillas knows his base location has been compromised, he can't evacuate without looking like he's running scared, and his pride would never allow that."

They walked down the same hallways they'd fled ten minutes

earlier. A guardsman came running forward to meet them. "Lord Commander Zyll."

Roden waved a hand through the air. "Well, get on with it."

"Yes, sir. The Grand Lord has requested the presence of you and your consort."

"I see his timing is as impeccable as ever," Roden drawled, the sarcasm dripping from his words. Hen held out a hand to Nalea. "It's time, my dear."

She slid her hand into his and focused intently on not showing any surprise that Roden had pressed a small blade into her palm.

Chapter 13

An hour later, Roden and Nalea were sitting in a different office, set up much like the one they'd sat in a couple of hours earlier. But much had changed. This time, Roden wouldn't let Nalea put space between them. Oh, she'd tried to take a lone chair when they'd first entered the room, but he'd held onto her hand, silently directing her to sit next to him on a small sofa.

No matter how convincing she was, he also knew he could not yet trust her. The only thing he could trust was that they both wanted Hillas dead. They may have different reasons, but that didn't matter. Within the night, Hillas would be gone, setting up the pieces for the endgame.

Of course, that meant he had to convince the daughter of Hillas that serving as the Draeken Grand Lord was the right thing to do—a feat he believed would be far more challenging than a royal assassination.

But the risk would be worth it. With Nalea at his side, they could end the hostilities between their peoples. Together, they'd have a better chance at brokering a lasting peace with humans, and the Draeken could make a home on Earth. But there was still much work to be done. Integrating his people into an established society meant they'd have new laws to follow, new customs and traditions to learn.

He glanced down to see Nalea watching him curiously, and he wondered if she could sense his emotions. Realizing his new vulnerability, he inhaled, forcing calmness to blanket him.

The door to his left opened, and two guardsmen stepped in to stand at each side of the door. Nalea tensed, and without thinking, he wrapped a protective arm around her, as they both came to their feet.

The Grand Lord entered. He wore the gaudy colors of his royal heritage. Bright yellows and purples bled into reds and blues. Since the beginning, the Puftan family had been anything but humble. Hillas' hair was pinned neatly by a long feather. His wings arched proudly behind him. He didn't look the least bit piqued that his base had just been infiltrated.

Hillas looked down his nose at Roden, who looked right back at his leader.

This moment had been coming for some time. After the poisoned rum, Roden had been looking forward to it. Within minutes, Hillas—or Roden and Nalea—would be dead. Roden had planned for both outcomes. If Hillas were dead, he'd lead his people. If Roden and Nalea were killed, his people would quickly learn of Hillas' betrayal and reject their Grand Lord. One thing was certain about the traditional Draeken: they would never forgive a Draeken who killed his own daughter.

"Lord Zyll," Hillas said as he took a seat across from them.

Roden lowered his head. "Your Highness."

"I apologize for my tardiness. After you first arrived, we picked up a beacon from somewhere on the base."

The insinuation was clear. Roden raised a brow.

"When the gold-skins breached the base, the reasoning for the beacon became quite clear. Nevertheless, we have turned the infil-trators away."

"For now," Roden replied with a slight tilt of his head.

Hillas waved a hand in the air. "But that's not why I brought you here. I'm far more curious about the Sephian in your arms. Have her come closer so I can better see her."

Roden released Nalea. With every step she took, he stayed by her side. She stopped only a few feet from his leader.

"Your Highness," Roden held a hand before the woman at his side. "May I introduce my consort, Lady Nalea Zyll."

Hillas scowled. "I'm disappointed that you didn't inform me of your intentions toward my daughter." He came back to his feet. His gaze examined her, starting at her face before moving downward. "You turned out nicely for a half-breed."

Nalea made no movement and spoke no words, but Roden knew she was fighting an internal battle to not leap onto Hillas and kill him. After all, Roden craved to do the same thing.

Hillas crossed his arms over his chest, aiming a stern look in Roden's direction. "A bit presumptuous giving your last name to my daughter. Her last name is Puftan until I declare differently."

But before he could speak, Nalea stepped forward and jutted her chin out. "Your blood may run through my veins, Your Highness, but that doesn't make me a Puftan. I choose my consort, and I choose the name I bear." She tossed a look at Roden. *And I'm not a Zyll,* he translated.

"Thank you for delivering my daughter to me," Hillas said, as though Nalea had not spoken. "Although, I see she has yet to learn common Draeken courtesy. We'll continue this discussion in private." He snapped his fingers, and the guardsmen at the door stepped forward. "Escort my daughter to my sitting room."

Roden stepped between the Draeken and Nalea. "Nalea *Zyll* is my consort and she stays." He glared at Hillas. "She will not die today." He then turned to the guards. "We have things to discuss, so get the *fyet* out of here."

The guardsmen looked to Hillas, and Roden glanced back,

giving the Grand Lord a hard look. "You want to try to take my consort, you have to go through me."

After a moment, Hillas dismissed his guardsmen with a distracted wave. "Return to your positions."

Roden tried not to show disappointment that Hillas kept his guardsmen in the room. Regardless, it wouldn't change his plans; he could easily handle two armed guardsmen. He moved to stand at Nalea's side. He spared a glance in her direction and was pleased to find her surprisingly calm.

"You should have brought her directly to me when you learned," Hillas said.

Nalea went to take a step forward, and Roden stopped her with a light touch to her hand. She gave him a questioning look, and he gave the slightest shake of his head. *Not yet.*

Roden faced Hillas. "We were unsure of where you stood on the matter, especially under the… *circumstances* of her lineage."

Hillas smiled, but there was nothing kind or genuine about it. "I have a daughter. That is reason to celebrate."

"It is, Your Highness," Roden said, but he didn't believe the Grand Lord for an instant. He knew about the other children Hillas had sired and subsequently killed. Everyone suspected Hillas had a hand in his younger brother's disappearance as well. "However, I doubt you brought us here purely for a family reunion."

"I'm disappointed in you, Roden," Hillas said. "I sense you have lost your respect for the office of the Grand Lord."

Roden heard the door open and the sound of three pairs—if not more—of bootsteps came up behind him, but none of the expected blows came.

Nalea tensed at his side. Roden turned once again to Hillas. "As we speak, a communiqué has gone out to all core ships announcing that we found your long-lost daughter and that she's become my consort. If you kill us, you will lose the support of the Draeken people."

Hillas guffawed. "I have no desire to kill my loyal subjects," he said a bit too quickly.

Roden belted out a laugh, and then his features straightened. "Did I also mention that if Nalea or I don't return to my camp unharmed by morning, a second communiqué will go out; one that contains a list of names—all within the Puftan bloodline—who met untimely deaths during your reign?"

The older lord's face reddened, and he jumped to his feet. "Lies!"

Roden lifted his brows.

Hillas slammed a fist on the desk. "They're my people and they'll follow me despite whatever propaganda you send out."

"Your reign is at an end," Nalea said from Roden's side. "My people have made peace with the humans. They'll be back to finish what they've started. If you don't submit, you don't stand a chance."

Roden admired her strength.

Hillas did not. His silver eyes narrowed onto the woman. "Submit? Never!" He swung a shock baton. Roden grabbed the Draeken's wrist as the metal connected with Nalea's skin.

She yanked the baton from his hand.

Roden was tackled from behind by two guardsmen. As he was pulled to his feet, Hillas swung out and punched him. Hillas was old and weak, and while Roden's vision flashed momentarily, he'd taken harder punches as a boy. He was tempted to return the favor, except he knew how delicate the situation was. Instead, he allowed the two guardsmen to restrain him.

He shot a hard look at the Grand Lord. "In case you haven't noticed, we're an endangered race. Without power, we aren't leaving this world. Without human support, we'll have to fight for the right to live here. If you don't make peace, and soon, you doom the Draeken to never-ending war."

"Bah!" Hillas cried out. He turned and walked to the wall, pressed several buttons, and a panel opened. He pulled out an octagon-shaped box covered by smooth dark metal on all sides. "The humans *need* us. The inhabitants of this planet have no technology to speak of. They couldn't breach our defenses with their best weapons. They got through today because of a traitor and with weapons the gold-skins stole from us. Humans, Sephians... they are *nothing*."

Roden eyed Hillas suspiciously and saw Nalea take a step to the side.

"However, this is everything. This..."—Hillas held out the box—"guarantees Draeken supremacy over this planet."

Chapter 14

Nalea stood frozen as Hillas' fingers ran across the dark surfaces of the box. A glow emanated from the box as it began to hum. She covered her eyes as the familiar thrum that powered all their ships brushed over her.

This changes everything.

If Hillas could recharge the power cells, the Draeken core ship would be unstoppable. The people on this world would be doomed. Even with few numbers, the Draeken could turn humans into slaves. It'd be Sephia all over again.

"It's been tested? It works with our technology?" Roden asked. His voice was steady, yet she could sense his unease. He, too, knew the implications, and wasn't happy.

Hillas beamed like a happy child. "The power cells work. It was simply trial and error to find the right solar frequencies."

Roden spoke. "How long before you have enough power cells to eliminate our power shortage?"

"Not long now," Hillas replied. "The Sephians will run out of power within weeks. Once they can no longer contact Sephia, nothing stands against me. This world is rightfully mine. She"— he gestured to Nalea—"must die today. But you, Roden Zyll, for your treachery, I will keep you alive just long enough to witness my glory."

She turned to Roden, and they exchanged a knowing glance. Battle-born, they both had an innate sense for timing. Roden pushed backward, knocking the guardsman off-balance. He pulled out his sword and killed one in a blink of an eye. He'd taken down the second guardsman by the time Nalea threw the shock baton.

Hillas roared in pain when the baton hit him, sending small lightning bolts of current over his skin. The baton clanged to the ground as Nalea launched at the Grand Lord, gripping the small blade Roden had given her. Hillas had no time to react. She tackled him, and he clawed at her flesh. Her first stab at his heart missed when he shoved at her, and she hit a lung instead. He grunted then started to yell something. Whatever he was about to scream was cut off when she sliced his throat from ear to ear.

Blood sprayed out from his jugular, splattering her face and covering her hand, causing her hold on the blade to slip. She stayed on him, pushing his hands away as he weakly pushed against her. After wiping her hand and the blade on his chest, she gripped the knife again.

It was a small blade—she'd have to go deep. Taking a deep breath, she plunged the blade into his heart, making certain not to miss this time. His hands wrapped loosely around hers, which were still around the blade. He looked genuinely confused as the life ebbed from his eyes.

She watched him die. *You're not immortal. You die just like anyone.*

There was no sound other than the ringing in her ears. She stared blankly at the Draeken beneath her. She brushed aside a blood-soaked strand of hair from his face. This was the lord who she'd spent a lifetime running from, a lifetime dreading. Covered in blood and lifeless, he didn't look like the great Draeken leader who'd raped her mother. He didn't look like a monster to be feared. He looked just like any other dead Draeken.

She pushed to her feet and stumbled backward. Numbness

wrapped around her heart in a loving caress, and she turned in a circle, trying to get her bearings. In a daze, she stared at the scene for a second or more before she remembered that she wasn't alone with Hillas.

The floor was littered with winged bodies. In the center of it all stood Roden, covered in blood and swinging his sword, slicing through tendons and muscles as another guardsman attacked. His opponent fell in a heap.

Roden glanced back to Nalea. Splattered with blood, she watched him move like a dancer. Suddenly, her eyes widened, and she leapt forward. "Behind you!"

Five more guardsmen rushed through the door. Roden took out one before the guardsman could fire. Another one got off a shot before Roden skewered his heart. Agony burned through Nalea's shoulder, and she cried out at the same time Roden snarled.

She grabbed at her shoulder only to find the skin smooth. Confused, she looked up and realized that she hadn't been shot; she'd *felt* Roden get shot.

The remaining three guardsmen dropped their weapons and went for their swords. They surrounded Roden, ignoring the practically weaponless Nalea to focus on the greater risk. Their mistake... She rushed forward and grabbed the wing of the guardsman who foolishly gave her his back. He twisted around as she slid her small blade into his liver. He went down, giving her a better angle to swing around and slice her taller opponent's throat.

Roden closed the ranks with Nalea at his side and held out his sword. "The Grand Lord is dead. Drop your swords," he commanded.

Neither of the two remaining Draeken dropped their weapon immediately. They both looked around the room, and it was almost comical how both attained the same expression when their gaze fell on the body behind Nalea.

One guardsman dropped his sword and bowed. The other lunged forward. *Fool*, Nalea thought as Roden parried the blow. Even with his injury, Roden swept to the side and made a direct hit to his opponent's side. The guardsman fell to the floor and Roden lifted his blade, bringing it down into the guardsman's heart, making it an honorable death.

Roden smashed against the wall. "Secure the door," he ordered to the only remaining guardsman, who obeyed without question.

Roden turned around and slid his sword into its scabbard, and Nalea rushed for him just as he started to sway.

"You got him?"

She nodded, glancing back. A river of blood continued to trickle from the dead guardsman's neck.

"Good," Roden said with a wince.

Nalea examined his wound. The skin was charred, but it'd been a clean shot through his shoulder and wing and into the wall behind him. He flexed his wing and winced again. "We have to get you medical attention," she blurted out.

"After we get out of here," he muttered. "Things will be chaotic for several hours. We need to ensure your safety."

Nalea eyed the other Draeken in the room. The young guardsman looked scared, but she couldn't fault him that. "You're safer if you come with us."

The guardsman gulped, and then nodded.

She paused, then turned and headed back to Hillas' desk. Bending down, she picked up the power cell and strode back to Roden. "Now we can get out the hells out of here."

A *whoosh* behind her brought both her and Roden around to see the wall open, and they found themselves facing the nasty ends of at least a half dozen blasters and several swords. Guardsmen filtered in and made room for an older Draeken to stroll through the middle. "Greetings."

Nalea gasped. *Impossible.* She felt Roden's frustration as strongly as her own confusion. "How can it be?" she whispered.

"Hillas' body double. Don't worry. You got the right one," Roden replied, attempting to step in front of her to protect her, only to have her move to cover his front. "I didn't realize you survived the trip, Otas."

"I think I'll go by Hillas now. And that's Grand Lord to you. Or, Your Highness, if you prefer," he sneered. He then motioned, and a shot was fired. The guardsman at Roden's other side collapsed with a thud. "I should thank you, Roden. I'd been looking for the right way to make the change more permanent for some time."

"The people will see through your disguise," Roden countered.

"They haven't yet," Hillas smiled. "I believe my people will gladly continue to follow Hillas over you. Look around you. The Draeken people have been swallowed by chaos. They need something consistent in their lives. Even the Grand Lord's guardsmen see the logic."

Nalea spoke. "The Grand Lord is dead. There's no reason to follow his doomed plan."

Otas took a step forward. "He knew what was needed to keep our people strong. The plan will work. It's infallible."

"The people won't follow you once they read the communiqués," Roden bartered.

"Ah, yes, the communiqués," the new Hillas replied. "Fortunately, I learned of them in time to intercept your second communiqué."

"But the first one was delivered," Roden rebuked. "Meaning the Draeken people know that you have Nalea and me. If you kill us, you won't like their response."

Otas nodded. "I'm no fool. That's why you are both players in my plan. That I wasn't born Hillas Puftan won't matter for much longer."

Roden barked out a laugh. "You're a fool."

"I'd rather die than serve you," Nalea shot out, trying to buy time to figure out an escape.

"Oh, you will do exactly that," Hillas' doppelgänger replied with scorn. "You will serve me or die." He motioned to the guardsmen.

Roden lunged forward to protect Nalea, but it was too late.

The guardsmen opened fire.

Chapter 15

As soon as she awoke to find herself alone in a small cell, Nalea shivered. She'd been a prisoner yesterday, but today was different. With Roden, she'd found comfort in the belief that he wouldn't torture her or kill her. He'd seen value in her. Now, she had none of that comfort.

She assumed Roden was still alive, but she suspected he was also in a small cell. A pang of remorse flitted through her. Despite everything he'd done, she believed he had tried to do the right thing by his people. He didn't deserve to die. She glanced around the stark cell. *Not like this.*

"*Suvaste*," she muttered as she tried to tuck her head against her shoulder. Even with her eyes clenched shut, the bright light burned, adding to her headache and the aches resulting from the stun blast. Protected only by the thin dress, her golden skin reflected the glare, multiplying the effect of the lights installed on the ceiling, walls, and floors. If her hands weren't restrained behind her back, she would've covered her eyes. White light nearly as bright as the planet's star scorched her senses and seared her skin.

She knew the routine. First, the light, then the torture. She held no illusions. She wouldn't survive this cell. Too bad; she had so much to tell Apolo. If only she could have gotten the power cell to Apolo, he could have returned to Sephia to be with his *tahren* Krysea again.

"Oh." In that instant, she felt something that hadn't come from her. *Roden's awake, and he's very pissed off.*

Her jaw tingled then her back burned like a nerve had been pinched in a cluster of cells near her shoulder. She leaned back against the wall. If she'd had wings, she would've been able to pinpoint where the phantom pain had been centralized.

Roden's torture had begun.

And they weren't taking it easy on him.

For what seemed like an eternity, she allowed herself to feel the echoes of phantom pain. Her face tingled, her lungs burned, and her leg throbbed. Her stomach felt as though she'd had the flu for a week. Then, as abruptly as they hit her, the sensations disappeared.

"*Fyet,*" she muttered and then added on a "*Suvaste*" after realizing that she'd spoken Draeken slang. She frowned as a new emotion emerged; one she hadn't felt in a long time. It took her a moment to find the right name for it. *Concern.* Not since she was a child had she actually worried for a *Draeken*.

A part of her still hated Roden, because he'd never given her a choice, really. Either way she would've died in a prison cell. At least this way, she'd had the chance to kill Hillas. *And I succeeded.*

Only to have another one take his place.

As she waited for Roden to wake and for the next wave of his torture to give her comfort that he was still alive, her mind began to form a plan. She had a chance at survival, but the only way to make it work meant that she'd have to do two things. First, her people would have to believe she betrayed them and, second, she'd have to make an enemy out of Roden Zyll.

"*F yet da*, Otas," Roden said after spitting out a mouthful of blood, the splatter hitting the doppelgänger's highly polished boots. The prim, older Draeken glanced down at his boots in disdain and took a step back with a frown. Ironic, since Otas Olnek had been born a beggar. Roden may have done his share of hypocrisy, but this Hillas was by far the biggest hypocrite of them all. Everything Otas had accomplished was simply because he'd volunteered to look like someone else.

Roden had awoken to find Otas standing over him 'and knew they were about to have a 'conversation'. The first round was just warm-up.

Otas looked down upon Roden. "Things would be so much simpler if only you'd died back at your base like Hillas wanted."

He chuckled, though the movement cost him dearly. "Sorry to disappoint."

Otas motioned to the guardsman at Roden's side. The guardsman swung the heavy shock baton, and it landed with an electric jolt on Roden's already injured wing. He snarled, only to have his restraints retract, brutally yanking him back against the wall. His limbs were taut and unable to move. He stood spread out before Otas, naked save for his kilt, which the imposter Hillas left on likely to reflect the real Grand Lord's sensibilities and certainly not out of civility for Roden.

"You really think you can pull this off, Otas? You've done nothing original in your life. Everything you've done was to imitate a once-great lord."

He tensed his muscles for what came next: first a hit to the gut, slamming the air from his lungs, then a battering on the limbs. Pulsing agony sent his body into spasms with each connection from the shock baton. An especially direct hit to his shin brought a grunt. The sound was all the guardsman needed; he turned up the intensity meter on the baton, and more hits ensued.

When he could breathe again, he ground out his next words. "Is that all you have, Meyt? I taught you better than that."

He had no idea what the guardsman replied with; his right ear was ringing too loudly from being struck, his ear drum likely shattered. At least he could see that he'd pissed off the guard, and he'd take every win he could get. A few more hits and he'd pass out again. It was the only thing he could do until he killed this bastard impersonator.

Meyt lifted the baton high above his head. Just as he began to swing, a hand grabbed the guardsman's forearm.

"Enough," Otas said before pulling his hand back. "We don't want him to be irreparably damaged. Not yet. He still has an important role to play. You've done enough for one day."

Meyt handed over the shock baton and left, only to be replaced by another guardsman.

Roden glared at the guardsman from his base. "I knew it was you who poisoned my rum, Elng. Tell me, what made you betray your people?"

Elng pursed his lips. "I'm looking at the betrayer of my people."

"You'd rather follow an imposter?"

Elng didn't reply. His jaw was clenched too tightly shut. He'd chosen the wrong side and he knew it.

Roden tried to keep his head lifted to watch as Otas walked over to the wall and pressed a button. Several pillars rose from the floor in a half circle around Roden, and he was forced to pull his wings even tighter to keep from getting skewered. He pressed another button, and a hum filled the room, nearly drowning his ability to reason.

Roden frowned. Why would Otas bother using a disjunctor around him? A disjunctor's only purpose was to prevent Sephians from sensing their *tahren*. What game was Otas playing to shield Roden from Nalea?

The elder strolled toward him, the bars and restraints the only things keeping Roden from biting out Otas's throat. Otas crossed his arms over his chest, putting his fat belly on display. "You will provide your staunch support to me onscreen. Your speech will be broadcast across every Draeken channel tomorrow."

Roden managed a sneer. "Why would I pledge my support to a pale imitation?" The restraints pulled at him, burning his limbs. An unquestionable *pop* sent a blinding pain into his shoulder. He sucked in a breath. *Dislocated.*

"If you don't play your part well," Otas said. "Nalea will die a long and painful death. I'll broadcast footage of you torturing and killing your own consort."

The restraints slackened a little and Roden struggled to stay on his feet, the muscles in his legs shaking, his lungs struggling for air. He forced himself to look up at the imposter. "I look forward to tearing the wings from your back, Otas. They'll decorate the walls of my office."

Red fury filled Otas's cheeks. He spun around and stomped toward the door. In the doorway, he paused. "If you don't help me, your consort *will* die."

Roden refused to show concern, refused to let Otas see any sign of weakness for Nalea.

After watching Roden for another long moment, Otas left the room, leaving Roden alone with Elng and the hum of the disjunctor. He sagged. His dislocated shoulder sent a screaming reminder, but he could no longer hold his own weight.

Elng watched him from across the cell.

"You're a fool," Roden muttered at the guardsman.

The door opened, and he inwardly cringed. *Another torture session so soon?*

A scuffle. An electrical charge filled the air, and then a loud *thud.*

Roden found the strength lift his head just enough to see Elng's unmoving form on the floor, and Wync hitting several buttons on the wall. He smiled and winced when the movement aggravated his split lip.

Roden's restraints retracted into the wall, leaving him to free-fall forward. The pillars disappeared into the floor and Wync lunged forward to grab him just before his head cracked onto the hard metal surface.

"Lea. In another cell," Roden murmured as his surroundings went in and out of focus.

An arm slipped under his dislocated shoulder, and he moaned.

"Sorry, but you're the priority. I have to get you out of here, Commander."

"No, she's—" Someone reached under his other shoulder—the one with the gunshot—and black fog bled into his vision. His wings and feet dragged along the floor as his guardsmen carried him into the hallway. He'd barely registered the alarms blaring. His troops clearly needed to work on their diversion tactics.

A blaster shot whizzed by his head. Wync returned fire while the second guardsman, Gix, covered his body with hers. He grabbed her neck and flattened them both on the ground. As Wync laid down a barrage, Roden pulled her ear close to his lips. "Gix, I need you to do something." Before she could respond, he relayed his instructions.

When he released her, she unholstered another blaster and handed it to him. "I'm not sure I—"

"Go!" he ordered.

After throwing an anxious glance over her shoulder, Gix ran back down the hallway the way they'd come.

Staying low and against the wall to avoid the gunfire, Roden turned and fired a strafing line across the hallway. Wync had downed one of the guardsmen already, leaving only one. Two blasters firing at him convinced the last guardsman that fleeing was the wiser option.

Silence reclaimed the hallway and Roden pulled himself to his feet with a grunt. Wync reached out, and Roden held a hand up. The larger Draeken stepped back with a shrug. Roden started moving forward as quickly as he could—which was pitifully slow—while trying to avoid stumbling in the spinning hallway. When they reached the next intersection, Roden took a left.

"Our ship is this way," Wync said, nodding his head in the opposite direction.

"We go this way."

"No time," Wync replied. "We're cutting it too close already."

Roden had spilled plenty of blood in his time. Being ruthless was one of his best traits. No life was worth even a hundredth of his. Until now. "You prep the ship. I'll be right there. We need her."

"But, sir…"

Roden didn't respond. The sounds of blaster shots erupted down the hallway he needed to enter. His body utterly without strength, he had to make this quick. The sounds of dozens of boots pounding on the floor came closer. He cranked a knob on his blaster, widening the blast path and stumbled down the hallway.

"*Fyet*." Wync threw his hand in the air, then grabbed him by the shoulders and twisted him around. "Sorry about this, sir."

Roden couldn't raise his arm in time to block the punch to his face. His vision blackened with white pricks of light. With consciousness fleeting, he brought a knee up hard to Wync's gut. The larger guardsman bent over with a wheeze.

Roden fell and waited as his tunneled vision widened. By the echoes in the hallway, they were vastly outnumbered. With his injuries, he was more of a ghost than a warrior, leaving Wync and him to certain death if they remained. He was useless in this condition. He scowled. "Let's go."

Wync helped Roden to his feet. By the time he stumbled into the ship bay, he knew he'd failed. The place had turned into a battle zone. Ships were on fire. Draeken fought Draeken. Sorrow filled him as he followed Wync to a small transport ship near the edge of the bay. Gix was already in the pilot's seat, plugging in navigational points, and Wync claimed the only other seat. Roden didn't argue. Mentally and physically, he was in no shape to give orders. With a sigh, he collapsed onto the floor.

He'd signed Nalea's death warrant tonight. He'd forced his troops to choose between himself and Hillas. How many Draeken would die for his decisions? Everything he'd done was to save Draeken lives, not destroy them. This was the last thing he'd wanted.

Movement at his side brought his eyes open. "Did you get it?" he asked, fighting for the strength to speak.

Gix nodded as she injected something into him. "This will help with the pain," she said. Her next words sounded distant. "You're safe now."

"No." He sighed as the drug began to steal his mind. "We just started a civil war."

Chapter 17

Nalea knew Roden was escaping when she heard the first shots. His pain flooded her with the tingled sensation again, and his fury tore at her. Of course Roden would escape. Of course he'd leave her behind. With Hillas dead, she was no longer of any value to him.

At least she wouldn't have long to sulk. The chaos outside her cell was merely delaying the inevitable. She sat cross-legged, arms bound behind her, in the center of the blazing hot cell and made her prayers to the great god of death, Uhl, as she forced her focus away from the bright lights surrounding her and away from the pain and angst coming from Roden.

And so she began to wait…

The night Nalea killed Lord Homs wasn't called Blood Night, not until days later. Ironic, really. The night started off not bloody at all. All three moons were full, with no clouds to block their pure beauty. Lord Homs had given Nalea a night off from her studies to go for a walk. She'd asked her mother to come along, but Nexa often chose to spend her nights in the company of Homs instead.

Nalea sulked, but Homs was a good lord. He'd been like a father to her. He'd even asked her once to call him so, but she'd snapped at him, and he never asked again. She walked her usual route. All the flowers were in full bloom under the night sky. It was getting late. She was just about to head back when she heard the yells.

Scrambling up the hill, she crawled under a shrub to hide. Fear gripped her. She couldn't move for forever as she watched. First the blood-charges rained down on Lord Weer's estate. Minutes later, Lord Weer was dragged, still in his sleepwear, into the courtyard. A horde of angry Sephians surrounded him. They tied the lord to a tree, and three large Sephian males approached.

In their hands they each bore a blood-whip. With each lash, Lord Weer screamed out in agony. The three continued until the lord cried out to gods he didn't believe in to help him. No one, not even his servants, came to his aid. Long after Nalea could no longer tell where the blood began and where the skin on his back ended, the Sephians stepped back, rolling their whips and fastening them to their hips.

Lord Weer hung limply from his restraints, moaning and whimpering as the poison coursed through him. The Sephians ignored him, instead talking to among themselves. One of them pointed to the west, and Nalea's eyes widened. That was the direction to her home!

She shuffled out from the bush and took off at a dead run back to her home. She had to warn Lord Homs! She ran until her chest burned and her breaths came in gasps. She kept running until her legs nearly gave out, but she never stopped. She jogged through the courtyard and up the steps, crying out when she tripped and landed hard on her knee. Pulling herself back up, she reached the top of the stairs and paused, panting.

Turning to the door, she didn't bother knocking. Just pushed the door open and stepped inside. In a rush, she jumped toward the massive bed. She reached out to wake him and froze, then ran to the window instead. Several vehicles had pulled up outside the estate, and Sephians were pouring out of them.

No! She turned back to Lord Homs, still sleeping soundly in his bed. Thought back to Lord Weer, who was probably still suffering in agony alone, but it was Lord Homs's face she saw. Homs, the only father she'd ever had, was about to suffer the same fate.

A tear fell down her cheek. Frantic, she searched the room for a place for Homs to hide. Her gaze froze on his nightstand. Silver glinted in the moonlight… The blade he always carried.

With a sniffle, she wiped her nose and stepped closer. Her body was shaking, her breath coming in short pants. When her fingers wrapped around the blade, she bit back a sob. She scolded herself. She had to do this. She had to make sure Lord Homs wouldn't hurt.

She held the knife out, and then pulled it down and toward her, as though cutting a roast. The cut was deep and jagged. Blood poured forth, looking like a dark river in the moonlight.

Nalea whimpered. The blankets next to Homs moved, and Nalea jumped back. A figure sat up, and Nalea dropped the blade.

Nexa frowned at her daughter, and then saw Homs. She raised a hand to her mouth. "Nalea, what have you done?" Yells from outside pulled her mother's attention to the window. Splitting her gaze between Nalea and the window, she went to the sill. She gasped. "It's begun!" she cried out in terror.

She pulled her daughter into her arms. "The death forces will kill me for this!"

Even with tears pouring down her cheeks, Nalea stood firm. She reached up and cupped her mother's cheeks. "Go. I will hold them off."

Her mother's eyes went wide. "I won't lose you, too."

She pushed at her mom, knowing that if she delayed, fear would make her change her mind. She bent down and picked up the bloody blade. "Go!"

Nexa glanced back at Homs and sobbed. She took another look at her daughter for a long, frozen moment, then spun and ran out the door. Nalea hastily wiped her tears and followed, but when her mother took the left stairwell, Nalea went all the way down the steps, not stopping until she walked into the middle of the courtyard.

The death force was already pulling together its ranks, and one of the three Sephians stepped forward. She held up the blade. Lord Homs's crimson blood dripped onto the ground. "We are free."

.   .   .

Nalea jolted to consciousness at the sound of the door to her cell opening. The lights were now dimmed, and the sounds of fighting had long ago melted into silence. She no longer felt anything from Roden, so he was likely unconscious again. Rather than opening her tender eyes, she laid on her back, unmoving, no need to look up to see who entered. "Hillas, or should I say, *Otas?*"

"*Daughter.*"

"Let's not play games. Hillas is dead."

The metallic *thud* of booted feet came closer. *Thud.* The shuffle of wings.

"Your *tahren* has abandoned you, just as he's abandoned his people. The coward fled without even trying to save you. I have it on video if you'd like to see."

"No, thanks." She forced her body to remain calm. *Breathe. Relax. Breathe.*

"I see you're not surprised."

"Should I be?"

"Look at me." When she didn't, he raised his voice. "I command you to look at me."

Exhaling, Nalea pushed up to a sitting position. Tired muscles protested the movement. She pried her dry, burned eyes open, and the air assaulted them.

A finger caught a runaway tear. Distorted, Hillas' face came into view. If she didn't know better, it almost looked as though he was concerned, though they'd never met before tonight. "They never should've left the lights on. It was never my intention to harm you. I'll see to it that you get medical attention."

She saw right through his tactics. The old sympathy ploy. "Why should you care?" she countered.

"We are family."

"Bullshit."

"Fair enough." He knelt before her. "I care because we can help each other."

While she'd spent her life hating Hillas and the Draeken, her hands were figuratively—and quite literally—tied. "Go on."

"We can help both our people by standing together." Hillas said. "I have no hatred toward the gold-skins. Together, we can broker a peace."

She came to her feet and he took a step back. "I saw the power cells. What's to stop you from just taking what you want?"

He blew out a puff of air. "A wise lord once told me that the threat of power was better than power. He planned to force peace upon this world. Now it is my place to bring peace; one way or another."

As he spoke, she realized that while he lacked the strength and wisdom of the Grand Lord, Otas had confidence. He just didn't have the gift for leadership. It was inevitable that he would be discovered for the fraud he was.

She tightened her lips. When that time came, if he wasn't aligned with a Puftan, he'd be publicly executed. He *needed* Nalea. Not only was her life safe for now, but she could turn Otas's weakness to her advantage. "If I play along with your little charade and act the good little Puftan, there can be no further aggressions against the Sephians."

He balked. "We haven't attacked the Sephians once since leaving Sephia."

"You attacked our base," she countered.

"We had no intention on killing anyone. We'd simply gone there to secure the base, nothing more."

Her lips curled. "You play with words."

He brushed her off. "I do not wish to launch an offensive against the Sephians, but if they continue to attack our people, I will be forced to retaliate." He began to pace. "Perhaps if you were to talk with your people…"

Nalea sighed. "I don't have that kind of authority."

His lips curved upward. "You underestimate your authority.

You're a member of a trinity. The Sephians will listen, especially if it's to save lives."

We'll see about that.

After a moment, Otas spoke again. "Do you agree to those terms?"

She lifted her chin. "I'm not finished," she said. "There will also be no aggressions against the humans."

He cocked his head, watching her for a moment. "We've never attacked the humans before and will not... unless we're forced. Satisfied?"

She watched him for a bit, and then gave a tight nod. "You have a deal, *father*."

He smiled then tapped something on his wrist-comm.

A guardsman entered.

"Release my daughter," he commanded.

The guardsman walked toward her without questioning the command. How many knew that the Grand Lord was dead? Outside of the few who'd ambushed Roden and her, she suspected Otas was misleading most of this base and the core ship.

The guardsman turned her around and she bit back the urge to try to fight or flee as he freed her from her hand restraints. As soon as her hands were free, she snapped around to face the two Draeken.

Otas was watching her suspiciously. "Tell me, what do you think of Roden Zyll?"

"I don't." The response was swift and hard.

"And yet you're his consort. I know enough about Roden to know the choice was yours."

"I was going to die." Either at Roden's hands or at Hillas', it didn't matter. The result was the same. "I had nothing to lose."

His lips curled into a grin. "The Puftan blood runs strong in you. A Puftan would always seize a chance. You remind me of him." He brushed his thumb over his lips. "If you had the opportunity to be released from the bond, would you take it?"

She raised her brows. "I don't understand."

"Answer my question first."

"I have no need to feel Roden."

"What if you could break the bond?"

She watched him closely. "The bond can only be broken through death."

"Roden will die in due time. Until then…" Otas pulled out a thick gold chain with a gaudy pendant hanging from it. The front of the pendant was emblazoned with the royal Puftan crest. "This is a portable disjunctor. While you wear it, you will feel nothing from him, not even the pain of his inevitable death."

"I've never heard of such a thing."

"We've rarely had a need to use it. Most *tahren* want to feel the bond."

The words stung. Steeling herself, she looked up. "Why are you offering me this?"

"It's a gift."

"*Hillas*," she scolded.

He held up a hand. "All I ask for is your support." He began to pace. "Roden has tainted his troops. They attacked this base. He has escaped and will likely begin a propaganda campaign. He can reveal the truth about me, but even he cannot dispute your heritage. With you at my side, we can stop this little uprising before the violence bleeds over to hurt your people or the inhabitants of this world."

She paused, longer than she needed, but she was in no hurry to capitulate to Otas. "If I refuse?"

"You'll remain here. Unharmed, but within this cell until you see the wisdom of my proposal. You must understand, I cannot allow freedom to someone unwilling to trust me."

Meaning she wouldn't get a chance to escape or a shot at killing Hillas—again—as long as she was in that cell. Her chin lifted. "I accept."

With a smile, Otas held up a pendant. "Allow me."

She swallowed and nodded. She stood still as he lowered the pendant over her head. The pendant was heavy; its humming metal cold.

"There. That's it."

Nalea turned around to face Otas. She brought her fingers up to feel the pendant. With a trivial hum radiating from it, the chain was thick, like the choke chains humans used on canines. It was too short to pull over her head, and she imagined it was not easily broken, but it could be done. She frowned before looking back up. "All I had to do was accept your gift, and now you're willing to trust me?"

"That's all there is to it." He smiled coldly as he stepped away from her and toward the door. "Because if you try to remove it or if I'm killed, the disjunctor will be deactivated. If you betray me, I'll deactivate it." He opened the door. "If it deactivates, it detonates, killing you and anyone within several feet of you."

Chapter 18

Furious, Roden steamed. Bracing his arms against the soft mattress, he pushed himself up and fell back with a groan. *Fyet!* He was as weak as a *fregee*. He was panting by the time he found himself on his feet, every muscle protesting. He rolled his shoulders. Fortunately, someone had put his shoulder back into place. As for the blaster wound, a thick balm covered light pink skin. While it throbbed worse than all twelve hells, he'd heal; just another scar to add to his collection.

Inch by excruciating inch, he stretched his wings. The agonizing burn of healing tendons and muscle was a welcome feeling. He would have worried if he felt nothing. It would've meant the nerve damage had been so severe he might never fly again. If only he had full Draeken medical facilities at his disposal, he'd be completely healed by now. As it was, with the extent of his healing, he suspected they'd kept him in a coma for days.

He walked toward the small window. The sunlight was bright. He shaded his eyes with a hand. A mossy well sat under the shade of lush maples. Movement caught his eye. Off in the distance a guardsman on patrol glided by, his wings outstretched. It was a calm day given how smoothly he flew. Not a single thermal to buffet the flight. Roden craved to fly again himself.

No longer able to watch, his gaze moved away from outside to the window. From what he could make out, he was in a quaint human house far from any city. Ivy invaded the edges of the glass. It was idyllic, and he wanted to destroy it.

"Lord Commander?"

Roden turned to find a haggard Draeken female. She'd always slouched, and her wings drooped.

"Can I get you anything, sir?"

He motioned. "Come in, Gix."

She nodded slightly and stepped inside the room. Taking a spot in the corner, her eyes flitted everywhere but to him. She was a small female but precious to his race, as there were far too few females remaining. Most were being coddled and protected. He refused to do that to Gix. He'd been amazed she'd survived the war, let alone the trip to Earth. She was classic prey, but yet somehow, in the moments that demanded it, she displayed more courage than males nearly twice her size. She needed those moments to feel strong. If she were tucked away in a protective shelter, the spark within Gix would fade. Hells if Roden would ever allow that to happen now that she was just discovering her potential.

She was also one of the few people whose loyalty he never doubted.

"It's good to see you up on your feet, sir."

"Bring me up to speed."

She fidgeted. "Well, sir, you've been out for fourteen days."

Fourteen days! He brought a hand to his forehead. The entire time was a chasm.

"For the first couple of days, we weren't sure you'd pull through. You kept shouting incoherently, mostly about a woman." She scuffed at the floor with the toe of her boot. "You tried to get out of bed. After you broke three more bones in your left wing, we were forced to sedate you."

As he suspected, they'd drugged him. He stared out the window, remembering back to when he'd been no more than a child, just coming into his body. Females had begun to notice him. No, more than *notice* him, they'd flocked to him like lightning to Sephia's red, iron-laden clouds.

Lightning filled the clouds that night, turning the red skies to passionate iridescence. In the orchard, he'd kissed her. She was married, but she hadn't cared. She came to him. He was young and too proud. Her husband had refused to hire him and Apolo that very morning, and so Roden would gain vengeance by taking his wife to bed.

As the most generous couple in town, they often threw parties to raise funds. He no longer remembered which charity was the focus that night. It hadn't mattered. Roden had come to take, not give, at this particular party. It only took a hungry look, a careful brush against her wings. She'd followed him out to the orchard.

She was zealous, and he'd had no problem enjoying himself. She was lithe and beautiful and clearly experienced. As he pressed himself against her, he'd felt the injection. "What is this?" he asked as he collapsed to the ground.

He was still fully conscious, yet he lacked motor ability. He could feel but could not move his limbs. As she undressed him, he cursed her through muffled lips. She responded by covering his mouth with tape. It was then he realized how depraved the zealous woman was. She lifted her skirts and straddled him. She'd grabbed onto his wings as she slammed down onto him. He'd always been told that sex was pleasurable. This was anything but, and he tried to will his hands to move, to grab her by the throat and strangle the life from her. Instead, he could do nothing as she violated him over and over.

She redressed when she'd finished with him and then left him lying on the damp ground as though he was nothing but garbage.

Roden couldn't even wipe away the tear that had betrayed him.

She'd smiled then. "I'll always be your first," she whispered. The soft words contained no sensuality like a lover's caress. Instead, it was taunting, like a conqueror's jest.

A lord stepped from the shadows and helped her to her feet. The lord looked down upon Roden as his wife straightened her skirts. At that moment, he realized that he'd been their prey all along. That she'd chosen him, and her husband had orchestrated everything.

The rains had come and gone before he could move his limbs again. As he lay on the cold, wet ground, he thought through how they had tricked him so easily, clearly with experience. When he could, he moved slowly, his body shivering nearly uncontrollably. Ripping the tape from his mouth, he pulled his soaked clothes back on and walked through the woods with dark plans formulating in his mind. That night had been his most valuable lesson. That night, Roden Zyll was born.

Without looking at Gix, he spoke finally and quietly. "Don't ever drug me again. Never again, do you understand?"

The cutting edge to his voice must've been clear because she stuttered in her response. "W-we were o-only to-trying to help."

"Gix," he cautioned.

"Yes, my lord. Never again."

"Good. Now that that's settled, give me an update."

"When we heard Hillas had imprisoned you, Wync spread the word as quickly as possible. Everyone supportive to you abandoned the base to set up a temporary base at the backup coordinate and at this rendezvous point while Wync and I went for you."

"And, please tell me, you took everything you could from the base."

"Not exactly," she said, her voice hitching with uncertainty. "The Grand Lord sent attack squads to the base the moment you were taken. Everyone grabbed what they could, but we had to get out of there fast. We have all our ships, but only the weapons and medical supplies we could carry." She sighed. "He continues to send out search parties but has had no success. The Sephians and humans have the Grand Lord's base surrounded and are watching his every move. With them restricting his movements, the risk of him finding both this location as well as our interim earthside base is nil. Using force to quell unrest was a strong reminder that Hillas Puftan is no longer fit to lead our people."

"The Grand Lord is dead." He swallowed. *Hillas is gone and my people are no closer to safety.*

Gix looked confused. "My Lord Commander?"

"Hillas Puftan is dead. The Draeken in charge now is his doppelgänger, and he plans to continue the Puftan legacy, even though he carries no Puftan blood in his veins."

The guardsman gasped. "We must tell our people. Once they know the truth, they will kill the imposter. You are the natural replacement."

Roden held up a hand. "A day more will not matter. I need time to discover what schemes Otas has initiated over the past two weeks." Roden paused. "Tell me, has there been news of Hillas' daughter?"

"I never knew the Grand Lord had surviving children."

"Answer the question."

"There has been no news about a daughter," she said.

Roden's jaw clenched. While he'd been on his back, Nalea was being tortured and executed.

He turned to the guardsman. "How many have sworn loyalty to me?"

"There's over a thousand Draeken loyal to you, earthside. More are on the core ships, but they can't get here with Hillas' stand-down orders. Most are at our new base, a short flight from here. There're still some imprisoned at the Grand Lord's—er.. I mean, the imposter's, earthside base. More yet are still in hiding on his base and on the core ships. We're ready to attack at your command."

"That'll be all," he said, dismissing her. "And quit slouching. Build those back muscles. Your wings will be stronger for it."

"Yes, sir." At the door, Gix paused. "The woman you wanted to go back for… was she Hillas' daughter?"

He cut her a hard look. "It no longer matters."

Roden waited until Gix scurried from the room before he turned back to watch the autumn trees swaying in the breeze. All he had now was the mission, but their numbers were pitifully few. Without help, they didn't stand a chance against the full power of the Draeken core ships. There was only one place where he could get the help they needed.

The same place that had orders to kill him on sight…

Taking a seat at an old wooden desk, Kreed sighed. Who would've ever thought that maintaining two identities would be so exhausting? Playing the good military commander while lining up the pieces so that all would fall into place at exactly the right time. Fortunately, he would no longer need both identities soon. Once his people had the support they needed, there would no longer be any need for Kreed The Grand Lord had declared war on anyone who pledged fealty to his Second. That directive had only made those already loyal to Roden all the more dedicated. Wync had even mentioned the growing list of names loyal to Roden from Hillas' earthside camp earlier today.

After decades, the tides were finally turning in Kreed's favor. Most Draeken felt that Hillas had failed them, but they were afraid of the break from tradition yet. A Puftan had ruled the Draeken people through centuries of peace and decades of war. Even Kreed had to admit he felt a pang of something akin to remorse for the change he was steering his people toward. But he knew in his heart that what he'd done—and was about to do—was the only way to preserve what remained of Draeka.

He stretched his wings. The bones cracked and popped a little more each year. Just one more task and then perhaps sleep would find him tonight. Kreed checked his room and set up the portable electronic dampener before dialing the secure code only he and Apolo knew. This setup wasn't as secure as what he'd had on the base, but he needed to get news of the war to Apolo. The risk of being caught was worth it. He needed Sephian support now more than ever.

Seconds passed. Seconds became minutes. Minutes became tens of minutes.

"Fyet," he cursed as he fell back in his chair. His wings flicked in irritation. Apolo had never missed a call before. *Never.*

He could only hope that some menial meeting detained Apolo. If the Sephians were no longer on good terms with the humans, what hope did the Draeken have? Unlike the Sephians, who could now return home, the Draeken were stranded there; the next closest planet would take several years to reach, and even with the upgraded power cells, the core ships weren't equipped for such a journey. Earth was their only chance.

Except, without Apolo, Kreed had no bridge to garner human support, and without human support, Kreed would be forced to rely on Roden to broker peace with humans. With the reputation Lord Commander Zyll had earned during the war, Kreed would have a better chance navigating the twelve hells than seeing peace come to fruition for his people. For his people's survival, Kreed must succeed.

Fyet. He thumped the desk with a fist. *Answer my call, ta deiti.*

If he were discovered now, the Draeken people may believe Kreed was the traitor, but he knew who the real traitor was. If he did nothing to stop Otas, his people would die. If he continued his plan without Apolo's help, he'd die, but his people might survive. No choice, really.

He leaned forward and dialed the secure code again, and again, no response. Apolo had always been there for him. Even when his father beat him within an inch of his life for not winning an archery contest, it'd been Apolo—not his Draeken friends—who sat by his side and nursed him back to health.

Goosebumps flitted across his skin, and he hated himself for feeling any kind of weakness. He'd come too far, sacrificed too much, to succumb to fear now. He would still succeed with his part. He couldn't afford to fail. And when he was finished, he'd have to count on his people's collective intelligence and need for survival to find an end to war.

Chapter 20

Like every night, Roden haunted Nalea's dreams. Tonight was no different. Just below the shell of consciousness, she'd known the fantasy wasn't real, because if it were, she'd punch him rather than seduce him. By morning, she'd label it a nightmare, the pleasure of it too much. Still, she let herself fall deeper into the fantasy.

A strong male body pressed hers against the soft mattress. Skin against skin, the tactile contact exhilarated her senses, made her crave more. It was as though she was a spoiled child and he was her favorite toy. Reaching up, she cupped his face. "You came."

"Always."

Broad wings spread out to form a protective cocoon around them. With his arms propped up on his elbows as not to crush her with his weight, he bent down and kissed her forehead, then her cheek, then—hesitantly—her lips. "Ah, Lea."

The words held so much depth, so much passion, she found herself sighing into his mouth as she opened to receive him. His tongue found hers, and the decadent taste of him reminded her of sweet, dark chocolate with the bite of whiskey.

Wrapping her arms around him, she caressed the thick muscle where his wings merged into his back. He groaned, and she knew she'd found a sensual hot spot on her lover. She'd known Draeken wings were sensitive, but she'd never considered that information useful except for battle. She ran her palms outward, across the smooth skin of his wings, and they fluttered in response. "They're as soft as a moth's."

He bit down on her neck, sending shivers across her skin. A deep chuckle vibrated from his chest. "And you're the flame that draws me."

She spread her thighs, wrapping her legs around his waist to pull him closer to where she needed him tonight. She gripped his arms and writhed against him, attempting to entice him with every movement.

Where Roden was patient in everything else, in bed he was demanding. He lifted her enough to angle against her opening. He pressed into her and gasped at the welcome intrusion. She begged him for more, to go deeper, to go harder, to never stop. She didn't stop begging when her words became nonsensical between moans and cries. His thrusts detonated an explosion within her. All the sensations in her body came together in her core and then shot outward. He came soon after but continued to thrust, and together they rode the passion that could only be found when two fractured pieces fit together to make a whole.

After the throes of their lovemaking lessened to tremors of raw, natural bliss, his wings blanketed them, and he kissed her, always holding her against him as though she was delicate, a dichotomy to how he fucked.

For only an instant, his weight had become like air. "Not again!" he cursed as he squeezed her against him. He held her tight enough, she found it hard to breathe, but she didn't care. She clutched at him, trying to hold him to her. Cold air assaulted her skin. She could see through his wings, into the void behind him.

As he faded in and out of the darkness, they clung onto one another in desperation. But it never did any good. As he became more and more incorporeal, she begged. "Don't leave me."

He yelled out in frustration before surrendering to the inevitable abyss. "I'll come back for you."

• • •

Awareness pulled Nalea from sleep. She would have preferred to stay in her dreams, to forget that she lay in a room deep within enemy territory. She was surprised she'd dreamed of Roden, having thought the disjunctor would've removed him completely from her thoughts. With it, she felt *nothing* from him. While she thought she'd find the absence of his emotions a pleasant break after the intensity she'd felt after the bond had taken hold, instead, she felt hollow from the *aloneness*.

Running her hands through her hair, she shrugged off the remnants of sleep. She had enough to deal with already, like pretending to be the daughter of the Draeken who looked like the father she'd hated her entire life. Talk about irony.

The door opened. She slipped on her dark glasses and came to her feet just as the white-haired Draeken stepped through the doorway, his wings just brushing the floor. He wore a formal uniform: a long black and crimson kilt met tall boots that showed no signs of wear. His shirt, simple crimson on the front, had been turned into a gaudy display of flare. Colorful ribbons—each signifying something for Hillas Puftan—fluttered with every step. Even with all that, her gaze was drawn to the royal crest proudly emblazoned over his heart. It covered nearly a third of his chest, clearly meant to be seen.

In some ways, Otas was no different from the lord he impersonated. He was a proud peacock, intent on impressing the world with his plumes so that they didn't notice his faults or lies.

Otas had spent most of his life mimicking the Grand Lord; his entire world was built on mirroring, not creating. It made sense that he would follow the dead leader's ambitions beyond the grave, simply because he couldn't come up with anything on his own.

Upon seeing her, Otas smiled. While the gesture was meant to be warm, it made Nalea uncomfortable. Shivers crawled over her skin. There was nothing fatherly or friendly about a smile that hinted at possession. When this Hillas looked at her, she always felt that whatever he was scheming was something very *un*fatherly.

"Good morning, Nalea. I see you've adjusted to Earth days with ease."

She nodded tightly. Even without shoes, she stood the same height as Otas, which made him very short for a Draeken—males were commonly seven feet tall. Other than the uniform, there was nothing militaristic about Hillas. His belly was round, his wings nearly transparent from lack of use. Right now, with the way he watched her, she felt as though she were a plump insect in a hungry bird's path.

As she stepped forward, he took a step back. Nalea gave a tight smile. "How can I help you, *Father*?"

He frowned, and she noticed that, while he demanded she play along with his farce, he disliked the term. "I trust you are doing well?"

She lifted her hands slightly in response. *I'm alive, aren't I?*

He moved closer, and she stood firm. He brushed a finger down her neck. "The disjunctor is working properly?"

"I feel nothing."

"Good," he said, a corner of his lip curving upward. "You are free from Roden Zyll. Now, if only we could all be free from him." He turned and began to pace, an annoying habit he did whenever he was thinking. "I do not hold you accountable for getting ensnared in the devious webs he weaves. After all, you were no more than a weapon to him, simply a ruse in his coup to destroy what I've built."

What Hillas built, you mean.

"His need for power knows no bounds."

Funny. Roden said the same about Hillas.

"And I look to you for help to prevent his coup from escalating further." He paused and turned to her. "You will make your public announcement tomorrow. In it, you will acknowledge that you are Lord Commander Roden Zyll's consort and, as you are of

Puftan blood, you wish to unite those under Roden to our cause."

Nalea frowned. "As long as Roden lives, people will remain loyal to him."

Otas continued. "You will also say that Roden has betrayed our people. You'll talk of how he tried to assassinate me in his bid for power and is hereby stripped of title and command. Those who continue to follow a pariah will not be tolerated."

Nalea's muscles tightened. "And what if your little civil war bleeds over? The Sephians and humans are both at risk. There must be another way."

"If the Draeken people aren't united, then how can they stand before the Sephians and humans in peace? Together, we can unite them." With that, he moved forward and kissed her.

Nalea jerked back. She threw a punch and hit him square on the jaw. Otas stumbled backward against the wall and fell flat to the ground. He jumped back to his feet, shooting a vicious glare at Nalea. She could've easily parried, but she let him slam into her, sending her against the wall. Air shot from her lungs, and her bones cried out on impact.

His hand wrapped into her hair and yanked. White-hot stars flashed across her vision, and the muscles in her neck burned.

"Look at me!" he yelled, his spittle hitting her face. His grip in her hair tightened.

Jaw clenched, she obeyed.

Otas held his wrist shakily in front of her. A black band with a small pad incorporated within it wrapped around his forearm, just below his wrist-comm. "You will never raise a hand to me again," he said, his words muffled from between his bloody lips. "All I need to do is press a single button and your head will be removed from your body."

She knew she'd made a mistake mid-swing, but it'd already been too late. "My apologies," she ground out.

The hand in her hair relaxed, then was gone, only to grip her throat, and she found herself choking, forced to look into hard gray eyes. "You survive at my mercy. Do you understand?"

"Yes," she gritted out, though she knew she could kill him before his guardsmen could arrive. The only problem with that plan was that she'd be dead, too.

"You will help me eliminate Roden," Otas said, cupping the back of her neck with his hand. "You will help me align with the Sephians. Then, when our peoples are united under my leadership, we will bring our bloodlines together. My blood—as well as Puftan blood—will continue as one. Only then will the Sephians and Draeken be fully united under me."

Bile rose in her throat, and she put all her strength into not showing revulsion.

"If you displease me," he whispered, "I'll have the core ships fire upon the Sephian bases. I will kill every Sephian on this planet."

Roden bolted awake. The intensity of the dream had left a sheen of sweat on his skin. He came to his feet and stretched. His healing wing cramped and spasmed.

In a matter of minutes, he was fully clothed. He reached for his weapons and paused. No, he could take nothing with him today.

"I'm going with you."

Roden turned to find Wync standing in the doorway. "No," he replied. "If they choose to kill me, they'll do it whether you're there or not. The only difference is that if you're there, you're dead, too."

"I don't care," Wync said, entering the room.

"I do." He placed a hand on the guardsman's shoulder. "I need you here in case things don't go well. Our people need you."

"I don't like this," Wync snapped back.

Roden gave Wync's shoulder a squeeze. "I'll talk to you tonight." *If I'm not dead.* He then stepped out into the hallway and went down to the kitchen.

He grabbed a quick breakfast and made his rounds. The guardsmen stationed at the house needed to hear assurances. They needed to know that everything would turn out all right.

When he took to the skies, the spark of confidence in their eyes gave him strength.

He flew low, almost skimming the trees. Without feathers or fur to protect their skin, Draeken were susceptible to cold. Unfortunately, when his people had abandoned the base, they had taken weapons rather than protective gear. And right now, he was missing the ultra-thin heated rider-skins that would have his wings blanketed in a layer of comforting warmth. *I suppose I must get used to living like a primitive.*

After a couple of hundred miles passed below him, a cramp in his left wing brought on a wince. His wings ached at the strain so soon after his injuries. Because of the cold, he'd been forced to fly below the thermals, unable to leverage the lift, but high enough to be noticed on radar. He had to work at this flight. Fortunately, if the two military helicopters forming up on both sides were any sign, he was nearing his destination.

"You are unauthorized in this airspace. You will land immediately," a masculine voice erupted from a loudspeaker mounted on the aircraft to his right. *"If you do not comply, you will be shot."*

He spared a glance to both sides to find himself in the sights of rather large machine guns. *How archaic.* As they repeated their commands, he ever so slowly reached into the outside pocket of his down jacket. That they hadn't fired upon him already was rather surprising. He certainly would've shot down any risk. He pulled out the fabric and held it up. The white flag flapped in the wind. He chuckled inwardly. *As though a white slip of fabric ensures I'll behave.*

Silence.

They didn't shoot. They flew alongside him for several seconds, maybe a minute, before they addressed him again. *"You will follow us. If you change your flight path, you will be shot."*

Roden dropped his white fabric and smiled.

Fifteen minutes later, he flared his wings and touched down on the concrete inside a military base surrounded by tall chain-link fences. His helicopter escorts now circled overhead.

He tucked his wings close to his back and held out two empty palms.

"Freeze!" The order was shouted by one of the humans closest to him from among the army of rifles aimed at his heart.

"I'm quite cold enough already, thank you." Roden made sure to not give them any excuses to shoot. "I come in peace. My name is Lord Commander Roden Zyll, and I request an audience with the leaders of the American Sephian forces."

No one moved in front of him. He heard plenty of movement from behind, however. He showed no resistance when he was shoved onto the ground, the edges of his wings pressing painfully against the abrasive surface as his arms were yanked behind his back. He bit back the pain shooting through his still-healing body.

His coat was removed, and the sudden cold air bit at his skin.

A pair of smaller boots with larger black boots on either side took over his vision. He cocked his head up to see fatigue-covered legs—one wearing a brace customized from a Draeken design—and up past the leather jacket to a human face so badly scarred on one side that he might not have recognized her if he'd not seen the other side. He'd already known that the scars that covered the left half of her face continued down her body, despite the numerous surgeries she'd undergone. And, he knew that her left arm no longer functioned fully.

Sienna's attacker had very nearly killed her. While Roden had no doubt it was Hillas who'd sent the suicide bomber, when he'd discovered precisely *who* had been sent on the suicide run, the news had curdled Roden's stomach. Hillas had sent Sienna's own mother to kill her. The Grand Lord's cruelty knew no limits.

Sienna was known to hold a grudge. However, it was the human capacity for forgiveness that gave Roden hope that Draeken and humans could find peace together.

"Hello, Sienna," Roden said. "You didn't have to go to so much effort for my visit."

A movement at his side, and he found his cheek pressed harder against the rough concrete. A flash of gold skin, and Roden suspected who held him down. He gritted out his next words as best he could with his face shoved against the ground. "Put a leash on your *fregee*, Sienna."

"You've got some nerve showing your face around here, Roden," Sienna said.

Hands patted him down. "He's clean," someone said from behind.

Sienna nodded, and Roden was pulled—none too politely—to his feet.

Legian—Sienna's feral *tahren*—now had Roden by the throat. He was tall for a Sephian, nearly Roden's height.

"Sienna. Leash." Roden choked out.

She scowled at him for a moment before placing her hand on Legian's forearm. "We need him alive. For now, anyway."

The pressure disappeared, and he could breathe again. He would have massaged his neck except that his hands were restrained behind his back, making his arms bind his wings tight against him. His lips tilted upward. "Now, where were we?"

With venom in her eyes, Sienna spoke. "We're going to have a long conversation." With that, she turned and, with Legian at her side, led them toward the large building with a smooth gray exterior. Roden followed none too gracefully with soldiers on both sides and behind, pressing him forward like a marionette.

Inside the building, guards of both races—human and Sephian —stood at attention. Roden glanced around. "Well, isn't this cozy."

Sienna hit a button on the wall, and an elevator door opened. "It's about to get a hell of a lot cozier."

He was shoved into the elevator. They'd been smart. Sephian guards surrounded him. Humans weren't nearly as strong—or as blood-thirsty—as their gold-skinned cousins. Legian stepped in with Sienna behind him. *Ever the protective dog.*

As they descended, he noticed her gaze upon him, and he lifted a brow.

"I still wake up at night with pain in my leg, you know," Sienna said.

Roden glanced down at her braced leg. He shrugged. "Then you should not have gotten in my way."

"I'm surprised you have the balls to show your face, especially after last time we met."

He pursed his lips before responding. "On the contrary, my dear; I gained my consort out of it."

The Sephians on the elevator seemed to let out a collective gasp. Sienna's jaw slackened. "Bullshit," she said.

Legian wrapped a protective arm around her as he glared at Roden. "You lie."

Roden smiled. "I am Nalea's *tahren*."

"*Suvaste*," someone behind him muttered.

Roden chuckled. "As you are quite aware, Sephians don't choose their *tahren*. Blame our pairing on your Sephian gods." Roden was thankful he had no religion. If he believed, he'd alternate between begging them, thanking them, and blaspheming them every day of his life.

The floor gave a small jolt, and then the door opened. And that was fortunate, because the air in that box had grown hostile.

Sienna eyed him as he was pushed out of the elevator and into the hallway beyond.

Waiting before them was a human with a short haircut, and a Sephian whose face Roden knew all too well. All Draeken recognized Apolo, Sephia's leader of Earth's Sephian forces and *tahren* to Krysea, the great leader of Sephia. Last Roden knew, Apolo had taken over half the Sephians to England, leaving the remaining in the States under Legian and Sienna. If Apolo was standing here now, things had changed.

Though the man looked rather haggard now, he was still a Sephian to be feared. His visage was lean and hard. "I've been looking forward to this day. You will atone for your crimes, Roden Zyll."

Apolo could potentially ruin everything. "Perhaps," Roden replied curtly. "But I doubt that day will be today."

Apolo's eyes narrowed as he scrutinized him. Roden hardened his features in response.

The human spoke next. "I'm Major Sommers of the U.S. Army, Division 51. We have much to discuss."

Roden gave a slight nod. "I don't believe we've met. I'm Roden Zyll, Lord and Commander of Draeken forces. I'd shake your hand, but,"—he wiggled his wrists—"as you can see, I'm otherwise disposed."

Sommers nodded to a guard, who opened the door closest to them. Roden was led into a windowless room with a large mirror —unquestionably two-way—spanning one wall. His guards were none too gentle about restraining him to the metal bench, and he grunted when one bumped roughly against his wing.

They left him there. The guards locked the door, and Roden sat alone in silence. Oh, he knew he was being watched all right, and so he sat there, watching the mirror, while his hosts planned their next steps.

They returned nearly an hour later. Surprisingly, they didn't torture him. Instead, two humans simply questioned him, and then left him alone once again. They were likely buying time as they figured out what to do with him. After all, it wasn't every day one of their most wanted waltzed up to their front door. Not that they needed the time. He planned to lay everything they needed on a platter and serve it right up to them.

The sound of metal on metal pulled his attention to the door as it opened. Sienna, Legian, and Major Sommers sat down across the table to face him.

"Why'd you come here?" Sienna asked.

"And I thought our friendship was off to such a fine start." He crooked his chin toward her scars. "Although it looks like you've run into some trouble since our last encounter."

She lunged forward and slapped him. Heat bloomed on his cheek.

Legian hit the table and snarled. "You ever speak like that to Sienna again I'll slice your wings and tie you outside for the scavengers to have their way with you."

Sienna rubbed her knuckles. "It's all right. I just let him rile me up." She turned to Roden and sat back down. This time she pulled out a blaster and set it on the table, the barrel pointing at him. "And he knows that's not a good idea. Answer my question, Roden. Why'd you come here?"

Roden nodded toward the weapon. "Is that the same blaster you used to execute your mother after she tried to blow up the base with you in it?"

Sienna grabbed the weapon and fired. The heat from the blast singed his wing spur before searing the wall behind him. "You sent my mother to her death. Her blood is on your hands."

He tsked. "That business with your mother was the act of an unsavory fellow who's no longer a threat."

"I should've killed you a year ago."

He shrugged. "You tried. You failed." Then he sighed. "Getting rid of me won't solve your problems."

"There's nothing stopping me from killing you now."

"With me harmless in a cage? How very *Sephian* of you."

"I'd take *Sephian* over *Draeken* any day."

He cocked his head. "What have my people done to you, Sienna? I'd wager your experiences all tie from making your alignment with the Sephians and getting caught up in the unpleasantness between two races. It's certainly not from anything between your people and Draeken."

"*My* people are Sephians as much as humans," she shot back at him.

"Enough small talk." Sommers brought his hand between them. "Roden, you came here alone and unarmed. While I appreciate the gesture, if you have something to say, now is the time."

"I came under the terms of peace."

"You came under the terms of surrender," Sommers reminded him.

He shrugged. "Semantics. I have information you need to keep humans from getting slaughtered."

"And in return?" Sommers asked, the woman at his side still glaring at Roden.

"In return, I ask for the same thing the Sephians have here. An alliance. A chance to make our home on your world."

Sienna shook her head. "We don't make deals with terrorists."

"A rather harsh label," Roden replied. "My people came in peace to this planet, fleeing genocide and seeking only a place to call home. We are refugees, not terrorists."

Sienna gave a combination of a choke and laugh. "You really believe humans will accept you, live side-by-side with you, when they find out that the Sephians were nothing but Draeken slaves for centuries? What's stopping you from doing the same thing here?"

"Slavery?" Roden raised a brow. "You should ask your *tahren* about the history of slavery on Sephia. It was there long before my people arrived. We continued a tradition merely because the entire political structure and millennia of customs depended upon it. I may not condone what my ancestors did, but I understand it. Who are you to judge, when slavery still exists in this world?"

She shook her head. "Slavery is outlawed. It's being stomped out. And we certainly don't have it in this country."

A smirk curled his lips. "Ah, yes. Your people are so altruistic.

Slavery hasn't been condoned in this country for a whole *century*. You're certainly an enlightened race."

Sienna fumed. "How about Club Mayhem then? Everyone knows that you were the one behind that breeding facility, using humans as slaves."

Roden lifted a brow. "You make it sound so clinical. It was a place for our peoples to discover one another in a social setting."

Sienna hit the table. "Bullshit. You were cross-breeding, using human women like cattle!"

"Were we?" he asked. "Did you find laboratories? Did you speak with any of the women from there? They would have a very different story."

"Those women were brainwashed," she countered.

"Really?" Roden belted out a laugh before going sober. "You're grasping at straws because you already know the truth. You know that everything in that club was consensual. Find me one person who was in any way traumatized or said they were forced." He leaned closer. "I'll bet the women were checked for drugs and yet none were found." He turned back to Sommers. "Club Mayhem was the first connection of my people with this world's inhabitants. We met on their terms. We hid *nothing*. We forced *nothing*. It gave us a chance to get to know one another under casual conditions."

"Why did you keep it secret then?" Sommers asked.

"It wasn't a secret. The place was legally licensed under the laws of this country. We simply did not widely broadcast our attendance since we had yet to meet with this world's leaders." Roden turned to Sienna. "You just don't like it because you're a racist."

"A racist?" She balked at his words, shaking her head in denial. "I'm a *tahren* to a Sephian!"

"A Sephian who wants to see every last Draeken dead, and I see you've aligned yourself fully with that same belief," he replied calmly. "You go straight for genocide without giving us a chance."

He shook his head. "The root of the issue at hand is that both the Sephians and Draeken underestimated humans. Their technology was so archaic, we both *inaccurately* assumed that they wouldn't yet be able to comprehend that they had brethren in the stars. The Sephians have begun to rectify that miscalculation." He turned back to Sommers. "How about you? Do you believe the Draeken should also have a chance to make amends with your people?"

"I'm still figuring out both of you," Sommers replied. "And what I've seen from *both* sides so far hasn't earned my trust. You brought your war here. You set up shop here uninvited. And neither one of you reached out to us until after we were onto you. In my eyes, you *both* have a lot of work to do."

Roden nodded. "Fair enough. I came here today to stop a war that started on Sephia and continues to bleed us."

"A war you propagated," Legian said. "A war you propagate still."

"Believe what you will." He turned back to Sommers. "We can all agree that unless we reach peace, this war is going to result in human casualties."

"What game are you playing this time?" Sienna asked.

"No game. I like this planet. *Earth.* It has a nice ring to it."

Roden turned to find Sommers studying him. "Why now?" Sommers asked. "What's happened that brought you here today?"

The human was smart. He could be a valuable ally. Or a dangerous enemy. "My people are undergoing a change in leadership."

"Hillas Puftan is stepping down?" Sienna asked.

"The Grand Lord is dead. Courtesy of your friend and my consort, Nalea Zyll. However, a doppelgänger is now in place. Unfortunately, this Hillas isn't so smart, and once backed into a corner, is likely to lash out like the rabid *fregee* he is."

"Meaning?" Sommers asked.

"Meaning Hillas had figured out how to modify our power cells to run off this system's solar energy, and this imposter—this copy

—has no qualms about using them to protect our people and his position."

Legian placed his other hand protectively on Sienna's shoulder. "If this Hillas has power cells," he said, "the Draeken core ship can decimate this world."

"On the contrary," Roden said. "He only has working prototypes. But it won't take long to modify the cells once he's ready. We don't have much time."

"How do you know he's not ready now?" Sommers asked. "We could be walking into a trap."

"Because we're all still alive," Legian said.

"That's why time is of the essence," Roden added. "Fortunately for you, I just happen to have in my possession a working prototype. Should we reach an alliance, I would gladly share it with my Sephian and human *friends*."

"We could return to Sephia," Legian murmured.

"Yes. The new cells would support travel both ways," Roden added.

"How can we trust you?" Sommers asked.

"You can't. Trust has to be earned," Roden said. "But we have one thing in common."

Sienna snorted. "And exactly would that be?"

"We all desire peace, of course."

Sienna clamped her mouth shut. No one spoke for several moments. Sommers was the first. "What kind of alliance are you looking for?"

Roden inhaled. "First, we need earthside support to go in and remove Hillas' doppelgänger from leadership. Once that's done, I will be able to ensure the integrity of my people. They will not be the aggressors on Earth."

"So, you're asking for our help in your coup," Sommers said.

Roden shrugged. "I'm asking for your help to prevent a war. Once that is done, I'd prefer to find an arrangement mutually beneficial for all three of our peoples to live in peace. I've seen enough bloodshed."

"Why should we help you instead of this Hillas?" Sommers asked.

"Because Otas enjoys the comforts of slavery," Roden snapped back. "If not for altruism, consider an alliance for that saying, *the enemy of my enemy is my friend.*"

No one looked convinced.

Sommers steepled his fingers. "I'd like to think peace is a real possibility and not just some pipe dream. We may be able to provide a certain level of mission support to eliminate the imposter in exchange for the working prototype. But I don't make a habit of taking anyone I've just met at their word. I need a lot more details and assurances first. And we need to see this proto-type. After that, for anything more lasting, a hell of a lot more negotiations need to take place."

Roden nodded. "That's all I ask for. I can have the prototype delivered tonight while we work out the details."

Sienna leaned forward. "Even if we have to work together, I'll never trust you, Roden; you know that, right?"

"The feeling's mutual, Sienna."

"You still have war crimes to atone for," Legian pointed out.

"No more than you," Roden snapped back.

"That's between your two races." Sommers stood. "I need to make some phone calls."

Roden rattled his chains. "You could take these restraints off as a sign of good faith."

Sommers chuckled. "We're not there yet." He then left, leaving Roden alone with two people who very much wanted him dead.

They sat in silence for several minutes. "I can't believe it," Sienna said finally. "You two really became *tahren.*"

Legian glared; his voice dark and cutting. "The gods would never punish anyone that much that they'd make a *tahren* pairing with you."

"Funny," he replied. "Nalea thought the same thing. Didn't change the truth." He leaned back. "Careful how you speak about my consort. And you'll be wise to watch your tone if you want my cooperation."

"How did she die?" Sienna asked; her words soft.

"We were ambushed after we killed Hillas. They got both of us," Roden replied, his voice flat.

"Where were you when she was being killed?" Legian asked from the corner.

Roden lunged forward, only to be held back by his restraints. "You want to know if I abandoned her? Yes, I did. I escaped, leaving her to die alone in a cold cell. Here's another human saying for you: *shit happens.*"

He was ready for the fist; he just hadn't expected how blasted strong the Sephian was. When Legian hit him, Roden's jaw made a thundering crack and his world spun in blackness and stars. It took a long time for his world to stop spinning.

When it finally did, Sienna watched him carefully, as though pondering something. "You cared for her," she said after another while.

He stared at her. "If you want vengeance on the one who killed her," he said, the words slightly slurred from his jaw not working quite right, "join me."

"*R*oden Zyll should be executed for crimes against humanity.*"* Sienna's words from an earlier discussion thrummed at Apolo's mind. Humanity? Crimes against Sephia, yes. But, despite memories of more than twenty years of war, the Draeken lord had yet to be found guilty of any crimes on this world. More so, there was something familiar about Roden...

He turned his attention back to the thick glass window. Apolo hated this corridor. Deep within the bowels of the base, this was where they kept the Draeken they had captured at Club Mayhem. One had already died from the tests. From the looks of the female currently being led from the testing room, today's tests couldn't have been pleasant.

Apolo had come here as a reminder of what could easily be done to his people. They had to be constantly *better* than the humans to simply keep the status quo. He didn't want this for his enemy. On Sephia, everything had been so clear, black and white. But here, dozens of star systems away, Apolo had begun to see things differently.

In the Noble War, race was all that mattered. Yet, as a child, Apolo's closest friend had been a Draeken. As the war continued, it had seemed like they fought merely for the sake of fighting; to end one another. His people had been triumphant, the Draeken had fled, and the Sephians had pursued them, intending to end the Draeken race as though they were evil. Apolo had become guilty of the same charges he'd made against the Draeken. It was time Apolo acknowledged the truth: Draeken weren't evil; any more than Sephians were. There were evil individuals, not evil races.

He refused to continue the charade.

The door opened. Jax Jerrick was nearly carrying the female Draeken. Her wings were banded. No obvious wounds showed on her body, but then again, many of the more painful tests looked completely innocuous to outsiders.

Apolo stepped forward. "Let me help."

The Draeken cursed at him, but he ignored her. When Jax gave him a small nod, he lifted her arm and took on as much of her weight as Jax would allow. Apolo was careful to not overstep Jax's lines when it came to Talla Kohlm, the Draeken prisoner to whom he was assigned as Leash.

"Roden is here," Apolo said as they moved slowly down the hall.

Talla jerked but said nothing.

"He is not a prisoner," Apolo continued. "He came for our help. He said that Hillas is dead."

She closed her eyes, lowered her head, and sighed. "It's begun."

Chapter 24

In the comm center on Hillas' earthside base, Nalea watched the screen spanning the wall in front of her. Her "father" stood at her side. The room, with its whirring machines, brought a cold tang to the air, amping up her restlessness.

Otas pointed at the screen. "Isolate that range and zoom in."

Two comm-techs sat at stations, tapping away on their screens as they analyzed the latest video feed.

The comm beeped, and Nalea's nerves gave a jolt. The past fifteen days of playing along with Otas had proved exhausting. She'd been careful to not displease him, but it was only a matter of time. He was paranoid, convinced Roden would make his bid for power soon. And, as an imposter, he wasn't confident the Draeken people would side with him over a war hero. Not that she disagreed.

She was surprised to see the guardsmen and comm-techs on this base loyal to a known imposter. Many she'd seen held disdain in their features whenever they were near Otas, yet they did as he bade them. It made no sense to her, but then, Draeken protocols often made no sense to her.

His scientists back on the core ship were working day and

night to upgrade the power cells. But the core ships had apparently been built with nothing in excess. They were a monument of technology but required all power cells for full functionality. Luckily, upgrading power cells was a tedious, manual modification and the only reason why Otas couldn't flee to a ship, let alone put up a force barrier around the base. Even with Draeken working earthside on power chips for the base, he didn't have enough firepower yet to cover an escape; not with the Sephians and humans surrounding them with heavy artillery.

"There," Otas said.

"I don't see anything," the older of the two comm-techs said.

Nalea eyed the Draeken, wondering if he was loyal to Roden.

Otas scowled and then placed his hand on the comm-tech's shoulder. "I know you see it. Stop your delays. Do I need to remind you that you should not displease me?"

"Your Highness," the comm-tech said as he typed on the screen. The video on the screen froze and enlarged. At first it seemed the normal amount of movement outside the base, given that they'd been under surveillance by the humans for a couple of weeks. The humans had been moving in more heavy equipment and troops daily, and patrols flew over every hour.

Soon, an impenetrable fortress would surround the base, yet Otas continued to gamble that he could modify enough power chips on the base to throw up a force barrier. Exactly where the ship—or ships—were currently located, Nalea didn't know. Otas trusted no one.

"Move the frame forward by three. What is that?" Otas said, and the image changed slightly. It'd been nearly ten minutes since the blip had appeared and disappeared, and they'd yet to decipher the images. The issue was blips simply didn't happen with Draeken technology. Their technology was far superior to both human and Sephian equipment. The split-second blip they'd picked up could have been a bird or a fleet, but it hadn't appeared again. Whoever—or whatever—was heading toward the base was using Draeken stealth abilities to bypass radar sensors.

Roden. Nalea shook the thought away the moment it hit her. It was futile hope thinking he'd come, even if it was just to finish the rebellion he started. And he would most definitely not come for her. Otas had been right about one thing; Roden had used her. If she didn't know better, with the way Roden had looked at her, she could've sworn he cared. He was the best actor she'd ever seen. When the bond took hold, she'd felt emotion from him. It had been deep and hot, and she'd been clearly mistaken.

Her fingers brushed against the metal around her neck. Warmed by her skin, she'd grown accustomed to its constant hum, a reminder that she was nothing more than Otas's slave. She'd find a way to kill Otas, even if it meant her death… though she preferred to live.

Some way, she'd find a way to kill Hillas before she died. Everything had seemed so much easier before, with Roden. His strength and confidence had suffused her. Now, her spirit felt empty, her mind dulled, and she felt completely on her own. Whomever that blip betrayed had Draeken support, but it couldn't have been from Roden. He was likely enjoying himself with a flight around his new Earthside base Otas had been trying relentlessly to find.

Her gaze dropped to the tattooed wings of the two comm-techs seated before her. Each pair was decorated with family crests that denoted honored lineages. One pair displayed names and scenes from battles he'd participated in. Neither pair of tattooed wings was nearly as complete as Roden's. His tattoos spanned the surface of his wings as a proud display of a life truly lived.

The wings blocked the comm-techs from her view. One of the guardsmen Nalea had met for the first time this week. He was young, barely a grown Draeken, and had been too young to fight during much of the war. Their numbers were so low that guardsmen were performing multiple duties now. The other comm-tech, she'd met in battle back on Sephia, and again on Earth when the Draeken attacked her base last year. She thought she'd killed him both times. As she stared at the screen, she wondered what else she'd been wrong about.

"I broke the encryption," the younger Draeken said.

The blip returned; this time as a group of blips filling the screen. Details on each ship were being added as the computer deciphered the images. At least a dozen rotor transports and another dozen Sephian and Draeken ships were closing in fast. Whoever had slipped the blocking encryption program past their defenses had known exactly what they were doing. An invasion was coming, and it was already nearly upon them. It had Roden's signature all over it.

"Immediate full lockdown. And be quick about it," Otas said, his voice shriller than usual. An alarm sounded. He lifted his wrist-comm. "Status of the upgrade?"

"Working on it," a voice replied curtly through his wrist-comm.

"Work faster!" He then stepped to the wall and tapped several buttons. When he spoke, his voice echoed through the speakers in the room. "The base is under attack. Do not show mercy, as they will show you none."

He waved curtly at her. "You need to make your announcement a bit earlier than I'd planned."

Nalea nodded, but he'd already stepped past her. Her breath quickened as she scanned the surrounding area, searching for anything that could be used as a weapon. Her eyes fell on a blaster holstered at Elng's hip, the elite guardsman at the door. She glanced up to find Elng watching her suspiciously.

She swallowed, lifted her chin, and walked past him to follow Otas into the hallway. Elng couldn't have been sure she'd eyed his weapon with her dark glasses on, which meant he didn't have enough evidence to take to Otas. She strolled confidently behind the Grand Lord imposter as he walked brusquely to the next door down the hall. He entered his office, sat down, and a panel on the wall immediately lit up, displaying the impending attack.

She waited until the door shut behind her before speaking. "You could escape in the chaos."

He eyed her. "Draeken never flee."

Your people fled Sephia.

He motioned to her side. "Stand in front of the wall, there."

She obeyed as she mentally went through ways she could incapacitate a neurotic Otas who'd only to reach his wrist to kill her.

The floor rocked, sending her off balance, and she grabbed the desk. The panel went blank.

"No!" Otas punched at the screen, but it remained blank. "It seems Roden prefers us to be blind and deaf."

A bolt of excitement shot through her. *Roden!* But she quickly tamped it out. Why he'd come for her after half of a moon's cycle had passed didn't make sense. If he came for her, it would've been two weeks ago.

He huffed. "Your announcement will come later. But, do not fear, Nalea; we'll kill him. Together."

She stood there, saying nothing as a chill climbed her spine. Though she told herself dozens of times every day that she never wanted to see Roden again, she'd also no desire to see him dead. On the contrary, the idea terrified her.

It was then she noticed the leftover dinner plate and utensils. A small chunk of charred meat with gravy remained. Resting across on the plate was a fork and a steak knife. She took a step forward.

Otas was saying something, and Nalea looked up.

"But they're not ready," a voice replied through his wrist-comm.

"They have to be ready!" he shrilled.

Nalea watched him carefully. "The power cells could explode if they're not functioning right."

"They'll work," he said, shaking his head. "They're just delaying." He continued to type on the blank screen as though the schema would come back online.

She edged closer to the desk. She put her hand over the two utensils and pulled them behind her back.

Heaving a sigh, he looked up exasperated. Then he glanced down at his desk, looked back up at her and grabbed his wrist. "Don't even think it."

Nalea cocked her head and then held the knife up. "Afraid I may try to slit your throat?" *You should be.*

He held up his wrist, the one with the black controller strapped around it. She rolled her eyes. "Even if you managed to kill me, my pulse stops, you die. That is, if I don't kill you first. Just the press of one button is all it takes."

His breathing hitched. Then she held it out, palm open, to him. "And lose my shot at killing Roden Zyll?" She smiled. "Not a chance."

Chapter 25

The Super Stallion helicopter was loaded with soldiers ready for war: Sephians, with their golden skin; humans, who looked like petite, wingless Draeken; Roden and his soldiers. All wore black. Kilts had been exchanged for battle gear with pockets for extra weapons.

He'd been a bit surprised when the humans and Sephians agreed to the terms of his proposed mission with only minor changes to his initial plans. Of course, he'd made it near impossible to refuse. It was simple. First, entice them with the prototype he'd snatched during his escape. Second, give them the opportunity to take down Draeken leadership for good, while keeping Roden within their reach. The humans and Sephians had been playing it too conservatively. Watching Hillas' earthside base but taking no action, unsure what awaited them on the inside, only gave Otas a chance to fortify his position.

Roden had given them all the answers they needed for an assault. Of course, they were assuming they could control Roden, and therefore his people. He'd been careful to do nothing to give them cause to think otherwise.

When it came down to it, Roden wouldn't allow his people to be massacred. The humans already knew the location of Hillas' earthside base—courtesy of Apolo's spy. It was only a matter of time before Otas had working power cells or the humans got antsy and moved in. Both would result in unnecessary deaths. And so Roden had laid out a plan for them to invade the base with minimum loss of life.

This way, everyone got something they wanted. The Sephians felt like they were making headway in eliminating the Draeken threat, and the humans were about to gain unlimited access to undreamed-of technology. Roden was fine with that. Both perceptions were necessary for the endgame.

Everyone figured Roden's stake in the game was to replace Hillas. They also assumed they could either control him or assassinate him. *How foolish of them.*

"He's a wild card. I don't like him here."

Roden glanced up at the sound of the voice to see two human soldiers watching him. He snapped his teeth at them. They scowled. One turned away while the other continued to watch him.

Roden liked the soldier immediately. Strong and loyal, the one called Ace would make an honorable guardsman. His gaze took in the assembly of soldiers sitting around him. Most avoided eye contact. One gold-skin in particular watched him, his narrowed eyes filled with skepticism. Apolo looked exhausted, but his eyes were as sharp as ever. Chills furrowed in Roden's body. *He sees too much.*

He lifted his chin ever so slightly. "Being separated from your *tahren* doesn't look like it suits you, Apolo. How's Krysea? I suppose serving as the grand leader of Sephia keeps her from the little things, like sending support to Earth."

Undeterred, Apolo continued to examine Roden. *He doesn't know,* he assured himself, but it didn't help his comfort level one bit. He leaned back in his seat as much as his wings would allow;

the loud *whoomp-whoomp* of the helicopter vibrated through the metal hull behind him.

Closing his eyes, he inhaled the pungent petroleum smell of hydraulics. He was mentally exhausted. Bringing a feud against his own people lay heavily on his heart, yet that wasn't the only thing weighing it down. Nalea had been the key to the survival of the Draeken race. With her gone, he felt as though his people's hope was gone. The only thing Roden could give Nalea now was vengeance, and that was something he was very, very good at.

It'd taken him years, but Roden was patient. This time, he came to her a Draeken in his prime, and she'd shown no interest. She didn't recognize him thanks to the surgeries he'd had done to alter his face.

He'd taken her to the same orchard. He'd already tied her husband to a nearby tree to watch. Roden had taped her mouth shut so she couldn't scream. He'd chosen drugs to ensure she felt everything. He shoved stakes through her wings and into the ground then pulled out the collection of blades he'd selected over the years for this night. He went to work, making a cut for every boy she'd abused. Throughout it all, her husband had begged for mercy.

When Roden had finished, he skewered her husband before turning back to the woman. Just before the life bled from her, he'd said, "You'll never add another to your collection."

"Jump in zero minus three minutes."

Roden jolted when the voice came over the loudspeaker. He grounded himself by looking around the interior. The helicopter was now humming with activity. Seatbelts were unhooked, and soldiers of all three races came to their feet. Draeken stretched their wings, earning curses from those around them. Humans and

Sephians situated their parachutes and checked their new blasters. Roden had provided weapons, all set to stun—a stipulation he had made very clear—as a way of preventing as many Draeken deaths as possible.

Otas needed to be removed just as a festering wound needed cauterizing. He only hoped that not too many would be lost in destroying the infected false heart of the Draeken people.

"Jump in zero minus six-zero seconds."

Roden and the eleven Draeken soldiers who'd volunteered for this mission took the lead at the wide opening at the tail of the aircraft, with the wingless soldiers filling in behind. Cold wind blasted their faces. They stretched their wings.

That they hadn't been shot at yet meant his encrypted blocking program had worked. He inhaled deeply. The cold air reminded him of his first kill many years ago. *It's a good night.*

A light flashed red and a buzzer sounded. With his wings held tight to his body, Roden leapt from the helicopter. Angling into the wind, he shot forward and waited for a mental count of five before spreading his wings. Pressure stretched his muscles to their limits as he caught lift and flew. Even in the black of night, the freedom of flight was exhilarating.

He couldn't imagine not having wings. It would be like wearing leaden manacles. Nalea was part Draeken. Had the desires to take flight soared through her veins like it did his? He'd never had the time to ask her things like that. *Too late now.*

He cursed, refocusing his attention on the mission. Moments later, he touched down, a bare second before the first human—who was clearly an expert jumper—came in silently behind him. The man who'd watched him earlier was impressive, already rolling his parachute before the first Sephian landed.

While humans might be wingless and not technologically evolved, they did bring some value. Their primary value being that their DNA was eerily similar to that of the Draeken, making them the key to the survival of Roden's endangered race. The most noticeable differences between the two races were that humans were shorter since they'd evolved on a planet with greater gravity. Also, humans had never developed wings, which Roden found strange given that their DNA supported it.

Being winged, Draeken bodies hadn't evolved to be overly muscled to support the wings. Instead, their wings grew larger in proportion to their bodies, and their bones became lighter. The result of mating with the heavier boned, smaller humans remained an unknown. It was a risk Roden wouldn't have to deal with, as it would take generations to reveal the new—and hopefully better—race his troops had already jokingly labeled *Druman*, a word ironically similar to a Draeken term meaning *changeling*.

So much faith pinned on the future. Roden hoped they wouldn't be disappointed.

As all the helicopters emptied, the soldiers split into six teams, each containing four members from each race; as much from lack of trust as to leverage the various unique abilities, even though the lack of experience working together was a risk. Apolo led his team away from the others through the tree line around the base. It would have been faster to fly, but unfortunately the two other races were inferior in that regard, and they burned four minutes running an outer semi-circle of the base.

Apolo halted and held up a fisted hand in human fashion. They'd discussed communication before going in. All were fully aware of how dangerous this particular mission was. That was why Apolo had demanded to have Roden on his team, although he suspected the Sephian had an ulterior motive in keeping him close.

Roden wasn't comfortable serving as a second on this mission, but he understood the whole conflict-of-interest thing. He could deal with it… as long as they didn't get in his way.

Apolo's team would be the first to go in, grab Otas before the rest of the base realized they were surrounded, and—hopefully—

have the base surrender without a drop of blood spilled. *Otas's sour blood excluded, of course.*

He glanced at his wrist-comm. *Twelve seconds to go.* Everything had to be precise for this mission to succeed. Roden had been planning this mission for over a year; he had spent countless nights awake planning how to end a tyrant's reign without casualties. There was no way around it though: there would be casualties. But ending the Grand Lord's rule wasn't the most important reason for this mission. The Sephians saw the Draeken as their enemy, and they'd already begun to sway the humans. For his people to have a future, he'd have to find all three races a common enemy—something to bind them together.

Enter the Grand Lord as the perfect scapegoat. In a way, Hilas Puftan would lead his people to a new future. His downfall and Otas's death would be the dawn of his people's future on this planet. Otas thought Roden was trying to take over. He didn't know the half of it.

Nine seconds. He waited. *Four seconds.*

Two.

One.

Apolo nodded to a bulky Draeken soldier Roden had hand-picked for the team, who prepped a huge door-punch to break in as close to the heart of the base as possible. It only took two ear-ringing hits before the door splintered wide open. The base comm-alarm blared through the opening and blaster fire burst forward, taking down the guardsman still holding the door-punch with a dozen shots to his body. Everyone took cover to each side of the door.

Fyet! They must have bypassed his program. The question now was how much time the base had to prepare. Not that it would change anything; it was too late to call off the mission. If they didn't get Otas now, the imposter would get to the core ship and launch an attack the planet would be defenseless against. Tonight, the Grand Lord's reign must be ended for good.

With a scowl on his face, Apolo punched a code on his wrist-comm to warn the other teams, and then raised his hand, holding up three fingers. The Sephians quickly slid on black glasses. Wync pulled out two chaos-charges, activated them, and then tossed them down the hall. The team turned away and grabbed their ears.

Light and screeches erupting from the hallway pierced the night. Sparing a quick glance over the four humans, Roden nodded. Given how little time they'd had to prepare, they remained levelheaded. He made a mental note to approach them later about joining his team on a more permanent basis. He imagined what they'd say, but it was still worth a shot.

He moved around Apolo to enter the brightened base as their tracker, knowing they were only steps away from Hillas' heavily protected comm-center. He took down the first two guardsmen with clean stun shots to the head as they knelt in the hallway, still recovering from the vertigo brought on by the chaos charges.

Shots fired from his sides, and the remaining guardsmen fell. No new guardsmen appeared, and Roden stopped. Something wasn't right. No sooner had the thought crossed his mind than the back door to Hillas' office opened, and a small orb flew out. The door slammed closed.

"Chaos charge!" Roden yelled. "Fall back!"

They sprinted back the way they'd come until light and sound sent out waves of vertigo, knocking the team to the ground. His eardrums rang shrill sirens, nearly breaking under the duress. Even with his eyes closed, the light caused an instant migraine. If the Sephians hadn't been wearing special dark glasses, they would have been knocked unconscious.

As the effects of the charge faded, Roden tried to drag himself to his feet, only to be thrown against the wall by a human, who was firing at a door in the hallway. Roden realized he was returning fire. Pulling out a weapon, he fired off several shots, knowing his aim was still skewed by the charge. "Thanks, Ace," he shouted over the noise of battle.

The human nodded and kept on firing, looking fully recovered from the blast. In fact, all the humans had recovered more quickly than both their Draeken and Sephian counterparts. *Impressive.*

A shot singed Roden's thigh but he kept firing, finally taking down the Draeken nearest to the entrance with a solid stun-shot to the shoulder.

The rest of his team recovered soon after, and they volleyed enough return fire that their assailants retreated behind the closed door. "Status," Roden called out before checking his latest injury. The laser had just skimmed the skin. He was lucky, because, unlike his team, Otas' guardsmen had their blasters set to kill. He'd survive this battle, just as he'd survived countless others. Sometimes it seemed he was doomed to survive.

"Everyone's good," Apolo said from off to his left. "And I'm leading this team."

Roden stepped forward, grimacing at the pain but refusing to limp. He pulled out a round metallic ball from his pocket and squeezed. Apolo gave him a nod, and then kicked open the door. Roden tossed the chaos charge inside and Apolo slammed the door closed. Light and sound bled through the cracks around the door, but it was nothing compared to what the Draeken were experiencing inside.

Apolo glanced back and, without waiting for a response, opened the door. With Apolo in the lead, the team charged into the large room and fanned out, laying down gunfire like a rainfall of falling stars. The Draeken guardsmen, blasting away in a wild spray of shooting, were taken out in the first seconds. The room fell silent, and Roden glanced over the team.

Apolo was leaning over one of his own. Roden placed a hand on the Sephian's shoulder. The soldier on the ground was conscious, dark golden blood pouring from her stomach. "I'm fine," she scolded while Apolo ignored her and slapped a coagulant wrapping on it. The soldier hissed, but the bleeding stopped almost immediately.

Apolo pulled her to her feet, and she clenched her teeth. He turned to Ace. "You get Sana back to Kilo Tango."

The human moved forward and the Sephian glared at him from her spot against the wall. "I don't—"

"Go," Apolo said, interrupting her excuse. "You're no good to us when you can barely stay conscious."

Her mouth clamped shut, but she didn't say anything as Ace grabbed her under the shoulder and took on some of her weight.

Apolo eyed Roden's leg. "How about you?" he asked with a gesture.

Roden took a look. The material was frayed where the blast had singed his pant leg, and a wet spot around the hole betrayed signs of bleeding. "A paper cut." He motioned to the Apolo's arm, which currently had a stream of gold running down it. "You?"

Apolo barely glanced down. "Paper cut."

With a nod, Roden turned walked through the room, in between the fallen Draeken, and toward the wall on the far side. Just as he'd expected, Otas had hidden himself away. *Spineless.*

He went straight past the wall with the obvious hidden door to where Roden knew the entrance to Hillas' battle shelter was. Otas couldn't have known Roden knew, but he was likely watching his doom walk toward him on video at that very moment.

Once the team filled in behind and Apolo nodded, Roden casually typed in the secure code to open the door. With a click and a *swoosh*, the wall slid back and to the side.

All their blasters locked onto the small room's occupant.

Roden froze. Make that *occupants.*

Otas stood facing him, clad in full protective gear. The coward held Nalea before him like a shield. She was wearing no body armor whatsoever. Her eyes were covered by dark glasses, so he couldn't tell if she was as surprised to see him or not.

"Hello, my dear," Roden said, fighting against every nerve in his body to show a response.

She stood like a silent statue. Why wasn't she trying to break free? She wore no restraints. She could easily overpower the fop. Yet she just stood there, draped in a long gown.

"Nalea?" Apolo asked as he came to Roden's side, his face mirroring the shock Roden felt.

Until that point, Nalea had been focused on Roden, but upon seeing her old friend, a smile filled her face and she stepped forward, only to have Otas yank her against his chest. She scowled.

Apolo eyed Roden before turning a hard glare on her captor. "Release her this instant, imposter, or die."

Ten blasters were aimed at Otas, but there was no way to shoot him without hitting Nalea first. Roden paused when light reflected off her necklace. The woman he knew wasn't one to wear gaudy jewelry. He narrowed his gaze on it and tensed. "Damn it, Lea."

She bristled but didn't say anything.

"Roden?" Apolo asked.

Roden sighed and lowered his weapon. "As much as I'd like to kill this imposter, we can't shoot him without the risk of harming my consort. A neck-charge, Otas? How *undignified*."

Apolo cursed.

Otas chortled as he pulled her back a step. "Dire times call for dire measures."

Nalea's eyes widened. "Behind you!"

The sound of pounding bootsteps broke through the silence. Roden snapped around to find guardsmen pouring into the office behind them. Wync flung himself at the wall and hit a switch. The wall moved back into place, cutting off the newcomers and Roden's team, leaving Roden and Apolo trapped inside the small shelter with Otas and Nalea.

Gunfire and shouts filtered through the wall. Otas smiled. "I believe we're at an impasse."

"Here's your only chance," Apolo said. "Stand down and we won't shoot."

Nalea stood firm, turning first to Apolo and then holding her gaze on Roden, as though she were contemplating what to do next. "Kill him," she said suddenly.

Roden looked into her eyes. She believed that eliminating the Grand Lord was more important than her life? *Never.* "No," he ground out.

She must've seen the truth in his eyes because she turned to Apolo. "Finish this."

Apolo, face hard, shook his head slowly.

Otas grinned as he backed up a step.

A low hum erupted around them. It'd been nearly three years since Roden felt that kind of power. "Oh, *fyet.* The power cells are active."

"Don't move," Apolo commanded.

With a sudden twist, Nalea yanked free and stabbed Otas near the collarbone with a small metal object.

Otas cried out, and pulled out the object, which turned out to be a fork. He went to press a button on a band around his wrist.

Roden pulled the trigger. A shot blasted through Otas's hand, and he screamed.

"Can't set off her disjunctor without a hand, can you?" Roden sneered.

"Damn you!" Otas snarled and pulled out a handgun with his other hand. A *human* gun. What the hell was the imposter doing dirtying his hands with human technology? "You will still die today, Roden!"

Apolo shot Otas in the leg; he stumbled with a grunt but quickly returned to full height. With protective body armor covering most of his body, blaster shots were easily absorbed by the material.

Roden aimed and fired at Otas' uninjured hand at the same time Otas began shooting, each trigger pull making his hand jerk. Apolo fired, knocking the Draeken down. Even then, Otas kept firing.

A sudden pain blinded Roden. He stumbled back, and Nalea grabbed onto him.

Otas jumped to his feet and barked out a command. A narrow door opened behind him and he leapt through the small door just before its jaws snapped closed.

Apolo lunged forward and searched for a touchpad.

Roden tried to move forward to help, but pain burned his side. He touched it and discovered wetness. A familiar, numbing pain climbed through his veins. *Poison.*

Nalea came down with him, pressing against the bullet wound, trying to staunch the blood flow, but Roden knew the tangy scent of the poison too well.

"*Tiscalin,*" he muttered. A common poison because of its effectiveness and often used in blood charges, it was both an anticcagulant as well as a deadly venom that would eventually paralyze his heart. He looked up at Apolo. "Tell me you've packed anti-venom."

Apolo was already pulling out a small syringe as he ripped open a bandage. Nalea held Roden's head up as Apolo injected the syringe full of anti-venom directly into the wound. Apolo then slapped a bandage over the wound, none too gently, and Roden cursed and glared at the Sephian.

Apolo smirked before backing away. "You'll survive." Then he turned and spoke into his wrist-comm. "This is Team Three. We need an evac at Kilo Tango. Multiple injuries. Prep for a *tiscalin* treatment and Draeken blood transfusion."

A voice coming through his wrist-comm quickly responded. "*Acknowledged. Pickup at Kilo Tango in three minutes. We're reporting a serious influx of power coming up around the base. Status of target?*"

Apolo scowled. "The target has escaped."

A pause. "*You better move fast.*"

"Sounds like you came prepared," Nalea commented.

The humming in the room grew, and Roden noticed a slight glow emanate from the direction Otas had escaped. The glow was slowly filling in the wall. He winced. "Otas has initiated a force barrier."

Apolo cursed. "Clearly we weren't prepared enough." He stood and hit another key on his wrist-comm. "Team Three, status report."

"Room is secure."

Apolo nodded to Nalea, who swiped her hand over the wall. The door opened.

Biting back the writhing tentacles of agony expanding outward from his wound, Roden staggered forward into the larger room. Already, an additional team was filtering in. They stopped at each fallen Draeken, disarming and restraining before moving on to the next one. One of Roden's least favorite Sephians, who now bore a nasty burn shot through his arm, came to his feet upon seeing them.

"Bente!" Nalea called out.

Cradling his arm, he smiled. "Good to see you."

"Pickup is on its way," Apolo said.

Bente nodded. "I heard."

Roden's muscles tensed as he tried to hold himself up. "Let's move."

Nalea watched him suspiciously for a moment, and then wrapped her arm around his torso to keep him from collapsing.

He gave a weak smile. "I've missed you too, dear."

She grunted in response.

"I say we leave him and let the force barrier take care of him," Bente added.

"Bente, grab that gear bag," Apolo said as he walked past the pair.

The Sephian lifted his own arm. "But I'm injured."

Apolo huffed. "That scratch?"

Roden glanced down at Nalea, and she looked up as though she knew his eyes were on her. He frowned, and then turned his attention to Apolo. "You have any people who know how to remove a neck-charge without detonating it?"

Apolo's lips thinned and he shook his head slowly.

Nalea stopped, swallowed. "I have to stay. I'm a safety risk to you."

"Like hells you are," Roden countered.

"What are you talking about?" Bente asked.

She pointed to her necklace. "There's a charge set on this. Otas has the detonator. He could set it off at any time."

"*Suvaste,*" Bente muttered.

Roden nodded toward the humming wall. "The force barrier is already filling in. There's no way to get to him."

"Don't be foolish. You're coming with us," Apolo snapped at Nalea.

She shook her head. "I don't know how big the blast could be if he detonates it. I won't risk your lives. I need to stay here and finish this."

"No," Roden said. "If Otas was going to detonate the charge, he would've done it already." He winced as he wrapped his arm around her in turn.

"I'm trying to protect your worthless hides," she muttered.

"You're coming," Apolo barked over his shoulder. "And that's an order, Nalea."

She cursed several colorful words but didn't push away from Roden as they walked through the hallway. Without the cauterization of the blaster injuries, his wound was excruciating. *Damned human weapons.* It took every ounce of strength he had to walk, but he wasn't about to show weakness.

He'd only stumbled twice—blaming it on debris both times— by the time they stepped through the collapsed door that led outside the base. A *whoomp-whoomp* sound brought his attention to the night sky. Three helicopters lowered to the ground as gently as birds to their nest.

Losing his balance, he fell to his knees, his strength now gone. A couple of medics jumped out of one of the aircraft with a long board. They rushed forward and reached for Roden. He hissed, drawing back from their outstretched hands. "Help the others first."

The medics froze, looking to Apolo, who stalked over and helped him back to his feet. "You go with them or else I'll shoot you myself."

He grimaced, but finally relented with a nod. The two medics pulled him onto the portable stretcher. They had Roden strapped down within seconds, and he pulled at the straps. "Imbeciles," he muttered as they slid him none too gently onto the floor of the helicopter.

Nalea backed away, touching the disjunctor. Roden motioned for her to come to him. She turned and walked away.

His head collapsed onto the cushioned stretcher. Pain coated his senses, numbing his mind. When he looked again, Apolo stood there, watching him with blank features, before stepping closer and grabbing Roden's hand.

His mind glazing, Roden looked out to where Nalea had disappeared. He squeezed the Sephian's hand. "She can stop the war. Take care of her, *ta deiti*."

"I will." He paused. "Old friend…"

Chapter 26

Nalea stood under the tree, hidden by low branches, as the helicopter lifted from the ground. The night air, even with its metallic hints of machinery and petroleum, strengthened her. *Freedom.* It'd been so long that she'd nearly forgotten the smell of fresh air. Closing her eyes, she inhaled deeply. Then she remembered the weight around her neck, and the air grew stifling and dull.

Every second she wore it, the disjunctor around her neck grew heavier. Why hadn't Otas killed her yet? What was he waiting for?

"He's going to be all right."

Nalea jumped at Apolo's voice. She turned and saw him walking toward her from where the helicopter carrying Roden lifted off. "I don't care," she blurted out a little too quickly.

His lips pursed, but he didn't have time to respond.

"Can we remove the collar without it detonating?" Apolo asked.

She jumped, not realizing he'd approached. She shook her head. "Otas is wearing the detonator. If he's killed, it goes off. He can set it off manually too."

"*Suvaste,*" Apolo muttered before turning back to the helicopter. He rummaged through a crate of gear and returned with a black vest. "We'll get that thing off you back at the base. In the meantime, try this," he said.

She frowned. "What is it?"

"A bullet-proof vest. I don't like you still being at risk, but it makes you safer to be around others. Cover that thing with the vest, and if it discharges, the vest should catch most of the charge."

Apolo helped her fasten the straps. "Now, we need to head back to the base and regroup."

When she opened her mouth to object, he cut her off with a wave of his hand. "Before you even think you're not coming back because of that thing around your neck, let me tell you this: if you don't get on that helicopter, I'll have you arrested and carried on board if I have to."

With a scowl, she snapped around and headed toward the helicopter. As they walked, a human soldier from her past jogged up to them. "Good to see you, Nalea," Ace said before turning to Apolo. "It looks like a contingent of Draeken has holed up within the central communications room."

Apolo didn't seem surprised. "Our target is there. With a force barrier in place, we may not be able to get to him, but at least he can't get out. We need to lock up any escape routes, and we need to do it now. I want you to take point. I'll apprise Sommers."

Ace nodded before taking off into woods, disappearing within feet of entering the darkness.

Nalea climbed on board, grabbing the closest seat. Bente lifted himself with his good arm and took the seat next to her. "The bastard said you were dead."

Nalea glanced up, knowing Bente was referring to Roden. Had Roden thought she was dead? *Presumptive fregee.* She shot a hard look at her friend. "Do I look dead to you?"

Bente belted out a chuckle. "Gods, it's good to have you back." Then his features hardened. "Wow, of everyone in the universe…"

Nalea sighed, leaning her head against the seat. "Tell me about it."

"*Suvaste*," he muttered.

From outside the plane, Apolo gave several more commands before climbing on board and strapping himself into the seat across from Nalea. Several bags of gear lay on the floor of the helicopter between them.

She frowned, still trying to figure out why Apolo wasn't trying to kill the second most hated Draeken of the Noble War. Apolo had pursued Roden relentlessly over the years and vice versa. They were stout enemies, each a major player in the Noble War. Yet they'd come against Otas, working side by side.

"How do you know Roden?" she called out over the jolting roar of the engines as they lifted from the ground.

Apolo's eyes narrowed only slightly. "I don't know Roden, but I know Kreed. And that Draeken is Kreed."

Chapter 27

F *yet.*

Roden awoke to find liquid fire running through his brain and lead clogging his veins. He forced his eyes open and a drab human medical facility came into view.

He rolled his stiff neck from side to side, wincing at his tight, sore muscles then brought his hand over to the bandage covering his stomach. *Damn, human weapons could do their share of damage, especially coupled with the nasty effects of tiscalin.* It would take days before he'd be back to full strength.

Nalea watched him from a chair across the room.

"How long have I been out?"

She shrugged. "A few hours."

She wore a thick, high-necked vest that didn't move when she shrugged. He frowned. "They let you run free around this place with a bomb still around your neck?"

She bristled. "No. I'm only allowed here or in my quarters. Evidently, they don't see your death as a significant risk."

He brushed off her comment with a wave. "We need to get that thing off you."

Nalea continued to fidget. "Wync brought a couple of your

people to Apolo to see if they could get it off without it detonat-ing. It seems that no one has experience with these things."

"We'll get it off." He grunted as he moved to a more comfort-able position. "Otas needs you alive to keep Hillas' title."

She looked up, and though he couldn't see her eyes, he knew the frustration and sense of helplessness those dark glasses hid. He felt the same way while lying in this bed. He'd expected the mission to take down Hillas' imposter as well as to show the humans that the Draeken were a fair and just race. Instead, it seemed he'd made no progress whatsoever in establishing an earthside home for his people. Without human support, they were nothing more than nomads.

He frowned when he realized Nalea was still watching him.

"Who are you?" she asked under her breath.

"You know me." The reply was quiet, confident.

Her head shook slightly from side to side. "That's the thing. I have no idea who you are."

He sighed, long and hard. "What do you wish to know?"

"For starters, you can tell me about Kreed."

He shot her a hard look and saw the truth in her eyes; even through the dark glasses. All that planning was wasted. Every-thing he'd done to maintain a dichotomy, gone. If she knew, that meant Apolo had figured things out, which could only mean his lifelong secret was now public knowledge. His people would never trust Kreed, and the Sephians and humans would never trust Roden. What he'd worked at keeping separate had come together explosively. He rubbed his temples, a headache overpowering the pain wracking his body.

"I don't get it. Why two identities?"

He sighed deeply. "As Roden, I could lead my people to lasting peace right in the open. As Kreed, I could guide my people from the shadows. Besides, many of the heroes in human legends had alter egos."

She belted out a laugh. "You're no hero." She shook her head.

"How can you say you worked toward peace when you led your people in war?"

His lips tightened. "Because, sometimes, to get to peace, people have to suffer enough that there's no other choice."

She flinched. It was the slightest movement, but Roden noticed. Then she sobered. "So, are you Kreed who used Roden's identity to betray your people, or are you Roden who used Kreed's identity to mislead my people?"

His eyes closed. "Neither." He paused. "Both." Speaking caused him to cough. "I was born Kreed Sylk, but I've been Roden Zyll longer. Regardless of the name I go by, peace has always been my endgame."

"You switch identities so easily. Even Apolo said he hardly recognized you, even though you grew up together."

"You think he was my slave?"

She shook her head. "No."

He let silence fill the room for a moment before speaking. "We went to school together. My family had no slaves. Even if my parents could have afforded them, they never would have accepted a slave. They were stalwart opponents of slavery and worked hard to integrate the races. That's how I ended up in the same school as Apolo."

"Yet you became a lord with hundreds of slaves to your name. Your parents must've been proud," she said sarcastically.

"They died when I was young," Roden said. "And I wasn't born a lord."

She frowned. "But that's impossible; on Sephia, commoners can't just *decide* to become lords. Bloodlines are sacred."

Roden shrugged. "I'd just gotten over a bad time in my life. On my course for vengeance, I ran into Lord Zyll, who was seeking vengeance for the death of his only son who'd been about my age. I promised retribution for his son. In return, I became his son to carry on the bloodline. I didn't like having slaves, but I couldn't release them without breaking my promise to Lord Zyll."

She studied him, and the pieces finally fell into place. "That's why you brought Kreed back. To do what Roden couldn't do."

Roden nodded tightly. "Yes, that was how it started. I've made mistakes, but I don't have regrets. Everything I've done has been to bring lasting peace to my people."

Her chair slid on the hard floor, and he looked up to see Naea standing over him. A gentle hand pushed his fist down, and he found a straw held to his mouth. The water was cool, at first burning his raw throat, then soothing. She pulled away the glass far too soon.

She returned to her chair. "I still can't tell when you're telling the truth or when you're lying."

He wiped his chin with the back of his hand before nodding toward the disjunctor. "When we get that thing off you, you won't need to ask. That's how Otas got you to wear it, I assume—you had begun to sense me."

She set the glass down. "Rather than having me read your emotions, you could just tell me the truth instead."

"I can try."

Her expression was sad, but he could have sworn he glimpsed hope in her features. "You know, things could've gone smoother if I'd known you were on our side."

He clenched his eyes closed, then glowered at her. "Still you don't understand? There is no *side*. I do what's best for our people. Our survival, Draeken and Sephian, is intertwined. Neither can thrive without the other. You are the key to making that happen."

She didn't look up, only shook her head. "It's not that easy."

"It's not that difficult. All you need to do is stand with one hand reaching out to each race, and the Draeken and Sephians will accept peace. With the humans, we'll broker peace together, and live in whatever inhospitable nook of this world they deem fit. If they refuse, with our power cells recharged, we'll move on to the next habitable world."

"None of that sounds easy," she said.

He shrugged and winced.

"Why did you tell everyone I was dead?" she asked.

He frowned. "I assumed Otas had had you executed."

"Not that time. The first time… before you left me with Otas, Apolo said that you—Kreed, I mean—said I was already dead. Were you planning ahead?"

"I wanted us to finish Hillas without distractions, like rescue attempts."

She blew out a breath. "I'm a living being, Roden, not some possession. Don't you realize these games you play destroy lives?"

For the first time ever, he realized that he craved this woman to find him redeemable, though he often suspected that there was nothing left to redeem. He'd crossed that line too long ago. "Sometimes, games are necessary, and yes, I realize lives are in the balance. Tell me, how many lives were lost during last night's attack?"

"What?" she asked, and then shook a fist at him. "Gods, you're infuriating. Can you not answer a single question directly?"

When he didn't answer, she pursed her lips. "Eight total: one Sephian, two humans, and five Draeken."

"Five?" Roden shot her a dark frown. "Why so many?"

"It seems that several Sephians and humans switched their blasters to 'kill'."

Bloodthirsty imbeciles. He shook his head slightly. He'd known there'd be loss of life when he took down Hillas, but when would it end? "Where is Otas now?"

She began to pace. "We believe he's locked down in his comm-center. The force barrier has been pulled back to cover just that area of the base. We suspect that he doesn't have enough power cells to maintain a larger barrier."

"The good news is that he and his guardsmen can't escape," Roden said.

"How can you be so sure?"

He shook his head. "The force barrier imprisons him within his comm-center as much as it holds us out."

"We have him surrounded," Nalea said. "We wait until his power runs out."

Roden sighed. "The upgraded power cells needed to run a force barrier won't run out. He'll run out of food first, and the core ships could be at full power by then." He'd thoroughly examined the power cell he'd snatched. The technology was impressively simple. Just a few algorithms adapted the technology to read the smaller discrete waves off this star rather than the continuous waves off Sephia's system. He tried to sit up, the sheet draping around his waist.

Her step faltered as her eyes dropped from his face to a distance lower. "You need to rest," she blurted out.

"I need to end this before Otas has the power of a core ship behind him." The only reason the core ships weren't in orbit already was that Otas hadn't converted all the power cells yet, giving Roden a very short window to prevent a catastrophic war on this planet.

Nalea gave him a choked look. "You're in no condition to stand, let alone go back to the base. Face it, your coup is on hold."

Holding the sheet around his waist, he managed to pull himself to his feet, flaring his wings for added balance. His legs were wobbly, forcing him to hold onto the bed for support. He glared. "Damn it, Nalea. It was never about power. We have hours, days at most, before the first core ship has finished upgrading their power cells."

Her eyes narrowed. "Exactly how many core ships are there?"

"More than one." His reply was curt. "Which makes taking down Otas quickly all the more critical. If Otas is at the helm when that happens, he'll enslave this world and destroy both my and your people in the process."

"Don't," she scolded. "Don't act like you're doing all this out of some altruistic urge. You don't care about my people."

He pushed off from the bed. "I owe as much to your people as I do mine." He miraculously found the strength to walk. With each step, the burning tension eased in his muscles. He stopped at the table across the room, where his clothes sat neatly folded. He grabbed the wrist-comm from the top of the pile and snapped it around his forearm. A female's voice came through the small speaker.

"Gix," he said. "Tell me you're finished with what I asked."

"I am, my lord. We're all set," Gix replied.

"Good. See you in an hour." His body ached all over.

His people moved fast. If only they'd been able to move faster, they would've ensured Otas was eliminated the first time.

"What makes you think the humans will let you out of here?" Nalea asked from behind.

He gingerly fastened his kilt around his waist. "I don't need permission, my dear. All my ships are equipped with the new power cells and on their way here as we speak."

Chapter 28

Nalea followed Roden past the guards posted at the doorway, out of the room, and into the hallway. It didn't take long to catch up. After several swaying steps, he leaned against the wall. With his eyes closed, he rested his head back and took a deep breath. His wings hung limply.

Despite still being angry at him for writing her off as dead, she took a step closer. Cautiously, she slid her dark glasses down her nose to look him in the eye. "And what happens when you take down Otas? What then, Roden?"

His gaze met hers then. "Then you'll have one less Draeken to worry about."

"Amen to that," Sienna called out as she appeared around a corner and into Nalea's line of sight. "But Nalea's right. You're in no shape to be out of bed."

"Eavesdropping again?" Roden asked.

"When it comes to my best friend being in the same room as my worst enemy, you're damn straight. And you better get used to it because *The Roden Show* is on twenty-four/seven around here."

Nalea pushed the dark glasses back up her nose.

Roden grunted and pushed off from the wall. "Get me Sommers."

"I don't follow your orders," Sienna snapped back.

"Please," Roden said, except the word came out as an order.

Sienna shot him a hard glare but picked up her cell phone.

Roden stepped forward, but his knee buckled. Without thinking, Nalea slid herself under his shoulder, taking on some of his weight. He grumbled but didn't push her away. As she hefted his dead weight, she looked up at Sienna. "A little help here?"

Sienna looked aghast as she slid her cell phone into her pocket. "Uh, hello? Cripple here." She motioned to her leg.

Nalea snorted. "I've known you long enough to know that you would never, ever consider yourself crippled."

Sienna rolled her eyes before sliding her arm around Roden's other side. They'd walked only a few steps before Sienna was pulled away.

Nalea glanced up to see a glaring Legian standing in the hallway with an arm wrapped around Sienna's waist. Major Sommers, along with three human soldiers, approached from several feet away.

"Glad you could make it," Nalea said. "It seems Roden is intent on killing himself, and we're helping him."

Sommers smirked. "Well, if that's the case..." He motioned, and two of his men stepped forward and took on most of Roden's weight. Nalea stepped back with relief. Being in such close proximity to Roden was unnerving.

Sienna and Legian led them down several long hallways before coming to a large room, one wall of which was covered in windows. His ships had already begun to arrive. Armed soldiers— all human aside from a few Sephians—flocked onto the tarmac. Humans and Sephians alike looked more than a little apprehensive, but Roden's people must've provided the clearance codes to land, or else they would've been shot down.

"I would thank you for the assistance, but I much preferred the company of the two women—ow!" Roden sniped, and Nalea noticed one of the soldiers had roughly grabbed a wing as they stepped away from the Draeken. Roden stretched his wing, glancing back. "Your people are quite clumsy."

"Mm," Sommers replied with a smile.

Roden leaned against a window, his pale skin even paler in the light. He looked absolutely exhausted, probably as much from blood loss as from the *tiscalin*. "Major, my ships will have room for more if you have any soldiers you'd like to send along. But, if they come, they're under my command for this one."

"Giving orders now? That wasn't part of our deal," Sommers said, his armed crossed over his chest. "You better tread softly, Commander."

Roden sighed. "If Otas has partially completed upgrading power cells on the base, then the core ships won't be far behind. We're on borrowed time as it is."

"And what do you propose?" Sommers asked, leaning forward in his chair. "We can't breach that force shield."

"Ah, but we can now," Roden replied. "My teams have just finished updating the power cells on several ships."

Legian frowned. "Who's to stop you from turning that power against us after we take down your competition?"

He won't. Nalea suddenly noticed everyone looking at her and realized she'd spoken her thoughts out loud. "It's true," she said. "Roden doesn't want another war."

"I do want peace," Roden said before turning back to Sommers. "And I also don't renege on my promises. I'll keep to the terms we agreed on. It is not my intent to cause friction at the onset of our relationship. However, we simply don't have the time to negotiate right now. Otas won't suspect that my teams have upgraded the cells so quickly, but he has to assume we've been working on them. We must move quickly, because I doubt you'll like the outcome if he's still in charge when the core ships are at full power."

"Do you propose the same mission plan as before?" Sommers asked.

"Same plan, but we use my ships this time. They have the power necessary to take down the force barrier."

Sienna held out her hands. "You can't be seriously considering this."

Nalea frowned at her friend. She'd never noticed how much Sienna hated the Draeken before. Then again, she'd never noticed because she had hated the Draeken so much herself. Roden was right: Nalea had lumped his entire race into one bucket labeled 'unworthy of living'.

"We can take your ships," Sommers said, ignoring Sienna. "But we're doubling the human troops. You run the show to take down the force shield, and I run the show on the ground."

Roden nodded. "As long as I lead the team that goes for Otas."

Sommers thought for a moment. "Yes, as long as Apolo goes with you. And I select your team. I want people who've worked together before. We won't succeed without cohesion."

"I have to be on that team," Nalea added. When everyone turned to her, she added, "Otas knows he needs me. We can use that to our advantage."

"As long as you wear that disjunctor, you pose a risk to the entire team," Roden said.

"I'll keep the vest on. If Otas sets it off, that should protect everyone from the blast."

"Except you," Sienna said.

"I'm not safe wherever I am as long as I wear this. I may as well do some good instead of sitting around."

Sommers nodded. "You have a point. You go with us. While that thing around your neck is still an unknown risk, we need to get to Otas quickly, and you might be the diversion we need." Sommers motioned to a soldier who pulled out a syringe and approached Roden.

Roden took a step back. "What is that?"

"This,"—Sommers held up the syringe—"contains a tracer. Consider this an assurance that you don't plan to leave us high and dry once this is done. Any Draeken *and* Sephian on Earth soil also gets a tracer."

Nalea stood there, holding her breath. A tracer would effectively put a bulls-eye on each of them. The humans could take out any of their people whenever they wanted.

Roden pursed his lips before speaking. "An assurance it is then. I'll make arrangements for my troops." He held out his arm.

Sommers shook his head. Then pointed to Roden's neck.

"I do believe that you enjoy this." Roden lowered his head and winced when Sommers injected him.

Roden looked back up, rubbing his neck. "Happy now?"

"Mm," Sommers replied. He then looked across the faces in the room. "We leave at 1730. That gives us nearly four hours to prepare our teams for the mission."

"One last thing," Roden said. "I'd like my people back."

Sommers frowned. "And exactly which ones would that be?"

Roden cocked his head. "Talla Kohlm, for starters, who I know for a fact the Sephians have had the pleasure of hosting for the past year, as well all my compatriots abducted from Club Mayhem."

"I can't confirm we have any of your people, but I'll look into it," Sommers said.

"You do that," Roden said, the challenge clear in his words.

The door opened, and a small Draeken female stepped inside, escorted by two human soldiers. She glanced around, and once she saw Roden, she headed directly to him. She pulled out a small black case from her pocket. He nodded in the direction of the Sephians. "That belongs to them."

"My end of the bargain," Roden said. "We've made adjustments to the prototype to make the update process more efficient. With this, you should be able to get all the Sephian power cells updated within a month, at which time any Sephians who wish to return to Sephia can. I'm working on the conversion on my base now."

"I'll take that," Sommers said, taking the package. "We'll work out the conversion timetable together."

Interesting. A sense of foreboding filled Roden. The humans had even more control over the Sephians than he'd first realized.

"Let me get this straight. Your entire base, not just your ships, will be running at full power soon?" Sommers asked, looking skeptical and not a bit pleased.

Roden nodded. "Soon, and I suspect you'd like to continue our discussions of a more permanent alliance after this mission because I can assure you, you don't want me for an enemy."

Sommers bristled. "You won't intimidate me, Zyll. And, don't forget, this planet doesn't belong to you. We'll fight tooth and nail to keep our home."

"As long as the alliance we reach is mutually beneficial, I assure you that things will go smoothly." His voice then lowered, the words more drawn out. "I would hope your people have learned from past mistakes, such as how the natives to this country were originally handled. My people would find that kind of treatment… unacceptable."

"We have no intention of mistreating our new guests," Sommers said tightly.

Roden's lips curved upward and he clapped his hands once. "Then we'll get along splendidly. I already have some ideas for how you can leverage our power cells."

Three hours later, Nalea sat in a lounge with Roden, Sienna, Legian, Sommers, and several other human officers, finalizing plans for the mission. A female Draeken stepped into the room as though she were unsure she should be there. She was the first Draeken Nalea had seen on Earth who was shorter than her. She watched with suspicion as the winged female pulled out a fabric case and opened it to reveal a syringe of black fluid. Nalea sucked in a breath and glared at Roden. "*Merr*? You can't be serious."

Roden glanced down at her. Hard truth shone in his eyes. "You want peace? You want a shot at Otas? Then this is it, my dear. There's no time to lose, and my body isn't strong enough."

"But that drug has a seventy percent death rate," she countered.

"Sorry to disappoint you, but I've used it more than once before and I'm still here," he said. He nodded to the Draeken at his side.

Nalea stared as Roden was injected with the highly illegal drug. He gave a sharp wince as the drug entered his bloodstream. *Merr* was a last resort drug, used to increase adrenaline for several hours, most often used during warfare to allow wounded soldiers to continue the fight.

She shook her head in disbelief. "You'll be helpless for days after it wears off."

Roden stretched his wings, then his arms, clearly still in pain but already moving with more fluidity and strength than seconds earlier. He glanced her way. "Then I'll be sure to be in bed and ensconced safely in your arms by then."

Nalea scowled at the comment. "I see the *merr* has already affected your brain."

Roden stood, at first wobbly on his feet, then more secure. "My ships depart for the base in fifteen minutes." With that, he walked outside.

Nalea jogged to catch up. "Hold up," she said, grabbing Roden by the shoulder.

Gix grabbed Nalea's wrist, but after a nod from Roden, Gix stepped away, glared at Nalea, and walked ahead.

Roden turned his attention on Nalea.

"There's something I can't figure out," she said quietly. "You went after Hillas before your ships were at full power. If you'd waited, you wouldn't have needed help from the humans and Sephians now. Why?"

His lips curved upward. "Hillas had bragged too soon. Until he had operating power cells, he was weak. It was the optimal time to bring in humans to take down Hillas with minimal risk. Battles are always good for alliances. If he hadn't initiated the force barrier, we would have succeeded in taking Otas down."

"But the mission failed."

He shook his head. "No. I rescued my consort."

"Ah yes, your endgame," she said drily. "After all, you need a Puftan to make everyone fall in line."

He glanced over to his ship, then back at her. In his eyes, she saw emotion; disappointment, sadness, and something else. "Yes," he said finally. "Everything is about the endgame."

Chapter 29

R oden sat on the ship, letting the *merr* surge through his veins. It was an unnatural adrenaline, burning and raw, but if it wasn't for the *merr*, he'd be on his back right now and Otas would have no one to prevent him from escaping to a core ship. Nalea had been right. A large percentage of *merr* users died with the first injection. Their hearts simply couldn't handle the extreme rush. Hells, he'd thought he was going to die the first time he took it. But he knew how much *merr* his body could take, had always been careful, and the drug had saved him in more than one impossible situation.

But he would never use *merr* once Nalea was safe from Otas and free of the disjunctor. He'd made the vow before he'd taken the injection today, when he awoke to find Nalea at his bedside. *Merr* was no longer worth the risk.

He could handle all the hostile glares coming from the Sephians, except Nalea, who watched him with suspicion. However, he was disappointed at how many of the humans glared at him. The Sephians had clearly been busy badmouthing the Draeken—and especially Roden—and it would take some time to change those initial impressions.

Fortunately, with his ship, the flight was much quicker than last time. It took only a few minutes before Roden's fleet of eight ships touched down outside Hillas' earthside base. There'd also been no need to hide their presence. This time Roden wanted Otas to know that his time was coming to an end. He looked outside to see the human and Sephian garrison around the base in full motion. Several trucks were already driving up to his ships.

As everyone departed the ship, he went to Gix in the cockpit. She was still at the controls, already scanning for the frequency the force barrier ran on. He placed a hand on her shoulder, and she turned around. "Yes, my lord?"

"You are doing well," he said. "I have complete trust in you."

She beamed. "Thank you, my lord. You have given me chances that most wouldn't."

He patted her shoulder and turned to leave.

"My lord..."

He turned back to Gix.

She swallowed. "I know you have our people's best interests at heart, and that's all that matters. If you needed another identity to do that, it's not my place to judge. I just want you to know that I still believe in you."

He smiled. "You're a good guardsman and an honorable Draeken, Gix. Any man would be honored to earn your attentions."

Her cheeks turned a rosy blush before she returned focus to the ship's controls.

There'd never been a Draeken civil war before, likely because his people had no religion to cause hate, or perhaps because they'd enough technology and wealth to bring comfort to all citizens. Regardless, because of Draeken contentedness, no countermeasures had ever been built into their technology. Roden had access to the same technology and systems that Hillas had. A risk Roden had noticed long ago and had counted on to protect his people. But he was also certain that Otas was feverishly working on less *universal* technology.

In this case, the force barrier surrounding a small section of the base ran at a specific range of frequencies. If a large blaster could be calibrated to just the right frequency, its sound could penetrate the wall of energy that cocooned the comm-center from the rest of the world. With that sound, dismantling codes could ride in and shut down the barrier, and even the best comm-tech couldn't prevent it.

With Roden's ships running at full power, they had the strength necessary to take down the force barrier. "Gix, keep running through the energy frequencies, but don't take down the force field until my signal."

She nodded without looking up. "Yes, my lord."

With that, he double-checked his weapons and left the ship. Already, the hum of the force barrier vibrated within his teeth. The afternoon sun was bright and hot. All the Sephians wore blackened wraparound glasses that were so dark, neither Draeken nor human could see anything through them.

Apolo walked out of the base to meet him. Roden's jaw tightened and he kept walking forward. Apolo met him halfway, turned, and stayed in step by his side. Apolo grabbed Roden's arm and pulled him to a stop. "Tell me you're still Kreed and not Roden."

"I am," he replied simply before pulling away. It was the truth... mostly. While he was first and foremost Kreed, sometimes he had a hard time remembering who Kreed Sylk was.

He could hear the Sephian still at his back, the sounds of gravel crunching under heavy boots. "We'll talk more later."

"I'm sure we will," Roden muttered under his breath before continuing toward the large, broken-down door to the base. A few dozen teams were all set, checking their weapons. Nalea stood just outside the door, keeping her distance.

"Sommers apprised me of the plan on your way over," Apolo said, spoiling Roden's view.

Roden paused. "Make sure everyone has their weapons on 'stun' this time. I'll personally break the neck of anyone who intentionally kills a Draeken."

Apolo's eyes narrowed. After a moment, he gave a tight nod. "I'm not used to taking orders from a Draeken."

"And I'm not used to giving orders to a Sephian."

Apolo smirked. "*Suvaste*. You've always been bossy."

With that, Roden grinned and grabbed Apolo's forearm, then patting him on his back.

His friend repeated the gesture.

Feeling a bit more at peace with the world, Roden turned to find Nalea giving him a frown, or perhaps more correctly, her usual expression. He strolled up to her. He placed a hand on the wall, nearly pulled it away from the pulsating hum of the barrier emanating from within.

"What?" she asked.

"As soon as Otas sees you, we'll need to move quickly. I'm counting on the fact that he's smart enough to not hit the detonator. Still, I don't want him to get twitchy fingers."

She nodded tightly. "Just in case, this vest should protect everyone around me, as long as they keep a distance."

"It's not them I'm worried about." He brushed past her to walk into the middle of the team. "Apolo says that you're all ready for this. Any questions?"

Not a one. These were professionals.

"Good," Roden said. "Some gentle reminders then. This is a grab-and-go, *not* a mission to kill anyone with wings. Be sure to have your blasters set to 'stun'." He turned and saw Nalea watching him from her place at the wall. "To give you an idea of the unsavory type of fellow we're up against, our dear Nalea is wearing a neck-charge, courtesy of Otas Olnek, that's primed to detonate if anything happens to him. If the imposter dies, Nalea dies, so I highly recommend you subdue rather than kill Otas."

Roden looked over the crowd. "Since Otas has disjunctors on this base, he also has the means to nullify the detonator. I've programmed an image of a nullifier into all of your wrist-comms. Be sure to memorize it. Should you come across one, get it to me as soon as possible."

All heads tilted down, looking at their wrist-comms.

Roden continued. "Any nullifier is probably in the comm-center, which is on the other side of the force barrier. When we find Otas, if you see him go for a black band on his wrist, disable him immediately. I'd like to incapacitate Otas without a single loss of life."

Roden turned once more to Nalea, who was shooting him a glare. "They need to focus on Otas," she hissed. "I'm not the primary here."

He nudged closer to whisper his next words in her ear. "You're far more important than either Otas or Hillas."

She huffed and started to curse and mumble under her breath.

He held a hand over his heart. "You wound me, Lea." He walked away with feigned nonchalance, while inside he feared that if they failed today, they would spend the rest of their lives at war.

Chapter 30

Adrenaline roiled beneath Nalea's skin. She gripped her gun while she waited. Ahead, two human soldiers scanned what lay around the next corner in the hallway. The one on the left motioned the team forward, and again they moved. With every step and with every turn, the hum grew louder. It now vibrated through her bones. Their team had done the same routine down seven hallways so far and had yet to come across any resistance. It seemed that any Draeken not on the other side of the barrier had fled into the surrounding wilderness.

She turned a corner and stopped cold. Half of her team stood stock still, all watching the glowing wall before them. Her heart raced as she found herself outside the door she recognized: the main entrance to the comm-center, just outside the force field.

Roden stood next to her, punching codes and snapping commands into his wrist-comm. She checked her wrist-comm. Red lights—each representing another team in the base—turned green one by one as they reached their assigned placement at a position outside the circular comm-center.

Once all the lights turned green, Nalea glanced up, locking eyes with Roden. "Ready for this?" he asked.

Every single one of her muscles tensed. She nodded.

Before she realized his intent, he grabbed her by the neck and kissed her. It was hard and fast and spoke of emotions she knew he couldn't possibly possess. She yanked away with shock and scowled.

His wicked grin transformed into all business the next instant. *"Leghat,"* Roden announced into his wrist-comm. *Show time.*

At first, nothing happened. Then, the glow faltered, and the humming became jagged. The floor trembled with vibrations until everything stilled. The silence became near unbearable.

"Wync," Roden commanded, and the Draeken soldier ran forward with a large torch. A thick purple laser shot forth, and the metal bars blocking the door began to melt. Seconds later—though it felt like minutes later—the last of the metal bars fell to the floor with a *clang.* Wync backed up, still holding the torch.

"Alpha, ready," Apolo announced on his wrist-comm.

"Charlie, ready."

"Echo, ready."

Roden waited until all teams had checked in before he announced, "Engage."

Everyone cleared the area in direct view of the door.

Wync started the torch again, this time at a centralized spot on the door. Slowly light shone through from the other side.

Once a small hole had been burned through, Wync took a rushed step back while Apolo pulled out two chaos charges. A light lit up on each one, and he tossed them through the hole in the heavily damaged door. An ear-ringing cacophony of noise and blinding white light bled into the hallway. Vertigo hit Nalea, but it was nothing compared to what those inside the room had felt, especially since chaos charges were being tossed in simultaneously by the other teams at each door to the comm-center.

As the sounds and lights muted, Roden nodded to two humans, who brought forward a door-punch. It only took one solid hit for the already weakened metal door to collapse inward.

They tossed the punch to the side and jumped out of the way so the rest of their team to enter. Nalea followed Roden in, with Apolo right behind.

Tens of Draeken were on their knees, haphazardly holding up their bare hands while trying to regain their balance. Stun blasts came from all directions. Each of the four doors to the room had been knocked in by teams at precisely the same time.

If the soldiers hadn't been so well trained, they would've run the risk of knocking out each other in the crossfire, but Roden and Nalea had provided a clear blueprint of the stadium-style room. Everyone knew exactly where to fire: low and center.

Nalea glanced around and frowned. "I don't see Otas!" she yelled out to Roden, who rushed toward a corner of the room. He didn't seem overly surprised and didn't slow to double check that the comm-techs and guardsmen were down. Roden yanked an unconscious Draeken off a chair stationed at a computer screen, dropping the guardsman to the floor. He typed furiously at the keyboard. Nalea came to a stop at his side, her breath coming in pants.

"Can you get to him?" Apolo asked, coming up to Roden's other side.

"Of course."

A click and a whir, and Nalea glanced up to see a stairwell open leading underground. *Suvaste.* She'd been in this room a dozen times and had never seen this before.

"Alpha, with me!" Roden yelled over his shoulder then lifted his wrist-comm. "Echo, heads up. You've got company coming your way." He lunged forward to the stairwell. Nalea rushed to keep up as they entered the belly of the base.

The hallway was narrow and long, a straight shot under the base. "Could he have escaped with the barrier still up?" she called out.

Roden shook his head. "The barrier would have gone below

the surface a good fifty feet. He can't be more than several seconds ahead of us."

Her hand flew to her chest to make sure the chain was fully covered by the vest. Her heart pounded. Otas could set off her disjunctor at any time, and she feared his plan all along was to detonate her neck-charge when she was standing close to Roden.

She kept pace a few steps behind Roden as he led their team in a sprint past evenly-spaced stark lighting, keeping her distance so that if the disjunctor blew, it would only take her. The tunnel had no turns or doors, only curves, until it came to a lone stairwell. Hillas' doppelgänger stood on it.

She pressed herself against the wall, separating herself from the rest of her team as much as possible.

One of Otas' guards had his back turned to them and was peeking through a slit in the floor above them, likely watching Sommers's teams and timing their chance for escape. The other two guardsmen either heard or saw the incoming team. They raised their weapons at the same time Roden, Nalea, and the rest of Alpha team did.

"Tucking tail and running? How *noble* of you," Roden sneered.

Otas jerked around, face red, and shook a bandaged fist. "I must survive. Our people are lost without me."

Roden belted out a laugh. "You seriously overestimate your value, Otas." He inhaled. "There was a time I would've followed Hillas to death, but that time is long past. And you're less than a shadow of him. You'd be the demise of our people. And that I can't allow."

"Surrender, Otas," Ace exclaimed from her left. "You are surrounded. There's no way out."

Otas' gaze jerkily scanned the team. He'd lost and knew it. Then his eyes homed in on Roden. No, not true. He was looking beyond Roden, at her. His mouth opened, and then closed.

When Nalea realized his intent, she backed up a step. "Take him down now!" she screamed.

Roden yelled out something indistinguishable.

Everything and nothing happened at once. Roden rushed her with a blaster in his hand. She tucked her head and dove to the floor but found herself yanked back by her hair. She felt a sharp sting alongside her neck, followed by the brightest, loudest explosion.

Blinded and deaf, she fell to the ground. Excruciating heat tore at her neck. She gasped for air, but the pain smothered her. She fell back, her head bouncing off the floor. Inky blackness poured across her; then, nothing...

Nalea regained consciousness with a gasp. Throbbing agony was everywhere. Her neck was a red-hot pin cushion, air turning to fire as it passed through her throat. She bolted forward, only to be pressed back down. Her mind fought to make sense of what happened, but the world around her was muted, as though she was entangled in grasses and caught swirling underwater in one of the hot springs of the Golran Sea.

As her vision came back into focus, she found Apolo kneeling over her. Sweat beaded his forehead as he leaned over her. He wiped his wet forehead with the back of a bloody hand before pressing it again to her neck. This time she felt the pressure and low tingle of energy through his palms.

Details seeped back into her mind as her healing wound burned and itched. They were on a mission to find Otas, but then…

The disjunctor.

She pushed at Apolo, but he slapped her hand away. "Not until I get you stabilized."

Frowning, she moved her head. *Suvaste*, her neck *hurt*. "I'm alive." The words so rough and scratchy, she didn't recognize her own voice.

"Because you're incredibly lucky," Apolo said, and he pressed harder onto her neck. She coughed, fighting to breathe through the pressure. Her mouth tasted of iron.

The scene replayed. She'd thought she could talk Otas down by negotiating with him. She hadn't considered that he'd lash out like a cornered *fregee*. If she hadn't been there, they could've taken down Otas without any injuries. She'd put them all at risk. "My fault," she coughed out. "Otas. The mission—"

Apolo shushed her. "Later."

Her skin continued to tingle as it pulled his energy to heal her wound. It was a natural ability of her people and required no conscious effort on her own. It worked much the same way as the *tahren* bond. Sephians were more connected to living energy than any other race they'd met.

Making only the smallest movements, she took in the scene around her. Most of the team had disappeared. Otas was nowhere to be seen. Wync was bent over someone several feet away. It was another Draeken—she could tell by the wings. Wings covered in soot and blood, but beneath the grime she recognized the tattoos.

She reached out weakly.

"Don't worry about him right now," Apolo said, his voice a bit too gentle. "Not until I get your wound sealed." He glanced over to Roden and lifted his wrist-comm. "We need med-techs down here now, godsdammit!"

She watched as Wync worked on his commander. No movement. His back to her, his wings were draped limply across the floor. Her jaw clamped shut so hard her teeth hurt. She clenched her eyes closed against the fury boiling in her blood. She'd been wrong to come on this mission, but what the hells had he been thinking? When Roden came at her with his blaster, her gut reaction was to defend herself, but she'd realized he was about to do something very stupid.

When Apolo finally pulled away, she brought her hand to her throat. Her fingers traced a thick line of hyper-sensitive scar tissue. By the feel of it, Roden had nearly hit her jugular when he shot through the chain.

She pulled herself slowly to a sitting position and the world spun.

"Careful," Apolo said, holding her steady, although he didn't look much better. He looked positively drained, and she wondered how much energy he'd used up helping her heal.

"Otas?" she asked, her voice like sandpaper, but slightly improved from before.

"The coward used the blast as a diversion. The rest of the team followed him. No word yet."

Clumsily, she got to her knees.

Apolo put an arm around her. "You need to rest. The med-techs will be here soon enough."

"I'll be fine," she said as much to convince herself as Apolo. "Help Roden."

His lips tightened. It was all the look she needed. As she started to crawl toward the Draeken, her palm slipped in blood, and she went down. Apolo's strong arms enveloped her, and she used him to steady herself as she crossed the seemingly endless distance to Roden's wingtip. Reaching out, she touched the smooth velvet skin. Without the disjunctor, she should now feel his emotions, pain… something, but there was nothing. No reaction.

She collapsed on an elbow. "You idiot," she muttered, wishing that he was Sephian so that he could pull her energy to heal.

He was lying on his side. Dozens of bleeding cuts from shrapnel covered his body. Fortunately, none of them looked too deep. Wync had bandaged Roden's arm, and crimson blood already soaked the gray cloth. Draeken couldn't heal from energy like Sephians could. They needed medical care. Worse, they got things like infections and illness. And there was so much blood.

She reached out and gingerly brushed her fingertips down his cheek. His skin was still warm, but he showed no sign of reaction. She plucked out a tiny shard of shrapnel from above his eye. A bead of blood took its place. She reached for another, only to be pulled back. She jerked free, but Roden was suddenly surrounded by med-techs—or medics, as humans called them. So focused on him, she hadn't even heard them arrive.

She leaned back and then noticed the other Draeken lying near him, clearly dead. It was Elng—one of Hillas' devout guardsmen. It looked like he'd taken the brunt of the blast. A messy, rough-edged hole had burned into his torso, and a glint of metal caught the light. A piece of the pendant with the Draeken royal symbol still lay embedded in his chest. Her disjunctor.

Roden had pulled it off her and tried to throw it at Otas in the split second between detonation and blast. Elng had died protecting his false leader. She shook her head. "Why?" she asked, but no one answered her.

The medics moved fast, loading first Roden then her onto stretchers. She tried to sit but found herself strapped down. She fought her restraints all the way back to the waiting ship. The medics set her next to Roden, and injected something that made her world spin and fade to darkness.

Nalea awoke to silence and the glow of the planet's single, pale moon illuminating the room through large windows. Pushing herself into a sitting position, something tugged on her arm. Glancing over, she saw a bag holding some kind of clear liquid that had a long, narrow tube connecting it to her arm. With a frown, she tugged off the thing Sienna had once called it an *ivy*, though it bore no resemblance to a plant.

She came to her feet. It took a moment before the floor felt solid beneath her.

A curtain enclosed her in a small area. Silently, she slipped between two fabric privacy panels, finding herself in a large room. *Definitely a human medical facility.* The walls were drab with an over-abundance of white. Cloth, paint, even the strange long shirt she wore, bore the same lack of color. And, unlike the med rooms she knew, small lamps were lit on tables throughout the area.

Dozens of beds lined the two long walls. Several held occupants, some with wings, but none held the one she sought. Barefoot, she marched out of the room and into the brighter hallway. Wincing, she covered her eyes and glanced in both directions. Two humans, a male and a female, each wearing a long white jacket, were approaching from her left. Upon seeing her, they paused. "Can we help you?"

She shook her head and turned away. She felt their gazes at her back for a moment, and waited until they finally went into the room she'd just come from. Closing her eyes, she concentrated on something deep within herself, focusing on sensations, searching for anything that didn't originate from her. *There.* Nearly too weak for her to catch, but the slightest sense of *bothness* was all she needed.

The tension in her muscles melted. Following the transparent thread, she turned left. Her footsteps slapped the floor as she progressed past several doors. Coming to a stop, she paused, turned, and returned to a door she'd just passed.

She pushed through the door to find a much smaller room with four beds and only two occupants. She stepped to the first bed, and her heart clenched. Roden lay on the bed, his eyes closed. More of those *ivies* hung from poles off to his side. Machines with electronic readings sat on a cart by his head. One machine made a recurring beeping sound. He'd been cleaned up, his wounds bandaged. Tubes went into his nose and arms. His long hair flowed down the pillow under his head, and his wings fanned out behind him, his bed twice the size of hers to accommodate his Draeken physiology.

His heavily bandaged arm was held aloft by straps and cables. She frowned. Even though the bandage was thick, it was too short. Rather, his arm was *too short*. She reached out but didn't touch. "*Suvaste*, what have they done to you?"

This time, Nalea awoke to find Roden, his eyes glazed, but watching her intently.

His voice was weak and rough when he spoke. "You're well, I see."

She didn't speak while she came to her feet. She bent over him, cupped his cheek, and ever so softly kissed his forehead.

He stared at her, surprised.

"That's for saving my life," she said. "Though you're an idiot for doing that."

He grunted then tugged at the cables, which brought forth a wince. "Damned primitives," he muttered as his head pushed deeper into the pillow. "Leave it to humans to cut off damaged appendages rather than repair them."

A pang of sympathy shot through her. "Is there anything your med-techs can do?"

He grimaced. "Not now. Not without a *fyet* hand left to work with." He yanked once more at the cables, the sounds echoing in the small room.

He lay there for several long minutes, staring at the ceiling. Finally, he spoke. "Tell me it was worth it. Tell me we got Otas."

"I haven't heard yet."

His lips tightened. "It doesn't matter. If we didn't get him, he's gone from earthside. We'll have to deal with him later. First, we need to get in front of the Draeken core ships to show them we are alive. When they see us together—"

"No," she interrupted.

He frowned before wincing back on the bed. It took him a

couple of deep breaths before responding. "You're Hillas' heir. It only makes sense—"

"I'm a Sephian first, and nothing will change that."

"Sephians. Draeken. On Earth, we're the same. We're both outsiders."

She shook her head. "I'm a member of Apolo's trinity, and right now my people need me more than ever. I can't abandon them."

"Can't or won't?"

She paused before speaking. "Both."

"But your place is with me." His words were demanding. "The endgame was always to have you and I rule our peoples."

She took his hand, and rubbed a thumb down his palm. "I won't deny that you're my *tahren*." Then she pulled away and backed up a couple of steps.

His gaze never left hers. It looked as though he'd climb out of the bed if he could. "Nalea…"

She paused at the door. "Good-bye." She rushed out of the room before she changed her mind. She couldn't stay with Roden any more than she could abandon her people.

It was the best for both of them.

Chapter 32

Several weeks later.

Frustrated, Roden massaged at the muscles in his forearm where phantom pain sent streams of fire coursing up his arm at regular intervals. The blasted humans had cut off his hand midway up his forearm without even trying to save it. Had they even apologized? Hells, no. To make matters worse, he was stuck without an appendage while his med-techs worked on an artificial replacement.

Even more frustrating was the fact that Otas had somehow managed to escape, despite all the ground forces around the base. He'd left his loyal guardsmen behind to die. Guardsmen like Elng, whose confused loyalties had stolen a life of promise.

Hillas' remaining guardsmen had been taken into custody while Roden worked at transferring them under his command. Elng was just another casualty in a war that never should have happened. Roden didn't believe in slavery; never had. The things he'd had to fake to not get caught while he worked to align the

Sephians and Draeken... he fought back the revulsion. He still found himself retching late at night when jagged memories returned.

He glanced up to see Nalea across the table, sitting on the Sephian side as a member of a trinity. She now bore a nasty scar across her neck from where his blade had nearly killed her. *She should be at my side, and she knows it.* When she caught his gaze, she shifted uncomfortably in her seat.

He flicked his wings intentionally, and grinned when her eyes narrowed then widened. The day before, he'd had her *soullare* tattooed across every inch of his wings. Darker than it appeared on her skin, the shade matched what a *soullare* would look like on a Sephian man. She jerked away before turning back to him with a frustrated glare.

Content, he turned back to the speaker. A human leader—an American general—was talking about their expectations from Roden and his people in exchange for a peace treaty, and—more importantly—amnesty for the Draeken. Earth was now entering into the next stage in its evolution. *Blah, blah, blah.*

Time was of the essence. With nearly all their power cells on earthside updated, the Sephians could now return to their home planet. In fact, Apolo would be taking the first humans to Sephia on his return trip next month. All the Sephians could return home if they wanted, but the humans had made it clear: no more came to Earth without prior clearance.

The situation was very different for the Draeken. Even if Roden signed a peace treaty with Apolo on Earth, his people wouldn't be welcomed on Sephia. Earth was currently their best hope, and he planned to make it work.

The humans had treaded carefully throughout negotiations. They knew Roden was the only thing standing between the core ships and Earth. As Sommers said, they were smart enough to not "poke the bear".

Until Roden could gain control of all four core ships, the war was at a standstill, but it was still a war. Apolo still called him Kreed in private, but they'd both agreed that Lord Commander Roden Zyll could accomplish far more for the Draeken people. He'd never given much thought about which identity he'd maintain. He figured he'd be dead by now. Surprisingly, Kreed had won him Apolo's support, while Roden maintained Draeken backing. Rather than canceling each other out, it seemed as though the two identities had merged seamlessly into one; the first—and only—thing that had been easy this month.

While the general talked of demands, Roden was confident of two things. First, the general couldn't refuse the Draeken technology and knowledge Roden offered, or else another country on this world would make a bid for it. The United Nations forces couldn't flat-out take the technology without getting a war on their hands. And second, Roden would accept any proposal to secure a place for his people on this new world. It made for a precarious peace indeed.

As if to sweeten the deal, the Americans had walked in Talla, one of his best soldiers, taken in the same tousle during which he'd captured Nalea. He knew it was the general's way of saying 'You want her back you sign the treaty'.

Talla looked unharmed and healthy, though her wings were banded and her wrists were restrained. A human soldier he recognized stood at her side. The soldier had positioned her in the corner, either for her protection or the protection of those in the room. Roden suspected both, and he made a mental note to keep tabs on that particular soldier.

Talla, with her head held high, scanned the room, finally coming to meet his gaze. Roden smiled, and she gave him a nod. It was good to see her, but what of Laze, Talla's brother, as well as the others taken at Club Mayhem? Roden suspected he wouldn't like the answer much at all. But he'd deal with that issue later.

"So, you will move all your people to this base, and we'll transfer any remaining Draeken we have to you," the general said.

"But you're a feudal race. How can we trust you to not attempt aggression toward us?"

They'd consistently misinterpreted Roden during the negotiations. While Roden had said he'd move his people on earthside to the human base, he'd said nothing about the core ships orbiting in this solar system, where most of his people remained.

Upon hearing of the death of Hillas Puftan, three of the four core ships had quickly pledged full allegiance to Roden. His people understood the value of Earth and the importance of peace.

The fourth ship, however, had never responded, making it clear which ship Otas had fled to. Though they knew their Hillas was a doppelgänger through Roden's communiques, that ship was clearly under the control of the imposter; either by force or apathy.

He glanced up at the general and cocked a half-grin. "You're incorrect, General. I've never been a feudalist. I've always seen myself as more of an anarchist."

That didn't appease the human. Roden sat back and listened to him drone on and on, knowing that within days, a week at most, they'd sign a peace treaty, and his people—at least those on earthside—would be safe for the time being. But he had serious doubts about the integrity of the humans in keeping their side of the bargain.

Two days later, Roden signed his name to a piece of paper filled with long words and flowery rhetoric. He smiled at the primitive custom. All Draeken currently earthside—four hundred and sixty-four, to be exact—would live on this base, brought in as full American citizens. Talla had been released, as well as the three survivors of Club Mayhem, but he'd yet to see them. Talla stood behind him, with a Leash—a human soldier who'd been assigned to watch her and keep her in line.

His people were to be incorporated into the current military structure, all with ranks comparable to their current positions, though Roden noticed that their ranks were all lower than their human counterparts. Roden would be a general, a rank lower than his current status, but deemed acceptable as he continued to be called Lord Commander by his people.

The Draeken and Sephian refugees would remain incognito until the United Nations apprised other governments around the world of their existence. Then, his people would be able to live where they desired, within certain constraints. In exchange, Roden freely offered their technology and knowledge, propelling human science hundreds of generations forward. Somehow, he suspected the humans would move very, very slowly.

The humans clearly felt like they'd won. They'd gained undreamed-of power while keeping both Draeken and Sephians under their control. And yes, a hard rock sat in Roden's stomach, knowing how fragile the balance of power was, but what the humans didn't realize was that these concessions were miniscule compared to the survival of his race and of a long-awaited dream being realized. *My people have a chance to live in peace.*

Instead of setting down the pen he'd used to sign his name, he held it out to Nalea, who stood several feet away. Her eyes narrowed before widening in understanding. Her jaw tightened.

Roden turned to the general. "As you said, the Draeken are a feudal people. I've signed my name, but a member of the royal family should also sign to ensure the Draeken people are fully represented."

The general looked confused, and Apolo stepped forward, clearly displeased. "You sure you want to do this?" he asked quietly.

Roden raised a brow at his friend before turning to Nalea. "Your signature ensures all Draeken will adhere to the treaty."

Apolo nodded, his lips thin. "It would make the treaty acceptable to any Draeken loyal to the Puftan bloodline."

"I thought Hillas was the last member of the royal family," the general said.

Nalea stepped forward and yanked the pen out of Roden's hand. She shot him a hard glare before addressing everyone in the room. "I'm Nalea Puftan Zyll," she said, making the two surnames sound like curse words. She glanced back to Sienna—who, Roden noticed, looked aghast—before she turned once again to the general. "I am the daughter of the late Grand Lord Hillas Puftan and consort to Lord Commander Roden Zyll. I sign my name on behalf of the royal family and in alignment with the Lord Commander to ensure the Draeken people are fully represented in this treaty."

Whispers erupted across the room as Nalea signed her name. She dropped the pen on the table and spared a glance in Roden's direction. Her thoughts were clear. *You better not screw this up.*

Nalea had done her best to avoid Roden after signing the treaty. He'd never made anything easy for her, and she didn't expect him to start now. Even though he was right, his actions infuriated her, outing her in such a public fashion. Begrudgingly, she saw his point: if she hadn't come forward, not all Draeken would support the treaty, leading to infighting and violence. *Suvaste*, there'd been too much of that already.

With her capitulation, she'd effectively united the Draeken under the same peace treaty as the Sephians while branding Otas an outlaw if his core ship did not surrender to Roden's rule.

But, damn, Roden didn't have to be so obvious. He'd tattooed her *soullare* onto his wings, for gods' sake.

She stood near her bunk, packing her small duffle. She'd heard her friend enter before Sienna spoke.

"I always knew you were hiding something, but this is a doozy." She placed a hand on Nalea's bag. "Do you have to go?"

Nalea frowned. "Yes. I committed myself to the Draeken back there. If I don't live on their side of the base, then signing my name back there meant nothing."

Sienna took a seat on the bed. "It feels like I just got you back, and now I'm losing you again."

Nalea turned to face her. "You're not losing me. I'll still be over here whenever I can."

"You'd better," Sienna said. "After all, I'm still expecting you to be the maid of honor at my wedding."

Nalea stared at Sienna and then grinned. "Nothing would make me happier."

Then Sienna sobered. "Whatever you need, I'm here. You know that, right?"

Nalea nodded shakily. "I know," she said, sounding unconvincing to even herself. She shrugged. "I'm doing the right thing. And Roden, well, he's my *tahren*, after all. It's time I came to terms with that."

Sienna put a hand on her shoulder. "If you don't want to be with him, then don't. When it comes to Roden, no one would be surprised."

"Roden needs me. He tries to do the right thing, even if he goes about it all wrong."

Her friend didn't respond, and so she turned around to find Sienna staring at the doorway and at Roden standing in the doorway, his eyebrow raised.

"I think I'll go check on… something," Sienna said. She limped out of the room, glaring at Roden on her way out.

Roden pulled the door closed behind him and strolled into the room, looking nonchalant. But she knew better. She could feel intense emotions radiating from him. Happiness? Pride? Even though he wore no smile, emotions didn't lie.

"I don't have time for this," she said, stuffing a tank top into the duffle.

He wrapped his hand around hers, his wings forming a semicircle around them. "Make the time."

"You won. I'm moving to the Draeken side, but it's going to take hells longer to trust you."

He smiled. "Challenge accepted."

"I need to know something." She turned to face him with her shoulders squared. "Why did you risk your life to save me back at the base?"

"You are the last surviving Puftan."

She watched him for a long moment. While his features betrayed no emotion, she focused on feeling what he was feeling. It was difficult. The emotions felt muted because he wasn't a Sephian, but she could still sense them. "That's not why you saved me," she said as a matter of fact.

"It's true. We make a good team."

She smirked. "That's not why."

He lifted a brow. "Oh?"

"You care for me. I can feel it."

He gave the slightest wince before regaining his composure. "Yes, I do. You make me feel..." He frowned, clamping his jaw shut.

Nalea's brow furrowed as she felt his turmoil. "How do I make you feel?"

He swallowed. For the first time, she saw honesty in his eyes. "You make me feel... *redeemable*."

She stood frozen for a second. One simple word, yet it cost him so much to say. She opened her mouth to speak, only to have Major Sommers rush into her room.

"There you are," Sommers said, coming to stop before Roden and Nalea. "Someone leaked this base to the press. It looks like everyone on this planet now knows we're no longer alone in the universe. We'll need to do a PR briefing. Are you up to representing your people as peaceful guests in an interview?"

"We will be a shining star for our people as peaceful *citizens*," Roden said, taking her hand in his.

Sommers gave a tight nod. "Okay then, meet in the officer's room in ten minutes." Without waiting for a response, Sommers took off at a brisk walk back the way he came.

"The military has less control over the media than they'd

anticipated," Nalea said.

"Or, the military is quite efficient at leaking news that leads to their benefit and ties our hands," Roden replied in a low voice.

A shudder brushed through Nalea as she suspected his words rang with a bit too much truth.

The military's PR effort turned into a fiasco, with canned news articles and prerecorded interviews only raising human suspicion and unrest. And so, three weeks later, the time came to introduce Earth's latest additions to its populace via a live press conference.

Nalea and Roden stood off the stage, ready to make their first public appearance to a new world. The general stood at the podium, with Sienna and Legian at his side, announcing that the United Nations was setting up an "extraterrestrial zone" for all Sephians and Draeken to live in peace on Earth. Flashes barraged the stage as photos were taken. Legian and Nalea both wore dark glasses against the light, though Sommers would've preferred them not to from a public relations perspective.

Someone had spent significant time on Sienna, adding makeup to hide scars. Nalea hoped Sienna's and Legian's optimism would show through in the media. She looked up at Roden. As though feeling her gaze, he glanced down.

"I think your friend Sienna's wedding is about to be postponed," he said, then added, "As well as the hunt for Otas. But we'll take him down. And we'll ensure our people—the Draeken *and* the Sephians—find peace here. *Together*."

Even now doubt nagged at her, questioning whether his race deserved redemption, let alone a comingled peace with her people. "You really think that's possible?" she asked.

"If you can give us a second chance, then humans can give us a first chance," he said and held out his hand. "Ready, my dear?" he asked, and she glanced toward the stage.

A question struck her, and she paused. "Do I call you Roden or Kreed?"

His lips nudged her ear, sending chills across her skin. "I was born Kreed. And I became Roden. You know me. I am both and neither. In public, I'm Roden. In private, I'm *yours*."

She swallowed, then slowly, tentatively, reached out and took his hand. "Let's create the future."

The general was just finishing up his bit on how the United Nations was working hard to ensure all three races could live in peace.

Loud applause rang out, and Nalea swallowed. Still holding Roden's hand, they stepped onto the stage as the others stood to the side. Human soldiers stood behind them. Whether they were there for protection or to guard them, Nalea didn't know and didn't want to think too deeply about it.

Beforehand, she'd agreed to let Roden do the speech. After all, he'd had a lot more practice and was a natural in front of large groups. She only hoped that she looked half as confident as he appeared to be. As Roden spoke, even when he raised a tablet computer that detailed early human-Draeken encounters, he never once let go of her hand, and she realized she'd lied to him earlier.

She *trusted* him. It had nothing to do with the *tahren* bond and everything to do with the bond they'd formed through blood, pain, and sacrifice.

She smiled, facing the onslaught of camera flashes.

In time, she'd let him know.

But not today.

END OF PART TWO

PART THREE: EXPLOSION

Chapter 1

U.S. Extra Terrestrial Restricted Zone, AKA the "Etzee"
1500 hours

"It's just been confirmed," Colonel Jerrick announced to his officers at the emergency briefing he'd called just five minutes prior. "Fourteen minutes ago we shot down a Boeing triple-seven a hundred miles shy of landing at LaGuardia. We are now at threat level Delta."

The briefing room broke out into murmurs, both questions and curses. Lieutenant Jax Jerrick muttered under his breath as he scrutinized his father for any sign of emotion. Of course, there was none. The ever-stoic officer wasn't one to show weakness.

Their world was turning into a mess before his eyes. Jax glanced over the twenty-odd officers in the room whose tense features summed up the anxiety that Jax felt. Each of them knew what this meant: the U.S. had just made its stand, declaring to the rest of the world that everyone else was on their own.

"I take it there were suspected cases of Omega on board, sir?" Major Bruce 'Six' Sommers, the colonel's second in command, asked.

Jerrick nodded. "They refused orders to change course. Instead, they just kept repeating over and over that they were running low on fuel." He paused. "It was an international flight from Hong Kong."

Ah.

No further explanation necessary. Hong Kong had been hit hard by Omega. All of Asia had turned into a mass exodus overnight. This wasn't the first plane to be shot down, but it was the first to be shot down by the United States military.

China had bombed several of its own cities to prevent the spread of the virus. Tokyo had quarantined itself, only to be decimated within days. What was first believed to be a strange recurrence of the bubonic plague turned out to be a virus developed in a lab. Omega brought on plague-like symptoms but with a much higher death rate, putting even Ebola's mortality rate to shame.

Omega began innocently enough, like a case of the flu, but as the body attempted to fight off the invaders, the lungs would fill with fluid. Lack of blood to the extremities brought on gangrene, the brain would swell, causing bleeding from all orifices above the neck, and intense fever brought on raving delusions. Within a day or two, victims drowned in their own blood.

So far, all they knew were two very important facts: first, the superior science that created Omega could not be human; second, Omega's starting point was on the exact opposite side of the planet from the Etzee. It was as if someone had skewered the Earth at the center of the Etzee and shot the virus out the other side. No one doubted the clear message.

The Etzee had just become the safest place on Earth to be human and the worst place to be an alien. The Etzee was a desolate, one-square-mile quarantine for Draeken and Sephian immigrants. Tall prison-style fences lined the perimeter, and U.N. and American troops were posted every fifty yards. The Etzee sat in the middle of a U.S. military operations area, which meant enough heavy equipment and troops to start World War III could be called in at a moment's notice.

Jax had understood the Etzee for what it was the day it had been established. The Etzee was not a temporary quarantine until immigration was processed. His people were afraid. The Etzee was a prison to maintain control over every alien on the planet. It seemed to be working, but the Etzee had one gargantuan Achilles' heel. Thousands more aliens were in Earth's orbit, and they were getting impatient with the U.N. delays.

"We've been given a new directive," Colonel Jerrick said. "The U.S. is officially closing its borders and shutting down the airways, effective immediately. So far, we have no cases of Omega here in the continental states, and we plan to keep it that way."

Murmurs and sidebar conversations erupted.

Colonel Jerrick held up a hand, and the sidebar conversations died down. "Only one person speaks at a time."

"What about the non-continental states like Hawaii and Alaska, and the territories?" Sommers asked.

The colonel shook his head. "They're considered no longer viable. We have to focus our resources on what we can save. Troops are being moved to police the borders and they need all the help they can get. This means that we will evacuate all units from the Etzee by zero-eight-thirty tomorrow morning. Inform your troops to load only essentials. No communication is to be made with the Etzee's residents regarding the evacuation."

Chills climbed Jax's spine. They had less than a day to load up and pull out with no replacements? And, all this on the down-low?

"The Etzee is no longer going to be policed by the U.N.?" Sommers asked. "Has the Triad been advised? Hell, has the U.N. been advised?"

"The U.N. has their hands full, so they've turned over full responsibility of the Etzee to us. This evacuation is purely a U.S.

Army initiative and does not concern the Draeken or Sephian delegates to the U.N.'s Triad."

Sommers shook his head. "There's a significant risk involved if we leave the Etzee unpoliced. While the Sephian and Draeken delegates of the Triad will be pleased to have control, those two races will be at each other's throats within a day."

"The Etzee is no longer our responsibility," the colonel replied a bit too quickly.

"Then whose it is, sir?" the officer sitting a few seats down from Jax asked. "The Etzee is on American soil. Are the residents to be given autonomy?"

"The General of the Army has been invoked and has assumed authority of the Etzee, as well as all military forces."

Everyone in the room took a collective inhalation of breath.

Sommers cocked his head. "The General of the Army is invoked only in a time of war. The last time I checked, we're not at war."

"Our country is facing a terrorist threat the like we've never seen before. As you are all aware, it's U.S. policy not to bow down to terrorists," Colonel Jerrick said sternly. "We have reason to believe the terrorists are associated with those in the Etzee, and therefore it has been declared enemy territory as of twenty minutes ago. All Etzee residents are to be considered hostiles. We are now at war, gentlemen."

"What's going to happen to the Etzee's residents? Most of these people are good folks. They came here in peace," Ace protested. Jax's best friend was the best staff sergeant he'd seen, but Ace never knew when to keep his trap shut. Basically, they were a lot alike and Jax had been thinking the same as Ace, but was smart enough to keep his thoughts to himself. Besides, he already suspected the answer and didn't want to hear it.

The colonel's lips pursed. "The loss of six hundred eighty-five illegal aliens in order to save billions has been deemed an acceptable loss."

Ace hit the table. "They've shared their knowledge. We've advanced decades, if not centuries, thanks to the knowledge they've shared with us over the past twelve months."

"And now some of them are using that same knowledge against us," a staff sergeant said from the back of the room.

"Can you blame them?" Ace snapped back.

"Sir," Jax said, steering the rising hostility levels of the room away from Ace. "Does the General of the Army realize that if the Etzee is destroyed, any chance for a cure will probably be destroyed along with it?"

Colonel Jerrick narrowed his eyes on his son. "All the risks were analyzed in the making of this decision. The General figured that if the terrorists were willing to offer a cure—if they even have one—they would've made their demands by now. We have to assume that Omega is germ warfare, plain and simple. We are in a crisis situation, gentlemen. Our best defense is to keep Omega outside our borders. Any infected—near or on our soil—are to be eliminated. Then, we wait out Omega. Aside from that, I have no further information. These decisions were made well above all of our pay grades."

Jax sensed the bitterness in his father's voice at the last words.

"What about the Leashes?" another officer asked. Every Etzee resident had been assigned, or 'leashed', to a human soldier upon entry to the Etzee. These soldiers served essentially as probation officers, ensuring their Leashes stayed in line. A few had become more involved, helping their alien assignment acclimate to Earth by teaching them about local culture and norms.

"All Leash orders are hereby cancelled, effective immediately. Every resident will still have a tracker, so should any escape after we leave, they will be tracked down and neutralized."

Thoughts poured through Jax's mind as his father went over the details of their new directive. Of all the officers in the room, he was being put between a rock and a hard place. Jax had been assigned as a consultant to the U.N. Triad—the governing body of the Etzee—made up of Sephian, Draeken, and human delegates. Officially, his allegiance was fifty-one percent to his country and forty-nine percent to the Triad. He *should* be informing the Triad of the new directive. He should be doing everything he could to save alien lives. In this case, however, a couple of percent points made a world of difference.

Country trumped world. Humans trumped aliens.

The sound of chairs scraping on concrete pulled Jax's attention back to the room as the colonel held up a finger. "Make sure you have your troops pulled out by oh-eight-thirty and not a minute later. We will not and cannot come back for anyone left behind."

"Yes, sir," chimed around the room as the officers departed, everyone looking nervous. Jax eyed Ace, who shot him a look every bit as strained as he felt.

"Jerrick and Monson, a word."

Snapping upright, Jax and Ace spun on their heels to return to the room. Ace, being the lowest ranking officer, waited for the others to leave before closing the door and catching up to stand at Jax's side to face the commanding officer.

"As you were," Jerrick said as he rustled around some papers before leaning back on his desk and facing the pair. "Staff Sergeant, you have more potential than just about any soldier I've met."

"Thank you, sir," Ace replied.

"Yet you manage to screw up every time your lieutenant isn't around to bail you out. I'm giving you one last shot. Lieutenant Jerrick is taking a temporary assignment. You will ensure Echo-Three company reaches Whiteman with the other companies tomorrow morning. Are we clear?"

"Clear as a bell," Ace replied without hesitation.

"That will be all."

Ace saluted the officer. "Thank you, sir," he said and left the room, closing the door behind him.

Jax's father looked around the room before leveling his gaze on his son. "What I'm about to say could get misinterpreted as treason if it fell onto the wrong ears."

Jax didn't respond, because how did one respond to that?

"We've never been fair with the Etzee's residents. The Sephians who are here could've gone home, but they chose to remain. I'm not worried about them, since they had a choice and could head back to Sephia. As for the Draeken, well, they have no home. We've been keeping several hundred of them restricted to the Etzee in the hopes that we could keep the several thousand orbiting our planet in those giant core ships of theirs in line. If we kill those residents now, I have no doubt their compatriots will retaliate, and that would make the Omega virus look like nothing more than a slap on the face. At oh-nine-hundred, we're going to royally screw ourselves by bombing the Etzee, and I doubt that the persons responsible for the Omega virus are even in the Etzee."

While Jerrick had spoken to the same effect at the officer briefing, having him spell it out—*Jesus H. Christ, we are going to bomb a camp where over six hundred people live*—froze every muscle in his body.

Jerrick cracked his knuckles. "I'm giving you a counter-directive for one hour in order to save our world. Save the alien delegates to the Triad—Roden and Nalea Zyll and their officers, Apolo's trinity, Sienna Wolfe, and whatever families you can. We can only hope that the Zylls will be able to keep their core ships from bombing the U.S. into oblivion. Do you understand what I'm saying?"

It took Jax a deep breath before he found the ability to speak. "Yes, sir."

His father watched him for a long second. "I've already put the paperwork through that you'll be driving a large supply truck with medical records. It's large enough for you to get the key personnel out. I'll have drones watching the roads, so be sure any passengers are well hidden."

"Understood, sir. Where do I drop off my passengers?"

"I'm counting on the Zylls to arrange pickups."

Jax nodded.

"Don't dally with dropping them off. You need to get your ass to Whiteman as soon as possible. You'll need to have some records on board to not raise suspicion, so have some troops load enough onto the truck tonight. Troops evacuate at oh-eight-thirty. It doesn't give you much of a window to sneak out the critical few."

"Thirty minutes is more than enough time," Jax said. "You can count on me, sir."

His father looked relieved, yet pale. It was the third time in Jax's life that he'd seen his father emotional. The first was when his mother died. The second was when Jax had been taken by the Sephians. "This is a high-risk situation, but you're the only officer the aliens trust. If you're caught with them, there's nothing I can do. You need to get them out of Etzee then let them fend for themselves. Once they're a few miles clear of the Etzee, they are no longer your concern. Do you understand?"

Jax swallowed and then nodded. "Yes, sir. Will that be all?"

His father came forward suddenly and embraced him. It was fast and hard, and over before Jax could respond. The colonel walked around his desk, sat down, and began to shuffle papers. "Those records are important. You've got a lot of work to do, Lieutenant. Better get to it."

Jax saluted before turning away. Feeling disjointed and edgy, he stumbled through the doorway to find Ace leaning against the wall. He pushed off and joined Jax's side as they walked outside.

"I'll get your guys out all right," Ace said.

"I know you will," Jax said.

Ace watched him for a moment. Ace was smart. He'd know something was up for Jerrick to pull the company leader at such an odd time. Ace suddenly pulled his buddy into a quick, hard embrace.

It was much like the one Jax's father had just given him, and spoke of the same heartfelt emotions that words couldn't relay. When they pulled away, neither said a word, instead going their separate ways. His father was right. They had a lot to do and not nearly enough time to get it done.

Chapter 2

2200 hours

"Excuse me." Talla Kohlm veered around the soldier blocking her path.

He mirrored her steps, blocking her way once again.

She heard the booted steps of his partner coming up from behind. Her only chance for escape was down the dark alley between the two empty trailers at her right.

Trap.

Refusing to appear kowtowed, she glared at the man before her and entered the alley.

Better to walk into a trap than to be shoved.

Broken glass crunched under her feet, which explained the lack of light in the foul-smelling alley. The nearest post stood empty, with no guard on duty. These men had planned their games well. The sound of footsteps echoed behind her, and she turned to face her assailants. It was difficult to make out their features, but she'd no doubt sneers of imminent success had already crossed their faces.

Each man took a cautious step closer, as though they'd

cornered prey like this many times before. In response, Talla took a step back, only to bump into a dumpster. One of the humans chuckled. "Don't be scared, dragon girl. We're not going to hurt you."

Talla clenched her teeth at the taunt soaking his words. Her wings, though banded tight behind her back, flicked in agitation. She couldn't scream for help. It would do no good, anyway. She couldn't attack, let alone kill, these bastards without severe repercussions against her and her people. There was one constant in the Etzee: the humans always sided with their own.

Hard to believe less than a year had passed since her people's so-called peace treaty with the humans. It had taken them less than a month to round up every remaining earthside Draeken and Sephian to be quarantined within the high chain-link fences of the Etzee. The Draeken, their wings banded to prevent flying, were in the same predicament as the wingless Sephians. Individuals of both races had had tracking devices implanted in their necks. None were allowed to leave the Etzee unless they were leaving the planet altogether. All of it under the guise of it being "for their own safety".

The humans had lied. They'd never wanted peace. They'd wanted power, control, and supremacy. They weren't ready to live as equals with another race, let alone two, and so they'd fallen into old habits of dealing with others who weren't like them.

Every day in the Etzee was a fight to retain her heritage. Twilight had already faded to black. She'd found it suspicious that the sergeant had kept her in the work center to finish a menial cleaning assignment while everyone else had been allowed to go home. The reason became clear when that same sergeant stepped into the alley behind the two, putting a hand of each of his men's shoulders. "I hope you're not starting without me, boys."

"Just warming up," the one on the left said.

With that, the sergeant stepped between the two men. Metal

clinked on metal as he unfastened his belt. With a man on each side, he stalked toward her.

"You're a pretty one," one of the soldiers cooed. "We've been watching you for a long time."

Talla clenched her teeth. If her wings weren't banded, she could've easily flown over their heads and to Laze's trailer. But the humans had given the Draeken a choice: have their wings banded or amputated. Like everything else the humans had done, ultimatums had been issued under the pretense of choice.

Talla was a soldier. She'd taken on far more dangerous foes than these misfits. But Roden had made it clear: all Draeken were to avoid giving the humans any reason to sanction her people, at least until they had established their own home on this planet. They had to take the abuse… for now.

As the men stepped closer, they spread out to block her in. Her heart raced and bile rose in her throat. She balanced on the balls of her feet, knowing she could take down one, maybe two, without leaving any distinguishable marks on their bodies. Three armed soldiers moved the odds out of her favor. She pulled her arms into a defensive position. "Leave me alone."

The sergeant paused. "We don't want to hurt you, honey." He gestured to his men. "We just want to talk."

Except the way he said the word "talk" sounded anything but harmless.

"Don't come any closer," she commanded.

"Or you'll do what?" the man on the right mocked. Moonlight glinted off the blade he now held.

The other one had already pulled out a handgun. "C'mon, dragon girl. Tonight's our last chance for a bit of fun. We don't have time for your games."

"Fyet da." Fuck you. Talla lunged to the right, swung around, and then dove at the man on the left. Her elbow connected with his sternum. He grunted, pulling his hands toward his chest. She twisted his wrist as she pulled the gun from his hand. As the same time, one of the others grabbed her long hair and yanked her off the soldier, who was now cursing up a storm. Pain shot through her scalp, but pain she could take.

Dropping the gun, she threw herself back onto the man pulling her against him, knocking him off balance. As they fell, she spun to straddle him and clapped his ears. He cried out, and his hold on her relaxed.

Just as she went to leap off the writhing man, she froze. Cold, sharp steel pressed against her throat. Warm blood trickled down her neck. Any movement would result in a severed artery.

She could do nothing while the first soldier, still wheezing and coughing from her blow, stepped around and reclaimed his weapon from the ground. Aiming it at her heart, he knelt and checked on his fallen comrade, who was whimpering while cupping his ears.

"We were going to go easy on you," the sergeant said from behind her. "Now it's going to hurt." The piercing pressure on her neck lessened, and she drew in a breath of relief, only to have duct tape slapped over her mouth. She found herself kicked forward onto her hands, knocking the breath from her lungs. Before she could get her bearings, he shoved her down and onto her back so that she faced him.

The soldier with the gun glared at her, fury in those weasel eyes. Then his fist swung out. Talla's vision went white as pain shot through her nose. A hand gripped her face. Blood trickled down her throat. With her mouth covered, she fought to breathe. As her vision returned through a haze of white stars, she found herself looking up at a cruel grin. "That's for hitting me."

"C'mon, quit playing. Hold her down. We don't have much time," the sergeant said as he pulled at her pants.

Talla shoved at his hands as she struggled to slide into a defensive position. While she was nearly as strong as one man, she was in too much of an awkward position to gain leverage. Two human men—with their heavy, solid bones—had overwhelmed her far too easily.

One of the soldiers grabbed her wrists and yanked her arms over her head. Agony overtook her as he knelt on her sensitive wings and held her against the ground while staring down at her. Her shout was muffled behind the thick tape.

Her nose was already swelling, reducing her air supply to nil. The tape prevented her from coughing as blood continued to run down her throat. The only good thing about her situation was that she'd soon pass out from lack of air. She wouldn't witness what they were about to do. While she still could see, she turned to face the human coming down on his knees before her. She focused on remembering the sergeant's face, as well as the faces of the other two men. She knew that, no matter how long it took, she would track them down and kill them one by one.

Her body fought for air even as she clenched her eyes shut, trying to will herself into blacking out sooner.

"Sarge! Behind you!"

Her eyes popped open.

The soldier kneeling on her wings shouted an instant too late. A newcomer had two large hands already on the sergeant's head, twisting. With a pleasant-sounding crack, his head fell at an unnatural angle on his shoulders. Her assailant collapsed forward. The new arrival shoved him to one side, revealing himself to her.

"Laze!" She shouted his name, but it came out as "Mm!" from behind the tape. The world swirled around her as she began to sink into oblivion. Her lungs burned. But, while the soldier with the gun was distracted, Talla used her remaining strength to yank her hands free. She ripped the tape off her mouth, sucking in a deep breath. She tried to pull herself up, but the soldier on top of her still had her wings pinned.

Metal pressed hard against her temple, though she could barely feel it through the piercing pain coming from her wings. It wasn't sharp like the knife had been. Then she heard the click by her ear. Gun. "Stop, Draeken scum," the human ordered. "Come any closer and the whore dies!"

Her brother didn't come closer. Instead, he leaped to the side and grabbed the third soldier, who was still attempting to overcome the nasty case of vertigo Talla had given him. The man feebly batted at Laze from the choke-hold.

"Let my sister go now, human," Laze gritted out. "This is your one and only chance. Do you know me?"

She felt the gun quiver against her temple, which she suspected was sign enough the soldier was quite aware of Laze's reputation.

"I will see that you are tortured more than any other human before you," Laze said as he came to his full seven feet, pulling the whimpering soldier up with him as a shield. The human's feet dangled a couple of feet above the ground. "I will take you apart, one piece at a time, starting with your teeth, then your ears. I wonder... how many pieces a human can lose before he dies?"

"We—we can work something out," the soldier stuttered out.

Glass crunched, and Talla tried to turn her head enough to see if friend or foe came. When he came into view, she realized he was neither and both. Her Leash had arrived.

"Lieutenant Jerrick!" the soldier with the gun exclaimed. "Thank God! These dragons attacked us!" He waved his gun wildly at Laze. "That one killed Sergeant Thompson!"

Lieutenant Jackson Jerrick—who his friends called Jax— seemed uninterested in the fact that Laze could kill the human he held in a heartbeat. Instead, his gaze fell first on Talla and her torn clothes. His look was hard. She knew that look well. He'd been assigned to her when she had first been captured by the humans.

That had been over two years ago. Little had changed. He was still assigned to her. And, unlike most Leashes, he was much more than her Leash. Jax was her shadow. The human soldier with haunted eyes crossed her path every day. Was it strange that she found comfort in his presence, that she *wanted* to see him, a human, each day?

Even more strange, she sensed that she brought the same reaction in him. He might be her enemy, but still her heart calmed at his arrival.

Jax's eyes narrowed and his lips soured. He glanced back up at the soldier above her. "She attacked you with her pants undone?"

"I had nothing to do with it," the man stammered in a rush.

"Then get off her wings," Jax replied drily.

The soldier pointed at Laze. "But—but that one threatened to kill me!"

"Based on what you did to his sister, I'm not surprised," Jax said. "Let her go. That's an order." He glanced at Laze. "Same goes for you. Let the corporal go."

Laze didn't move. "They must be punished."

Jax nodded ever so slightly. "Agreed. But you messed up tonight by killing an NCO. Don't make things worse than they already are. You got a kid at home. Don't leave him without a dad."

Scowling, Laze looked from Jax to Talla before dropping the man to his knees, then kicking him away. Similar to the humans, Draeken males were stronger than their female counterparts. Where Talla was as strong as many human males, Laze could crush human bones in his grip. The human scraped himself across the ground for several feet before unsteadily pulling himself back up and moving closer to the lieutenant.

When the excruciating weight disappeared from her wings, Talla came to her feet in a battle stance.

"It's not going to matter after tomorrow!" the one soldier yelled.

She knew that if she and Laze remained at the Etzee, they were doomed. If they fled, their fellow Draeken would suffer repercussions. A human was dead—someone had to be punished.

Laze strode over to her and clasped her arm. "Sheescaten, ta deitan," he said in a soothing voice. You are safe, sister. And she knew his words were true, even if for only that moment.

She turned to Jax. He had the control now. The lieutenant's face was hard, set in uncompromising lines. She'd learned many times over that once that man set his mind to something, a mouse would have an easier time moving a boulder than it would be to sway his will.

Jax watched her. "Get out of here; both of you. And be sure to take first breakfast. You're going to have a busy morning." He turned his attention back to the two soldiers.

With a frown, she glanced at Laze, who looked just as confused. The Sephians took breakfast early, before the sun rose and hurt their sensitive eyes. Since the two races didn't get along, her people waited for the second, later breakfast. Perhaps it was Jax's way of warning her that they'd be coming in the morning to take Laze and her away.

She tugged on her brother's shirt. "Let's go," she whispered. She knew Laze craved to kill those two humans as badly as she did, but he was also smart. And as long as they were confined to the Etzee, they were forced to put logic before emotion. With her shoulders squared, they walked past the soldiers.

"You're going to die," one of her attackers taunted.

She never looked back; just kept on walking. Whatever Jax had planned for the soldiers, he was waiting for her to leave.

They didn't speak once during the ten-minute walk back to their small trailers. There was nothing to say. They'd screwed up, and they knew it. Killing a human was a death sentence for them both.

Chapter 3

0500 hours the following morning

Talla discovered she and Laze weren't the only Draeken in the food line for early breakfast. Laze had arrived before her. He nodded as she approached, and the two Draeken with him turned.

The taller guardsman, Wync, spoke first. "Morning, Talla." His smile fell. "What's the story behind the bruise?"

Talla had been surprised to find her nose hadn't been broken by the soldier, but his strike had left her with darker than natural circles under her eyes. She forced a smile. "Nothing that Laze and I couldn't handle."

Wync scowled. "I hope you punished him appropriately."

"We did," she said.

"Good," Wync said, and his smile returned. "You could tell me about it over dinner tonight."

Talla knew not to let Wync's flattery go to her head. His interest had more to do with Draeken males outnumbering females by twenty to one than anything. Still, she found herself smiling. "Perhaps another time. What brings you and Qan out so early?"

Shy Qan stammered, then started to say something. Wync nudged him, and the shorter guardsman clamped his mouth shut.

"Just doing a quick thing for Roden," Wync said.

She raised a brow and glanced at Laze, who gave a questioning shrug in response. Laze and she were Roden's primary guardsmen. If there was something going on, they always knew about it.

The hairs on the back of her neck prickled. Peering into the shadows, she found Jax leaning against a trailer. Even though the sun hadn't risen, he was wearing sunglasses, making it impossible to see where his gaze fell, but she knew it was her and Laze he watched. To her, his presence echoed his warning last night.

The soldiers would be coming for them this morning.

"They say millions are dead in China already," she overheard Wync say.

"And it's spreading," Qan tacked on.

She turned back to the group. "What's happened?"

Wync wrapped his arm around her, leaning closer than was proper. Draeken propriety had suffered since they'd been forced from their home planet. "Remember those rumors that the humans have contracted a nasty plague?" he whispered in her ear. "Well, they're true. It started a few weeks ago. We're just finding out about it now. It's hit several major cities in Asia already. Who knows how many lives it'll claim." Satisfaction interlaced the words.

Like Wync, Talla had no love for humans; not after being their prisoner only to be later released into the Etzee.

"Nearly a hundred percent death rate within three days of contracting it. Humans drown in their own blood." Wync gave her a toothy grin. "If we're lucky, this will clear the humans out. Then we can be free from this camp and everyone on the core ships can join us."

Talla nodded in response. She knew better than to speak of such things the humans may consider inappropriate. Microphones and video cameras monitored everyone across the Etzee. She even suspected the trackers implanted on all of the Etzee's inhabitants were more than simple GPS chips.

Lord Commander Roden Zyll, her people's leader and the Etzee powerhouse now that the Sephian Apolo had returned to Sephia, continued to take the high road and allowed the humans to keep the earthside Draeken and Sephians at the Etzee. Although, even he was growing tired of the humans' delays and oversteps. The U.N. had promised to turn control of the Etzee over to the Triad three months ago, yet nothing had changed.

Foolish humans.

The Draeken had traveled to Earth on four core ships, the largest and most powerful battleships in the Draeken fleet. A single core ship could lay an entire planet to waste within days.

Three of those core ships—the Striga, the Artox, and the Evo—were under Roden's command. He could call in any of those ships to rescue the earthside Draeken any time he wished. But to abandon the Etzee would be to abandon negotiations for land. As such, he had the ships keep a safe distance from the planet while the Draeken on Earth put up with the inconveniences of dealing with humans.

The fourth core ship was a wildcard. Controlled by a vile traitor, the *Grax* was all that remained of the blood feud Roden and his consort, their new Grand Lord Nalea Puftan, had stomped out a year ago. The *Grax*, under constant surveillance from the other ships, frequently changed orbit, but had yet to show aggression or any sign of retreat.

In her darker thoughts, Talla sometimes wished Roden would order the core ships to bomb the largest cities to thin out the human population and take the land they needed. Once the humans fully understood Draeken firepower, perhaps then her people could live in peace on this planet, free from the desolate Etzee. But core ship weaponry would be a sledgehammer to a world's landscape; it would be difficult to destroy the human population without leaving the planet as scarred as Sephia now was. And so Roden continued to let the humans believe they were in control while he and the other Draeken and Sephian leaders negotiated for land each race could call home.

"It's party time."

Talla snapped her attention back to find two Sephians, Bente and Legian, joining their group. She knew the pair better than many Sephians. As members of Apolo's trinity, they were roughly her equals in status, as they all served as elite guards to their respective leaders.

Wync and Qan stepped out of the line. Wync curled his upper lip and then nodded. "Let's go, gold-skin."

Talla and Laze watched the four men leave.

"What do you suppose Roden is having them do that includes Sephians?" she asked.

"I have no idea," Laze replied as he turned back to the food line and grabbed a tray. "I intend to ask Roden about it."

Talla grabbed her tray. She glanced over her shoulder to see Jax head off into the shadows. She frowned, wondering if his disappearance bade good news or bad news for her. She set down the tray and stepped away from the food line. "I'll see you back at the trailer," she called out to Laze over her shoulder.

She jogged over to where Jax had stood seconds earlier, only to see him leave through a gate—where she couldn't follow. She scowled, giving his back one final glance, before heading back to breakfast.

Jax slammed the door of his Jeep. He'd had to hustle through the gate or else Talla would've caught up with him. And, while he was glad to see her up early, he didn't trust himself to talk to her without giving up what he'd done last night or—more importantly—not to preemptively give up the details on the shit show headed for the Etzee.

He'd always had a crappy poker face.

He pulled out the flask from his leg pocket and took a long draw. The whiskey burned, but it felt good. It grounded him, numbed him.

Red bled over his vision when images from last night flashed in his mind. He'd seen that type of scene a hundred times before, so it was nothing new to him. Where there were slums, there was crime. And that's what the Etzee was becoming. But to see it happen to the person he was supposed to be protecting... he wanted to see the bastards suffer. He wanted to pull their fingernails out one by one.

He had planned to trade the soldiers' silence in exchange for Jax not having them arrested. Instead, the two fools had attacked him. He'd killed them in self-defense. He should've reported the event, but that would bring blame onto Laze and Talla. Instead, he'd stashed the bodies in the dumpster in the alley. The same dumpster where the men had likely planned to dump Talla's body after they'd finished with her.

With the confusion of the evacuation, Jax was counting on the three soldiers' CO assuming the screw-ups had gotten mixed up and loaded onto another truck. It could take them hours, if not days, to figure out the three had never left the Etzee, and by then it would be too late.

Jax tried to convince himself he was only there to protect her but that would be a lie. She was beautiful, and beautiful in the Etzee wasn't a good thing. She was tall for a female; at six foot she was nearly his height, with glistening silver hair. Even with her wings banded tight against her back, he could recall every tattoo that covered them.

A rock formed deep in his gut. There wasn't much time. He downed the rest of the flask—the whiskey burn followed by a pleasant, numbing buzz—then grabbed his keys and headed back to the Etzee.

Time to play hero to the aliens and traitor to his people.

Chapter 4

0600 hours

"**Y**our timing is impeccable," Roden commented after dropping his feet—which had been casually propped up on the desk—onto the floor with a thud. Despite his words, he didn't sound the least bit pleased.

The idea of adding her problems onto Roden's already heaping plate of Etzee woes grated on Talla's nerves. But if Laze and she hadn't come forward, if Roden learned what happened the night before from the humans, he'd have no chance at helping them.

"Neither of you are speaking a word about last night to anyone," Roden said. "It hasn't been brought to anyone's attention yet, and I plan to keep it that way. The other two soldiers who assaulted you last night are already dead... and I'm glad. The matter is closed," Roden said. "There are bigger matters to deal with right now."

Talla stiffened. "Dead? How—?"

Roden cut her off with a wave of his hand. "We're evacuating everyone here onto the Striga today."

"You mean your evacuating all of *our* people," Laze corrected.

"No. I'm evacuating the Sephians as well."

Talla shook her head. "Why would you help them?"

"If they stay, they die," Roden muttered. "Besides, this isn't the first time I've had to get people other than ours off earthside."

At that moment, Nalea and Jax stepped through the doorway. Tension emanated from Jax's hard features. Nalea fared no better. Even with her golden Sephian skin, she looked pale. Clearly, their conversation had been similar to the one Laze and Talla were having with Roden.

"Grand Lord," Talla and Laze said in unison. Already on their feet, they showed respect with a slight bow of their heads toward Nalea.

Nalea had replaced her father, Grand Lord Hillas Puftan, a year earlier, during peace treaty negotiations. The fact that her mother had been Sephian didn't matter. As the last living member of the Puftan bloodline, Nalea was the natural heir. Despite Nalea's Sephian heritage, Talla had come to respect the new Grand Lord. Nalea had left Roden to manage the Etzee and coordinate logistics with the core ships, while she worked on building Draeken-Sephian-human relations. Without Nalea's help, the Sephians and Draeken cooped up together on the Etzee would've killed each other off the year before.

Nalea walked past them to lean on Roden's desk and look at Talla and Laze. "The humans are blaming us for the virus. That's why they're going to kill everyone in the Etzee."

"They're idiots," Roden hissed. His eyes narrowed on Jax. "Has the Sephian leadership been apprised of everything we discussed last night?"

His lips tight, Jax nodded. It was one of the few times Talla recalled being able to read his emotions. "All U.N. troops evac in just over two hours," he replied, his tone hard. "That leaves us a narrow thirty-minute window to smuggle you out under the noses of drones stationed three miles out in every direction."

His words swept through Talla's mind. Her eyes widened.

"How can we slip nearly seven hundred out of the Etzee in only thirty minutes?"

Jax slipped a quick glance at her. "We can't. I have only one truck. My orders are to get the Triad and key staff out. I'm taking everyone in this room along with the Sephian trinity and a few others."

"I will not leave my family behind," Laze said from Nalea's side, agitated.

"They can have my seat," Talla said.

"No," Jax said. "I've already made room for anyone with children on the truck. But I can't take more than forty without running the risk of being spotted. Everyone's going to be packed like sardines the way it is."

"I refuse to leave my people behind to be slaughtered," Roden said. "There are far too few Draeken remaining. Every loss brings us one step closer to being erased. The Striga will be here in six hours, but when it breaks through the atmosphere, the world will know. There's nothing stealth about ten square miles of Draeken technology hovering in the sky. Humans don't have anything to damage a core ship, but there's nothing to prevent them from shooting at innocents on the ground. We've got to find another way to protect the Etzee until everyone can be relocated to the Striga."

Jax shook his head. "I have no control over the timetable. They'll send everything they've got if they see anyone trying to escape." His lips tightened. "I wish there was another way, but the Etzee is not in a defensible position, and we can't get everyone off the Etzee before the bombing." He paused, then turned to Roden. "What if you promise a cure for Omega? They'd have to delay the attack if they believed the cure was on the Etzee."

Roden glared. "You think I released Omega? Fyet! I've been playing nice for the past year despite the transgressions against both the Draeken and the Sephians. The last thing I would do is something stupid like release a virus that could just as easily mutate and kill my own people."

Roden ran a hand through his long hair. "I'd wager Otas is behind this. The sniveling imposter is stupid enough to try something like that. And he has my people's two best scientists on board the Grax. Though viruses themselves are easy enough to build, creating antidotes without the initial formula is nearly impossible," he said with a grimace, rubbing the stump of his arm where he'd lost his hand over a year ago, courtesy of the Draeken traitor, Otas Olnek.

"But if Draeken technology is behind it, can't you recreate the formula for Omega?" Jax asked.

Roden sighed. "I've had people working on it, but there are far too many variations built into the design to hack it. Otas has likely spent an entire year planning this little game. He's using the virus to clear the board without losing a single guardsman in the process. But he's playing with fire; that virus could mutate and target Sephians or Draeken just as easily as it does humans. Our DNA is far too similar."

"It was poor planning on his part. He didn't plan on the humans coming after the Etzee and killing his fellow kinsman earthside," Nalea said.

"I suspect he did," Roden said. "It would be a rather easy way to get rid of me; assuming he's willing to waste a few hundred brethren to see it done."

Nalea frowned. "It's safe to say the peace treaty we made with the humans no longer matters."

Jax scowled. "If there's still a chance at peace, I'll take it. We won't survive a war with the Draeken." He looked at Roden and Nalea. "Your people respect you. As long as you're alive, there's still a chance at peace. But I need to get you off the base."

"What if we escape en masse? There are too many of us for the troops to contain, and the bombs are targeting the Etzee, not us."

"Don't forget the trackers in your necks. Any survivors after Etzee is bombed are going to be tracked down and neutralized." Jax muttered a string of cuss words before continuing. "The trackers monitor your pulse, so there's no way we can cut out all trackers at the same time. And then there are the spotters, who will report in anything they see."

"The spotters won't be an issue," Roden snapped.

Jax snapped his gaze to Roden's. "What did you do?"

Roden lifted his chin. "I sent out four of our best this morning —two Draeken, two Sephian—to take out the spotters at precisely eight thirty."

"Damn it," Jax said, running a hand through his hair. "I didn't want any—"

"Any what? Casualties?" Roden stepped forward. "Yet you're willing to leave over six hundred innocents behind to get slaughtered, in the hope that I will feel like preventing my people from decimating your world."

No one spoke. When Jax opened his mouth, a glaring Roden held up a finger before opening his desk drawer and pulling out a small device and fastening it around his forearm.

"I thought all wrist-comms had been seized," Jax said.

Roden tapped several buttons on his wrist-comm. "Can you get tools to remove our wing bands?" he asked while continuing to type.

"Heavy-duty cable cutters should do the job," Jax said. "I'll see what I can round up."

"It won't do much good," Talla said. "Our wings have been banded long enough that our muscles will have atrophied too much to fly far."

"But many of us could glide a mile if we had to, which could make the difference between life and death," Roden countered. He looked up from his wrist-comm. "We'd better get moving. We have six hundred eighty-five people to plan an escape for."

Jax raised his brows. "And exactly how do you plan to make this mass exodus work without getting everyone slaughtered?"

Roden smiled, cold and hard. "A diversion is on its way."

Chapter 5

0730 hours

The Draeken and Sephians were absolute soldiers. War had flowed in their veins for over twenty years. Their homes were wherever they closed their eyes, be it bunks, ships, or trenches. They were ever ready to pack up and leave at a moment's notice. Without the oversight of their Leashes, they needed no time at all to pack.

Talla, like her kinsmen, had grown up on battlefields. Yet, despite the fact she'd seen enough battles to know that her instincts and training would take over when things turned dire, she was still scared. Hands steady, she slid a small shiv into her cargo pocket and walked out of the simple trailer where she'd slept for the past year.

Even though the humans were trying to be covert about their evacuation, it was easy to see the soldiers packing up and moving out. Good thing that the troops were distracted because the Draeken-Sephian information relay system was underway, right under their noses.

Within weeks of their move to the Etzee, Roden had worked

with Apolo's trinity to develop a simple, yet fail-safe, relay network to communicate news and orders across the Etzee. Everything was verbally relayed three-fold. Each officer relayed information to two of their troops and one of another's troops. This relay continued through the ranks until each person, regardless of race, had received the same information three times. This was to ensure information hadn't been tampered with anywhere along the relay. If information was found to be faulty, it would be easy enough to trace back to the source.

It was this relay that Roden, the Draeken member of the Triad, and Sienna, serving as the Sephian member of the Triad as an interim stand-in for Apolo, put to use. It took eleven minutes for Talla to convey and receive back orders in triplicate. By six forty-seven, every Etzee resident was ready to initiate Roden's plan. Now came the waiting part.

"Need any help?" Talla asked, stepping into the trailer her brother shared with his wife and son. Laze sat with his arm around a very pale Sarah on the sofa. Sarah was watching Jacen playing on the floor with a deadpan stare.

Laze looked up, relieved. He glanced at his wife, then back to Talla. "How about you carry Jacen to the truck?"

Talla walked over to the toddler, but Sarah bolted forward as though she'd just awakened. "I have him," Sarah said before she grabbed Jacen.

The boy whimpered and flapped his wings at being taken from playing with his small blocks but then giggled, returning his mother's hug. "Mama!"

As Sarah walked past Talla, she paused, reached out, hugged Talla with her free arm, and mouthed the words thank you.

Talla gave her a warm smile.

Laze came to stand at Sarah's side, his eyes filled with concern. Sarah was holding up as well as Talla had expected. One of only a few human residents restricted to the Etzee, she'd grown up in a small town, never knowing violence aside from what she'd seen on the news. She'd gone from college student to new mother to Etzee prisoner in little over a year. After she was taken during the Club Mayhem raid, her parents and friends had been sent reports that she'd been killed in a car accident. She'd lost everything she'd ever known because she'd fallen pregnant by—and in love with—a Draeken.

No longer fitting in anywhere, Sarah was constantly ridiculed by the soldiers. "ET whore" was one of the less cruel names Talla had heard her friend called. But another thing Talla had seen in both Jax and Sarah was that humans were resilient. The ridicule slid off Sarah, whose spunky, Gothic-girl exterior rarely showed cracks. While Talla knew Sarah struggled with depression, she never showed any regrets at the decisions she'd made that had led her into Laze's arms and to the Etzee.

Laze cupped Sarah's cheeks and kissed her forehead. "Everything will be all right."

There was much more to Laze and Sarah's relationship than the fact that she had borne him a son. Ever since Laze had met her at Club Mayhem, he had adored her, even if it had taken him some time to change his flirty ways. He'd even gone so far as to marry her in a traditional human wedding a few months after Jacen was born. He doted on her and Jacen.

Talla suspected Laze blamed himself for Sarah being taken when the Club was raided, forced to carry out the remaining seven months of her pregnancy in a military hospital. Laze hadn't been allowed to see her until after their son had been born. He'd been imprisoned, repeatedly undergoing torture and invasive tests, until the peace treaty had been signed.

Their son, Jacen, was the first Draeken-human hybrid. Not yet two years old, he could already glide short distances with his wings. Even at his age, it seemed that the Draeken-human hybrids, with their smaller human stature and wings built for larger bodies, would prove to be better fliers than their pure-blooded Draeken counterparts.

Though Sarah didn't have it easy, poor Jacen had suffered worse than anyone at the Etzee. From the day he was born, tests had been conducted weekly, sometimes daily, by the humans, ostensibly to check his blood and better understand the impact of Draeken DNA on human physiology. It wasn't until the Etzee had been established that Jacen found any relief. One of Roden's stipulations in relocating his people to the Etzee was that no child could have tests done without their parents' permission. Approved tests required to have a parent present at all times.

The threat of Draeken firepower looming in Earth's orbit had been just enough for the humans to carry on the charade of behaving when in the Etzee.

While Jacen continued to have night terrors, Laze and Sarah had forced the tests to be cut back to only blood work and x-rays, and even then, no more than once per month. But Jacen was no longer the only hybrid tested. Six other hybrid children had been born in the months following Jacen's birth. Four were born with adorable Draeken wings. The remaining two carried the latent gene, but no wings; no one knew if they'd develop the extra appendages at puberty or if they'd remain flightless.

The children had brought hope to both the Draeken people and the humans, but for far different reasons. Draeken saw a future. Human doctors became fascinated with the dominant wing gene, which they saw as changing the face of warfare. Talla suspected the humans would try to take the hybrids, and so the first objective was to protect their youth at all costs. Any trailer with a hybrid had two dozen 'visitors' standing watch inside and out.

Sure enough, soldiers had come to each trailer, requesting the children for an *innocuous* test, only to be turned away. With the number of Draeken—and even some Sephians—guarding each trailer, the humans were sorely outnumbered. Rather than face the risk of a possible riot, the humans had returned to the doctors empty-handed. A small win, but a win, nonetheless.

"Looks like you're all set," Talla said, eying the hilt of a blade in Laze's boot. His blade made hers look worthless in comparison, but hers was sharp enough to slice cleanly through a carotid artery.

She had a second, even smaller, blade tucked into one of her boots. While weapons were prohibited, the soldiers never managed to find every hidden weapon. Most of their blasters, which had been taken for 'safekeeping', had long ago disappeared from the Etzee, but some had remained, in locked storage, in case riots broke out. The soldiers couldn't have removed them during the evacuation without looking even more suspicious than their actions already foretold. Those critical weapons were to be retrieved and distributed the moment the soldiers closed the gates.

While Talla, Laze, and his family could sneak out with Jax, the others weren't so lucky. They'd realized that, even without spotters, there was no way to get everyone out of the Etzee without being noticed. They'd have to take their chances, hiding in the woods for the dangerous hours until the Striga could land and whisk them away to safety. They would cut out their trackers soon, but even so, they expected planes and troops to be scouring the area.

Roden had acknowledged that the time for compromise was over. They would carve out a home on this world, regardless of what the humans thought. The façade of peace would end this morning.

Sarah glanced at her watch and then looked from Talla to Laze. "It's time."

Talla grinned and pulled out a small bolt cutter from a cargo pocket. It wasn't much, but it was all Jax could round up in any quantity. "Want me to do the honors?"

Laze shot a matching smile before giving her his back. "You don't know how long I've been waiting for this."

She pulled away the back-straps of his shirt to better access his wings. It took a couple of tries to fit the cutters around the tight bands. She scraped skin as she fitted one end of the cutter under the thick plastic restraint, but Laze didn't flinch. Talla grunted as she squeezed the handles together as hard as she could for a long second before the band broke with an audible snap. As the band fell to the floor, Laze slowly spread his wing, the bones cracking. The skin that had been directly beneath the band was red and inflamed. He winced but didn't complain.

She cut the band from his other wing then handed him the cutter. Turning her back to him, she tried not to grunt as Laze fitted the cutter. He cut her bands off more quickly and smoothly than she had cut his, and she waited until both bands were removed before stretching. Her wings protested the movement, and she hissed through her teeth at each painful inch.

"It gets better after a few more stretches," Laze said, still flexing his wings as Jacen reached out, trying to grab them while giggling.

"It's a good burn," Talla said as she moved her wings about. The pain was akin to trying to walk on a foot that had been asleep for hours, times exponential multiples of twelve. But the sensation of stretching such an integral part of her body made her feel like a Draeken again, like she'd suddenly become whole after being a shell of herself for too long.

Sarah ran a hand down Laze's wing. "I've missed these," she said with a glint in her eye.

He turned and embraced his wife. With Jacen pinned between them, he kissed her. "And I look forward to what you'll do to them later."

He gave her another kiss before releasing her and picking up two bags on the floor by the sofa. After helping Sarah into her backpack, one arm at a time so she could continue to hold Jacen, he slid his bag over his shoulder. Backpacks and wings didn't mix. "No bag?" he asked.

Talla shook her head. "Everything I own is on the Striga."

Laze gave her a knowing look. Like her, when he'd been taken prisoner, they'd been stripped of their weapons and their Draeken clothing.

No one spoke as they left the trailer that had served as both home and prison for the past year. Keeping her wings tucked tight against her back in case humans still lurked, Talla glanced around. For one minute, the entire Etzee seemed desolate. Then, as eight-thirty came, shapes began to filter out one by one. Some Draeken spread their newly-freed wings in the sunlight, and Talla followed suit. Her outspread wings soaked up heat from the sun, and the warmth felt incredible. Freedom!

The Sephians, who lived on the opposite side of the Etzee, migrated to meet in the open area on the south end, setting aside lifetimes of hatred for a common goal. A cornfield and then trees sprawled beyond the tall fence. It was deemed better for hiding than the bean fields and roads leading away in the other three directions.

As the dirt walkways became crowded, Sarah was the only human in sight. Turning east, Talla led Laze and his family toward the rendezvous point. They met a group of Sephians laden with heavy black duffels. They eyed Talla and Laze and were continuing past, but one Sephian, upon seeing Sarah and Jacen, paused and threw a quick glance to Laze. "Need a blaster?" he asked.

Laze shook her head. "No. We're good."

The Sephian looked surprised, but then moved along.

Laze and Talla had Jax to see them to safety. Those who remained needed protection far more than they did. A blaster could buy precious seconds should the humans attack while they waited for transport to the Striga. Whether the Sephians and her people could put aside their distrust long enough to live together on a single core ship, or not, remained a risk no one was ready to discuss yet. Getting out of the Etzee alive was the more imme-diate problem.

It took a couple of more minutes to get within sight of the main gate. Still no sign of soldiers or their fleet of trucks. The gate was closed and locked. Dust billowed from the road leading off into the distance. The humans had cleared out. Except for one truck, which was backed up against the closest—and now open—unloading ramp. Her heart pounded with anticipation.

In the shadow of the truck, a lone soldier stood. He gave her a slight nod, and she smiled, jogging straight for the open gate. Jumping up on the metal platform, she noticed that the other five families were already inside. The truck was full.

As Laze helped his family on board, she remained on the ramp. "When you said it would be tight in here, you weren't joking," Laze called out to Jax through the gate.

Instead of a reply, Jax glanced at his watch then looked to his right. "We need to move faster." A small group walked toward them, led by a Draeken and a Sephian. Roden's wings were outstretched in the morning sunshine, as though flaunting his impending freedom. Nalea walked at his side. Her soullare, the tribal-like markings covering her gold skin, were identical to the tattoos spanning Roden's wings. It was a bold display of respect for his Sephian consort. Most Draeken would never dare, but Roden had always dared much.

Roden glanced to the sky. "Fyet!" He yelled into his wrist-comm, "Get here now!"

Talla followed his gaze and squinted into the sunlight. At least a mile or more upward, jets were closing in fast from the east. She turned to Jax, who was trying to make out what she and Roden had seen. "They're coming," she said.

Jax looked at his watch and cursed. "Twenty-one minutes early." He snapped at Roden. "Tell me your distraction is ready."

Roden, who'd been jogging toward them, came to a stop. "They'll be here in less than a minute."

Dots appeared in the sky. Talla sucked in a breath. "They'll be too late," she whispered. She watched the dots grow bigger as they fell toward them.

———————————————————————

Chapter 6

———————————————————————

Jax stood in numb silence for the next interminable second. Nothing existed except for the dark mass of H6 bombs carving their unerring path toward the Etzee. Someone had grown either suspicious or antsy, and had initiated the attack too early. He suspected the former, but it didn't matter. They had approximately zero chance of outrunning the several kilotons of H6 about to rain down upon their heads. But still…

He snapped around and grabbed Roden's arm. "Get in the truck now!"

Roden shoved off him and continued shouting commands into his wrist-comm. "I don't care about the risk! Destroy anything above these coordinates. Now!" Roden shot Jax an uneasy look. "You'd better take cover."

Roden sprinted off. Jax cursed. He twisted to his right, and then to his left. With everyone else on the truck, he found Talla hurrying Laze as he loaded his family onto the truck. Jax lunged, taking her down with him off the edge of the dock. They dropped four feet and hit the ground hard. She grunted and yelled something, and he ignored her, rolling them both under the dock.

She pushed against him, but he held her down, covering her body with his at the exact moment several explosions rocked the world around them. Dust and pebbles showered down from the dock above.

Talla looked upward, past Jax, her open mouth in the shape of a silent oh as the first shrapnel from the bombs or jets, or both, hit the earth.

"Roden," Jax said, as though it answered everything.

The ground shook, and screams erupted in the distance, as though a meteor shower had picked out the Etzee as a target. A cacophony of impacts, smaller explosions, and screams took place all around them.

Though it lasted no more than a minute or two, the bombardment seemed endless. Jax, muscles hard, held onto Talla. They watched each other, flinching at each too-close impact. Only after the deafening sounds lessened to thumps of less substantial debris did Jax loosen his hold.

He lay his forehead against hers for a brief moment before pulling back enough to watch her. "You okay?"

She nodded. "You?"

Something sharp and hot landed on his shoulder and he hissed.

Talla brushed the debris off his back. "We have to move. It's not safe down here."

He glanced over his shoulder to see light flicker between the wood boards of the dock. Burning material sprinkled down through the cracks, twinkling like red lightning bugs as it fell. "Ah, hell," he muttered as he rolled off her, staying at her side as they crawled out from under the burning dock.

Talla jumped to her feet while Jax took in the scene while still down on a knee. Debris from bombs—and likely from the jets that had released them—sat in burning piles across the Etzee. Some of the debris was many feet wide, large enough to rend trailers in two. Most was far smaller, inches, maybe a foot or two at most.

All had splattered the buildings and land with intense heat and deadly shrapnel. Walls and people alike were shredded. Bodies looked like small boulders through the haze.

The Etzee looked like a war zone.

But they were alive, proof enough that Roden's incoming support had blown the bombs out of the sky before they could detonate.

The stench of jet fuel and burned explosives scraped at his nose and throat. The sound of crackling fire blended with the cries and moans of the injured. Names were shouted, and he blocked out the noise to focus. At least three of Roden's small Aggressor ships circled above. A Transporter was already on the ground, ready to take on passengers. Each Transporter held twenty to thirty passengers. They'd need a hundred Transporters to clear out the Etzee, and Jax suspected Roden didn't have the fleet for that kind of extraction.

Roden's attack would not go unnoticed. The Etzee stood in the middle of a military operations area. It was just a matter of time before they'd be swamped with troops. Those who'd survived the falling debris would not escape quietly.

"Laze!" Talla shouted.

Jax turned just as she ran toward the truck where all the children were. Shrapnel and debris had pelted the truck. Metal was blackened. Fire shredded the oiled canvas tarp covering the back, leaving flaming tatters swinging across the entrance.

He looked around for anything he could use, but the Etzee had been kept barren in order to prevent common items being turned into weapons. A backpack lay near a Sephian woman who sat cross-legged, rocking back and forth with her head clasped in her hands.

He rushed over and grabbed the bag and ran back to Talla's side. Talla was dragging out a Draeken clutching a crying baby. More coughing and cries came from the truck. Talla gave him a quick nod and stepped back. He took the bag and swung it against the tarp, knocking the flaming tatters to one side. With one more swing, he was able to pin the burning tarp against the side of the truck, using the bag to hold the flames away from the entrance.

Several lunged out of the truck, nearly toppling Jax on their way to safety. After a couple of more staggered out, coughing, no others came. Talla jumped onto the truck. "Laze!"

No response. She stepped into the darkness.

"Talla, no!" Jax yelled, but she disappeared. At least twice as many had entered the truck as had come out, and a knot formed in Jax's gut. He peered into the smoky blackness but could make out nothing but a tangle of unmoving limbs. He glanced up at the tarp. Flames had engulfed what was left of the cover, and charred, liquefied pieces were breaking off. "I can't hold it much longer." he shouted into the truck.

She emerged then, soot on her face, dragging two bodies, one coughing, with her. Laze emerged next, his arms full. One of his wingtip spurs was snapped off.

"Are there others?" Jax asked as Laze went by, but the Draeken didn't even look his way. His lips thinning, Jax dropped the bag and moved away, careful to avoid the burning sections of the dock that looked about to collapse.

On the ground, Talla had left the coughing pair she'd rescued and now stood at Laze's back. He was crouched down, still holding those he'd carried from the truck. Flowing over his arm was long brown hair with black streaks that had once been smooth and straight but was now singed and curled. The woman's legs draped on the ground. In Laze's other arm, Jax made out a much smaller figure, and glimpsed tiny wings hanging slack.

Silent, Talla placed her hand on her brother's shoulder.

Laze didn't say anything. He didn't move, didn't shake… nothing. He just continued to clutch the lifeless bodies of his wife and son to his chest.

Above the shouts, cries, and coughs, Jax heard something else. Then he felt it: a vibration below his feet. He jogged over to fence and saw dots on the road in the distance. "We've got company!" he shouted over his shoulder.

Talla jerked up and frowned. He scanned the area, but Roden and Nalea were nowhere to be seen. He went straight for Talla. "We have to get out of here," he said, looking from her to the top of Laze's head and back to her again. "They'll have orders to finish off anyone left."

The whoomp-whoomp of helicopters added to the drone of far-off engines, but Jax wasn't worried about them. As long as Roden's Aggressors were in the skies, no aircraft could get close to the Etzee. Ground troops would be another story altogether. Roden's air support was feeble compared to the size of the army driving toward them. Despite their superior firepower, they didn't have enough ships to hold the fleet of heavy artillery heading their way at bay.

Talla gripped Laze's shoulder. "You have to leave them." Her words were quiet and commanding.

Laze looked up then. He looked at Talla, then at Jax, then down the road. As though not to wake them, he carefully laid his wife and son on the ground before he straightened Sarah's figure, then bent down and kissed her lips. Ever so gently, he rolled Jacen onto his stomach. With a roar that clenched Jax's heart, Laze tore the wings from his son's back.

Jax winced at the alien custom. He'd never seen it done before, but had heard rumors about it. A human would see it as desecration, but to the Draeken it was a ritual. To memorialize them, they preserved the wings of their loved ones and displayed them in their homes.

Laze came to his feet and tucked the tiny, bloody wings into his belt. He stood before them. Jax knew that flat, deadpan stare. He'd been there before. He wanted to say something meaningful, something epic. Instead, he blurted, "We have to run."

Laze pulled out a long shiv instead and turned to face the approaching trucks.

Talla watched Laze before giving Jax a tight look. Then she pulled out a smaller shiv and went to stand at her brother's side. "I'm not leaving Laze behind," she said.

"Like hell I'll let you both kill yourselves." Furious, Jax stomped forward. Hanging around was suicide, plain and simple. He reached out to grab Talla's arm, but Laze swung and punched Talla. She collapsed, and Jax caught her just before she hit the ground.

"I'll buy you the time you need to get away," Laze said, staring straight ahead. He took off running toward the truck, its cargo bed now in flames, not looking back.

There was no time for Jax to respond let alone convince Laze to come with them. Knowing he'd need every second Laze could buy, Jax slung Talla's unconscious form over his shoulder and ran down the fence line. He struggled with her; she was nearly his height, and that made her difficult to manage without risk of injury to her wings.

He stopped at the next gate, the one nearest the offices. This gate was small, no more than a steel door between the Etzee and the rest of the world. He pulled out his badge and swiped it over the black pad next to the door. The lock clicked, and he shoved the heavy door open. His Jeep sat where he'd left it earlier, still in one piece, much to his relief. With no time for gentleness, he dumped Talla into the cargo area of the Jeep and jumped into the driver's seat.

He had the Jeep in reverse by the time the engine caught, and pebbles kicked against the fence as he backed up. He slammed it into gear and twisted the wheel, tore across the gravel parking lot and onto the road, and then turned in the opposite direction of the approaching trucks. The bat-bat-bat sounds of heavy gunfire came at him from behind, but he kept the pedal on the floor, expecting to get a fifty-caliber round through his skull at any second.

He risked a glance at the rearview mirror to see the truck of flames barrel between Jax and the .50s. It was a beautiful sight.

Jax didn't slow down as Laze drove the deathtrap toward the trucks. Laze was as hardheaded as they came, but Jax would've fought alongside the guy any day of the week.

It should've been Jax in the truck and Talla with her brother. Scowling, Jax kept driving, refusing to look back until the tremendous head-on collision snapped his eyes back to the rearview mirror. Trucks were already picking their way through the ditches, but Laze's barricade had slowed them down enough to buy an extra mile for Jax and Talla.

"Damn you," Jax muttered. Laze didn't deserve to die, but war wasn't about what people deserved. War was violent and brutal, and it didn't care who died. War was what his government had started today. For the first time in his life, he knew that his people stood on the wrong side of the line separating right and wrong.

Gripping the wheel, he scanned ahead for side roads. They were on the northern outskirts of the Ozarks—a good area to hide in. He whipped the Jeep into a small driveway and parked it. Leaving the engine running, he pulled out his knife and glanced back at Talla. She was just beginning to stir. He needed to move quickly.

Crawling to the back, he nudged her onto her right side to better expose her neck. Running his fingers over her skin, it took him several seconds to find the rice-sized tracker implanted near her spine. He pinched her skin around the tracker, brought up the blade, and made a narrow cut, just deep enough to pop the tracker out. A small groan escaped her lips, but she hadn't yet fully awakened.

Jax set the tracker on the metal side of the Jeep and smashed it with the flat end of his Ka-Bar. After knocking it to the ground, he sheathed his blade and hurried back to the driver's seat. Even though the trucks had all turned into the Etzee, he wouldn't make the mistake of thinking no one would come after them. By now, the troops would have orders to track down and neutralize any survivors.

Jax didn't have much time. He pulled back onto the road and stepped on the gas. A column of black smoke filled his rearview mirror, and artillery sounds echoed in his ears. A battle was raging. Jax's people hadn't reckoned on the cunning of Etzee's inhabitants nor the sacrifices they would make so that some would survive. Sephians would align with Draeken, and those survivors would come back at Earth with everything they had.

____

Chapter 7

____

Consciousness tugged at Talla's mind. The entire left side of her face throbbed, and her thoughts swirled. She gingerly touched her nose and cheek. Fortunately for Laze, nothing felt broken. That lunatic brother of hers was going to get it good this time.

Her wings were pinched against a rough surface. It took many long seconds before her mushy thoughts firmed up. The last she remembered was Laze's fist coming at her just as the human troops were bearing down on them.

Why am I still alive?

She opened her eyes to find herself squinting into bright sunlight. She was on her back in a small open cargo area of a Jeep. The wind blanketed the rumble of engine noise, but otherwise the world around her seemed deceptively quiet. The road was of typical earthside variety, filled with potholes and cracks, and the Jeep jumped and swayed. Pulling herself up, she climbed off the gear and bags and into the passenger seat, snagging her wings on her way to the front.

It took her a while to position her wings around her in order to sit upright comfortably. Her neck was cramping, and she rubbed it with her hand. Pulling it away, she frowned as she noticed fresh blood on her fingers. She turned to Jax. "You cut out the tracker."

He shrugged. "I couldn't risk us being tracked." He gave her a quick once-over. "Are you okay?"

She nodded, but the motion made her cheek throb. She winced and rubbed her cheek. Laze had always had an impressive right hook. She'd participated in hand-to-hand combat before, many of those times with her brother. The swelling would be down within the day, but it would take at least a week for the bruising to face. She rolled her neck from shoulder to shoulder, her neck cracking with each motion.

Jax looked her direction and winced. "You're going to have quite the shiner."

Since she could barely see out of her eye, she could imagine what she looked like. Then a sudden tension crept through her body. "Where's Laze?"

Jax's lips tightened.

"Where's my brother." An order, not a question.

The steering wheel creaked as he clenched his hands around it. He replied after a long pause. "He's not coming."

"That's impossible." She sat for a moment, unable to focus. "What happened?"

"He bought time for us and others to get away."

"No." She shook her head. Ta deiti.

A surge of numbness spiked with intense emotions took control. "I should've been there. He was a warrior. He shouldn't have had to die alone."

Jax's hand squeezed her knee. The movement was awkward, clumsy, and meant all the more for it. Her good eye blurred, and she clutched the dashboard for support. The tears burned her swollen eye. She liked the pain. It made Laze feel real. He was her older brother. He'd taken care of her since she could walk. He was brilliant and strong and good. He couldn't be dead. He couldn't.

She took deep, cleansing breaths. It took endless minutes to tamp down the agony; to bury it deep within her until she could grieve properly for him. She fought the tears. There was a Draeken saying that tears added salt to a wounded spirit, turning a warrior into a casualty. Talla refused to be a casualty from Laze's sacrifice.

Clenching her jaw, she inhaled the fresh air through her nose to force herself back into the present. She was alive. Her people would need her. Grieving would come later. Only when she felt back in control did she lean back in the seat.

She stared absently at the trees flashing by as the Jeep sped down the road. She let her wings spread just enough to catch the cool breeze. The sun had not yet reached its highest point, which meant that they couldn't have been on the road more than an hour; two at most. The attack, Laze… everything started to feel like an eternity ago. With each minute, she reclaimed a bit of herself again. Sensations returned to her skin. The clouds lumbering in her mind dissipated, to be replaced by a sense of duty.

"Where are we headed?" she demanded.

Jax eyed her for a moment before answering. "Not really sure. I've just been driving away from the Etzee to give us some breathing room. We should be far enough out to be safe from any scouting units."

The Jeep slowed and Jax turned off the road onto a driveway overgrown with weeds. He parked behind the cover of several shrubs and trees and cut the engine. He reached behind him and pulled out a folded paper and a bottle of water. He handed the bottle to her. The water was warm; it had a slight plastic taste to it, but it was refreshing. Her throat felt raw from smoke inhalation. After another drink, she passed it back to Jax, who took a long swig. He wiped his mouth with the back of his hand and handed the bottle back to her.

He unfolded the paper and started scanning the green layout. "We should be safe here for an hour or two until we figure out our next step."

"Is that a map?" she asked.

"Yeah, I need to get a fix on our location. I had to ditch my phone so they couldn't track it," he replied without looking up.

"But it's paper. Is the tech weaved into it?"

"No. It's just paper."

"But it doesn't show where you are or where you're going. What good does it do?"

He cocked his head and watched her for a moment. Then he pulled out a small compass and laid the map over the emergency brake that separated them. "Here. I'll show you."

Jax began to show her how to use a map, but he paused and looked up.

Talla should have noticed its approach. She was still off-balance, distracted, until the high-pitched sound wouldn't be denied. Two pairs of eyes widened at each other when they recognized the unmistakable small engine sound above them at the same time. They shot out from the Jeep in opposite directions just as they heard the pzoosh of a small missile launch from the drone overhead.

The missile whistled through the air and impacted the hood of the Jeep. Talla ducked behind a tree, covering her head with her arms and wings. The explosion shook the ground and sent a wave of hot wind past her. She braced herself with a hand. A storm of leaves tumbled down on her back.

Coming to her feet, her ears ringing, she chanced a quick look at the drone. It now hovered just above the tree line, scanning the ground. A narrow red laser-line crossed over the wreckage and spanned a good ten feet on either side. After a second scan, the tiny camera disappeared with a whir inside the drone. Another larger slot opened, and something was shot into the ground several feet from the wreckage.

The drone moved off and Jax jumped out. "Talla?"

She was already running toward him. "I'm fine. You?"

He nodded and then glowered at the object the drone had left behind. It reminded her of a chaos-charge connected to several arrows. The top round portion had several lights and indentations. It was attached to metal sticks, which stabilized it in the ground.

"We weren't far enough out," he grumbled.

"What is it?" she asked.

"A tracker. They'll send a cleanup team here."

She pulled out her shiv. He held out a hand to stop her from approaching it. "No. If the tracker goes offline, they'll know we're alive and send in a team right away. Either way, they're coming. No need to tip them off any sooner."

"Fyet." She sighed, looking around. But, while the vehicle was out of commission, the blast had been contained. The engine area was gone, and the seats were charcoaled, but the back end remained somewhat intact. The cleanup crew would notice the lack of bodies.

"How much time do you think we have?" she asked.

"A couple hours, maybe more, depending on how things are going back at the Etzee. The Ozarks cover a good chunk of land. It will help us evade troops for longer. That they're using drones right now instead of helicopters with troops for tracking runaways is a good sign. I'm betting that the Etzee is still keeping their hands full."

"We were not the only ones that got away," she said with certainty.

Jax stood before her. His expression was intense yet sympathetic, as though he was looking to her for forgiveness. Everything about that man was a dichotomy. Talla wondered if she'd ever discover the person hidden the masks he wore.

Then he frowned and stepped away. It felt like he couldn't risk someone seeing inside him, and he'd close himself up tighter in response.

"Did Roden say anything about a rendezvous point other than the Striga?" he asked.

"Roden did say that if we can't get to the Striga, his earthside base is the backup plan, but that's over a thousand miles from here, and without my wrist-comm, I don't have the exact coordinates. All I know is it's in the northwest corner of the United States. Do you think you could get us there?"

Jax grunted. "So, the core ship it is. And we'll have to hoof it from here." He turned back to the wreckage. "They must have put a tracker on the Jeep. I should've thought of that."

"You'd have no way to know they'd be tracking their own people," Talla said. "Good thing it was on the Jeep and not you, or else we'd be dead right now."

The tracker had to be the drone's target. Its targeting system hadn't even tried to scan for heat signatures. The first bit of luck they'd had all day.

Holding a hand out to protect his eyes from the heat, Jax stood by the cargo compartment, reached to unbuckle the ammo boxes, and yanked his hand back. With a muttered curse, he pulled off his shirt, wrapped it around his hand, and then unstrapped the two metal cases. Each case dropped onto the ground with a thud.

She watched as Jax poured out the contents of one box then moved to the other. The contents snagged her attention. Talla came down to her knees to sift through the items. A small first aid kit, a bottle of water, a protein bar, an emergency blanket, and a large Swiss Army tool.

"I go off-roading on the weekends. I like to keep a few bare essentials in an overnight kit just in case." From the other box, he pulled out another knife and a handgun in a small black holster.

She gave a low whistle. "That's quite the overnight kit."

"I wish I'd packed a hell of a lot more." He stood abruptly and pulled on his shirt. He fastened the holster around his chest and checked the M9. He picked up the knife and tossed it to Talla. "This will work better than the shiv you have."

"Thanks," she said as she tied the sheathed blade to her thigh. It was a solid six-inch blade and would be far more useful than the short tape-wrapped metal in her pocket, even though she kept that as well.

The pair stuffed their pockets with the remaining gear. "We better get going," Jax said. "We should find somewhere to hide before nightfall."

Talla would have volunteered to fly over the area to scout for caves and holes, but the risk of being seen by a human was too great. They'd have to do this the old-fashioned way. She grabbed a medium-sized branch off the ground to use as a walking stick. "I'm ready."

He turned, headed down the embankment, and up the other side. Talla kept pace as they moved deeper into the forest. Her long wings, made for flight, not hiking, swayed with every step, brushing against fallen leaves. She raised them to lessen the noise, but within an hour her back muscles were cramping, and she found herself dragging her wings once again.

She craved a break to rest and rub her shoulders, but there was no time. She'd been on the lam before. It was how her people had ended up on Earth. Running wasn't fun, but she was confident they could avoid their pursuers if they stayed smart.

Soon, however, their pursuers wouldn't be the greatest risk to their survival. There was no way to hide her wings. They couldn't blend in any populated area. Worse, they didn't have enough water to get them through one day. How long could she survive in this alien environment?

Chapter 8

The birds chirped as though it was just another day, as though Jax and Talla weren't running for their lives. He'd been on the other end of the chase plenty of times. Hell, a couple of years back he'd hunted Sephians through woods much like these. Being on the flipside of the coin wasn't much fun.

There were few clouds to block the afternoon heat, and the tall trees, with their thin needles, did little to buffer the sun's harsh rays.

His stomach growled. They'd shared the protein bar, and there were only a couple of drinks of water left in the bottle. They didn't have the time to stop and purify water, which meant they'd have to find a house to restock from.

Talla muttered a curse behind him.

He turned to find her trying to dislodge the sharp bone spur that tipped her wing from a clump of low branches. Closing the distance, he reached up and pushed the branches away from her scraped wings.

"The trees here are so much bigger than on Sephia. I swear

they're snagging me on purpose," she complained as she pulled a burr from a wing.

"They're better than the desert," Jax said.

"The open space would feel good right now."

"At least trees offer shade. Try wearing full gear during an Afghan summer." He'd seen plenty of brutal terrain in his life, but he'd also always had the latest gear and equipment, courtesy of Uncle Sam. Today brought back some not-so-pleasant memories of advanced training camp to become an Army Ranger. He'd been driven to his breaking point—beyond, really—and he'd managed. This felt similar. He kept waiting for his lieutenant to shout out another command.

He gave Talla a once-over. Her silver hair clung to her sweaty face, and her left eye was nearly swollen shut. Blood trickled from dozens of scratches on her tattooed wings. "Do you need a break?"

"No. We need to keep going." Even weighted down with the extra appendages, she stood tall.

He watched for a second longer.

She lifted her jaw. "I'm fine."

He didn't believe her. Still, he turned and walked ahead. They continued on in silence for some time until the trees opened to a gravel road. "Shit," he cursed as he scanned for traffic. They were lucky no one had been driving down the road at that particular moment. Talla stayed in the shadows, and he retreated into the cover of the woods and walked parallel to the road.

"Let me guess. That paper map of yours will take us where we need to go."

He faced her to find a twinkle in her eye, and some tension eased. "If we follow this, we're bound to come across a house." A house meant water, food, and—more importantly—a vehicle.

Jax's throat was parched. If they didn't find potable water soon, they'd start losing their edge. The cleaning team should have found the Jeep by now, which meant the military would know there were Etzee runaways in these woods. Jax and Talla needed their minds and bodies sharp to survive.

Sounds of a scuffle tore Jax around with the gun in his hand. Talla was shaking her walking stick at a tree. He scanned up the tree and squinted. "That's a squirrel."

Her eyes were wide. "I thought it was a fregee."

He holstered his weapon while trying not to smile. Her assailant was standing on a lower branch, angrily flicking its tail, no doubt as agitated as Talla for having its foraging interrupted. When Talla still looked afraid, he added under a chuckle, "Don't worry. It's harmless."

"It moved like a fregee. It even looks much like one. That's how they get you, you know. One goes in to distract their prey, and that's when the entire pack moves in for the kill. They've been known to take down entire herds of tion before."

He laughed. "I have no idea what a 'fregee' or a 'tion' is, but I assure you, there's nothing to worry about with squirrels."

"A *fregee* is much like what you call dogs, except they are vicious."

"Ah, like Chihuahuas then."

She furrowed her brows, confused, then continued. "And *tion* don't compare to anything I've seen on your world. They are large, bigger than your horses, but hairless and incredibly dumb. Back on Sephia, they were our most popular meat source."

He holstered his gun. "You don't have to worry about too many predators around here. Now, there's rattlesnakes to watch out for, but there's not many this far north. Cougars and bears, but they tend to avoid attention. Rednecks are the biggest threat around these parts, though they're more territorial than anything."

She watched him for a moment before lowering her eyes. He followed her gaze and realized he was still rubbing her ankle. He yanked back and stood. Feeling guilty for acting like a jackass, he held out a hand. "Can you walk?" he asked gruffly.

She glared at the squirrel before she continued walking.

The distant rumble of thunder had them both looking to the sunny sky. Jax turned just as the sun was blotted out by a giant metallic shard. It was moving slowly, still at least twenty thousand feet in the air, but descending. The ground vibrated under the deep thrum. He stared up as the massive ship crossed the sky. He stood in awe.

"The Striga's arrived," she said, the pleasure in her voice unmistakable.

Jax's body thrummed with tension. Even though he knew the Striga was Talla's best chance at protection, he dreaded returning to the eye of the storm. To reach the core ship, that eye would be more of a warzone than calm. He spoke quietly. "You know how many troops stand between us and the ship? It could leave before we can get to it."

"Humans have nothing to damage it," she said. "It will remain until everyone's on board."

"We could die if we head back there."

Sadness filled her eyes. "We all die," she said softly, then met his gaze. "This way, if we can get to the Striga, we at least have a chance to make a difference."

It had been three Earth years since Talla had last seen the Striga. The pride of the Draeken fleet, it was the newest and grandest of all the core ships. Its cold metallic beauty breathed hope into her lungs for the first time in far too long. She watched the ship pass over until the trees cut it from her view. Still, she continued to gaze up to the sky reminiscently as they walked, a smile now in her heart.

The core ships had saved what was left of her people from certain death on Sephia. While each of the massive military ships could house tens of thousands, only a few thousand Draeken had survived to make it to each of the four ships the night of their evacuation from Sephia. There'd been twelve core ships ready to depart that night. Four had escaped. Nine thousand six hundred and fifty-one Draeken had survived of the once superior race. How many remained to carry on their legacy after this morning?

Sucking in a breath of tepid woodsy air, Talla kept pace a few feet behind Jax, though the heat and dehydration was wearing her down. Her muscles felt weak. Branches snagged her wings and fought against her for every step gained.

Jax, on the other hand, didn't show the slightest sign of weakness other than the sweat glistening on his skin. Talla had fallen into a hypnotic rhythm of watching his wingless stride until he came to a stop behind a large tree and held up a fisted hand. While she didn't know the meaning of that action, she'd been on enough missions to know that if he was still and silent, she should be, too. She stopped against the same tree, propping a hand against the trunk.

"There's a cabin about two hundred feet ahead," he whispered.

She thought back to their pursuers. If she were hunting prey, the first thing she'd take control of was any shelter in the area. "Is it safe?"

"We need wheels." He gave her his handgun. "I don't see any movement, so I'm going in to check it out. Stay out of sight until I give a signal."

She gave him a curt nod and he stepped off, moving low from tree to tree until he disappeared. With slow steps, she followed his path until she had a full view of the cabin. Crouching behind a shrub, she rested her wings on the ground to get in a more comfortable position. From this vantage point, she could see the cabin and a cream-colored SUV parked in front.

Jax had already made it to the vehicle. He checked something through the glass then moved around the vehicle and toward the cabin. He shot a glance through the large front window before moving to the front door. The main door was open, leaving a screen door as the only barrier. He stood there, body pressed against the cabin, for several long seconds. In a quick move, he opened the screen door and disappeared inside.

Talla held the gun, waiting for Jax's signal. A child's laughter from somewhere off to her left froze her spine. Looking around, she saw a large, well-camouflaged branch thirty feet above her. Stretching her wings, she spread them out to find just enough space for them to work. In a rush, she flapped her wings.

In prime health, vertical take-off required strength and energy. Unfortunately, Talla hadn't used her wings in two years. After lifting from the ground no more than a few feet, she fell back to the ground.

With a silent curse, she folded her wings back. Careful to move quietly and crouching over as much as she could, zigzagging around trees until she had a view of the other side of the house. A rock trail sloped downward from the back deck and led to a dock. There, she could see a woman lounging in a chair under the full rays of the sun, and a man standing in shallow water with two small children lodged in colorful tubes. Tension eased from her shoulders when she saw no sign of a dog.

Her mouth watered watching the lake in front of her. She was so thirsty. Her head throbbed like a bad hangover. They were surrounded by water, but Jax had warned her it wasn't safe to drink.

The sound of an SUV engine turning over startled her. She turned back to the cabin. Fyet! She glanced toward the family, which continued with their play. Confident they hadn't heard the engine over the sound of water splashing around them, she dashed back, staying only as quiet as she necessary to not be noticed.

Jax was standing half inside the driver's side and anxiously scanning the area. She sprinted forward, opened the passenger door and was in by the time he had the vehicle in gear. She waited to shut her door and he did the same. He pulled out of the driveway, careful to not rev the engine.

"They're out back, in the water," Talla said, her voice a whisper.

Jax nodded and then stepped on the gas. They shut their doors as they picked up speed. "I told you to stay put," he said through clenched teeth.

"No," Talla replied. "You said to stay out of sight, which is what I did. I heard voices and checked it out. Those people had small children," Talla said. "They'll return to their cabin soon and discover their vehicle missing. It won't take long for the soldiers to know we have a vehicle."

"We'll stick to side roads."

"This vehicle doesn't have stealth capabilities. How will we get close to the Striga?"

"Pray like hell?"

Her brows rose. "Has that ever worked before?"

Jax ignored her question and nodded toward the back seat. "Right now, the most important thing is to keep our energy up. There's water in the back."

Talla snapped around, pinching a wing against a seat belt latch. She writhed into a better position and found an entire case of bottled water. Next to it was a bulging plastic bag. She grabbed a couple of bottles and the bag.

"Here," she said, handing Jax a bottle before resettling in the front seat. After drinking half a bottle, she rummaged through the plastic bag to find different kinds of deli meats and cheeses. "You've been busy."

"I got lucky. It's a vacation home, and they must've just gotten in this morning. I grabbed the bag and water from the fridge and left."

Talla shoved an entire slice of ham in her mouth. While chewing, she pulled out a package of sliced turkey and handed it to Jax, who took it with an amused smile.

She swallowed. "What?"

"I've never seen anyone eat so fast before."

"I've eaten more meals on the battlefield or while flying than at a table. I've learned that there is rarely time to eat at leisure," she said bluntly and ignored his flinch. She broke out a slice of white cheese filled with holes. As she let the cheese soften in her mouth, she had to give the humans credit. Their food was a dozen times better than dull Sephian cuisine. Draeken cuisine was good and spicy, but lacked the salt of human food. Earth was loaded with the mineral, and Talla wanted to enjoy salt on everything.

It didn't take them long to go through three packages of meat and two packages of cheese. Replete, Talla leaned back in her seat, sipping from a second bottle of water.

Jax gave her a thoughtful look. "Why don't you crawl in back and take a nap?"

"I've slept plenty," she replied, touching her still-swollen cheek. Her mood sobered, and she swallowed back recent memories. She turned to Jax. "How'd he die?"

Jax's mouth tightened. He took another swig of water. "He rammed the truck into troops heading for the Etzee. Slowed them down enough to put some distance between us and them."

"Sounds like Laze," she murmured. She gave a silent thanks to her brother for his sacrifice. Sheescaten, ta deiti. *Peace, my brother.*

A chill of loss worked up her spine and she gave an involuntary shiver. Abruptly, she downed what was left in the bottle, crumpled it, and tossed it into the back seat.

Neither spoke for the next couple of hours. Jax kept his eyes on the road while Talla scanned the countryside and sky for any sign of their pursuers. Fortunately, this vehicle had a paper map, and she soon learned how valuable it could be in avoiding highways.

Rather than making a direct line back to the Etzee, they'd agreed that taking winding back roads would be their best chance at throwing off any pursuers. The troops would suspect they were trying to put as much distance between themselves and the Etzee. Instead, they drove east, winding back toward the Etzee, where there were more side roads but fewer trees.

Twilight had set in, and Talla squinted as she scanned the countryside. "Without tensatlen, I can't see at night."

"I wore a pair of those before, except Sienna called them drades. They were a big improvement over our night vision goggles. We'll stop for a break."

The SUV slowed, and Jax turned off the road and onto a dry creek bed. Talla held onto the dashboard as he drove down the ravine until the road behind them was out of sight. Then he drove a bit farther. When the dirt turned into mud, he revved the engine, and the large SUV lurched onto the embankment, snapping small trees unfortunate enough to be caught in its path. He pulled under the cover of a huge pine and cut the engine.

Talla took in the vicinity. They were surrounded by the old creek bed and trees. Any deeper into the woods and the SUV would get hung up. Without the engine and road noise, the sudden silence boomed.

"If anyone comes through this way on foot, we'll stand out like a sore thumb. Who the hell came up with 'iridescent pearl' for a paint color?" Jax turned and grabbed a bottle of water. "This is as good a cover as we're going to get. We should at least be hidden from any vehicles passing by—and possibly drones overhead—as long as they don't home in on this exact spot. If we have to run, we're not going far. We don't have enough gas to make it to the *Striga*."

"I sometimes forget the limits of these vehicles. Power cells on our vehicles back home constantly recharged themselves. It's unfortunate that this vehicle can't get us back to the *Striga*."

Jax scanned over the thick booklet of maps they'd found in the glove compartment. His fingers pinched air in a couple of different directions. "Looks like we can get back to your ship in a couple of hours if we keep sticking with back roads. That's assuming they don't set up roadblocks, but the Striga's arrival means that everyone in the area knows something is going on. So, I'd be surprised if they didn't have checkpoints set up on every way to the Etzee by now. The dark won't help with checkpoints, but it'll help us grab another car. It looks like there's a small town in just a few miles." He closed the map and set it on the dash. "We'll head out when most locals will be in bed. I'll take first watch. Get some rack time."

Talla noticed the dark circles under his eyes. Though he didn't act the least bit tired, she knew he must be exhausted. "You didn't sleep after you sent Laze and me away last night, did you?"

"I had to contact Sienna and Roden. You?"

"A little." She took a deep breath. "Listen… I'm sorry that you had to kill your own kind."

He shrugged, but the motion was tight, abrupt. "They were criminals that should've been locked up years ago." He reached for the door handle, and she put a hand on his arm.

"Let me take first watch tonight. I can scan the area from overhead without being seen."

He frowned. "Can you fly?"

With a running start, maybe. "Yes."

He didn't seem convinced, but exhaustion seemed to win. "All right. Wake me in thirty."

Chapter 10

Two hours later, Talla watched Jax step out of the SUV, his brows knitted together as he scanned the landscape for her. She jumped off the top of the SUV, startling him.

"Why didn't you wake me?" he muttered, scratching his head.

"You needed the rest, and the *Striga* will wait." She motioned around them. "It's been quiet. I scanned the area three miles out in every direction." Surprisingly, she'd discovered she could still fly—well, glide, anyway—short distances with a good running start. It had been magical; feeling the air break around her felt exhilarating after too long being grounded. And the cool air had invigorated her. She could've flown until morning.

He looked around. "Did you happen to see any good spots for cover nearby?"

She thought for a moment. "There's a rock overhang down by the creek not too far off that way," she said, pointing deeper into the woods. "Why? I thought we were heading out."

"I'm heading out. You're staying here."

She frowned. "Why?"

He shook his head. "I can blend in. Your wings will give you away if we're seen. And this is the safer location for now."

She hated to admit that he was right. Her wings were a detriment when the rest of the world wanted her kind gone. After a moment, she gave a tight nod.

He leaned inside the vehicle. He pulled out two bottles of water, and she grabbed both from his hands.

"If I'm not back in two hours, that means the shit hit the fan, and you'd better hightail it out of here." He turned and pointed in front of her. "Fly that way until you find the *Striga*. Watch out for drones and scouting units."

"If you don't make it back here well before your two hours are up, then I have overestimated your skills."

He shot her a smile. Then he was in the SUV and backing out the way they'd come. She stood there and watched him disappear in the darkness. When she could no longer hear the engine noise, she turned and headed down the creek bed for the tedious task of waiting.

Seeing it from the ground, the large slate overhang was a perfect concealment. She lay down on her stomach and cocooned herself within her wings. She tossed leaves over her shoulder, letting them sprinkle down onto her back, and willed herself to sleep.

Talla was dreaming of a wingless man with brown eyes and matching hair when she jolted awake. It was still dark. She came up on a knee, bending to accommodate her long wings.

She waited for any sound, but heard nothing. Still she waited. Minutes later, her muscles started to cramp from tension and lack of movement. A spider crawled up her forearm. It moved, one willowy leg at a time, over her skin. A leaf crumpled off to her right. She couldn't see anything through the shrubs and saplings, but the sound was unmistakable. Footsteps. Careful, deliberate footsteps. Unless there was a group of people walking at precisely the same time, there was only one pair of steps cutting through the natural harmony of the woods.

She wanted to call out for Jax, but her gut warned her against doing so. She inhaled, priming her body to spring, and tucked the gun into her waistband. She started a mental countdown as the steps came closer. Three. She unsnapped the sheath holding the knife. Two. She gripped the handle. One. She pulled the blade free. Leghat. *Showtime.* She lunged forward, coming behind the soldier in full gear.

The soldier wasn't as well trained as Jax. He'd been holding his rifle, but fumbled for it, stunned by Talla's sudden presence. He whipped around just as she moved with him, grabbed his chin and, pulling him toward her, sliced his neck ear-to-ear. The blade was sharp; it went clean through the man's throat.

She yanked the rifle from his hands before dropping him, jumping back before he could bleed on her.

The man collapsed to his knees, clawing at his throat, unable to scream, before falling forward.

Another sound snapped Talla's attention up to find Jax's venomous gaze leveled on her. "What the hell are you doing?" he whispered as he relinquished her of the rifle. Then he got down and checked the now-dead man. "Damn it, Kohlm. You should have incapacitated him, not killed him."

She bristled, keeping her voice low. "I'm not one of your soldiers, so quit throwing orders at me." She pointed to the soldier. "I couldn't risk him making noise."

He lowered his head. "He didn't need to die. He was just a kid."

She looked around. "Do we have to discuss this now?" she whispered back.

His mouth thinned. Rather than going through the soldier's

gear, Jax came to his feet, and motioned her forward. "Follow me." He took off at a jog, then a near-run, down the creek bed.

When they reached the muddy tracks where the SUV had been, nothing was there. Talla paused. "Where's the vehicle?"

"This way," he said, slowing but still moving forward. "The car I got can't handle these off-road trails."

She followed him until they reached the road. A small, two-door, blue vehicle sat nearly hidden by shrubs. "Well, that one is certainly easier to hide," she said.

"It was unlocked, and the gas tank is full," he said, opening the door. "That's why I grabbed it."

Talla had to move the seat back all the way to fit in. Even then, her wing spurs pierced the fabric in the roof of the car.

Jax gunned the engine. "We've got to move. There's no way one scout would be out this far without the rest of his unit nearby. When he doesn't check in, it won't take them long to close in on our location."

Jax focused on the road as they headed north and east along back roads toward the Etzee. Though Jax was often silent, Talla knew he was still upset.

"I wouldn't have killed him if there was any other way."

"I know," he replied after a long moment.

The cadence of the engine and movement lulled Talla to sleep. By the time she awoke, the earliest hints of dawn gave an outline to the horizon. She rubbed her eyes. Too many hours with a power nap here and there were beginning to cloud her mind. Fields had begun to replace trees. The landscape began to resemble the flat lands that surrounded the Etzee.

Getting to the Striga wasn't going to be easy, but the Striga couldn't come to them. Core ships were massive monuments of technology that required equally massive amounts of power. It wasn't like the Striga could just lift and relocate to new locations to pick up stragglers.

She turned to the man next to her. His muscles were tense; his lips were a thin line. "Thanks," she said quietly.

He turned, startled from his thoughts. "For what?"

"For giving up everything to help out those who are nothing like you. For risking your life for me."

"Why wouldn't I have?"

"Most wouldn't."

"I'm not most," he said.

"No. You certainly aren't." Suddenly nervous, she stared straight ahead, and she focused on breathing slow and steady, focused on not fidgeting. There was something about Jax that made her feel like foolish, like a child. But her self-consciousness quickly faded as she scanned the countryside again. Cold fear took over her thoughts as her gaze narrowed on the road ahead. What she'd first thought were low-level clouds in the far-off distance were gray plumes of smoke.

A battle was underway. The Etzee had become a theater of war, and they were heading straight toward it.

Chapter 11

Jax wanted to snap the car around and head in the opposite direction. To take them any place, other than the mess they were heading for. He wanted to hide with Talla until this whole thing blew over, but he knew better. Neither of them had anywhere else to go. He was a traitor—hell, there was a dead soldier in the woods to prove that—and Talla was condemned merely for being different.

"Fyet," Talla murmured at his side.

The Draeken curse word summed it up perfectly; it even sounded like its English equivalent.

Thirty miles out and already the Striga was a gray colossus, like an elephant about to smash an anthill caught in its path. He couldn't see the heavy iron yet, but he knew they were there. Dots of smoke from surface-to-air missiles bled into the haze surrounding the ship. The military must be throwing everything they had at the Striga. Even so, the shimmer across the core ship's smooth, untarnished hull shone a one-finger salute in response to the bombardment.

Neither spoke through the next few miles. At ten miles out, Jax cranked the car off the gravel road and into a corn field.

Talla grabbed a handle above the window. "A little warning next time."

He gunned the engine. "Hang on."

It was midsummer, and the corn stalks were already as tall as the car. He was regretting the decision to ditch the SUV. He maintained just enough speed to move forward, knocking down the two rows of corn before them. One of the headlights went out. The car's small engine would last only few minutes at this rate if the windshield didn't give out first. The green stalks were like battering rams, whipping at the heavily dented hood with one thud after the next. Bugs, leaves, and tassels broke free and smacked against the windshield. Every couple of minutes, he ran the windshield wiper to clear the sticky debris. When he reached the end of the row, he plowed through the fence, lined up, and started through the next field.

Talla craned her head toward the sky. "We're lucky there've been no helicopters so far."

"I'd lay bets that they're still focusing on the core ship."

"The Striga should be watching for survivors. We need to find a way to signal them so they will send a Transporter to pick us up. A few chaos-charges would come in handy right about now."

"We could light this piece of shit on fire and hope they spot us before the ground troops do," Jax offered.

"That's putting a lot of faith in hope, but it's also our best option." She scowled. "If only I had my wrist-comm. They could come get us anywhere then."

"I've got a whole pocket full of 'if onlys' here," Jax said drily, "but they're not going to get us onto the Striga."

At that moment, a raptor flew over low, loud, and fast. "Do you think he saw us?" Jax asked.

"If he was looking or had cameras on, then yes, he saw us," she replied.

"Whether they think we're one of theirs or if we're just gawkers is another story." The car sputtered, died, and rolled to a stop. He unbuckled. "Looks like this is as close as we're going to get. Ready?"

She gave him a hard look. "Always."

He grabbed the atlas, opened the door, and stepped out. Talla grabbed the rifle and a bottle of water, and walked around the back of the car. Steam was now seeping out through the hood's edges from the overheated engine. She stepped over broken rows of corn, and Jax met her midway as he walked back to the gas tank. He unscrewed the cover to see what shape he had to work with.

He tore pages out of the atlas and rolled them into cylinders. He slid the first cylinder into the gas tank, deep enough so that only the top edge remained. The next cylinder, slightly narrower, slid into the first. He repeated the process twice until he had a foot-long paper tube sticking out of the tank. He crumpled up a small ball of paper and stuffed the open end of the tube.

He rummaged through his pockets and pulled out the small flint from his Jeep's emergency stash. He turned to Talla. "When this lights up, we have no way of knowing which side will see us first."

She pointed to his left. "We run in that direction. My people will be able to track us from here."

Checking the flint, he brought it just above the crumpled paper. With a quick move, he snapped the flint against its steel. Tiny sparks flew. He snapped the flint again and again until a small piece of the paper blackened and then disappeared under a flame. He watched until half of the crumpled paper was engulfed before stepping back.

With a quick nod at Talla, she took off at a sprint, leading the way down a row. After a dozen seconds, a hearty *whoomp* sounded behind them. They slowed, stopped, and turned. Intense flames of crimson and gold hues had swallowed the car and licked at the air.

"It worked," he muttered with genuine surprise.

Contrary to the movies, it wasn't easy to set a car on fire. He was thankful there was no explosion to draw attention from troops on the ground. Not that he'd expected one. A good-sized, sealed, air pocket was needed for any Hollywood-style explosion. The car, at just under a half tank and with the gas cap gone, wasn't set up to blow. But even in the night sky, the dancing flames and smoke show were glorious. Now, if only the Striga saw the signal first, they'd have a chance.

He looked at the woman at his side. "Leave the rifle. If the troops see it, they'll open fire."

"They'll open fire anyway."

"I want to minimize kills."

She turned to face him. "A smart man told me that doing the right thing leaves little room for compromise and none for mercy."

"He sounds jaded."

"He was my brother."

Jax cast a glance her way. She stood stoic, her face expressionless, but she clutched the rifle to her as though it was her child. He inhaled. The air was now carrying hints of burning metal and gasoline. "What now?"

She stalked toward the burning vehicle, and went down on one knee a safe distance from the flames. She handed him the handgun. "We wait."

He took the M9, checked the magazine, and crouched, his back to her wings as he scanned the area to their north.

With every passing minute, tension tightened and weighed down his muscles. They were cutting it too close. They were less than ten miles from the Etzee. Troops would be here any minute. The flames had already morphed into black smoke, dimming their signal. "We have to assume we're on our own," he said, coming to his feet.

Talla lowered her head and slowly pulled herself up as though it pained her to do so. "They didn't see us."

Her words sounded hollow, her demeanor that of a small girl

lost. "We'll find another way." They'd come too far to give up now.

Corn rustled behind Jax. Her eyes widened, and he snapped his head around.

Then he and Talla leapt to the side. They crashed through rows, pushing through the scraping resistance from the corn stalks. They broke from the line of sight of the first soldier, which brought them into the sights of another soldier two rows over.

"Isn't that—?" Talla yelled.

"Yeah." Of all the shit luck, it had to be his own company hunting them down. Echo-Three was the best. *Of course they'd be first on the scene*, he thought as he plowed headfirst through another wall of unyielding green corn.

"Can you fly?" he yelled above the ruckus of crashing stalks.

"Yes."

"Go. Stay low so they can't get a fix. I'll distract them. Go!" He pushed her from him and turned direction, running down a row and directly toward his company.

Talla yelled something, but he never looked back, trusting her to get airborne. At least this way, she had a shot at getting away.

The soldier raised his rifle, and Jax lifted his M9. The man was too far away to get a body shot with a handgun, but Jax pinched off three shots anyway. The soldier never moved except to return fire. There were several pops. Something punched Jax in the gut, and a sharp sting knocked his right leg out from under him. He went down hard, but was more surprised that the other soldier hadn't gone for the kill shot. Jax had trained his guys better than that.

He raised his M9 to fire again, but a second soldier crashed through the stalks next to him, and the dark blur of a rifle butt came down on his head. He collapsed on his back, his world a dark and swirling mess. He felt the gun yanked from his hand. "Don't move, Lieutenant."

The sting in his leg had become a sharp burn, but that wasn't the only place he hurt. He touched his stomach and felt wetness. Gut shot. That was the nasty trick with adrenaline. A guy didn't realize he was screwed until it was too late. He grimaced as he stared up the barrel of an M16.

The rustling of leaves surrounded him, and he realized the rest of the company was closing in. Rifle fire erupted several feet to his left.

Several dark objects lobbed through his line of vision. "Shock grenade! Fly, Tal—" he yelled out, but his air as well as any ability to speak was cut off when someone stepped on his chest.

Off to his right, the air exploded with reverberating booms when the grenades exploded. The plants around him rustled with the vibrations.

Someone shouted commands, and many of the troops disappeared to the south. Two remained. The boot left his chest. He wheezed, sucking in fresh air.

His best friend came down on a knee. "Damn it, Jax," Ace said, grimacing as he scanned his friend's battered body. He pulled out a field dress kit and lifted Jax's T-shirt. "What the hell are you doing here?"

"Heard this was where the action was," Jax replied, coughing as his air supply returned.

"Christ, you look like shit."

Jax grunted as Ace slapped the dressing on his stomach wound. "You always say the sweetest things."

Ace reached out a hand. "Give me your kit, Moss."

Corporal Moss, who'd served under Jax until two days ago, dug into his pocket and slapped a small package into Ace's palm. The soldier continued to keep his rifle leveled at Jax, and Jax barked at him. Moss jumped and both Jax and Ace chuckled.

Jax heard fabric rip and looked down to watch Ace patch his leg. "Who shot me?" he muttered.

"Gabe, I think," Ace replied.

Jax scowled, holding his hand to his stomach. "I'm going to kick his ass."

Ace smirked but sobered. He got in close. "Whose side are you on, Jax?"

His response was immediate, no doubt of any kind. "Our side. Just like always."

Ace patted Jax's shoulder. "That's all I needed to hear." He came to his feet. "Stand down, Moss. Lieutenant Jerrick isn't part of our directive."

Moss wavered, but didn't lower his M16. He was the youngest and one of the newest members. A regular straight-shooter. Reminded Jax of what he'd been like when he first enlisted. All piss and vinegar. "But sir, the directive states that anyone aiding or abetting a demon or goldie—"

"I said, stand down, Corporal. That's an order."

Moss hesitated, and then lowered his weapon.

Something blotted out the sun, and Jax looked up to find a Draeken Transporter hovering above his position. He chuckled. Too damn late.

"Looks like the cavalry's here." Ace waved the Transporter down. "They'll get you patched up, brother."

As the Transporter descended, rifle shots came from a half dozen guns off to Jax's right. Bullets ricocheted off the ship with sparks. Moss got antsy. "This ain't right, Lieutenant. They're the enemy."

"You want Jerrick to die, dumb ass? They can help him. We can't. Now. Stand. Down."

Moss's eyes flitted from the Transporter to Jax to Ace. If it had been anyone else on Jax's team, he would've obeyed without question, but Moss was the new guy. That special bond of brotherhood hadn't been formed yet. Moss pulled up his M16, this time aiming it point-blank at Ace. "I can't let you do that, sir."

Ace didn't look scared. He looked pissed off. "What, Moss? You going to shoot me now?"

Moss's hesitation cost him. Jax grabbed the corporal's ankle and yanked. Moss flew backward, pinching off several shots on his way down.

More shots were fired, this time from Ace's direction, and the corporal lay motionless on the ground.

By now, the Transporter had landed a couple of dozen feet away from Ace and Jax. He turned to Ace. "Aw, hell."

His friend was holding his chest, a clean shot through his lung.

"Well, doesn't this suck," Ace said, a small trail of blood running down from the corner of his mouth. He fell forward, and Jax caught him. Pulling himself up with his good leg, he heaved Ace around his shoulders and trudged toward the vessel.

The ship opened suppression fire in a wide arc as its door opened. The sounds of gunfire lessened but continued. He could hear yelling and screams from not too far away. Jax screamed for them to stop, but his shout was swallowed by the Transporter's blasters. These were his men being chopped down. He'd stood at their side in battle, only to abandon them now to slaughter. "No! Stop firing!" he cried out.

Two Draeken ran out, each holding a full-length clear shield against the incoming rifle fire. When they reached Jax, the first one asked, "Is one of you Lieutenant Jackson Jerrick?"

Jax limply raised a hand, then motioned to Ace. "He's also coming with me."

Both Draeken were at least a half foot taller than Jax. One relieved him of Ace while the other dragged him toward the ship, which was still laying cover fire in the direction of the car.

Jax grabbed onto his rescuer's uniform. "Talla's still out there!"

"We know," the Draeken carrying him said. "We're picking her up, too."

The moment they carried him inside the door, he was dropped on the floor next to Ace, and the two Draeken left the Transporter again. Glancing around, he found only the pilot, who was focused on whatever lay outside the windshield. "Move faster," he commanded into his wrist-comm.

Jax rolled Ace onto his back. With a collapsed lung, he had minutes of air if he was lucky. Without a spare field kit, he pressed his palm against the wound to staunch the blood flow. "Stay with me, Ace," he said to the unconscious man on the floor.

The echoes of gunfire faded, and Jax suspected that every man he'd been proud to call a brother now lay bleeding or dead in a cornfield. A cold stone lodged in his heart. He was the reason they'd been killed. He'd slaughtered his own men. Who else would die if he continued down this path?

A Draeken lunged into the Transporter, and Jax startled. A second Draeken was right behind, carrying Talla. The door closed, and the guardsman set her down on the floor before hopping over to the front of the cramped ship.

He wanted to let go of Ace and grab Talla, but she was at least conscious. Bloody and disoriented but conscious, while Ace needed every extra second Jax could buy.

"Talla?" he asked.

She winced and turned her head. Her good eye blinked open. She smiled. "Hey."

"You okay?" he asked roughly.

"Just a hard landing from those shock grenades. They're a lot like chaos-charges." She scrutinized him, and her eyes widened. "You're shot."

"I'll be okay," he said, not believing himself. He'd seen gut wounds before. They rarely had a happy ending. He sobered. "Ace is going to need help fast. Let's hope your medical technology is as good as you say." He turned to the pilot. "Can't this thing go any faster?"

She looked over at Ace and nodded tightly. "I'm sorry, Jax, but I think he's already gone."

Talla left Jax's side to clean up and have her body repaired. They'd even injected her atrophied wings with muscle enhancers. With every flex of her long wings, she could feel invigorating strength returning.

When she returned to Jax's bed, she found him sleeping. She was surprised to find him fully clothed, which meant he'd regained consciousness and dressed himself after she'd last checked on him.

On the Transporter, he'd started screaming about saving Ace and his team, so their rescuers had been forced to sedate him so he wouldn't make his injuries worse.

Color had returned to his face, and his wounds would now be covered with fresh skin. Human and Draeken DNA was so similar that Draeken medicine was compatible with the human anatomy without any kind of adjustment needed, though it was obvious Jax hadn't had access to her people's medical technology for much of his life. When she'd come in earlier, he had still been unconscious and covered only by a blanket. She'd seen the scars that littered his arms and chest. Many were small, a slice here and a puncture there. She was curious about the four-inch scar on his shoulder and wondered what had led to that wound.

She set down the bag she'd been carrying. Jax's eyes opened. "You're awake."

He pulled himself into a sitting position with a nearly inaudible grunt. "I feel good. How long have I been here?"

She looked at her wrist-comm. "A little over four hours. It is night now."

"Only four hours?" He dropped his head back onto the body-conforming bed. "I thought I was a goner."

"Our medicine is superior to yours."

"That's an understatement." He gingerly moved his leg. "I don't feel anything more than a dull cramping in my stomach and leg."

"That will continue for another day or so until your body is fully repaired," she said. "Then you'll get muscle spasms and you'll notice weakness until you're at full strength. That is all a normal part of recovery."

He looked around the room, and Talla wondered what he saw. After all, this was the med-hub. Everything was clinical, with few comforts on display. Shades of gray and streamlined metals conveyed a strange beauty in its stark modernism.

He spoke. "Earth really is in the dark ages. Your people offer so much, and all we did was spit in your face for it."

"Yes, you did."

"After everything humans have done to you, do you still want to stay on Earth?"

So much honesty and pain in those eyes. Bristling under his gaze, she thought for a moment, stretched her wings before pulling them back. Her voice softened. "I want a home. I've seen enough bloodshed to last a hundred lifetimes. All of my people have. On Earth, for the first time in our lives, we have a chance to put that behind us and start fresh. Who knows how long and far we'd have to travel to find another habitable planet. It could take years, even decades. We're not going to give up a chance at a home here, even if we need to fight another war."

He shrugged. "With Omega, this planet will probably be all yours anyway."

"I see they found you suitable clothing," she said, not wanting to talk about the virus.

He glanced down at the black and gray outfit. "All the Draeken shirts have strips in the backs cut out, so they gave me a Sephian shirt. Not sure who they got it from."

"I brought you the clothes. And I made sure to find you Draeken pants, so you are at least half-styled," she said and gave him a small smirk.

He grunted.

"You've been cleared to leave med-hub, and your sanctuary is ready," she said.

"Sanctuary?" he asked as he accepted the bag from her.

Talla thought through her English vocabulary for the right word. "Quarters? Residence? Yes, your new residence. They are designed for you to be as comfortable as possible. Your sanctuary is eight floors up from here." She picked up the small gray bag. "I've brought you an orientation kit to help you acclimate to the ship."

He motioned to the door. "Show me the way."

As they walked through the open hallways, Talla realized that she'd seldom walked this hallway before. She'd always flown to where she needed to go. She'd thought being back on the Striga would make everything feel normal again. But she'd realized familiarity had nothing to do with her emotions right now. The last time she'd been on this ship, Laze had been with her. They'd always been inseparable.

She paused. "I need a drink."

"Yeah," he agreed quietly. "Me, too."

They walked in silence through the next several corridors.

"You know, I really didn't think we'd make it here," Jax said.

"Me neither." She smiled at him. "Perhaps I should try out your prayer thing."

He chuckled. "There's a bit more to it than that, but I figured it can't hurt." His neck craned to the side as he scanned the larger vestibule they were now crossing. "Hell," he muttered. "When I saw the Sephian base in Arkansas, I thought that was impressive. This ship blows it out of the water."

Talla looked up. She looked around, imagining what it would be like for someone to see it for the first time. Doors spotted the wall at their level, but higher up, the walls climbed for fifty feet before curving in to meet in the center, forming a dome. The night sky played across the panels, bringing a feeling of open space to the core ship's inhabitants.

Smaller video panels showed a variety of scenes. Some were officers providing updates, while others showed human troops surrounding the ship. Though the Striga had a single, massive window by the command room, its inhabitants could obtain the status of the battle at a quick glance and receive more information than any person on the ground.

"I'll give you a tour tomorrow after you're fully healed. How do you feel?"

"Fine. Better than fine, actually." He shook his leg. "You're right about the spasms, but they're just annoying. It doesn't feel any worse than a nasty bruise right now."

"Good. This way."

They walked to the bar. When they entered, all faces turned toward them briefly before returning to their own drinks. Talla avoided the section where the Sephians sat, which had the lights turned off. She led Jax through tables, keeping her eyes focused straight ahead to avoid being pulled into any conversation.

"Don't mind the looks," she whispered to Jax.

He leaned closer. "It's not me they're looking at."

She nodded stiffly. "There are not many Draeken women left," she replied, her voice low.

A guardsman cursed at Jax before downing his drink.

"I'm not very popular around here," he said, not sounding the least bit bothered.

"They don't like competition." Her eyes widened. "Not that you're—we're—"

"Don't worry. I know," he said. Then he froze. He pulled away and headed toward one of the square bars in the huge room. "Ace?" he asked, his voice barely above a whisper.

The dark-haired human sitting at the bar, bundled in a thick blanket, turned. A smile crept up his face. "Jax, you ugly bastard. I was wondering when you'd get here."

Jax looked from Ace to Talla and back to Ace, his face full of wonder. "You're alive?"

"Alive, yeah. Surprised the hell out of me too."

Talla pursed her lips, eyeing the orientation kit on the counter before him. "What are you doing here? You should still be in med-hub. You suffered a very serious injury."

Ace spoke before taking another drink. "Funny. That's what the doc said too."

"Man," Jax said, dragging the word out over a sigh.

Ace nodded. "I know, right?"

"After he went into cardiac arrest, they lowered his body temperature to not risk brain damage while they repaired his chest," Talla said.

"They froze you?" Jax asked.

"It's a common practice," she said. "It minimizes risk of infection and gives the patches time to take hold."

"Yeah, I think my balls froze off," Ace said, reaching shakily for his beer. "Definitely not the best meat house experience I've ever had."

Jax shook his head with a smile. "It's good to see you, brother."

Ace held up his beer. "Cheers to that."

Jax pulled out a chair and Talla followed suit.

"So, is the beer any good in this joint?" Jax asked.

Ace shrugged. "It's cold and not too skunky. Let's leave it at that."

Jax held up a finger, and the bartender came over. "Beer." Jax glanced at Talla. "You want one too?"

Talla shook her head. "Beer is a poor substitute for bolgt." She nodded at the bartender, and he smiled before heading off to get their drinks.

He was back in seconds with two mugs. Jax's had foam on top, while Talla's contained the dark liquid of bolgt. She took a drink and cringed. Not horrible for a bolgt substitute, but it still wasn't the real thing.

Jax was eyeing her. "What's that?"

"This, when made properly," she said, "is what your gods would call ambrosia."

"I don't do sissy drinks," Ace said.

Talla smirked and held out her mug. Ace took a drink. His eyes widened, and he handed back her mug with an exhalation. "That's good." He motioned to Jax. "Tastes a bit like rum but without the syrupy taste."

Suspicious, Jax tried bolgt. He turned to the bartender. "I'll have what she's having."

"Make it two," Ace said.

When their fresh mugs came, Ace held his up. "To Echo Team Three."

"To brothers lost," Jax added.

"To brothers lost," Talla echoed.

They drank.

Over the next few hours, Jax drank two for every one of Talla's drinks, while Ace was somewhere in between. He'd discarded the blanket after the bolgt took the edge off. They stopped when the bartender came over, typing something on his wrist-comm. "I apologize, Staff Sergeant, but it seems that you've reached your quota. It says you've been confined to bed rest."

"I'm just dandy," Ace said.

"Doctor's orders," the bartender said and walked away, taking Ace's mug with him.

Ace came to his feet. "Well, I guess the fat lady has sung then." He picked up the gray bag in front of him and turned, scanning the room. "Uh, either one of you happen to know where this 'sanctuary' of mine is?"

Talla stood, her bolgt buzz hitting her full force. "Yours is next door to Jax's. I'll show you both."

They strolled through the hallways and up several more floors. Jax lifted his small bag. "What's in here anyway?"

Talla reached for it and pulled it open. "Everything a Striga passenger needs. Guides, a translator, and most importantly," she pulled out the largest item, "your wrist-comms."

"Wicked," Ace muttered, sifting through his contents. "I've always wanted to try out one of those."

"I take it they're counting on Ace and me staying for a while?" Jax asked.

Talla spoke. "I believe the Striga is the safest place for you both right now, but neither of you will be kept on the Striga against your will. Oh, here's your hall." She pointed out the hallway. "Right now, there are only humans in this area until everyone's comfortable with integration."

"Where's your room?" Jax asked.

"It's one floor down. You can find anyone on the wall screens, which are in every hall. Our wrist-comms are connected to the Striga's main comm, so you can track us, unless we set our comms to non-tracking, such as in meetings." She took his wrist-comm from his hands, entered in her code and then fastened it around his forearm. "There. You can track my location from your wrist-comm as well."

She stopped at the third door in. Jax's full name and rank was posted in Draeken and English next to the door. She motioned to Jax. "Your wrist-comm is your key. You must be wearing it for it to work. Then, just swipe your arm like so." She moved her arm over his name plate. The door remained closed. "It will open for you, but it won't open for anyone else unless you grant them access."

He mimicked her action, and the door opened. He stepped inside, and she followed.

Ace whistled behind her. "Damn, this is bigger than my first apartment."

"Yours will be identical," she said, tugging Ace's wrist-comm out of his hands. "They're all set up the same, but you can personalize them any way you'd like." She strapped the wrist-comm onto his forearm.

"Over here is your food center," Talla gestured to a section of the wall, bypassing the small lounge area. She pressed a button, and the wall lifted.

"That looks complicated," Jax said, staring at the food processor.

"There are guides in your kit, and they're also programmed into your wrist-comm. But it's quite simple to use. You enter what you want on this pad, and it is produced." She moved past the two men and into the bathroom. "Everything here is pretty straightforward, except you'll notice the shower doesn't use water."

She pointed out two buttons. "Enzyme cleanser and enzyme wash. Make sense?"

"Sounds boring," Ace said. "There's nothing like sex in a steamy shower."

"This is good, too," Talla blurted out. Her cheeks heated.

Ace chuckled, and he ran his hand down the edge of her wing.

She shivered, the touch sending tingles through her body. She slapped him away. "Stop that. Wings are… sensitive."

"I know," Ace said. "Although the word I'd heard was 'erotic'."

"Don't you have your own room?" Jax asked.

"Yeah, yeah, fine." Ace winked at Talla on his way out. "Hopefully you have a twin sister who's waiting for me."

"I should've warned you about him," Jax said after the door closed.

Talla smiled and waved him off. "He's not so bad."

A silence came over them. They stood there, watching each other. Neither took a step closer.

A loud beep resounded through the room. Jax jumped. "What was that?"

"You have a message," she answered quickly, thankful for the interruption. She walked to the wall and hit a button.

Roden appeared on the screen with a summary in text. "It was sent to all officers."

She pressed the button once again to play the message.

Roden smiled. It was neither warm nor friendly. "Sheescaten, friends. I expect you to be in the command room by sceinan—that's eight o'clock sharp for you humans. This message includes an automated alarm to ensure you don't oversleep. Get some rest tonight, because you've got plenty of work to do starting tomorrow."

Chapter 13

Talla left Jax's room. The empty hallways echoed with her footsteps. Her pace increased to a jog before she spread her wings, lifting herself into the air. The late-night flight through the tall wide hallways helped clear her buzz, though she felt as though she weighed twice as much due to fatigue.

Back at her sanctuary, she didn't even bother removing her boots or clothes. The physical and, perhaps even more so, mental exhaustion from the previous two days had crept up on her.

The alarm blared, and she woke to find herself in the same position she'd fallen onto her bed in a few hours earlier. She took a long shower and dressed.

With time to spare, she let herself take in her surroundings.

This room had been her home for over a year, during the three-Earth-months trip to the planet and the several months watching it from the dark side of the moon. She knew every inch of the layout. Nothing had been touched since she'd left it. The air filtration system kept dust off things; much different from her trailer at the Etzee that seemed to have a thick layer of permanent dust on everything, despite her relentless cleaning. This was home; from the purple fabric she'd draped on the walls to her collection of unique Earth finds, which mostly included seashells and stones.

As she picked up a conch shell, her heart ached. She pressed the shell against her chest. She'd found this prize while on a scouting mission with Laze. Her gaze fell across her collection. She exchanged the shell for a stone with brilliant lines of blue and black running through it. Laze had given this one to her on her lifeday, a day similar to the human birthday, but more meaningful to the Draeken, in that each Draeken selected his or her own lifeday once they reached the age of maturity.

Nearly every piece in her collection had a connection to Laze, and she leaned against the wall. She couldn't fathom adding another item to the collection. It felt like a betrayal to his memory.

Sheescaten, ta deiti. Peace, my brother. She'd been just a toddler when the Noble War broke out, and her parents were murdered on Blood Night, the night that started the collapse. She would have died if her father hadn't sent Laze and her into the woods to hide. Laze, a few years older than her, had become a man that night, at the ripe age of seven.

He did what their parents could no longer do. He'd found them shelter in the basement of a burnt-out estate and only left her side to scavenge food and supplies. They survived like fregee for two years until Laze returned one morning with a tall man with eyes that saw into her soul. His name was Lord Roden Zyll, and he took both of the Kohlm children back to his base.

Roden could never be mistaken for a father figure. Though he revealed a softer side now and then, he'd seen them as assets and treated them as such. But they'd been treated fairly. At the base, they were sheltered and fed. In exchange, they learned how to become guardsmen. Talla killed her first Sephian at age eight, and fought in her first battle at nine. She'd been small and fast for her age, which made her an excellent messenger. She could crawl into tiny spaces and fly though narrow pathways to relay orders.

Talla had been beaten, shot, cut, and starved. Yet, she'd survived. And she'd continue to survive. With forced calm, she pushed off the wall and headed straight for the briefing room. *I will survive for both of us, Laze.*

People were starting to move about. When she came across a familiar face, she smiled and moved on. She was a guardsman. Guardsmen weren't driven by emotion. They weren't laden by remorse or guilt or grief.

By the time she arrived in the command room, she'd built a stone wall around her heart, tucking away precious memories.

"Morning, sweetheart," Ace said as she walked in.

She dipped her head in response. Ace was sitting down next to Jax and three other humans—soldiers she recognized from the Etzee. She wasn't surprised to see them defect to the Striga. All three had treated the residents fairly and made no secret of their dissent with the Etzee's hard regulations.

Even with his darker skin, Ace looked pale. It would take him at least another day before his lung was fully repaired. Jax, on the other hand, looked exceptionally healthy. She perused his body before giving him an affirming smile.

He watched her with that same intense look he'd given her every day at the Etzee, and certainly not the intimate gaze he'd given her last night. She chose to ignore him, like she had done in the past.

Several others entered over the next few minutes. She noticed how the room was divided into three sections, the fences around them invisible. Human, Sephian, Draeken—each sitting with their own race while warily eyeing the other two.

The next Draeken guardsman who limped into the room had Talla's mouth drop open. She sprung out of her chair. "Laze!" she exclaimed, and ran to embrace her brother.

"Ta deitan," Laze murmured, embracing her, though his voice sounded weak.

She clutched him to her, and he grunted. Relaxing her grip, she stepped back to study him. He was slumped over, using a cane for support. One of his wing spurs had been replaced by a metal spike. Many of his tattoos were missing from his wings, which meant that the skin had been patched.

Her eyes widened. He must have been nearly a corpse when he was rescued. "Your body is still repairing. You should be resting."

He snorted. "That's all I've been doing for two days."

"I don't know how you pulled it off," Jax said from Talla's side and she startled, having not noticed his approach, "but it's good to see you. You saved our lives." He held out a hand.

Laze accepted, returning the human tradition of shaking hands. "It was a rough go for a bit."

Jax shook his head. "I saw the collision. How did you make it out of there?"

Laze's eyes widened. "I'm not crazy. I bailed just before I rammed the truck down their throats. I took to the air, but one of their fifty-cals knocked me down. I was lucky they left me for dead. I was even luckier that one of the scouts from the Striga found me." He sobered. "Luckier than many."

Silence filled the space between them, and Talla rested her head on Laze's shoulder. After a moment, she pulled back and gave a little smile. "Fyet, deiti." She punched Laze lightly on the arm and he winced. "Don't you ever scare me like that again."

He held up a hand in defeat. "It wasn't my intent. I stopped by your room last night, but you weren't there." He glanced at Jax and then smiled. "Can't say I'm surprised."

"It's not what you think," she replied, perhaps a bit too quickly.

"We were just blowing off steam," Jax said.

The chime for *sceinan* sounded.

Talla touched Laze's face. "Deiti…"

"Deitan," he said, returning the smile.

She led Laze to where there were still two open seats in the Draeken contingent.

A badly scarred human entered right behind them and, not surprisingly, took a place with the two Sephians in the room. Sienna Wolfe, human representative for all earthside Sephians, watched the Draeken with less disdain than she had a year ago, but the animosity was still clearly there. The human blamed Talla's people for her mother's death and knew how to hold a grudge. Talla had no problem glaring right back. The Sephians had killed Talla's parents and kicked her people off Sephia. Everyone in this room had suffered plenty of loss.

When Roden and Nalea entered, Talla stood along with the other guardsmen in the room and nodded in respect to Roden's consort, the Grand Lord Nalea Puftan. Despite being a Draeken-Sephian hybrid, Nalea led the Draeken people with confidence, strength, and—the one thing her father had lacked—mercy.

"It seems we have a conflict of interest," Roden said, taking the seat next to his consort. "The United Nations wants us dead. We want to live."

He paused for effect. "The peace treaty we signed a year ago is now officially null and void. Since we aren't lining up to be executed, they are treating us like outlaws, though they are the lawbreakers. With the firepower on the Striga alone, we could destroy all the military forces ranged against us."

That last sentence raised a murmur across the room: consent from Talla's side, and dissent from across the room on the human side.

Roden held up a finger. "However, that serves no value to our end game."

"The Draeken people have never been the aggressors. It is not the Draeken way," Nalea said at Roden's side.

"You may not have much say about that," Sienna said. "How about Otas's core ship? Can you prevent him from attacking?"

"The Grax has not responded to any of our communication attempts," Nalea replied. "We know that Otas Olnek has taken control of the ship. The Artox and Evo are maintaining orbit near his coordinates. Should the *Grax* attempt to fire upon Earth, the Artox and Evo will destroy the *Grax*. But that is the worst-case scenario. There are over fourteen hundred Draeken on that ship; nearly all of whom are innocent. We have no intention of condemning them for a single traitor's actions."

Otas Olnek, who had once been the body double for Nalea's father, the Grand Lord Hillas Puftan, had been deemed a nobody. It was a horrible mistake in judgment learned painfully a year ago. Otas had shadowed the Grand Lord for so many years that he'd learned Hillas's secrets, spies, and plans. No one had suspected Otas had any ambitions, let alone ability to carry them out, until the minutes following Hillas's death. Then, it had become all too clear that the doppelgänger had been the greater threat all along.

Somehow, Otas convinced Hillas's guardsmen to follow him, and gained control of the core ship Grax, putting himself at the helm of a planet-killer. But that wasn't Otas's only weapon.

"How about the virus?" Talla asked the room. After all, that was what had caused the recent events. "Has any progress been made on an antivirus?"

"Since we cannot connect to the Grax's systems," Nalea replied, frowning, "we can safely assume Otas does not wish to share the antivirus. But he also can't make a move while under the watch of the Artox and Evo. We'll get to Otas when we can, and we're working on plans to infiltrate the Grax, but you are all aware of the power of a core ship. We cannot afford to lose any more lives."

Roden came to his feet, bringing all the attention to him. "That brings us to our mission. Everyone on this ship, we are no longer Draeken, or Sephian, or human," he said, looking at each contingent in the room. "We cannot afford to be. We are the Resistance. And we plan to resist death and imprisonment and segregation to the end. We will take the best approaches of each race and lead Earth into something better, stronger." He held up a fist.

"I won't declare war on my own people," Jax called out. Ace patted Jax's shoulder, and words of praise echoed his words.

Talla glanced over at him and frowned. Hadn't he essentially done that when he sided with the Etzee's residents?

"I never said anything about war, Lieutenant Jerrick. Quite the contrary to taking lives, we plan to save them," Roden said. "We have two objectives." He raised a finger. "First, find an antivirus. We can't sit back and wait the virus out, especially since these things are known to change and adapt. It could take months, and the people of Earth may not have that long. But we do. Right now, we're the only chance Earth has. We have people working day and night on this, but we need more help."

A knot of anxiety formed in Talla's stomach. She'd sat in on the early meetings with Roden when they'd first analyzed the virus. When Roden had asked when they could design an antivirus, the med-tech at the time had said, "Never. It's impossible." Had things changed, or was Roden giving them false hope?

"That brings me to our second objective." Roden raised another finger. "We have survivors to locate. With the virus out there and with the U.S. firing on us every minute of every hour of every day, the Striga will remain our base of operations for now. It's safer than anywhere else on Earth, especially from the Omega virus.

"We'll run search-and-rescue missions every hour to find survivors and gather new recruits. Out of the six hundred eighty-five residents on Etzee, we picked up two hundred fifty-one yesterday. We know more of our people are still down there. Furthermore, hundreds, if not thousands, of humans have trickled into what's left of the Etzee to aid us. It's likely they think that by joining us they won't get sick, but we'll take support any way we can get it. This ship can support sixty thousand, and we have fewer than two thousand aboard right now, so capacity will not be an issue for some time to come.

"Blockades between the Etzee and the Striga are a problem,"

Roden continued. "The human supporters settling at the Etzee can't get to us safely, and we can't get to them without getting fired upon. We'll drop supplies every day and watch their situation. There are many more supporters out there who are on their own and need us to pick them up. Our first priority is to bring more scientists, soldiers, and medical personnel on board."

Sienna held a brief sidebar conversation with the Sephians, then leaned forward in her chair. "I don't always agree with you, Roden. Everyone knows I don't trust you. But for this one time, you have full Sephian support."

Ace and Jax had been whispering to each other, drawing Talla's attention. Jax spoke first. "This is a solid plan. How do we help?"

Roden smiled. "Excellent question. Everyone in this room is either a Draeken guardsman, a human officer, or a member of a Sephian trinity. You're leaders, and that's what we need to pull our three races together. As of today, you will each be assigned a team of recruits. Wync and Legian have been going through the roster to divide all able-bodied people on the Striga into teams. Each team will be composed of all three races, though right now Draeken outnumber Sephians, and Sephians outnumber humans. Some of us have been at war against each other for decades, and many of our human recruits won't have any military training. Our focus will be on bringing everyone together as a cohesive force. Your team roster will be delivered to your sanctuaries within two hours."

"We can fight better with people we've fought alongside before," Jax said. "New teams will hurt us out there."

Nalea came to her feet. "Collaboration was my idea and believe me when I say I understand the challenges in bringing the three races together. However, I know that the only way we'll survive—not just until tomorrow, but until the next day and the day after—is to put our lives in one another's hands." She took Roden's hand, and they left the room before anyone could ask questions.

Talla stood when Laze did. He looked exhausted.

"Why don't you head back to your sanctuary for some rest," she offered. "I'll stop by later."

They embraced, and she watched Laze limp out of the room, not moving until he was through the door. A warm hand pressed against her back, and she turned. Ace was smiling. "I've been trying to figure out how to use my shower and was hoping you'd show me."

She considered grabbing his hand, pinching a nerve, and knocking him to his knees. Instead, she gave him a droll stare. "Do you shamelessly flirt with every female?"

Ace shrugged. "Yup. And doubly so on the pretty ones."

"You're hopeless."

He continued to watch her, smiling.

"And the answer is and always will be 'no'." It was bad enough she had half the eligible Draeken males vying for her attention. She certainly didn't need human complications, although she seemed to be doing that just fine herself.

Ace pouted and then shot her a grin. "All right, but you can't blame me for trying. See you around, Talla." He tried to jog, but grabbed his chest and opted to stroll ahead and join up with the trio of humans several paces ahead of them.

Talla made rounds to catch up with old friends, and then went to check in on Laze only to find him sleeping. She didn't wake him. Seeing him alive was enough to convince herself that as long as her brother was alive, everything would be all right.

Chapter 14

Jax went the opposite direction of everyone leaving the meeting room. He headed for the one place he could always count on...

He drank until his guilt dampened, though his mood hadn't improved. Five drinks later, the bartender scanned Jax's wrist-comm. He shoved off from the bar and headed back to his room, scowling at anyone who'd dared make eye contact.

After swiping his wrist-comm over his name on the wall, the door opened with a nearly silent swoosh. He stepped inside and just stood there, ignoring the intermittent tone reverberating through the room. There was nothing about this place that qualified as a 'sanctuary'.

He snapped around to the wall. Hitting the flashing button, his roster appeared. Another team. He didn't want another team. It meant just another team to get massacred. The truth was a bitter pill as he sent the details to his wrist-comm. He scanned through the list, recognizing half of the ten names. He could work with that. He didn't want to get to know any of them.

They were scheduled to meet in training room 153N4, and he was already twenty minutes late. That wasn't going to help them get off on the right foot. With a renewed sense of purpose, Jax pulled up the map and located the training room. Fifteenth floor, third quadrant, section N, room four. The ship's layout was pretty straightforward, and it didn't take long to grasp the codes and locations, especially since the Draeken had had the courtesy to add English to everything.

Walking through the hallways wasn't much different from any military base. Well, if one didn't pay attention to the Draeken's extra appendages or Sephians' odd skin color. Strangely, Jax felt at ease here. If his leaders had grasped the size and power of a core ship, he was pretty certain they would have handled the Etzee differently.

The Draeken could decimate the world with several well-placed shots from the behemoth now resting on American soil. The Draeken were desperate to find a home, and they had decided Earth was it. They weren't going anywhere.

The Sephians were different. As soon as Apolo returned, they could return to Sephia. Hell, he couldn't blame them if they all left, since Jax's own military had tried to eradicate them from the planet. He suspected the millions of Sephians back on Sephia wouldn't take the murder of their compatriots on Earth lightly. A fleet of Sephian ships were no trifling matter.

We should've let sleeping dogs *lie*.

By the time Jax got to the training room, he was amped and ready to work his team into just that… a team. If they were going to get killed, it sure as hell wasn't going to be from lack of effort on his part.

He found them segregated. No surprise there. He recognized the Sephians and three of the Draeken from the Etzee and his time with them.

The two Sephians stood off to the side. He'd known both for over a year. Sana was an excellent soldier, and he'd already assumed she would serve as his Second. Tanel, on the other hand, was a reliable comm-tech, but no soldier. The pair was just standing there. That they weren't conversing didn't alarm Jax. Sana was someone who spoke only when she had something to say, and from his experience, she never had much to say.

The two humans off to the other side were new faces. A man and woman who, if their clasped hands and sharing the same last name meant anything, had known each other before arriving on the ship.

And then there were the six Draeken standing proudly in the center of the room. He knew Qan and Gix to be good, solid soldiers, and Elc was a quick learner. But Christ, how was he going to get this crew of people from different races that hated each other to overcome their divided loyalties and work together?

He opened his mouth to say, 'fall in', but realized that they wouldn't understand. He'd have to start at a level below baseline. "Listen up, team. It's time for my first-day spiel. I'll only say it once, so pay attention," Jax said, cutting over all the voices as he strolled into the room.

The gold-skinned Sephians and dark-haired humans moved in closer, still keeping a noticeable distance from their winged team-mates, who had their arms crossed over their chests.

"As you know, everyone on the Striga has been assigned to a team in addition to whatever job they've been assigned. It's not a bad deal in exchange for safe room and board. You work five solid hours per day on your job and two hours per day with me. That leaves seventeen hours to do whatever the hell you want. That means that for those two hours, you're mine. You will do what I say, no questions asked."

"Don't you mean an hour and a half?" someone said.

Jax eyed the older Draeken who spoke. "What's your name?"

He looked down his nose at Jax. "Hert Hesmat, and I was here on time."

Jax's lips curled. "Your bio says you were a successful busi-nessman before coming here."

Hert held his head higher. "I was the most renowned clothier on the Golran Coast."

"That's nice," Jax said. "If I tear my fatigues in battle, you can fix them."

Hert stiffened. "I had slaves who sewed. I'm a designer." He said the last bit while touching his chest.

Jax glanced at Sana and Tanel. Both Sephians looked like they were ready to tear Hert apart.

"Listen, because I don't like to repeat myself," Jax said. "Like it or not, we're in this together. What you did before doesn't mean shit. What you do from this moment forward is all that matters If you were a screw-up before, then here's your chance to start afresh. If you were a hotshot success story, here's your chance to prove that wasn't a fluke.

"We're safe from the virus and from attacks while we're on the Striga, but we're not going to live out the rest of our lives on it. At some point, we're going to have to leave the safety of this ship to set up permanent homes outside. And when we do that, it's a few thousand of us against a world that doesn't want us here. We need to count on each other or else we're screwed."

"But we're not leaving while the virus is out there, right?" the human man asked.

Jax turned to the human couple. "They're working on an antivirus, but it could take some time. The virus hasn't made it to American soil yet, so it may never be a risk."

The man wrapped an arm around his wife. "But what if it spreads?"

"The plan is that we stay on the Striga until it's safe. Any other questions?"

Silence.

"All right, then," Jax said, reading over his wrist-comm. "Let's get the housekeeping out of the way. I'm Lieutenant Jax Jerrick, U.S. Army. In case you hadn't noticed, I'm a human, and it's my job to turn you all into a team. Now let's go down the roster...

Sana, Qan, Gix," he said, looking from the Sephian woman, then to the Draeken man and woman. "You all have solid military experience, and I'll count on you to help train. Tanel, you're in charge of comms. I know you have Sephian and Draeken tech down; get up to speed on human tech if you haven't already."

"Yes, Lieutenant."

"Let's see," Jax continued, looking up to inspect the rest of his team. "Starting with you..." He pointed at the humans to his left. "Tell me your names and your skill."

The man spoke first. "I'm Scott Edmonds, but you can call me Grease. I drove trucks and was a diesel mechanic before that, and they have me learning the engines on the Aggressors now. I'm good with engines."

Jax nodded. Mechanical ability was a valuable skill set. "Whatever vehicles we get assigned—no matter what they are—it's your job to keep them running. Understand?"

The man nodded. "I can do that." Grease turned to the woman at his side. "And here's my wife, Jeannie. She's—"

"—Going to speak for herself," Jax interrupted.

The petite redhead gave a sheepish smile. "Hi, everyone. I'm Jeannie." She waved at the others on the team. "I'm a senior at ISU, a Poli Sci major. Grease and I came on board last night, so everything's still really new. As soon as we heard what the government was doing to the Sephians and Draeken, we hurried down here. We want to help in any way we can. I've been assigned to work in Supply."

She spoke with enough passion that Jax couldn't help but feel a prickle of pride in his recruits, even though they were as green as they come. At least they had potential. "And you'll do the same for the team. You need to get up to speed on gear, weapons, and ammo. Got it?"

Her eyes widened. "I don't know anything about bullets."

"You'll learn," Jax said before turning to the Draeken standing nearest to Jeannie.

The thin man's wings flicked with nervousness. "I'm, uh, Nurn, and I was an office administrator. I guess I'm pretty good at organizing things."

"Good," Jax said. "You're in charge of scheduling our training times around everyone's work schedules."

His head bobbed. "Yes, I can do that, yes."

The youth next to Nurn was the same height, but where Nurn was all lankiness, this kid was lean and strong. "I'm Grept," the young man said. "And I didn't have a job. But I was a messenger on the trip here. And I played sports."

"How old are you, Grept?"

The kid stiffened. "Old enough."

Jax raised a brow. "How old, son?"

Grept stood defiant. "Nearly sixteen in human years."

Sixteen? Way too young. The kid should've been in school, not preparing for war. But according to the kid's bio, he had no family. He probably knew more about war than Jax did. "You were a messenger. You fast, kid?"

"Fast as the wind, Lieutenant. Both on the ground and in the air."

Jax smiled. "We'll be able to use you." He turned to the next man in line.

"You know me already. I've done a bit of everything," Elc said, but then turned to the human pair. "I'm Elc, by the way. Welcome aboard. It's good to see that not all humans hate us."

"It's good to have you on the team, Elc," Jax said, and meant it. The Draeken was a literal jack-of-all-trades. If they needed something, he had no doubt Elc would get it for them. There was a reason Roden kept him as a gopher.

When Jax turned to the older businessman, he eyed him for a moment. "Hert," he said. "You say you're good at designing things. That true?"

"I'm the best," the Draeken with long whitish-silver hair replied.

Jax grinned. "Our team needs an insignia. Something that isn't Draeken, or Sephian, or human, but encompasses all three. You up for the challenge?"

Light twinkled in the man's eyes, and he managed to stand even taller still. "We will have the finest insignia of all teams."

"That covers it," Jax said. "Each one of you brings something to the table. We're going to use that to build some semblance of a team." Jax realized that his team was much more than individuals from three different races coming together. His team was a microcosm of the new Earth. Human, Draeken, Sephian… at some point, those labels would no longer apply; their common cause would unite all three as one new Earth race.

Several of his team looked past his shoulder. Jax turned to locate the distraction and found Roden standing in the doorway. Jax headed toward the newcomer, commanding over his shoulder, "We have one hour left. We'll start on basic self-defense. Sana, you take Nurn, Hert, and Elc. Qan, you got Jeannie and the Kid. Gix, you get Grease and Tanel."

Draeken and Sephians alike had looks of unpleasant surprise.

Jax cocked his head. "Anything wrong? 'Cause if you think that I'll allow segregation in this team, then you're dumb as shit."

"You have such eloquence to your leadership style," Roden mused.

"What do you want?"

Roden inhaled and then frowned. "Fyet. You've been drinking. Bolgt, no less."

Jax ignored the comment, looking back to see his recruits busy in training.

"I have a mission for you," Roden said.

"They're not ready yet."

"Pick your two best. I need you to exfiltrate an ally. He sent word that it's no longer safe for him. And he requested you by name."

"Damn it, Roden. Send some other lackey."

"It's your father."

Jax stopped cold. He knew his dad disagreed with the orders coming down from the General of the Army, but to defect? What else had happened since he'd last spoken to his dad? Jax turned to his team. "Sana, Qan, you're with me. Gix, take over the training."

"I'm impressed at how well you function as a drunk," Roden said at Jax's side. "You must have experience."

Jax flipped him the bird.

Scowling, Roden walked over to the service station and hit several buttons. He returned with a small cup of thick dark liquid and held it out to Jax. "Drink this."

"What is that?" he asked, eying the inky drink.

"It'll sober you up for this mission."

"I'm fine."

"If you don't drink this, I'll send Talla to pick up your father instead."

Jax snatched the glass, downed the contents, and coughed. He glared at Roden, his eyes watering. "God, that's awful."

"Give it a second. It gets worse."

Right then, Jax's stomach cramped and he doubled over. Cold fire shot through his veins and doused his brain, leaving no traces of liquored bliss in its wake. Only hard, cold reality remained.

Roden took the glass back just as Sana and Qan joined their side.

Jax took a deep breath before speaking. "We have a sortie to make."

"Grab whatever you need from Supply," Roden said. "I've already reserved an Aggressor for you in hangar fourteen. I'll have the logistics sent to your wrist-comms in a few minutes." With that, Roden left the room.

"I can fly an Aggressor," Qan offered.

"Good," Jax said with a nod. "Then we don't need to pull anyone else. Get the ship ready. Sana and I will grab gear for you."

Qan took to the air and headed down the hallway away from

Sana and Jax. They didn't speak all the way to Supply, not even after they picked up their weapons and gear. They were nearly to the Aggressor when Jax asked, "You cool working with Qan?"

"I have to be, don't I," she replied.

"You chose to stay behind with the Draeken rather than returning to Sephia. Why?"

"I don't trust them." Her response was simple and honest.

He grabbed her shoulders. "I appreciate your honesty, but I need to know that you have Qan's back. I already know he'll have yours. You're good, Sana, but I can't have you on my team if I can't trust you."

She frowned, but then her face cleared of emotion. "You can trust me."

"Good." Because if his dad needed help, then this would be no easy grab-and-go mission.

Chapter 15

Heavy storms attacked the Midwest just before noon. The previous day's clear skies and warm breeze were swallowed by ominous clouds spitting hail and roaring thunder.

Talla watched the wall screen, which showed the Etzee getting pounded. The winds battered the new tents that were spread out across the remains of the camp. The troops had bulldozed everything after the attack. Trailers, debris, and bodies... it hadn't mattered; they had leveled the place, leaving no protection against the weather for newcomers.

By the time the military set up roadblocks around the Etzee, hundreds of people had made it into the restricted zone. And the military, rather than garner negative press by rounding up the protestors, allowed the humans to remain and newcomers to arrive.

Humans in plastic ponchos and rain jackets shoved against the barricades. They'd given up holding signs. The wind blew the boards away, and the rain melted the messages. Now, they used their bodies to make their point. They shook their fists at the soldiers on the other side. While the screen had no sound, Talla imagined their shouting waged a battle with the torrential rain and thunder.

There had to be thousands of protestors now. Their selfless actions gave Talla hope that her people could live on this world side by side with the humans.

The violence of the storm seemed to infuse the protestors with strength. They surged and pressed against the barricades, causing the fencing to bow and stretch. The individuals became a group, and they found a rhythm. As one, they pushed forward, stepped back, and pushed again. The metal stretched beyond what Talla thought it could. The troops on the other side looked jittery, raising their rifles and yelling back at the mob.

Lightning flashed across the sky and the protestors pushed forward once again. This time the barricade collapsed just as another bolt of lightning flashed across the sky. Talla's eyes widened. It was as though the humans' God had helped them. The mob spilled over the fallen barricades and spread out. The first soldier disappeared in the crowd. Pulsating light flickered from the barrel of another soldier's rifle.

Talla gasped, raising a hand to her mouth. "No! They're unarmed!" Her shout attracted attention in the hallway, and others stopped to take in the scene unfolding on the screen. The crowd scattered, some being crushed, as they sought to escape the gunfire. Tiny lights flashed off more rifles.

"We can't leave them to die. They'll get slaughtered," the petite human redhead at her side said.

The ship's lighting went from white to blue, and a loud siren sounded. A live feed of a Draeken man appeared on all the Striga's wall screens. "An attack is underway earthside. All military personnel: grab your gear and proceed to your assigned hangar immediately."

Talla sprinted toward her sanctuary, which was closer than Supply. It took her less than twenty seconds to get the backup gear she kept stashed in her room and strap it on. Once out of her room, she flapped her newly strengthened wings and lifted. She soared above the human and Sephian traffic in the tall hallways and headed toward hangar five, her designated hangar.

When she got there, a Transporter and two Aggressors were taking off. She touched down and ran toward another Transporter, its engine already running. Pires, the only member of her team who was considered military personnel, came running around the corner and joined her at the ship. He was fast for a Sephian, and experienced. She'd made him her Second before she even met with her team.

She looked him up and down, noticing he had more than a half dozen blades strapped to his chest and two blasters on his thighs. She'd brought two blades and two blasters, and had three chaos-charges inside the pocket of her body armor.

She gave him a nod and led the way onto the Transporter. Good thing he was on her side, because Talla never wanted to meet him in battle. Pires was tall and well-built, and filled out his body armor. He could handle himself in hand-to-hand combat as well as take down an enemy from a distance. But his shadowed eyes were what intimidated Talla. They were haunted. Like he'd seen too much and killed too many to ever return fully to civilization.

He followed her onto the Transporter, and they found two pilots already on board. Like Aggressors, Transporters could be flown by a single pilot, but it was standard protocol to bring a backup pilot into any battle. "You ready?" the second pilot asked.

"Yes," Talla said, strapping herself in. "Let's go."

"What are we up against?" Pires asked, taking the seat next to her.

She reached for the wall screen and pulled up the logistics. "Rescue mission." The human troops had switched from firing on their own kind to targeting the incoming Aggressors and Transporters. "Looks like we grab every breathing protester we can while minimizing enemy casualties. Let's see," she said, scrolling through the details. "There are four full battalions out there, and they're not playing nice."

His lip curled into a sneer. "And orders are to minimize casualties?"

"*Minimize* can be subjective." She leaned back as the Transporter vibrated and lifted off the hangar floor.

Pires was battle-hardened like Jax, but they were otherwise two completely different men. One was a killer, one was a protector.

Talla was thrown forward hard against the seat belt. She looked out the front windshield to utter chaos. Anti-aircraft artillery had begun to bombard the Transporter as soon as they left the safety of the Striga. The core ship was grounded a few hundred meters from the Etzee, its hull the same distance from the ground. It took mere seconds for the Transporter to claw through the storm of nature and humans to reach the Etzee.

Shredded tents blew like banners in the wind. Bodies dotted the ground. Survivors ran out, waving their arms at the incoming ships. They hadn't the sense to find cover. "Idiots," Talla cursed, and unbuckled. She lunged forward and pointed outside. "Put us between the tank and that group there."

The pilot nodded, and Talla pulled out a blaster. She turned around to find Pires already opening the door. "Wait!" she called out.

He jumped.

"Damned Sephian." She grabbed two shields from the wall then threw herself out of the Transporter after him. She landed gently on the ground. He was already moving toward the tank. She shoved the shield at him. "This is a rescue mission, not an offensive attack."

"It's too cumbersome," he snarled.

"It's to protect the refugees!"

He shot her a hard glare then holstered one of his blasters and took the shield. With Pires taking the lead, they rushed toward the nearest huddle of protesters. The approaching green tank was changing its course and heading for the Transporter. While it couldn't destroy the superior armor of the ship, a couple of direct hits this close would do some damage. They had to move fast.

In a rush, Talla did a cursory scan of the humans. "Can you all walk?" she shouted above the engine noise and gunfire all around them.

"Help." A woman meekly raised her hand, and Talla noticed her knee was bloody.

She pointed at the two closest to the woman. "You and you, help her. We're taking you to that Transporter over there. Stay behind our shields and you'll be safe."

She sidled up next to Pires. He nodded and then they crabbed their small group toward the Transporter. With the body-length shields their only defense, less than a third of the twenty-plus humans had any safety behind them. The remainder huddled close in, as though proximity would help.

The tank fired, and the Transporter rocked from side to side. Talla's ears rang from the explosion, but they didn't slow. Within a couple of seconds, they were at the Transporter, and the door opened. Talla and Pires held their shields against the tank, even though she knew that if the tank fired on them now, they were both dead.

The humans scurried onto the Transporter, stumbling over one another in desperation to reach safety. "Hurry!" Talla shouted behind her as she stared down the massive barrel of the tank. It could fire on them any moment. Why it hadn't done so already confused Talla. Then, the tank jerked and started to back away. Talla glanced at Pires, who looked just as confused, but it made sense when she saw the tank aim for a low-flying Aggressor.

It looked like the troops had some semblance of humanity left in them after all. Once the protesters were all on board, they almost seemed thankful, and no longer tried to destroy the Transporter, instead moving on to new prey. Perhaps, like Talla, they were also trying to save whoever they could.

But it wasn't a time for deep reflection. The ship was full.

"Wait!" someone screamed from the distance.

Talla turned to find several more humans run toward them. She motioned them forward, and they jumped onto the ship at full speed. Talla glanced inside. The Transporter was packed, all seats taken and everyone else standing shoulder to shoulder.

She made eye contact with the pilot. "We'll round up another group by the time you get back." With that, she stepped back and watched the door close. She looked around before pointing at one of the massive pylons anchoring the Striga to the ground. "There," she said. "If we can get the humans there, they can hide behind the pylon until the Transporters pick them up."

"Looks good," Pires said, scanning the area, "but we have company."

She noticed the incoming troops at the same time. "To the pylon!" she yelled just as the first bullets pounded their shields.

"I'll take the flank," Pires said, and she moved. He was stronger. He could handle the barrage longer. With her back to his, their clear shields enveloped them in a protective shell. Talla stepped forward when she felt Pires press against her. They made slow progress, but Talla knew the hazards of stepping backward over rough terrain. She supported Pires with her back, and together they reached the pylon.

Talla pulled Pires to the side, and they stood panting against the gray metal. She wiped the rain from her eyes. She wanted to peek around their shelter to see their odds, but knew the information would dishearten her. "They've got us pinned, and they know it."

"The grenades will come soon if we stay here," he muttered.

They resituated their shields to form a cocoon around them. It would buy them time, but there was only so much a shield could take. Talla checked her blaster, switching it from *stun* to *kill*, and looked at Pires. "Then we don't stay here."

He glanced at his blaster, and she noticed that it had been set to *kill* all along. He smiled. "Are you overriding your 'minimize casualties' order?"

"Temporarily," she said. "I take high, you take low?"

Pires gave a quick nod.

They each strapped their shields on their backs and stood. Laying her hand on his, she tapped one, two, three. They spun and started firing around the edge of the pylon. Together, they abandoned their shelter, Pires running to the left while Talla took off into the sky.

And found themselves outnumbered twenty to one.

Jax lay on his stomach, scanning the base's layout through his binoculars. Colonel Jerrick was taking lunch in his office at HQ, like usual. Jax had been stationed at this base several years back and nothing had changed, other than the fact that it looked like only a skeleton crew remained.

Mesh wire covered all the office windows as a protection against flak and burglary, but the wire also prevented an easy in-and-out. The hallways looked empty, but given that it was the lunch hour, that wasn't uncommon. He handed the binoculars to Sana.

"It looks like we'll go through the front door."

"Wait until he leaves for the night," Sana offered.

"See that cot in the corner? He's not leaving." Jax knew his father as well as anyone, which wasn't saying much, but one thing he did know was that the colonel never came home anytime the DEFCON level was raised. Hell, he didn't come home if he was even remotely busy. When Jax had been a kid, the neighbor lady would stop over and check on him after getting a call from his father. She was called at least once a week. Sometimes, Jax would go two weeks or more without seeing his father. In the regular world, what his father did could be seen as child abandonment, but the military was a far different place. For Jeremiah Jerrick, the military came before family.

Just like now. Jax knew his father wasn't joining the Resistance for his son. If the colonel was joining the Resistance, it was because he was going where he could do the most good for his country. Not that Jax was complaining; they'd be gaining a powerful man with significant connections out of this.

Jax glanced at his watch. Twelve thirty-six. Staff would start returning a few minutes before thirteen hundred.

Pulling himself up on his knees, he took back the binoculars and scanned the building one more time. "If things go bad, be ready to run. Don't wait for me," he said to Sana before coming to his feet and handing the binoculars back. He jogged forward through the small parking lot, his blaster holstered, hoping that anyone who saw him from a distance, especially in this rain shower, wouldn't notice anything other than a Ranger in regular fatigues.

Jax strolled through the front door of the one-story office building as though he'd done it every day, which he had for eighteen months. Just inside, a clerk Jax didn't recognize sat at his desk, raptly engaged with his computer screen and a sandwich. Jax had planned on incapacitating the clerk, but the man didn't even look up as Jax walked by and headed down the hallway. A couple of office doors were open; most were closed. He headed straight to the large office at the end of the hallway.

Not bothering with a knock, he stepped inside, closing the door behind him. Colonel Jerrick looked up, piqued, but upon seeing who it was, a smile broke out across his face. "You came."

"We have to hurry," he said, motioning his father to him.

His father came to his feet. "Jackson, it's good to see you, boy."

"Later," Jax said, gripping the door handle. "We have to move."

"Wait. I need to grab something out of my lockbox."

"Leave it," Jax said. "Let's go."

Instead, his father sorted the keys on his hefty keychain. "It won't take long."

"We don't have time for this!" Jax hissed.

"Just give me a minute." Jerrick's gaze flashed to the side for an instant before returning his focus on Jax. The movement was quick enough to prickle the hair on Jax's neck.

Jax's eyes widened. "No." He yanked the door open at the same time two armed soldiers—one from each side—emerged from the corner shadows. Boot steps pounded the floor, coming to a stop behind him.

He leveled a hard gaze at his father. He should have figured it out right away. The lax clerk at the front desk, the lack of troops walking outside. Even for the lunch hour, he should have seen more people out and about. Everything had been too easy. He'd been set up... by his own father.

Jax moved his hand away from his holster and a soldier disarmed him. He glared at his father. "Why?"

His father stiffened to his full height. "I had to do what I could to save you, Jackson."

"Save me?" Jax belted out a laugh as his wrists were restrained behind his back. "You're saving me by bringing me in so I can be hung for treason?"

Jerrick's mouth tightened. "I've called in some favors. You'll be sent to the brig but not executed. What matters is that you'll live. We can work on reducing your sentence later. Hell, I might be able to get it knocked down to a six, six, and a kick."

"Don't act like you're doing this for me," Jax said. "Saving my life is for you, not me. You know damn well leaving me to rot in the brig is not saving me. You're doing this to keep your conscience clean because of what you ordered me to do back at the Etzee. Isn't that right, Dad?"

His father bristled. "I'm not going to let my son die with aliens. Not if there's anything I can do about it."

"With the Omega out there, being with those aliens is the safest place to be right now."

"Not for long."

Jax furrowed his brows. "What the hell are you talking about?"

"Things are changing. I may not agree with the General of the Army on this, but it's my duty to obey. What's left of the Etzee, and the core ship, neither of those things will matter in another week."

Jax's temper roiled. "That's insanity! All that will be accomplished will be to guarantee a war that we don't have a prayer of winning."

"Perhaps," his father replied, the pain clear in his voice. "But the General of the Army is a man of action. Peace talks and delays don't become him. We did what we could to prevent war. Now that war is upon us, as soldiers it is our duty to defend our country."

Jax opened his mouth, but a soldier fell onto him, and they tumbled to the ground. Jax twisted out from under the unconscious soldier and struggled to his knees. Another three men dropped from blaster fire coming through the window from the tree line. He spun around and shot one final glare.

His father reached out for him. "Don't do this, Jackson!"

Jax turned and ran, his gait made clumsy by his wrists restrained behind his back. The clerk was standing by his desk, his eyes wide in shock. When he saw Jax, he scrambled for his piece. Jax ducked, lunged, and headbutted the soldier. He sprinted out the front door to see Humvees heading in from the east. He ran west.

Adrenaline sang in his veins as he crouched, weaving through cars. If he was seen, he was dead, so every movement was slow and careful. At the last car, he looked up to see Sana still laying down cover fire on the office building.

He took a step forward and was yanked back. Jax kicked out and Qan blocked the blow. The Draeken glared but grabbed Jax's bicep and pulled him toward Sana. When they neared, she came up on a knee, still firing, then moved to a standing position.

Qan pulled out a knife, and Jax turned his back to him. "Get the ship ready," he ordered as he felt the plastic restraint fall away.

"On my way," Qan said before taking off for the ship.

Sana continued to fire. Jax counted to five and then tapped Sana on the shoulder. "Let's go!"

She fired off three more rounds before spinning. They sprinted toward the Aggressor.

The engine was running and Qan was strapped in. Jax and Sana tumbled inside and Jax hit the switch. The door closed, and Jax went about untangling himself from Sana. The interior was cramped. It had two seats—one for a pilot and one for a gunner—and two jump seats for passengers. Jax took the seat next to Qan, leaving Sana in the back.

"No pickup?" Qan asked as he pulled the Aggressor off the ground.

Jax grimaced. "No pickup." He shouldn't be surprised his father thought to protect him by betraying him, but his betrayal was acid to his gut all the same.

Qan throttled forward and Jax was thrust hard against the back of his seat. His fault for not paying enough attention to brace himself for the acceleration. The hard rain they had encountered earlier was nothing but a light drizzle now, granting them miles of unhindered visibility. Their speed and the aerodynamics of the streamlined Aggressor were a perfect combination so that rain glided over the windshield without touching.

Even the Air Force's fastest jets couldn't keep up with a Draeken Aggressor. The one hundred sixty miles back to the Striga took precious few minutes, and they weren't even at full power. Jax still couldn't believe that he'd been set up. Screwed by the colonel, no less.

My own father.

The reality of the soul-deep betrayal seeped into his already drenched pores, dousing his mood all the more. While they had never been close, he had trusted his father. Hell, he had idolized that man for much of his life. That his father thought that bringing Jax in was the right thing to do went to show that he didn't understand his son in the least.

What a wake-up call.

Jax and his father had one thing in common. Duty was everything. But they had different ways of accomplishing that. The colonel was all about orders: making them, following them… it didn't matter. Jax, on the other hand, believed the end result was more important. They both sought peace but had such different approaches.

Jax was where he needed to be. There wasn't a doubt in his mind. He knew war would decimate the United States, if not the world. The best shot he had at saving lives was on board the core ship, in the middle of discussions with Sephian and Draeken leaders. Damn his father for screwing things up.

Though there was one new piece of information Jax had learned today. It was unlike Colonel Jerrick to share confidential information, which meant that he'd wanted Jax to know. And, that was very much like his father. He'd shared critical information that would help people in case the shit hit the fan and Jax returned to the *Striga*. His father hadn't become a high-ranking officer for not covering every base.

Time was of the essence for Jax to get back to the core ship. Once he shared what he'd learned, there was still a chance for preventing an all-out war, though he was no longer confident that chance still existed.

His seat moved, and Jax jerked his attention back to find Sana leaning over him, looking out the window. His gaze followed hers and narrowed on the battle scene before them. Several Aggressors were in the air, hovering around Transporters on the ground. They were taking heavy fire. "What the hell is going on out there?"

"I'm pulling up the details now." Qan's fingers flew over the comm. "The Striga is on alert. The humans fired on their brethren, and teams were sent out in waves to retrieve survivors."

They had begun shooting at protestors? What had happened in the last three hours? "Do they need air support?" Jax asked.

"No. The last Transporters are lifting off now," Qan said.

He scanned the area. "Okay, then. If they don't need us, we'll head straight to the—wait a sec." He first thought he was seeing things, and leaned closer to the windscreen. Of all people, Talla was on the ground, huddled next to a Sephian, both standing right smack-dab in the middle of an onslaught from several dozen troops. She and the Sephian were standing facing each other with shields on their backs as they fired in opposite directions.

Jax pointed to the ground. "Clear a path and pick up our guys!"

"But we're not supposed to engage," Qan said. "Orders are to pick up survivors."

"Then there will be one less Draeken female on the ship."

Without hesitation, Qan engaged the troops on the ground, firing a barrage of shots at the tanks.

"Get us down there and start a counterattack now!" Jax unstrapped his belt and lunged toward the door. Sana was at the door and had it open. Qan was holding the trigger down, blasting non-stop at the ground below.

Later, Jax figured he'd think of how many fellow soldiers he'd just killed, but now wasn't the time to weigh the consequences. He had to save his people.

Chapter 17

The Aggressor Jax rode in hadn't even touched down before he was out the door with no shield. He landed on the ground next to Talla and had moved in between her and Pires's shields the instant before several shots fired in the direction of where he'd been standing a fraction of a second earlier.

She glared. "Are you trying to get yourself killed?!"

"I'm trying to save your ass!" he snapped back over the blaster fire.

The Sephian woman accompanying Jax stood on Talla's other side, and the four of them fired shots out in every direction.

The Aggressor turned around to make another strafing run of suppression fire. The barrage sent the soldiers around them scattering. Knowing they were nowhere near to attaining a battlefield advantage yet, they remained close together, each shooting at the escaping troops.

"Back to the pylon!" Talla yelled, and the four moved as one, step by slow step, closer to the thick metal. When they were feet away, they broke rank and dove behind the cover of the pylon.

Pires and the Sephian woman stood near the center of the

ten-foot wide pylon. Jax pinned Talla against the metal as he held out his blaster, scanning the area, and Talla moved just enough to glance around the edge. At least a third of the soldiers who'd encircled Talla and Pires lay unmoving on the ground. The remainder had committed to a retreat, heading to the safety of the tanks, a couple of which were retargeting the pylon with their large cannons. Cannon fire couldn't get through the pylon, but there was little to protect them against shrapnel and debris.

"Get down here now!" Jax yelled into his wrist-comm. He let off a couple of more shots around the edge of the pylon.

The small Aggressor landed in front of them, forming a barrier in case anyone shot at them from this side of the pylon. No one needed orders. Talla and Pires used their shields to cover their flanks as all four piled inside the tight craft. The other Sephian took the co-pilot's seat, and Pires took one of the jump seats. Jax pulled out the other jump seat and motioned Talla to sit.

He stood over her, glaring at her, and she glared right back as she took the seat.

"What the hell were you doing out there?" he demanded.

Her mouth dropped. "My duty!"

He wrapped a hand around the back of her neck, and he took a deep breath, and Talla sighed. Despite his cowboy approach, he'd saved her and Pires. The soldiers had been closing in. If Jax hadn't shown up…

She pulled away. "I'm glad you made it," she tacked on quietly.

He gave a tight nod. His eyes spoke of feelings he denied having. The warmth from his palm infused her, and she craved to snuggle deeper into his embrace. But he pulled his hand away from her then, and she immediately regretted the loss of connection.

"You sure you're not injured?" he asked, his voice rough.

"I'm fine," she replied aloofly, frustrated that Jax continued to deny the truth between them. She glanced over at Pires. He was leaning back in his seat, golden blood running down an arm. Her focus shifted. "Fyet, Pires. You've been shot."

He glanced down and frowned. "Guess so."

Pires was on her team. He was her responsibility. She made a move toward him, but the other Sephian must have overheard because she pushed abruptly between Jax and Talla to reach Pires. He flicked her hand away, and she punched him in the shoulder. He winced, and she placed her hands over both the entry and exit wounds and closed her eyes.

To anyone, it looked like the woman was applying pressure to minimize blood loss. Sephians were highly attuned to energy, and they could feed energy to another to speed the healing process. There'd been many, many times during the Noble War when Talla had wished for the Sephian ability to heal rather than having to rely upon getting to a Draeken med-hub center in time.

After several seconds, the gold blood spilling out through the woman's fingers slowed and then stopped altogether. She stumbled on her feet, and Pires held her up with his uninjured arm. She looked angry at his action, but she needed his help after feeding much of her strength into him. When she stepped away, fresh scarred skin covered the bullet hole.

That was the downside with speeding up nature. Skin could heal only so fast; to push it was to cause scarring. And Pires had an impressive scar collection. He ran a finger over the new skin, like he was saying, Look, *I've* got another one.

Sephians. Talla didn't understand them. Their nonchalance about life reminded her of Jax. Like how he'd jumped out of a ship to land in the middle of a battle zone without any sort of defense. Then again, neither the human nor Sephian race was on the brink of extinction. She looked up and found him still watching her. As though he disliked the connection, he broke eye contact and stared straight ahead.

Jax neither moved nor glanced her way until after the aggressor touched down in trip back to the hangar. The two Sephians were out the door first and several paces ahead of Talla and Jax by the time they exited. Both her and Jax's wrist-comms vibrated the moment they stepped onto the hangar floor. She pulled up the message. "Roden has called another meeting," she said aloud.

Jax grunted. "I was on my way to see him, anyway." He paused and turned around. "Hey, Qan," he called out. "You did good today."

Qan blushed before rushing off in the other direction, no doubt to tell his friends about his adventure. Talla smiled at the departing figure of the shy guardsman. Her lips then tightened, as she knew there'd be many more battles to face over the coming days.

She leapt and flew to the command room. She landed outside the door and entered, choosing a seat near her fellow Draeken. A couple of minutes later, Jax entered and took a chair farther down the table.

Roden was already on his feet. "The numbers are still coming in, but we've taken in over eight hundred human refugees and lost three of our own today. While the loss of anyone is great, to die saving many more lives is an honor to be remembered. The names of Exed Dehem, Tyn Scohm, and Badrin will be added to our wall of heroes."

A moment of silence fell across the room. Talla knew both Draeken. She'd come across them in the halls every day on the journey here. She hadn't met the Sephian yet, but she mourned his loss all the same. They were all heroes, though she hadn't expected Badrin's name to be added to the wall. He would be the first non-Draeken on the Striga's wall, and Talla suspected he wouldn't be the last.

"We can expect more refugees to show up in the days ahead. News of today's events will be broadcast. It may garner us more support," Roden continued.

"This is about to become a non-viable zone for anyone wishing to come near the Striga," Jax said.

Everyone turned to face him. Roden spoke first. "Is Colonel Jerrick joining us?"

"No," Jax said, with a hard edge to his voice. He turned to the room. "They've thrown everything they have at the Striga, and they haven't even scratched the ship. They only have one weapon left in their arsenal."

"Ah, hell no. Don't tell me they're going nuclear," Ace muttered, loud enough to be heard from across the room.

Jax nodded. "They're willing to sacrifice much of the Midwest to take out this ship and everyone on it."

"A nuclear bomb cannot harm this ship, but it poisons the land," Roden paced around the room. "Fyet! The fools are fighting us when they should be fighting the virus."

"Any response from the Grax?" Laze asked from several chairs down. While he looked—and sounded—much stronger than he had earlier that morning, he still wore the residue of battle fatigue.

Roden frowned, shaking his head. "No response yet, but soon it will no longer matter. We've had a breakthrough in analyzing the virus. We'd been using our computers for analysis, but one of the human scientists we brought on board had an archaic, but practical, idea. Rather than recreating the virus using our technology, he has brought on board a plant native to this world that provides an enzyme that looks promising. We should have something for testing within days, a week at most."

Murmurs erupted across the room. Talla smiled. It was the first good news since… she couldn't even remember. It was what the Striga's collective morale needed.

"In the meantime," Roden continued, "we continue with our plan. We scout for resources and pick up refugees if their lives are in danger. With the risk of nuclear attack, this is more important than ever. We will make no aggressive actions unless the humans are foolish enough to cross a line from where there's no return. Yes, I'm aware we were forced to fire upon troops today, but that was to protect refugees and the Striga's people. If they wound this planet with nuclear technology, they will discover that we are its saber of vengeance."

Talla sucked in a deep breath. Was it wrong that a part of her wanted the humans to bomb the core ship so the waiting would be over? She craved to have the violence end, and sometimes a sword was the only way to force peace. Even so, the more logical part of her knew that bloodshed bred more bloodshed, and that they'd never reach true peace without working for it.

Roden stopped his pacing and looked at his wrist-comm. After several moments, he looked back up, his face tight with emotion.

"The Omega virus has breached American soil. It's taking over the east coast as we speak."

Chapter 18

J ax watched the screen while he did sit-ups in his room. He should be on the ground, helping save who he could, rather than watching the world end from the safety of an alien ship.

It was nearly a week since Omega had hit the east coast. It had taken the virus less than twenty-four hours to unravel its tentacles all the way to the west coast. Even though authorities had shut down all air traffic, trains, and buses as soon as the first case was confirmed, it had already been too late. The U.S. was being attacked by an enemy it couldn't see.

Twenty-four/seven broadcasts on every television channel reported news of Omega as well as propaganda about the aliens. The Draeken had been blamed for the virus, and the government wanted to make sure everyone knew it. Still, the clear message did little to stop the onslaught of refugees coming to camp outside the Striga.

As a precaution, the Striga had gone into quarantine mode as soon as Omega hit the coast. Except for sorties and heavy drops of supplies for the refugees, not even Sephians and Draeken were allowed off the ship in case the virus mutated. For that, Jax was glad. He'd been avoiding Talla all week. The trackers on their wrist-comms made it easy, but that didn't mean he didn't want to, see her safe. Now that he was no longer her Leash, he wasn't quite sure how to handle her, and it put him on edge.

Accepting the fact that exercise was not helping to dampen his impatience, Jax pulled up a map of the ship on his wrist-comm and wrote in Roden Zyll. A small bleep indicated the man he was looking for was currently in the sick bay. Pulling himself to his feet, Jax headed out of his room to hunt down the one person with some answers.

Halfway there, he bumped into Nalea and Sienna, who had been friends since before he'd learned of the Sephians and Draeken. Of course, he'd known Sienna long before that. Her husband, Bobby, had been a Ranger alongside Jax, but he'd been killed by a texting driver. Sienna had never had it easy. Not long after Bobby's death, Legian had come crashing—literally—into her life, which was how Jax had ended up in the middle of everything.

"How's it going?" he asked the two women.

Nalea was busy typing on her wrist-comm, but Sienna's face lifted into a bright smile right away. "Hey, Jax. I haven't seen you around."

"Been keeping busy." Not really.

"I get that," Sienna said. "It's been chaos. It'll be nice when Apolo gets back. I could use the break."

"Apolo's coming back?" Jax asked. Apolo, who'd led the Sephian forces to Earth and was the tahren of the *tahcayaren,* or Great Leader, of Sephia as well as Roden's childhood friend, was not a man to be trifled with. If the military leaders thought it was tough dealing with the Draeken, they wouldn't enjoy having the Sephian military against them, too.

"Yeah," she replied. "I check in with him once a day. He's working with Krysea to pull together several ships as we speak. It will take him nearly a year, but once he's back, I imagine most of the Sephians will return to Sephia with him, and he'll leave enough firepower for those who remain to make a home here on their own terms."

"Good to see you, Jax," Nalea said, looking up from her wrist-comm. Exhaustion paled her golden complexion.

"You all right, Nalea, er, I mean, Grand Lord?"

She rolled her eyes. "Don't you dare call me that, Jax. We're friends. The title feels so formal."

Jax chuckled. "It's supposed to. You're the Krysea to the Draeken people."

She sighed. "It gives me a new appreciation for what Krysea has gone through as *tahcayaren* of Sephia. I'd always thought that when she ordered, people obeyed."

"Not the case?" Jax asked, raising a brow.

"Definitely not the case," Nalea replied. "Take the Grax, for instance. That ship contains a quarter of my 'people'," she said, emphasizing her words with air quotes. "I hail the Grax every hour, and still I get no response. I even sent an envoy. They were ignored. They hovered outside the Grax waiting for clearance to land for three hours before giving up and turning back."

"At least they weren't shot out of the sky," Sienna countered.

"Good point," Nalea said.

"I'll talk to you later. And get some rest," Jax said.

"Yes, sir!" Sienna said, giving a mock salute.

Jax gave them a lopsided grin before continuing on his way to the med-hub, though his smile faded as he recalled Nalea's words. They were still on their own in finding an antivirus. Omega served no purpose other than death. Otas had made no demands. It was as if the bastard wanted Omega to run its course and decimate the human population, which wouldn't surprise Jax. A virus was an easy way to level the playing field without stepping a foot onto it. Jax would skewer the bastard's cold heart if they ever came face to face.

At the rate things were going, it wouldn't matter much longer. Refugees flocked around the Striga in the tens of thousands. They milled around outside like a horde of zombies. Many were clearly sick. People not showing symptoms tried to avoid the infected, but it was difficult. Even with the Striga making several heavy drops of supplies to the refugees every day, they looked like a sorry lot.

Jax had watched the infected for the first two days, and then changed television channels because it was too damn depressing. Omega started simply enough: chills, swollen glands, and high fevers; but within hours of infection, the infected would begin to show signs of gangrene on their nose and fingers.

"Zombie" was the closest term, because once the high fever hit, they often walked around in delirium, crying out and attacking others in between vomiting blood, infecting those around them. This phase lasted up to a day, and the images would be seared into Jax's memory forever. The final phase was almost a relief to every-one. At that point, seizures would overtake the infected until the person drowned in their own blood. Sometimes they were in a coma by then, their brains gone. Other times, they weren't so lucky.

The only good thing in this whole mess was that the troops on the ground had pulled back, cut their losses, and reassigned to the more grueling task of quarantining cities. They were counting on the nuclear order having either been rescinded or put on hold, since the week timeframe his father had mentioned was nearly up. Jax hoped for the former, because the latter could signal that any kind of peace was impossible.

Would the General of the Army drop a nuke on a core ship surrounded by tens of thousands U.S. citizens? He hoped to God the answer to that question was a big resounding *NO*.

He could see why Roden didn't want to risk getting the virus on board, but hell, watching innocents die while being unable to do anything was maddening. There were so many infected out there, but there were also uninfected people in encampments separated from the larger herd. The Draeken had run the first wave of protestors they'd rescued through some kind of screening process when they'd brought them on board to make sure none had Omega. Yet, now, they were doing nothing. Roden had said the risk of contamination was too great.

Jax disagreed.

"We've got to help the ones outside who aren't infected yet," Jax said as soon as he walked through the med-hub's door and spotted Roden.

The Draeken turned and cocked his head. "We are. We're working on an antivirus."

"What if we quarantine the ones not showing symptoms? Like we did with the ones we picked up last week?"

Roden shook his head. "Like I told you before, it's too risky now that there are confirmed cases of Omega outside."

"We need to do something," Jax countered, holding out in his hands in frustration.

"And we will," Roden said, taking a step away from the man he'd been talking to when Jax arrived.

He'd been so intent on Roden that he hadn't noticed Talla behind him, standing near a bed where a human man lay.

"What's this?" Jax asked.

Roden spoke. "Jax, I'd like you to meet Mike Ryan. Two days ago, Mike was injected with antivirus number forty-six, which included plant extract."

"Forty-six? What happened to the first forty-five test subjects?"

Roden continued. "Yesterday Mike was injected with the Omega virus. Today, his vitals are still normal. No signs of Omega are in his blood."

Jax's eyes narrowed before widening. "You've found the cure?"

Roden smiled. "More than a cure. Also a vaccine."

"That's good." He sucked in a breath. "No, that's great. We have to get it distributed ASAP. When will forty-six be ready?"

"Patience, Lieutenant. We need to wait a full twenty-four hours to ensure that forty-six cures infected humans as well as prevents transmission or reinfection. By tonight, we will begin producing forty-six in mass quantities. Until then, everything is housed in this room. We've been keeping this area off-grid so that it can't be hacked by the Grax."

"How about the U.N.?" Jax asked. "Can you share the formula with them so they can start producing batches, too?"

"I plan to do so as soon as they agree to a cease-fire."

Memories of the past two weeks flitted through Jax's mind. He'd gone from Army Ranger to traitor to Resistance fighter. His own father had tried to imprison him. "Fair enough," he said. "How soon can we distribute forty-six to the refugees outside?"

"As early as midday tomorrow."

"Good." Jax's gaze fell to Talla, and then to the man. He stared despondently at the wall, oblivious to everyone around him. The lights were on, but nothing was going on. Jax swallowed. Were the cure's side effects worse than the disease itself?

He motioned toward the human. "Forty-six do that to him?"

Talla shook her head tightly, the motion one of burden. "Mike's wife and newborn succumbed to Omega yesterday."

Yesterday. If they'd found forty-six just twenty-four hours earlier, Mike would still have his family. Talk about irony. To have the one thing that could have saved his family now flowing through his veins. No wonder the guy had volunteered to get injected with Omega. Not only did he have nothing to lose, but he'd already given up.

He gave a tight nod and turned to leave.

"One more thing," Roden said.

Jax's muscles tensed. Something in Roden's voice led him to pause and turn back to face the Draeken.

Roden's features were hard. "Your father's contracted Omega."

Air refused to fill his lungs. "How long?"

"Nearly a day."

The colonel would be delirious by now. His father had never

lost control; the man was an unwavering pillar of leadership. Now, the image of his father with a blackened nose and puking blood seemed impossible. Tension pressed against his lungs, and he clenched his jaw. He refused to imagine Jeremiah Jerrick as an infected. His father was another casualty of a senseless war, that was all. "Then it's too late for him," he said bluntly and left the room without another word.

"Wait up."

Jax kept walking down the hallway even though he could hear Talla jogging to catch up. When she closed the gap between them, she kept pace at his side.

"I'm sorry about your father."

"Like you said before, we all die sometime." He looked straight ahead and kept walking.

"Trying to convince yourself to not feel anything doesn't work."

"Who's to say I'm even capable of feeling anything?" he countered.

She grabbed his arm, pulling him to a stop. "When I thought Laze had died, a part of me died with him. I know you must feel something similar for your father."

He went to pull away, but she tightened her grip. She opened her mouth

to speak. An explosion rocked the floor as a thunderous boom sounded from the direction of the med-hub. Jax and Talla stared wide-eyed at each other for the split second before the alarms sounded. Talla took to the air at the same time Jax took off at a sprint back toward the sick bay.

Roden must have left not long after them, because Jax found the Draeken flying toward the sick bay from the other direction. The three of them stopped outside the blackened hole where they had all been standing minutes earlier. The ship's systems had already extinguished the fire, and cold oxygen was now being reintroduced to clear the air.

Everything in the room was charred. Beds, desks, and cabinets had been blown apart. At least three unrecognizable corpses were tangled in the wreckage.

Roden cursed. "Everything we had on forty-six was contained in that lab."

$$\text{\rule{3cm}{0.4pt}}$$

Chapter 19

Without forty-six, they were doomed. Weeks of research had been destroyed. They would have to start from scratch. At the rate of Omega's progression, it would be impossible to get a new antivirus developed in time to save the humans. Omega would have run its course in the Americas and Europe within two weeks; Asia in under a week. Humanity's hope was lost.

Talla's conscience gritted at the thought of yet another race facing extinction. Regardless of what the humans had done, no one deserved to experience the near-genocide her people had faced. She nudged the shredded metallic skeleton of a cabinet with her toe as she sifted through the wreckage. The bomb had been effective in destroying everything within the room. A charred corpse lay in between two beds, and she knew it was Mike.

The human had risked everything to help, and now his sacrifice meant nothing.

A wrist-comm chimed behind her, and Talla jerked to see Roden scowling at his wrist-comm. "Surprise, surprise," he said, glancing up. "It looks like Otas wants to talk now. How convenient." He spoke the next statement into his wrist-comm. "I'll be there in under five minutes, my dear." She said something, and he chuckled. "No. I'm coming with you because I don't trust you to not kill Otas as soon as you see him."

Roden tapped several buttons and then spoke into the device wrapped around his forearm. "Escalate all security to maximum alert. Search the rooms for everyone assigned to med-hub 071E2. Oh, and give Otas Olnek a temporary security code to land one Transporter and no more. Nalea and I will meet him at the hangar."

Talla's eyes widened. "You're letting that imposter onto the ship?"

"Talla's right," Jax added. "That bastard is behind this attack, as much as he's behind Omega. You can't trust him. For all we know, he's bringing Omega onto the ship with him."

"You think I don't know that?" Roden asked. "The humans' interference pulled us a step back, just enough for Otas to take the lead. We've been playing catch-up ever since. He knows it as well as we do. He's come to make his demands because he knows that as of sixty seconds ago our hands are tied when it comes to helping the humans."

Talla balked. "We can't give in to his demands. He's nothing but a terrorist."

"But he's a terrorist with the power to destroy the entire human population," Jax said, scowling.

"I had just given approval to make backups of our research and prepare to broadcast the formula," Roden said. "I don't know who Otas got to, or how, but I'd venture to guess it was one of the scientists lying charred to a crisp in there." He motioned toward the room. "No one else could've detonated a bomb at a more perfect time. Otas won this round. Now, let's go see what he has planned next. I'll see you both at the briefing room."

Roden left, and Talla spared a glance at Jax, who looked as furious as she felt. Emergency crews had now arrived on scene.

With a sigh, she started walking toward the command room. Jax caught up with her.

"I won't trust Otas one iota while he's on board," Jax said.

"Agreed," Talla replied. "But if we can get our hands on the Omega formula, Otas is unnecessary."

He grimaced. "Otas probably guards the formula for Omega with his life."

Her gaze narrowed. "There are always methods to get Otas to surrender the formula."

Jax eyed her, but said nothing.

"Although I'm more curious why he's suddenly come forward. He's a powermonger. He's obviously working some angle."

"Yeah," Jax said. "I don't like this situation one bit."

When they reached the command room, the first face Talla came across was Laze's.

Laze and she talked, but she found it was hard. Laze, who'd always been so easygoing and sarcastic, was now serious and quiet, his mood somber. Talla was careful to avoid the topic of Sarah and Jacen, knowing that he needed more time to cope with the loss. She had seen Jacen's wings displayed in Laze's sanctuary. So small and delicate. Seeing them wrenched her heart.

It was never easy seeing innocents killed. But that was war. The thought of another war on another planet made it hard to breathe. Gripping the arm rest, she focused on breathing deeply, watching everyone in the room tense.

She was almost relieved when Otas Olnek finally arrived. The traitor showed up less than an hour after the bombing, strutting into the room like a proud peacock. He came with a single guardsman as though to flaunt his confidence. He wore the bright colors of the Grand Lord, yet he had no relation to Nalea Zyll and no right to the colors. He'd been a body double for Nalea's father, Hillas Puftan, a job he'd clearly taken too far. Instead of wearing the Puftan crest on his chest, he wore a new emblem, one Talla had never seen before. Trying to create a new royal bloodline?

He looked down his nose at the attendees in the room, frowning when no one acknowledged his authority, not that he had any royal blood in his plebeian heritage. One chair remained open at the large round table, yet Otas continued to stand, even when Nalea and her consort Roden—arriving last per Draeken custom—entered the room.

All the Draeken in the room rose and bowed their heads. Otas smiled at Nalea, the *real* Grand Lord of Draeka: She eyed him, but make no further acknowledgement, and Otas bristled.

The guardsman at Otas's side bowed to Nalea. Talla knew that man well. She and Meyt had dated when she was a teenager, and she knew him to be one of the best and most noble of the late Grand Lord's personal guardsmen. They'd remained friends and occasional lovers throughout the years. Their bed play had helped pass the long trip to Earth. It didn't make sense that he served Otas now, but knowing Meyt, there had to be a good reason for it. He spotted Talla and smiled.

A slight movement at her right brought her gaze to Jax, who was now scrutinizing Meyt like a bird of prey homing in for a kill. Despite his words and actions, Jax clearly cared, and it somewhat lifted the pressure on Talla's heart. There was still hope. Hope!

She turned to the guardsman and winked, her lips curved upward. If another man's interest was what it took for Jax to come to terms with his buried feelings, she had no problem spurring things along. In fact, she would enjoy making a little payback. Intentionally avoiding Jax's gaze, Talla kept her focus on the traitor and his guardsman.

"Otas Olnek," Nalea Zyll said from Roden's side. "Over a year ago, you took control of the Grax and refused to acknowledge the Grand Lord. Have you come to make amends?"

The older Draeken smiled then. It was wide and false. "On the contrary, Your Majesty. I've always acknowledged you as the Grand Lord. Rather, I've come to offer my assistance in your time of need."

Nalea raised her brows. "You've done a poor job at showing your allegiance."

"I heard of the unfortunate accident with the antivirus. My condolences for your losses. One of the deceased had family on the Grax."

Talla clenched her teeth to keep from speaking. There was nothing sympathetic in Otas's statement. His words were as close to an admission of guilt as could be. He knew it and didn't care that everyone knew he'd destroyed the room. He'd even inferred that he'd gotten to the scientist by using his relations against him. It was one of the oldest and most trustworthy methods to get results. Blackmail.

"How timely of you," Nalea said, "considering the accident happened less than an hour ago."

"I like to keep up to date on Draeken events," he replied.

"Yet you've missed out on so much," Nalea said. "How it is that you knew of the accident immediately while you've refused all hailing attempts for over a year? Taking control of a core ship without authority is piracy."

Meyt made no movement, but Talla noticed his face was hard, holding back strong emotion. Talking with him afterward may help her learn more about how an unranked Draeken had managed to take over a core ship.

"We had communication issues," Otas replied.

"And those communication errors prevented you from sending Transporters to other ships, or accepting my envoy onto the *Grax*?" Nalea asked.

"I did not know if Roden Zyll was in charge or the Grand Lord. I am a patriot and do not follow traitors," Otas said, glaring at the man to Nalea's right.

Roden belted out a laugh.

"*You* are the traitor here," Nalea retorted. "Roden is my consort, and anything he does is with my approval. Ignoring his commands is disobeying the Grand Lord's commands."

Otas bowed lavishly. "My most sincere apologies, Your Majesty; I had not been fully apprised of the arrangement."

"Well, consider yourself apprised as of now," Nalea said.

"If I may make amends," Otas said. "Ever since learning of the Omega virus, I've had my scientists working on an antivirus."

"It should have been easy, since you designed the virus," Roden said with a sneer.

Otas ignored Roden. "It was auspicious for us all that Omega started on the other side of the planet, far away from posing any risk to Draeken life."

"Until last week," Nalea said.

Otas smiled smugly. "Yes, you must have been quite distraught watching humans outside die."

Nalea didn't respond.

"Fortunately," Otas continued, "I now have the antivirus in sufficient quantities for immediate mass distribution. We can begin with everyone on this ship."

Nalea and Roden glanced at each other. Nalea spoke first. "Billions have perished from Omega already. Why do you offer the antivirus now? What is your payment?"

He held out his hands with open palms. "I merely wish to free humans from the threat of obliteration. Perhaps they've suffered enough to gain a new perspective. All I ask is that the Grax be allowed to land on Earth and be reintegrated with the Striga, Artox, and Evo. The Draeken people must stand united if we are to survive."

"And you?" Roden asked. "What are you asking for?"

Otas glared at Roden. "I wish to serve the Grand Lord as she sees fit."

"That is quite altruistic of you, Otas. And quite unlike you as well," Nalea said, not looking convinced. "And if we should reject your generous offer?"

Otas smiled. It was cold and cruel and knowing. "Then the humans will die."

Chapter 20

The Grax landed, with the Artox and Evo touching down on either side. The ground shook with tremors from the force as the three massive core ships landed as one. These ships landed with no argument from Jax's government this time. Those still breathing were too busy standing in line for the antivirus.

Jax himself was stuck in line right now, a rock lodged in his gut. He didn't trust Otas, and he could tell no one else did either. He waited until after the Draeken departed for the Grax before heading to the med-hub for the antivirus. Roden's people had had the antivirus tested. The results showed that, while the formula seemed overly complicated, it got the job done.

Jax was glad. He'd been going stir-crazy stuck on the core ship, safe from Omega, while his countrymen died all around him. The line moved quickly since there were fewer than a thousand humans on board the Striga.

When Otas advised all Draeken and Sephians to also take the antivirus, Nalea had laughed out loud, instead saying they would be prepared to create more batches "just in case". She clearly placed no trust in Otas. She'd proved herself a good judge of character time and again, which gave Jax a bit more faith in Roden. He still didn't like the guy. Too smug and cold-blooded for Jax's tastes.

After Otas had returned to the *Grax*, Roden's mood was grave. When Jax asked him about it, the Draeken said that Otas was up to something but, with Jax being a human, the risk of not taking the antivirus was greater than any new risk taking the pill could present. In other words, Roden said Jax and his fellow humans were screwed either way.

Jax wasn't happy about the circumstances, but Roden had a point. Omega was still a very active virus. All it took was contact with a single infected person or contaminated item and he'd be dead if he couldn't get the antivirus in time. He'd asked about carrying a pill on him and taking it if needed, but it turned out the shelf life of the antivirus was eleven days. Just one more convenient argument for Otas to press for all humans to take the antivirus right away.

Every Transporter on all four core ships had been sent out already, with an ample supply of antivirus on board, to every government across the world. All the member countries of the U.N. welcomed the antivirus with open arms. It was amazing how one's scruples could take a one-eighty given the right circumstances.

Jax took a step forward. Six people stood in front of him. The antivirus was a simple pill. He figured they'd have enough on hand to pass out to every human on the ship, but these med-techs took their jobs seriously. There were two stations every recipient of the antivirus had to go through. A med-tech dispensed pills and water at the first station, and people moved quickly through. At the second station, a med-tech scanned each recipient to make sure the pill had "bonded" with their DNA—whatever the hell that meant. Plenty of Draeken technology seemed strange to Jax, but he was no medical expert.

Near the second station stood the Draeken guardsman who

had accompanied Otas to the *Striga*; Jax didn't trust the guy, and especially didn't like that he was overseeing the antivirus distribution. He had looked at Talla in a way that seemed way too intimate. The guy was tall and strong, and looked like he knew his way around a weapon. He would be a good match for Talla, and that made Jax hate the guy.

The Draeken turned and caught Jax watching him. He stared, making no move to turn away. Jax's lip curled into a sneer.

"Lieutenant Jerrick?"

Jax snapped around to see a Sephian med-tech holding out a pill and a glass of water.

"Thanks, Valyn," he muttered, taking the pill. He glanced back at the Draeken, who was now looking in another direction.

Grease and Jeannie Edmonds were in front of him at the second station. Jax's brows tightened as he watched the med-tech run a scanner first over Jeannie's face, then Grease's. Why the face? Why not the arm or chest? His suspicions hackled, he stepped between the med-tech and the Edmonds.

"Pardon me," the med-tech said, as though a question.

Jax held out his wrist. "No. Scanning our wrists should be enough."

The med-tech shook his head. "But I must scan your face."

Jax took a step closer. "Tell me why you need to scan our faces for DNA."

The med-tech stammered. "Because it's my directive."

Jax grunted and then turned away to find the Draeken guardsman in front of him.

"Is there a problem here?" he asked.

"He refuses to be scanned," the med-tech said.

"No," Jax said, his features hard. "I said—"

The guardsman had turned away, and Jax strained around the guy's wing to see Talla heading their way.

She glanced over the faces and frowned. "What's going on?"

Jax thumbed the first station. "I took my antivirus."

He heard a slight whir and spun to find his profile getting scanned. "There. That should work," the med-tech said, seeming satisfied with himself.

Jax pushed him and the scanner away. "Get that out of my face."

She looked at Jax with a question in her eyes, and he gave a slight shake of his head. "Scanning is just a precaution, anyway. There's no danger, Jax," she said coming between Jax and the other two.

"If you need to scan DNA," Jax said. "Why must it be the face?"

"What?" she asked, sounding genuinely confused, looking from the med-tech to the guardsman, and back to Jax. "You don't. Facial scans are necessary only for confirming identities. DNA can be scanned from any part of the body."

Jax glared at the guardsman. "Why does Otas want records of everyone who's been administered the antivirus?"

"It's the directive," the guardsman replied.

Talla didn't speak for a while. "It's more than for recordkeeping. Facial scanning can couple an exact DNA-specific dosage—in this case, a pill—to an identity. But it doesn't make any sense. The virus was not DNA-specific, therefore the antivirus shouldn't be. What's going on, Meyt?"

Meyt opened his mouth, shut it, and thought for a moment before speaking. "I cannot say."

"Can't or won't?" Jax threw out.

The guardsman's mouth tightened.

Jax chuckled drily. "Yeah, that's what I thought." He typed in a quick email to the one Ranger he still trusted who wasn't on the Striga. "I think the more folks who skip the scan, the better." He turned to the remaining humans in line. "You hear that? Don't allow facial scans."

The med-tech sputtered. "But..."

"I'll see that additional Striga guardsmen are posted here

immediately to ensure things proceed without issue," Talla said, eying Meyt with suspicion. Meyt responded by lifting his chin. Her lips were a thin line when she faced Jax again. She motioned toward the door with her chin. "Let's go, Jax."

Once they were out of the med-hub, Talla asked, "What the fyet is going on?"

"I don't know," Jax said honestly.

"I don't like that they were able to get your facial scan," she said, her voice strung with tension. "We need to share this with Roden and Nalea immediately."

"Ditto. This entire thing stinks. Otas's henchman definitely knows more than he's letting on." Jax noticed her quick glance back at the med-hub, and his muscles tightened. "You were coming here to see Meyt."

"He's an old friend."

Neither old nor friend seemed to fit when it came to the guy. "Yeah, sure."

She straightened. Without another word, she turned and headed back toward the med-hub.

He watched her for a moment, knowing she was pissed off. His wrist-comm chimed, and he glanced at the screen. He hit a button. "I'll call you in five," he said and headed toward his room. As he walked through the halls, he typed out a message to Roden and Nalea, being sure to send it as an emergency priority.

Four and a half minutes later, Jax was in his room, safe from prying ears. He dialed the number to his CO.

"Jerrick," Major Sommers said when his face appeared on the small screen.

The wrist-comms were handy in how they could connect to smart phones. "Major," Jax said. "Tell me you skipped the facial scans."

"Affirmative. I also pulled everyone left in my battalion who hadn't been scanned already. Thanks for the intel, but I nearly had a war on my hands with the medics in refusing to be scanned."

"Something's up, Six. They're scanning our faces to tie each of us to the antivirus pill we took. I don't get it yet, but I plan to find out."

"Good," Sommers said. "Keep me posted. And, Jax?"

"Yeah?"

"Sorry about your father. We'd hoped he'd hang on in time for the antivirus."

"That's what I figured," Jax said quietly.

There was a brief silence before Sommers spoke. "I have to go. The General of the Army has a videoconference with Otas Olnek right now, and I need to be there."

His suspicion went on full alert. "Why is Otas meeting with him?" Jax asked.

"Don't know," Sommers replied. "I'll be in touch."

"Roger, Six." Jax sat down on the low-back sofa. What the hell was Otas up to? There was no way Roden and Nalea knew what that Draeken was doing. First the scanning, now the meetings.

Jumping to his feet, Jax headed out of his room. He typed in Roden's name and placed the call.

"What do you need, Lieutenant?" Roden asked.

"Did you get my message?"

"Yes. I've already sent the word out. Come to my room. I'll give Nalea a call to let her know you're on your way."

Jax hit the disconnect button and headed through the hallways and elevators. Roden was several floors away, and it took him ten minutes to reach his quadrant. Before he turned the corner to Roden's hallway, his wrist-comm buzzed. He glanced down. Frowning, he answered. "What's up? I wasn't expecting to hear from you so soon."

Sommers's features were as hard and stoic as a statue. "The General of the Army has just dropped dead."

The air in Jax's lungs hardened. "Had he been scanned?"

"Yes."

Chapter 21

By the time Talla reached the command room for the unscheduled briefing, the room was at maximum capacity. At the front of the room stood Fayel, the senior Sephian doctor on earthside.

"Is this about the scanning?" she asked Laze in a whispered hush.

He shrugged. "No idea."

She leaned back, letting her wings relax out to the sides of the chair. Talking with Meyt had brought her little new information, aside from the fact that he was still interested in being more than friends.

As for information she could use, she'd learned that Meyt wasn't happy with his current predicament. Even though he refused to share any details about how he'd come to serve Otas or why he continued to serve him, it was clear that there was something forcing his hand.

A human officer entered with Jax, and she nodded in his direction, not trying to hide her surprise at the newcomer's presence. Major Sommers had been one of the commanding officers at the Etzee, but he'd always been fair. Still, she'd never expected to see him on the Striga. Despite his fairness, he'd always made it clear that he'd side with the humans each and every time.

Roden stood. "Now that everyone's here, we have some disturbing news." He motioned to the golden-skinned man to his left. "Fayel, if you would…"

The older Sephian man cleared his throat. "Yes, well, it seems that Otas Olnek hasn't been entirely forthright about the antivirus."

"It doesn't work?" someone asked from across the room.

Fayel shook his head. "Oh, it works fine. It prevents infection and can reverse infection if taken within the first twenty hours of exposure. The issue is that it seems there is some secondary programming underneath the antivirus. We missed it in our analysis. We'd thought the antivirus was more complex than it needed to be, but we didn't think much of it at the time. It wasn't until Lieutenant Jerrick and Major Sommers brought to light recent events."

Sommers came to his feet. "Otas Olnek has been meeting with leaders across the world. He met with the General of the Army this morning to discuss an alliance with the United States."

Talla's mouth opened in shock. First, Otas took over the Grax. Now, he was going after Earth.

"He does not represent the Draeken people," Roden stated.

Sommers held up a hand. "I know that, and the General knew that. He rejected Otas's offer, and one instant later the General was dead on the floor."

"Sounds like Otas doesn't handle rejection very well," Jax said.

Talla's heart pounded. The scanning was beginning to make sense, and she dreaded where this was headed.

"The secondary programming works much like a pika tablet," Fayel explained. "Only instead of running immediately, it waits for a signal to activate."

"Pika?" one of the humans asked.

"Oh, yes," Fayel replied. "Pika roughly translates to 'mercy'.

The tablets bring instant, pain-free euthanasia to patients with no hope. I've never seen them used as a form of biological warfare before, since each recipient would have to be connected to a detonation system. Linking a pika tablet's programming to an individual using a facial and DNA scan for a targeted release is simple, and quite brilliant."

"You make it sound easy," Jax replied. "Then why you didn't catch it before?"

Fayel lowered his eyes, as though ashamed.

Jax was right. They should have analyzed the antivirus further before release. They'd been so desperate to stop Omega's spread that they'd bypassed testing protocols they would never have done otherwise. Talla had pressed Meyt about the facial scanning, but he'd refused to say. Now, anyone who'd been scanned…

Jax had been scanned.

"We were in a hurry and got sloppy," Roden said, slamming his fist onto the table. "We thought Omega was bad. It was just Otas's way of thinning the population before setting up the remainder to live at his mercy. We tapped into human computers before we neared Earth to learn the languages and customs. It would be nearly instantaneous to link a scan to an identity stored on human networks." He looked at the doctor. "How many humans had facial scans?"

Fayel swallowed. "We estimate eighty percent of the remaining human population. As soon as Lieutenant Jerrick notified Roden and Nalea, we sent out warnings. Otas's med-techs had already been directed to pull the remaining antivirus. Fortunately, they refused his orders and continued to administer the antivirus, withholding facial scanning."

"At least we know he doesn't have unlimited control over the Grax," she said, though the relief was small compared to the number of humans now facing a deadlier risk than Omega.

"No wonder Otas recommended all Sephians and Draeken take the antivirus," Roden said. "It would have placed everyone, even his own people, at his mercy. How many have the pika now and are linked to Otas's detonation system?"

"Over two billion out of the estimated three billion survivors." Fayel's voice was quiet, squeaky.

Otas could kill over two billion in an instant…Talla glanced at Jax, unable to breathe.

"How about the remaining twenty percent?" Laze asked, bringing her attention back to the room. "The ones who took the antivirus but didn't get scanned?"

"As long as they remain decoupled from the system, we believe they are safe," Fayel said.

Not the most convincing response. It would be far too easy to scan someone without their knowledge. A person could get scanned while on an elevator or walking down the hallway. Talla's jaw clenched. She came to her feet and leaned on the table, directing a hard look at Roden and Nalea. They had to put an end to the madness now. They'd let a madman go on unrestrained for too long. "Where's Otas now?"

"He's on the Grax," Roden said. "We've put up a force barrier around the core ship, so he's not going anywhere."

"A force barrier can't prevent him from killing over two billion innocent people with the push of a button," Sommers said, his expression hard. Something vibrated, giving off a plastic hum, and he glanced down at the phone in his hand. "Excuse me." He stepped out of the room.

Jax said. "We can't just sit on our asses when Otas has got his finger on that trigger."

"We aren't," Roden said. "That fregee can't leave the Grax, and—"

"If we do nothing, he will take over the world," Jax interrupted, his words heavy with sarcasm. "Don't think he'll stop with just my kind."

Roden's lips thinned. "We are considering options."

Sommers had returned while Roden spoke, and he was not pleased.

"We have to take down Otas," Jax said. "The future of the Earth is at stake."

"And we will," Roden said, sounding exasperated. "But we need to be smart about it."

"It's already too late," Sommers muttered.

Talla's blood ran cold. She gripped the table. "What do you mean?"

Just like everyone else in the room, Roden narrowed his eyes on the major. "What have you done, Sommers?"

Sommers was about to answer but was thrown down when a massive blast rocked the ship.

Talla fell onto the table as the entire core ship felt like it was being lifted from the ground. The blast was worse than anything she'd ever felt on the Striga, even worse than a meteor storm. Alarms blared, and the lights switched to emergency mode. No one yelled or screamed, a tribute to their military discipline.

After the initial blast, the ship tilted, and Talla tumbled to the floor. Once the ship righted itself, she looked up to see Jax pull Sommers to his feet. Jax looked seriously pissed as he held the other man by his lapels. "I can't believe you let them nuke us."

Sommers placed his hands over Jax's hands that were clenching his lapels. Jax released him and took a step back. Sommers looked as crestfallen as Jax felt. Jax gestured to the nearest external wall. "Do you know how much collateral damage is lying dead outside? People who'd just survived Omega to be murdered by a warhead courtesy of their own government?"

Sommers winced and looked pleadingly into Jax's eyes. "I had nothing to do with it. The President ordered the first strike. He had a shot at Otas and took it. He thought if we could take out Otas, we could prevent him from killing eighty percent of what's left of this world. Can you blame him for trying?"

"A nuclear bomb can't damage these ships," Roden said, helping Nalea back into her chair. He knelt before her, concern in his eyes, until she scowled and swatted him away. He stood. "It's no worse than a strong solar flare. Bombing a core ship is like dropping a grain of sand on a boulder and hoping it will break. Already the power fluctuations on board are leveling out."

"Otas is going to put two and two together. By now he knows that we're aware of the pika pills," Jax said.

The door banged open, and Jax spun to find one of his team

barging into the room. "What are you doing here, Tanel?" he asked.

Tanel glanced at him as his fingers flew over his wrist-comm. The large screen in the center of the room lit up. "I think you need to see this."

Filling the screen was Otas Olnek, healthy and not a silver hair out of place.

"He's broadcasting on all television and radio stations world-wide, even on the Draeken channels," Tanel said, backing up a step.

Jax, and everyone else, turned to the screen. By the looks of things, Otas was already well into his speech.

"I am disappointed in you," Otas said, as though chiding a young child. "I gave you the cure for the Omega virus, asking for no payment in return, only for the chance to live alongside you on this wonderful planet. How do you repay me? You drop a nuclear warhead on my ship. Fortunately, no damage was done to my ship or crew. But, take a look at what you did to your own land and people."

Otas's face was replaced by a video of utter desolation. Where trees and fields had stood before was a barren landscape, with slivered stumps spotting the monotone ground. A toxic haze clouded the pictures. Seconds of exposure to that poisoned air guaranteed death. The camera must have been on a small ship, like an Aggressor. There was no music or words accompanying the video, just the eerie sound of wind and silence. As it moved farther from ground zero, the stumps grew larger and debris could be seen. Some pieces of debris were the size of people. Countless gnarled limbs and misshapen torsos came into view.

Bile rose in Jax's throat, but he refused to look away. Color crept into what had been a shadeless brown before. A dust covered the grass, and some trees still stood, though many were broken. Movement off in the distance brought the camera closer. People, dozens of them, still by their cars, stood on the interstate.

They were waving at the camera as if it would bring help. Instead, it zoomed in on blistered faces. Cries and moans filtered through the sound of wind. Some victims were throwing up, while others lay on the ground.

The camera hovered over a woman trying to get her crying baby out of a car seat. She fumbled, her red fingers swollen, the skin no longer resembling skin. When she unlatched the seat, the buckle took the baby's skin with it. The baby screamed. Its mother cried out, "Why?"

Jax bent over and sucked in deep breaths, one after another, to keep from puking his guts out. Murmurs of sympathy erupted in the room. He looked up to see a tear run down Nalea's cheek as she held a hand to her stomach. By the time he could look at the screen again without tasting his own stomach acid, the camera was skirting over the landscape, back into the heart of the desolation. It panned out as it got within several miles of ground zero. There, through the haze, stood four unscathed core ships, radioactive dust on their shiny hulls the only thing marring their cold mammoth beauty.

The image faded, and Otas's face reappeared. "None of those innocents had to die today. As you can see, you will murder your planet and people long before I can be harmed. Their deaths fall on their own government's heads. To protect you, I am forced to disband all governments, effective immediately. I will take care of Earth now.

"To ensure peace, the antivirus included a safety measure. For anyone found guilty of a crime, punishment is immediate death. As of five minutes ago, every country's leader and their next two in succession were executed for crimes against humanity."

"Son of a bitch," Jax muttered.

"Fyet," Talla whispered at his side. Her expression was that of utter shock. She stared blankly at the screen, her face pale. He reached out and gripped her hand. It broke her daze, and she threw a thoughtful glance his way before watching the screen once more. He didn't let go of her hand, even if he could, because she had it in a death-grip, as though he were her anchor. And, she was sure as hell his anchor.

"He's not bluffing," Sommers stated on Jax's other side. No one responded because everyone in the room, including Sommers, already knew the answer.

"…We must all work hard to achieve a future without war. For now, stay in your homes. I will begin to roll out a new, more effective government structure later this week."

The screen went blank, and the room swelled in uproar.

"Pompous ass," Sommers said.

Someone's wrist-comm chimed, and Nalea spoke. "Otas is hailing me." She looked at Tanel. "Put him on the screen."

The Sephian comm-tech rushed, and Otas's face appeared on the screen once more.

He glanced over the room and smiled. "It's good to see you again, Nalea."

Using her first name was an outright breach of Draeken protocol and a blatant act of familiarity. Nalea narrowed her gaze on him. "Nice speech."

"I'll get right to the point," Otas said. "I need the support of the Striga, Artox, and Evo."

Jax was surprised when Nalea didn't laugh outright. Whispers and mutterings erupted throughout the room. "Why would I give you more resources to enslave this world?"

"I saved this world," Otas replied, his voice rising with each word. "Without me, the humans would all be dead."

Roden barked. "Bullshit! It's because of you that the Etzee was attacked. You sent out the Omega virus, and now you expect homage for killing billions? Everything's that happened in the past year falls on your shoulders."

"You will pay for your crimes," Sommers bellowed from Jax's side.

Otas frowned. "Major Sommers? Why do you still live? You

were found guilty of crimes against the future." He was busy working on something off-screen.

Sommers belted out a laugh. "Can't find my scan to terminate me, can you?"

Otas's gaze snapped back to the screen. "It's only a matter of time."

Jax glanced at Talla to find her eyes wide in stark fear.

"Don't worry. I'm too low on his radar," he whispered.

She nodded tightly.

"Omega—and now pika—are mere symptoms," Nalea added. "You, Otas Olnek, are the real plague this world faces."

Otas shook his fist, his face darkening. "I control this planet! War will be eliminated. Only *I* can guarantee absolute peace."

Nalea shook her head. "You demand unconditional power. That only guarantees absolute corruption."

Otas shook with fury. "Release the force barrier around my ship and give me full support."

Nalea rose to her feet. "I am the Grand Lord of Draeka. You do not give me orders. You are a common criminal. You are nothing. I charge you, Otas Olnek, with treason against the Draeken people. You impersonated the Grand Lord Hillas Puftan, my father, and now you declare war against your Grand Lord, which means you declare war against the Draeken people. You will be executed for your crimes."

"You killed the Grand Lord!" Otas shouted. "You do not deserve to wear the title!"

A smile crept onto Nalea's face. "Yet, I wear the title, and you don't. I carry the Puftan blood in my veins, and you don't."

Otas opened his mouth and then shut it. He glared for several long moments. "The time for talking is over. You will release the force barrier and turn control of all four core ships to me. For every ternion—three Earth hours—you delay, I will erase a country."

He glanced off-screen once again. "Switzerland is a so-called peaceful nation, yet they conspired with the U.N. against us."

Nalea's face hardened. "Do not do this."

Otas sneered. "Everyone of Swiss nationality has just had their pika programming activated."

Jax could have sworn his heart stopped for a moment. Switzerland? They were a neutral country. They were known for watches, cheese, and chocolate, not war. How many lives had been lost at the push of a button?

"You bastard," Nalea gritted out.

"You have a ternion to release the barrier before I activate the next country." He closed his eyes and pressed his forefinger against a screen showing a map of the world just on the edge of their view. He leaned closer to the map and smiled. "It looks like Zimbabwe is next."

"You are a madman," Nalea said. Roden now stood at her side.

Otas glared at Roden before looking at her once again. "Things would be different now if you accepted my offer a year ago."

"Yes," she agreed. "You'd be dead already."

His face reddened, and his features tightened. He moved, and the screen went blank.

"What's he talking about?" Talla asked.

Nalea smiled grimly. "While you were imprisoned by the humans and Sephians, Otas invited me to take him as my consort." She glanced at the man at her side. "However, I already had a much better option lined up."

Roden looked across the room. "It's time to run. We'll move the Artox and Evo to Alaska as soon as they can get prepped, but with the nuclear fallout blocking the sun, it may take them a couple of extra days to recharge their power cells enough for the short move."

"Why Alaska?" Jax asked.

As locations went, Alaska wasn't ideal. The U.S. had bombed the core ships. They should be looking somewhere in another country. And, while Alaska was relatively remote, much of its land was treacherous. Not the best military setup to his mind.

"Alaska and Hawaii didn't appreciate getting abandoned by their government when Omega hit," Roden replied. "They reached out to us. Brazil has also offered us land in exchange for our resources. For now, we've selected Alaska. It's the least inhabited, and we can land in the northern region to minimize risk to local inhabitants in case there are further attacks.

"Yes, we have a home, for now," Roden continued with a smile though it soon faded. "However, the Striga will remain here to maintain the force barrier. We cannot allow Otas the chance to flee or use the *Grax*'s offensive power."

"Millions more will die every three hours," Sommers said. "Until we do something."

Roden and Nalea looked at each other and both of their faces hardened. It was Roden who spoke, though it was clear the words came from them both. "There's nothing to stop him from killing every scanned human already. If we succumb to his demands, this planet doesn't have a chance. These three core ships and pockets of unscanned humans are all that stands against the power-hungry lunacy of Otas Olnek."

"I'm not disagreeing," Sommers said, "but we need to get on board that ship and take Otas down."

"Are you saying you're with us?" Roden asked.

Sommers nodded. "I can learn the secret handshake later. I can vouch for my company and pretty much guarantee you'll have more military forces at your back. Give me ten minutes to see who I can get here in time. I may be able to pull together some semblance of a coalition."

Jax looked at the man who'd trained him and who'd led him through some pretty sticky situations. Six had always been a hands-on leader. It was clear he was hankering for action. "It's good to have you on board, Major."

Sommers turned his attention onto Roden. "Can we get through the force barrier and onto the *Grax*?"

"Of course," Roden replied. "But once you're on the *Grax*, there's no guarantee the ship's sensors won't pick you up."

"It's a risk we'll have to take," Sommers said.

Nalea looked over the faces in the room. "Going after Otas is a high-risk mission, so it will be volunteers only. Who will accompany Major Sommers?"

Nearly every hand in the room raised and voices yelled out, "I'm in."

"You can count on me," Jax said.

Roden spoke. "Everyone with Sommers, meet back here in ninety minutes for details. That gives you time to see your families and pull gear together. When you get back here, be ready to go."

There was a silent pause before everyone moved and funneled out of the room. Jax reached for Talla. "You didn't raise your hand."

"I'm sitting this one out to protect the Grand Lord."

"You're sitting this one out?" he echoed. Talla had never turned down a mission. Dubious, he asked, "Do you have a minute to talk."

She watched him and then nodded. "Sure." Except at that moment her wrist-comm chimed, and she looked up a couple of seconds later. "I'll catch up. I have to do something first."

Chapter 23

Talla took flight to hangar 022W1 where she found a lone Aggressor being prepped. She flared, touching down on her toes and coming to a gentle stop before Roden and Nalea.

"Does anyone suspect you're here?" Roden asked.

"No," Talla replied. "Everyone thinks I'm staying behind to protect the Striga."

"May the gods be with you," Nalea said. "I'd go if I could—"

"But you need to be safe here," Roden finished. "For the baby."

Talla snapped her gaze from Roden to Nalea.

Nalea smiled. "We wanted you to know."

Talla burst into a wide grin. "Congratulations." She paused. "Thank you for sharing that with me."

Another Draeken stepped out from the Aggressor, and Talla looked up to see Meyt. "Are we all set?" she asked.

"We're ready to go. I've got full landing clearance for the Grax. They believe I have bribed a comm-tech to get through the force barrier."

"They bought that?" Talla asked.

"Yes," Meyt replied. "Otas is cocky. He believes I can't betray him." He headed back up the steps and disappeared into the Aggressor.

Roden's features turned serious when he faced Talla. "In and out, exactly like I trained you. Meyt will have the ship ready to go when you're finished. Let Sommers's tactical unit handle the rest of the Grax."

Talla nodded, afraid her voice would crack if she spoke. Nalea hugged her and Roden patted her on the arm. Taking a breath, she headed into the Aggressor and strapped herself in next to Meyt. She closed her eyes and focused. In and out. This was the one chance to save her people and humans alike. She would not fail. After all, she was the best assassin Roden had.

Jax stood in the command room with his entire team. They hadn't even flinched when he'd brought up the mission. Even stodgy Hert Hesmat had volunteered on the spot, bringing with him their team's new patch: a winged star inlaid in gold.

Despite their varied exteriors and diverse personalities, each and every member of his team was a hero. It reminded Jax of his own company in the fifty-first division. They'd never backed down from a challenge, taken every order head-on, and he still claimed responsibility for their loss.

Sommers was still on his satellite phone. With the nuclear fallout, none of his battalion could get close to the Striga, and so they'd been arranging rendezvous points for the Transporters to pick them up. With fewer than ninety minutes until Otas eradicated the next country—if they could trust Otas to wait—they were running out of time to get those troops on board.

To assault a ship the size of a mountain, numbers counted. The more experienced soldiers they had the better their chance for success. Right now, they had maybe a hundred battle-hardened troops in the command room, with a couple more trickling in every few minutes. Not nearly enough.

Sommers slid his phone into his pocket.

"We going to have support?" Jax asked him.

"Yes, a full tactical unit has been formed," Sommers replied, but he didn't look pleased. Then he said louder, "All right, let's get started."

Sommers started on logistics. Jax scanned the faces in the room. He frowned when he saw no sign of Talla. It didn't make sense that she'd miss such a big mission.

"Additional troops will be here within two hours."

Jax's gaze snapped to Sommers at the words. "But Zimbabwe has less than an hour and a half," he said.

"Understood," Sommers answered. "We're going in as the first wave ten minutes before the deadline, with support coming in a second wave."

"Is that wise?" Laze asked from the side, looking healthier than he'd been recently, but still lacking facial color. Jax would have left him behind, but they needed manpower, and Laze had proven time and again that he could more than hold his own. "Once we lose the element of surprise, we're not going to get another shot."

"I agree," Jax said. "We can't go in half-cocked."

"The main objective is to secure the Grax," Roden said, entering the room. "We already have a covert team on the Grax, ready to take down Otas the instant you engage. With the force barrier, the Grax is essentially disabled. All you'll have to do is keep the Grax's guardsmen busy until Otas is eliminated and additional support can arrive."

"We're a diversion?" Jax asked, his eyes narrowing with suspicion.

"No," Roden replied. "Your mission is to liberate the Grax. Anyone who allies with Otas should be eliminated with prejudice.

Teams from the Artox and Evo will also hit the Grax. We anticipate the Grax to not put up much of a fight, but we can't know that for sure until we're on board. Every core ship has the same layout. You will rendezvous in the ship's command room once you've secured the ship. I've distributed clearance codes for landing on the Grax…"

Jax's thoughts overtook the words in the room. Roden had sent in another team for Otas already. The team had to be Draeken, someone Roden trusted. Jax glanced over to see Laze still in the room. With his wings still healing, Laze wasn't yet at a hundred percent, which meant…

"Son of a bitch."

"What is it, Lieutenant?" Roden asked.

"You and I need to talk."

Roden gave him a knowing look. Yeah, he knew exactly what had tripped Jax's outburst. His nerves ground on his patience until Sommers wrapped up, and people filtered out of the room. He grabbed Laze's arm on his way out. "Did you know Talla's already on the Grax?"

Laze's face froze, and he looked over at Roden. "No," he ground out. "I did not." He stepped off to the side by Jax, waiting for the room to clear out.

The room emptied, leaving only Roden, Laze, Jax, and a Sephian still sitting in the corner. It was the man who'd fought alongside Talla on the ground. Pires was his name. Jax eyed him, and Pires crossed his arms over his chest. "I heard what you said. I'm staying."

"Talla is the other team you sent," Jax said to Roden.

"She's not alone," he answered.

"Who else went with her?" Laze asked.

"Meyt."

"Just Meyt?" Laze countered.

Tension crawled up Jax's spine. "You trust that guy?"

"Not at all," Roden said. "But he could get her close to Otas."

"You should've sent me with her," Laze said, sounding pissed. "Talla and I are a team."

Roden shook his head. "Meyt could cover one extra passenger, no more. Plus, with their history, no one will suspect Talla if anyone saw her with Meyt. If we sent you after Otas, he'd be suspicious. Everyone knows you and Meyt have never seen eye to eye. Talla and Meyt can get close enough to stop Otas before he sets off any more pika programming."

"And how is Meyt going to get her close to Otas?" Jax asked, fury burning the air in his lungs.

"She's going onto the Grax as his consort," Roden said. "It's her cover," he tacked on, eying Jax.

Jax bristled. "I didn't ask."

"You didn't need to."

"Where is Otas at on the Grax?" Jax said, changing the subject.

"You're not going to break from the mission directive," Roden said.

"Eliminating Otas is the number one priority of the mission, right?" Jax replied.

"Yes," Roden replied.

"So," Jax continued. "If shit hits the fan, we need a back-up plan. This may be our best shot at Otas."

"Talla has never failed," Roden cautioned before waving a hand through the air. "However, continue."

Jax nodded. "Once we get to the Grax, Laze and I can divert to extract Talla and Meyt. If the target has already been neutralized, great, if not, then consider us the contingency plan."

"I'm in," Pires said, speaking up for the first time.

Jax eyed the Sephian for a moment and then nodded. "We could use you."

Roden didn't look convinced. "And who's going to lead your teams? We need seasoned leaders out there." he asked, looking between Laze and Jax.

"Sana will take point," Jax said. "She has more than enough experience to lead the team, and I trust her."

"Bente can handle my team along with his," Laze said.

"Bente already has Talla's team," Roden replied.

Laze pursed his lips. "Then how about Sommers? His other units aren't arriving for the first wave."

A knowing smile crept up Roden's face. "Excellent choice. Laze, open file 26-5878-98. It is a map of the Grax, with indicators on Otas's possible locations. You need to memorize it, because things will likely become chaotic. I've already set aside an Aggressor for you three to take onto the Grax."

Jax cracked his neck while he thought through Roden's words. "You had this planned all along."

Roden didn't deny it. "If Talla and Meyt knew they'd have a backup team, then they might not take a chance if things get risky."

"You're a bastard," Jax said.

"I like to ensure the best probability for success," Roden replied as he headed toward the door.

"I'll grab our gear," Pires said with a dark grin before heading out of the room without another word.

The Sephian was one of those who thrived on battle and loved bloodshed. Jax understood the type; he'd had men like Pires on his teams and he'd taken down countless Pireses in war. While Jax would rather have Pires on his side than against him, the man was impossible to control, making him perfect for this particular mission. Taking down Otas could get messy. Jax needed a guy with no regard for self-protection to see the criminal killed.

Laze was already pulling up the map of the Grax. "I'm sending copies to you and Pires," he said just as Jax's wrist-comm vibrated. "After I analyze the layout, I'll also send you the best place for us to start." He headed toward the door. "I'll see you at the hangar."

Talla let go of Meyt's hand as soon as they stepped inside his room. "I can't believe no one was suspicious," she said.

Meyt shrugged. "They're just happy to see us together again. They'd heard you shacked up with a human and were worried you'd be a lost cause."

"That was nothing, just something to pass the time," she said with a blunt edge to her words.

"Good." Meyt stepped forward. Then took another step, forcing Talla to take a step back. He continued until her back was pressed against the wall. Lifting her chin, he lowered his head and kissed her. When she made no move to pull away, his kiss went from tentative to deeper and more passionate.

They'd done this many, many times before. After all, Meyt was the ideal Draeken: tall, strong, gorgeous in a militant sort of way, smart, and incredible in bed. But this was the first time his kiss felt wrong. Empty. It wasn't Meyt. His kiss was as perfect as ever. Talla had changed. She frowned, then pressed her palms over his heart and gently pushed him away.

He backed up and looked at her. "Thought so," he said and

turned away.

"Meyt…"

He held up a hand. "Otas would've known we were on board the moment we landed. He'll demand for me to update him soon. He's superstitious. He uses twelve rooms, changing the room he stays in each day, so now we wait until he notifies me which room to come to."

"It would be so much easier if he didn't disable his tracking on his wrist-comm." Talla watched as he went about checking his weapons. She ran her fingers over a painting he'd done several years back. "Why are you helping me?"

He turned to face her, his brows furrowed in confusion.

"I need to know that I can count on you. I mean, you've served as Otas's right hand for a year. Why the sudden change?"

Meyt opened his mouth to speak and snapped it shut. After what seemed to be a long internal debate, he went to his wall screen and turned on a sound dampener. Then he approached her, held her close, and whispered in her ear. "We all knew Hillas's days were numbered, but we were counting on Roden taking over. The thought of Otas never crossed my mind, never crossed anyone's mind. No one paid him any attention." He lowered his head. "That was our mistake."

"What happened?"

"A few days before Hillas was killed, Otas impersonated Hillas and had everyone on the Grax take pika injections under the pretense that they were inoculations."

Talla covered her mouth with her hand. "I had no idea."

Meyt pulled back and frowned, his next words coming out softly. "You thought I'd willingly follow an imposter?"

"No, maybe, I don't know," she stammered, running a hand through her hair. "I guess I didn't give it much thought." She paused. "He also injected all of Hillas's guardsmen on the earth-side base, didn't he? That's why all you follow him. That's the reason, isn't it?"

Meyt pursed his lips before giving a solemn shake of his head. "No, he didn't inject everyone. Just a few."

Confusion and anger pressed her brows together. "I don't get it. Why would you stand by and watch all the humans get scanned if you knew what Otas was doing? Did he threaten to kill you if you don't do what he says?"

Meyt glared, stepping away from her. "You think I give a fyet about what he could do to me?"

"What did he do?"

Meyt turned, paced the room a couple of times, before facing her once again. "At Hillas's earthside base, the first time Otas gave me an order, I laughed in his face. You know what he did then? He pulled up a screen and had me watch as he killed a mother and her baby on the Grax. He laughed as they collapsed."

Bile rose in her throat. Draeken numbers, especially females, were far too low already. To kill a mother and a child spoke of a raving lunatic. She'd known Otas needed to die before. Now she craved to kill him even more, to clean their race of his darkness. "That monster."

"You don't know the half of it."

She watched Meyt pace, and dread crept in. "Was she yours?"

He glanced up. "No," he replied, before waving his hand in the air. "Just someone on the Grax. But they weren't the enemy. It was a mother. An infant, for fyet's sake. They died for no other reason than for Otas to prove that he was the one with the power."

She stepped closer, placing her hand on his arm. "I'm so sorry."

"They weren't his first victims, and they won't be his last."

Talla thought for a moment. "I take it you're not alone in wanting Otas dead?"

Meyt belted out a laugh. "He may hold the Grax by its balls, but there's not a single person on this ship who willingly supports the imposter." His wrist-comm vibrated, and he jerked away. After a moment, he typed in something. "I've been summoned. He's in a sanctuary on the fourth floor. It's not a heavily populated floor. All the surrounding rooms are vacant, since the *pika* programming activates if anyone gets within twelve feet of him. That you don't have *pika* must be making him nervous, because he specifically said for me to come alone."

"Onto Plan B then," Talla said. She stepped forward, only to pause. "There's still one thing I don't get."

"And that would be?"

"Why do you need me? You're with him every day. You are one of the most talented guardsmen I've seen. There had to be a moment when you could've killed him before he set off the pika programming on anyone else."

His lips thinned. "The *pika* is instantaneous. There was no way I could restrain him in time. The risk was too great."

"Until now, you mean."

He nodded tightly. "I didn't know if we had support until now. The Grax will do the right thing once Otas is gone. I needed to know they would be safe."

"They'd better not put up a fight when the others come to free them, or else they will be treated like traitors." She glanced at her wrist-comm. "Speaking of which, we'd better hurry. We have twenty-six minutes. Roden wanted the troops to engage the Grax three minutes before the deadline. We need to have Otas contained before we breach the core ship's force barrier. Knowing that Otas could kill everyone on this ship at the press of a button makes it all the more critical to take him out of commission."

Meyt double-checked his weapons. "You ready to do this?"

Talla checked her blaster and blades a final time and nodded. "Leghat." *Showtime.*

They strolled into the hallway as a couple.

As they walked, something he said earlier nagged at her thoughts. "Exactly how is it that Otas can't see me?"

"When Otas summoned me, I notified a comm-tech to replay a video of me walking alone to this particular sanctuary."

"How did you know that he'd be in this particular room?"

"I didn't," he replied. "The comm-tech made videos of me walking to each of the twelve rooms alone a few days ago."

"Not bad," she said, impressed. "Wait, so us holding hands is for everyone else's benefit?"

"No," he said with a boyish grin. "That's for my benefit."

She chortled and pulled free. She watched him and then chuckled more. "You never change. You're still one to take advantage of a woman's situation."

He shrugged. "You used to like me taking advantage of your... situation."

She smiled, but didn't take his hand again.

When they reached the fourth floor, their mood sobered. Neither spoke until they reached the door Otas stood behind.

Meyt grabbed her arms. "Otas is like a rabid fregee. He's vicious, but he's not smart. But if he has any other guardsmen in there, don't worry. They'll follow my lead. No matter what he does, you must disable the system on his wrist-comm. Do you understand? No matter what he does in there."

Talla cocked her head. "You don't need me for this plan. When we talked about this mission, why did you accept?"

He brushed a hair from her cheek. "I could never say no to you." His gaze bore into her. Then he kissed her again. "For luck."

Before Talla could object, he swiped his wrist-comm over the identification pad and the door opened.

Inside, Otas lounged on an opulent sofa. Alone. Meyt had been right—the fool trusted his guardsman to not betray him.

Upon seeing Talla, Otas sprang forward. "I ordered you to come alone."

Meyt bowed. "My apologies. I misread. I had assumed you wanted to meet my consort as soon as she arrived on the Grax."

Talla forced a fake smile and stepped forward. Adrenaline heightened her senses. "I wanted to present myself and ask for your blessing for me to stay."

"Keep your distance, Talla Kohlm. Oh, yes, I know who you are. You're Roden's lackey," Otas said, reaching for his wrist-comm. "Do not come any closer."

"Talla means you no harm, my lord," Meyt said from behind her.

Otas was still at least seven feet away. One good leap and she could be on him. She prayed it was close enough. She took one small step closer, watching the traitor fidget under her gaze. Close enough. Her smile became genuine. "What's wrong, Otas? Upset because I didn't take a pika injection?"

Otas glared at her and then at Meyt. "I believe you've outlived your usefulness, guardsman."

"She doesn't wish to be under your rule." Meyt pulled out a blaster. "And neither do I."

Otas screamed in frustration and looked down at his wrist-comm. Talla lunged forward, pulling out a curved black blade the instant before she wrapped her arm around his throat. "I wouldn't do that if I were you," she murmured in his ear.

"Nuleet, Otas Olnek," Meyt said. "The Grand Lord has found you guilty of treason."

"Ha!" Otas yelled. "You kill me, and you kill everyone with pika programming."

Talla tensed.

"Fyet," Meyt muttered, coming to the same conclusion as Talla.

Of course, Otas would've wanted a safety measure for his own protection. "You're willing to kill your own people—a quarter of the remaining Draeken blood—for your insanity."

Otas sneered. "If I'm dead, why would I care what happens to them?"

Talla looked up at Meyt. "Help me restrain him. If he can't reach his wrist-comm, he can't set off the programming."

Meyt grimaced, before leveling his gun on Otas. "I'm afraid I can't come any closer, but I'll cover you from here."

Talla was just about to ask when the realization hit her. "You've been injected with pika."

Otas reached for his wrist-comm.

Meyt fired.

Otas screamed out, reaching for his wing that now sported a six-inch charred hole.

Talla tackled Otas to the ground and slammed her blade through his palm, pinning it to the floor. She went to do the same to his other hand, but he flung her off him.

He was stronger than she'd expected, and she remembered that Otas was actually much younger than Hillas Puftan had been, that he'd been surgically aged to become the Grand Lord's doppelgänger.

"Don't move, Otas!" Meyt yelled.

Rather than trying to free himself, Otas yanked out his blaster and began to fire madly. Meyt fired several times, hitting Otas once in the other arm, but it wasn't enough to disarm him. Talla came back to her feet to find Otas weakly leveling the blaster point-blank at her chest with a look of cruel joy. It was a shot impossible to miss.

She couldn't duck in time, so she knew to not even try. She jumped straight at him. Meyt flew forward the instant before Otas fired. Talla was shoved to the side. Blinding hot pain burned her stomach. She stumbled forward. Otas was fighting to get out from under Meyt, who was no longer moving. She used the precious second to switch her blaster to from *kill* to stun. Just as Otas shoved Meyt's body off him, she stood over him, keeping both hands on the blaster to steady herself.

He laughed, reaching for his wrist-comm. "If you kill me, you kill them all!"

She fired three shots into his chest.

His eyes widened as though he hadn't expected her to shoot. Then he toppled backward, unconscious.

She fell to her knees with a wince. Every movement sent

searing pain through her abdomen. With clinical detachment, she glanced down at the charred hole in her stomach. It hurt, but already numbness was beginning to creep in. The shot had hit several major organs. Without immediate repair, she was doomed.

With her vision already tunneling, she rummaged through her cargo pockets and pulled out black restraints. Leaving the blade embedded in the floor, she ripped Otas's hand free and hogtied him, making sure to break several wing bones in the process. She cried out at the movement, but she didn't stop. Can't risk him getting free, she reminded herself when all she wanted to do was collapse.

Adrenaline saw her through her mission. When she went to stand, she fell back hard. Curling around her stomach wound, she sent the all-clear to Roden to pass onto the troops. Target ready for pickup. She paused and then entered the next line in case they didn't get there in time. Keep alive until pika can be deactivated.

A reply chimed back. Are you injured?

Ignoring the message, she used the last of her strength to drag herself to Meyt. He had no visible injuries, of course. The pika was devious like that. It ended life in a blink of an eye, giving the look of peace even in death. If he hadn't tackled Otas, Talla would have had a blaster shot through her heart rather than her side.

"Damn it, Meyt. Why did you have to be a hero?" she muttered, brushing his hair from his face and noticing how this was the first time she'd ever noticed his features softened.

She was tired of losing friends in this war. When would it end? She chuckled to herself, holding her wound. Guess it ends now.

Her wrist-comm chimed. They were on their way to free the Grax.

With no strength left, she lay down next to Meyt. Her world was getting darker, the tunnel closing in. She hadn't much time left. Jax was safe.

She smiled.

She'd taken the genocidal tyrant down.

Chapter 26

"We've got news," Laze said from the pilot's seat. "Otas is restrained. Guess everyone's pika programming is linked to his vitals. He would be selfish enough to do that."

Talla had succeeded. Jax leaned back in his seat, letting out the first easy breath in hours. "And Talla?"

Laze grimaced, his words gritted through his teeth. "No word yet."

Jax's blood froze in his veins. He rested his head against the back of the seat. "What is Roden-code for 'shit hit the fan'?"

Laze opened his mouth to speak. Right then, every hangar door opened on the Grax. A voice came through the common frequency. You are cleared to land.

Jax turned to Laze. "You send the landing codes?"

Laze was frowning. "No. And no Transporter has hailed the Grax yet."

Pires came between them, a smile on his face. "They know we're coming,"

"No screwing around," Jax said. "Anyone looks at us funny, blow them out of the sky."

"You don't need to tell me twice," Laze said.

Going off plan, Laze throttled forward, zigzagging around the Transporters to enter their targeted hangar first. Laze slowed, and the small Aggressor settled onto the metallic surface, keeping the turret pointed at the control station. No one shot at them, even though there were plenty of Draeken standing in the hangar.

No one was armed. All of them were cheering.

Jax eyed the other two men in the cockpit. "Unless they're decoys, they seem awfully happy to see us."

Pires, on the other hand, didn't look the least bit happy, and stalked several feet ahead as though looking for trouble.

"I don't buy it," Jax said to the Draeken by his side. "How could one man enslave an entire core ship?"

Laze shrugged. "I have no idea."

Behind them, the first Transporters were landing. Jax pulled up Talla's coordinates on his wrist-comm. Thank God she'd left her tracker turned on. "Looks like she's on the fourth level, not too far from here." He pinged her. No response. Adrenaline sent a shiver up his spine. "Let's move."

The three of them emerged from the jet, blasters raised, at the growing crowd. Chants of 'We're free!' and 'Thank you!' echoed around the tens of thousands of feet of hangar space. Keeping an eye on the crowd, they jogged forward, fingers next to the triggers. "This way," Jax motioned to a hallway.

They ran down the hallway, the Grax's residents cheering them on from the sides. Every wall screen showed the same. Jax slowed down to read. "The Oppressor has been detained! We are free!" messages were displayed across the screen, over an image of Otas hogtied on the floor. That wasn't what caught his attention. It was the tattooed wingtip of a Draeken female lying a few feet away, on the edge of the screen, and she wasn't moving. "Christ!" he yelled and sprinted toward the blinking dot on his wrist-comm.

Laze took to the air and broke ahead of Jax. Pires kept alongside Jax. The short minute felt like torturous hours to get the room. By the time he reached the closed door, Laze had already touched down and was busy firing a line around the doorframe. Jax and Pires joined in. It took several long seconds to melt enough of the metal away, leaving a red-hot glow tracing the door. The largest of them, Laze kicked out once, twice, and the door fell inward.

Laze leaped into the room with Jax on his heels. He followed Laze's motions and headed to the right. Laze collapsed to his knees by Talla.

Jax kicked a still-unconscious Otas out of the way. "Keep an eye on that bastard. And we need an emergency med-evac now." he ordered Pires before turning to Talla.

Laze was already ripping open a field kit. Jax scanned her before touching her. She had a blaster wound to her abdomen. It looked like half of her waist was charred. With Laze working on her stomach, Jax got as close as he could without jarring her.

Lifting her neck, he nestled her head into his arm. He cupped her cheek with his other hand. Her soft skin was still warm, but so pale.

Her eyes fluttered open, unfocused.

"Stay with me, Talla," Jax said, rubbing her cheek with his thumb.

She mumbled something and then her eyes came somewhat into focus, her heavy-lidded gaze on him. She tried to lift a hand, but it dropped. "You'll be safe now." Her words so slurred that he had to piece together her words.

"All thanks to you." Jax kissed her forehead.

She smiled and said something he couldn't make out.

"Be still, sister," Laze said, opening a packet of gel. "I need to stabilize you."

She hissed when he swiped the gel across her stomach and then sighed.

A ruckus of shuffling feet entered the room. Jax glanced up at the med-techs and additional troops. "About time," he muttered.

"Otas cannot be allowed to touch his wrist-comm or speak into it under any circumstances, got it?" He didn't wait for a response before shouting out his next command. "And this woman needs to be repaired from a blaster injury now."

It was then he noticed the third fallen Draeken in the room. He flinched at seeing the dead man getting loaded onto a stretcher. Meyt. Not that he cared for the guy, but Talla had cared for him. For that reason alone, Jax wished the guy had survived.

He turned his attention back to Talla as they loaded her on a stretcher. Her eyes fluttered before they shut once more, her features smoothing out just like they did before someone passed out.

"Her breathing's stopped," a med-tech said while scrambling with a scanner.

"Damn it, Talla. Stay with me," Jax ordered, but she didn't respond.

Chapter 27

Talla burst awake from the same nightmare. The one where she found herself wading through a thousand bodies, the bodies of all the innocents she'd killed by not stopping Otas Olnek in time.

Sitting up, she tried to push aside the images. She rocked back and forth, rubbing her temples. "Not real. Not real."

It was three days since she'd been released from the *Grax*'s med-hub and returned to the Striga. She was mostly repaired, and was now at the stage of cramping and muscle spasms. But she was alive.

She had kept herself busy dealing with Otas's aftermath, since the entire Triad, with all its delegates and consultants, including Laze and Jax, had to travel immediately to the U.N. to renegotiate peace and a more permanent arrangement for the Draeken and Sephians. The scientists on board the Striga had finished with a pika neutralizer so that it would be ready for distribution as soon as the U.N. could agree to peaceable terms.

She wondered if negotiations were going as smoothly at the U.N. as Otas's execution had gone. It hadn't taken comm-techs more than a few minutes to disengage his wrist-comm from sending out a pika signal. They didn't even try to repair him. He was summarily and very publicly executed by the Grand Lord Nalea Puftan for treason against Draeka and crimes against humanity. People from all three races had cheered. For the first time, the three peoples had come together on something.

But there was still so much work left to be done.

The door to her room chimed. Talla glanced down at her wrist-comm. Seven A.M. Frowning, she looked at the display to see a disheveled Jax. She hit the unlock button on the wall. "Come in."

The door opened, and Jax looked inside before taking a tentative step in. Talla stepped closer. If there was one thing Jax wasn't, it was tentative. "Jax?"

"Sorry for waking you." He glanced at the floor before looking back up. There were dark circles under his eyes. "I wanted to check in on you."

She noticed he still carried a backpack. "Did you just get back?"

As if realizing he still carried it, he nodded. "Yeah. I wanted to let you know that they're going to release the pika neutralizer at eight," he said. "Want to watch?"

She grinned. "I wouldn't miss it for the world."

A half hour later, Talla and Jax stood before the Striga's massive window outside the command room. They were surrounded by a hundred people waiting for the same event. The room was filled with smiles and good spirits.

"I take it negotiations went better than expected," Talla said.

Jax gave a dry chuckle. "There were no negotiations. Everyone at the U.N. stayed quiet during the discussions. The Triad laid out the terms, everyone agreed. There wasn't a single dissent. I think it was the closest thing we'll ever hear to an apology for saving their asses."

A rumble vibrated through the core ship. What looked like giant missiles shot out from the *Striga* and *Grax*, many of them heading off in as many different directions. The same thing was happening at the *Artox* and *Evo*. The missiles climbed and disappeared into the clouds. Then, moments later, lightning-like flashes illuminated the clouds. Four seconds went by before real lightning flashed, and a couple of drops of water hit the window. The sky opened. Rain poured down, carrying with it the *pika* neutralizer. The rainstorm was worldwide, delivering the neutralizer to the water supplies everywhere. The neutralizer had already been introduced to the core ship's water supplies last night. The Earth was safe again. No one would ever set off the deadly programming. But the planet had changed, nearly beyond recognition.

The past month had been a reckoning. A time for people to unite or fall. Fatal mistakes had been made, but the survivors would move forward grounded by lessons learned from the past. They would lay the groundwork for a new, united planet. All three races would have a chance at redemption and a chance to build a better world.

As the rain washed away the war and refreshed Talla, she found herself feeling lighter. The burden of stress she'd carried for the past few years rolled off her. "I can't believe it's done," she said. "My people can finally make a home here."

"And you have plenty of options," Jax said. "After the Omega fiasco, both Alaska and Hawaii seceded from the Union. They're breaking from the U.S. to form their own countries. With everything going on, the government decided to allow it, though it's going to hurt the economy. Since Alaska's environment is proving a bit harsh for Draeken wings, the Artox and Evo are going to relocate. The European Union has established Switzerland a port for immigrants. I think most of the Sephians staying on Earth are headed there since all immigrants, regardless of race, are guaranteed equal rights by law. Roden has negotiated a good deal with Brazil: Draeken and Sephians—hell, even I—have been given full citizenship and a chunk of land to build homes. In exchange, I suspect their economy will see quite an improvement. I think we're looking at the next world power."

"You're coming with me—I mean, with us?"

He reached for her hand. "I'm coming with *you,* ta eani," he whispered, just before kissing her.

They broke off the kiss, both smiling.

"I'm shit at languages, so you'll have to learn Portuguese," he said.

She chuckled. "I already have."

Epilogue

One year later

"It's time," Sana said from the doorway. It was the first time Talla had ever seen the Sephian soldier smile. Well, it was almost a smile, more like a slight tilt of the lips. A human stood off to the side. Jeannie was her name. She, on the other hand, was grinning from ear to ear and dabbing her eyes with a tissue.

Talla grinned while she examined her wings in the mirror. She'd just had Jax's name—in Draeken and in English—tattooed across them yesterday. She was already formulating what tattoos she'd get next when she realized the room had fallen silent. She glanced up and startled. Sienna stood to her left and Nalea to her right. They were looking in the mirror as well. "We're beautiful," Sienna said.

Talla nodded. It was true. At this moment, they were a vision. Sienna, even with her scars, looked like an angel in the white gown decorated with black pearls and the lace veil over her hair.

Nalea, in contrast, was a tall beauty in a floor-length black silken gown. But Talla preferred her simple silver gown. Panels of fabric hung loosely off her back so they would flutter when she flew.

"Let's do this," Sienna said as she grabbed her cane and limped toward the doorway. Sienna, with her slow walk, set the pace. Entering the huge Communal Room of the Striga, Talla, Nalea, and Sienna walked down the open pathway through the crowd. Everyone on the Striga was present. Every Draeken had come on board, and several hundred humans had arrived for the world-wide-broadcast event.

Laze stood near the front, a human female on each side. As she walked by, he gave her a full-blown smile. Surprisingly, Laze hadn't punched Jax when he'd asked for Talla's hand. It was the first sign that Laze was finding his way out of the darkness. Seeing him now, surrounded by pretty human "groupies," was the second sign. Talla smiled at her brother. You'll be all right.

The three women finally reached the end of the pathway, where three men stood. Each man reached out for his woman. Legian, the large Sephian, nearly lifted Sienna off the ground as he embraced her. Roden merely smirked as he tugged Nalea to him.

Jax held out his arm, and Talla looped her hand around his elbow. He placed his other hand atop hers. She leaned closer as the three couples were united by ministers from each race, and they became the three first families of tomorrow's world.

Talla looked into Jax's eyes and found in them the same joy she felt. A tear built at the corner of her eye. She wasn't one to cry but, after all, it was their wedding day.

***

END OF PART THREE

Available Now

Black Sheep

An alien ship. Stolen colonists. All Throttle wanted was a vacation...

Fifteen years into a twenty-year voyage, war veteran Captain Throttle Reyne is looking forward to taking a break from dealing with malfunctions, glitches, and the hassles of monitoring a thousand colonists in cryo-sleep.

But when her colony ship breaks down in the middle of nowhere, Throttle and her crew must leave the colonists behind to search for help. They find a ship that's not only missing a crew... it's clearly not from their star system.

It's the discovery of a lifetime. All they need to do is tow the mysterious vessel back to their colony ship for further study and Throttle won't ever have to work again. One problem. While they're away, the colony ship is stolen—with the colonists still on board.

Throttle gives chase to a lawless star system on the outer rim. To get their colonists back, they must take on the pirates and gang lords who will do anything—and sell anyone—to make a buck.

They play dirty. But Throttle and her crew play dirtier.

Strap on your restraints and experience the start of this new space opera thrill ride. It's perfect for fans of Jay Allan, Jennifer Foehner Wells, and Star Wars.

Available on Kindle, Audible, and paperback.

About the Author

Rachel Aukes is the award-winning author of *100 Days in Deadland*, which made Suspense Magazine's Best of the Year list. She is also a Wattpad Star, her stories having over six million reads. When not writing, she can be found flying old airplanes across the Midwest countryside and catering to an exceptionally spoiled fifty-pound lap dog.

Subscribe to Rachel's spam-free newsletter to hear about new releases: www.rachelaukes.com/join

Acknowledgments

With many thanks to Laurel Kriegler and Terri King for making my stuff look good; to my beta readers Rob Shores and Kay Smillie for catching the little things that could cause big problems; to Brian for the hugs; to Ellie for the endless supply of doggie kisses; and to *you* for picking up this story and opening the worlds within it.